An Irishwoman's Tale

PATTI
LACY

Kregel
Publications

An Irishwoman's Tale: A Novel
© 2008 by Patti Lacy

Published by Kregel Publications, a division of Kregel, Inc., P.O. Box 2607, Grand Rapids, MI 49501.

Library of Congress Cataloging-in-Publication Data
Lacy, Patti
  An Irishwoman's tale : a novel / by Patti Lacy.
     p. cm.
  1. Family—Fiction   I. Title.
  PS3612.A3545I75 2008
  813'.6—dc22

                        2008016808

ISBN 978-0-8254-2987-3

Printed in the United States of America
08 09 10 11 12 / 5 4 3 2 1

ACKNOWLEDGMENTS

With warm gratitude to the dozens of people who made this book possible, yet wish to remain nameless, including Irish travel agents who seemed not just willing but eager to get late-night, toll-free phone calls, librarians employed by both public and private institutions, psychiatrists, teachers, sheep farmers, a soul food restaurateur, kaleidoscope makers, university disciplinary officers, interior designers, airline employees . . . the list goes on and on.

A special thanks to these sharp-eyed, big-hearted readers who weren't afraid to hammer at the manuscript until rough edges had been smoothed: Eileen Astels, Walt Baertsch, Arlene Deerson, Paula Crowley Deneen, Jan DeWitt, Helen Fritzen, David Hirst, Eve Lomoro, Becky Melby, Mary Mertz, Carol Pierskalla, Ann Qualls, Joan Qualls, Camy Tang, Debbie VanHoorn, and Anna Wells.

Thanks to Beverly Verdery for praying me to the rocky west coast of Ireland and back and tossing in for good measure the use of her all-weather coat.

Love to my parents, who told me the stories until they taught me to read them for myself; and my husband and children, who surely tired of hearing the stories yet encouraged me to capture them on paper.

A final thanks to Mary, the Irishwoman who shared her story and is still sharing her life.

PROLOGUE

Get 'er out of here." Moon-shaped faces stared at Mary across the round, oaken table, then guzzled tea. Stared. Guzzled. Cup after cup of the steaming stuff.

"Ye can't mean it," Mam screamed. "Not now. She's all o' a bloody five."

"The little eejit. Get 'er out."

A fist crashed to the table. Cups and saucers and cigarettes flew. Tea splattered onto the wall, onto the front of Killian's shirt.

"Ye swine." Mam was in Killian's face. "For the sake of St. Patrick, she's my flesh and blood."

"She's got to go."

Mam's screaming curse sent a chill up Mary's spine. "Ye lured me here, promised to take us in."

"She's got to go. Now."

"All right, she'll go." Mam's words slapped Mary in the face. "And you'll be cursed, all of ye."

Mam? No. Not you, Mam? Mary flung herself on the floor, legs and arms flailing. *Mam on their side?* Her heart broke in two, not by the others, but by her own mother.

Mam jerked her to a standing position, letting those horrid, horrid faces burn holes into her. Still, Mary stared at them, refusing to be the first to look away.

They glared back at her and sloshed watery tea all over themselves and the tabletop. Words floated overhead. *Harris, Chicago, America.* What did they all mean? She heard a slap and cowered, but the blow did not fall on her.

One of the sisters half-carried, half-dragged her to bed.

"Why, Mam, why?" Over and over Mary sobbed the same thing into her pillow. She knew the foul-smelling faces that loomed over the table didn't want her, but Mam? The black reality engulfed her, and her body convulsed with waves of despair.

Chapter 1

Run the straight race through God's good grace;
Lift up thine eyes and seek His face.
—John S. B. Monsell, "Fight the Good Fight with All Thy Might"

Terre Haute, Indiana, 1995

Mary Freeman had done all she could to make it special. The skillet was hot. Creamy yogurt waited to be dolloped onto nutty granola. Raspberry scones cooled on a wire rack. Steel-cut oats from County Kildare simmered on a back burner. She whirled about, trading a spoon for a spatula, determined to suit the palates of her husband, Paul, and her two teenage daughters, Claire and Chloe. Every morning, the four of them ate breakfast together in this big kitchen, with its copper pot rack and granite countertops. Then Paul would leave, heaving this tool or that box into the old farm truck, a quick hug to suffice for a day without him. The girls would leave too, armed with backpacks and racquets and changes of clothes. The house would be empty—except for her and Mother.

For now, Mary's world became Paul and the girls. She checked her watch, then stepped out to the garden and clipped purple asters off spindly stems. It pricked her to think of the approaching void, when she and Mother would coexist within the walls of this cavernous Victorian Painted Lady. Bustling back inside, she arranged the flowers and twigs of hypericum in a crystal vase, hoping to add the final touches to a memory she could cling to when the walls closed in.

She stepped back and surveyed her handiwork, plucking off a rogue leaf, then headed to the laundry room. Three more loads, which she could easily wedge in between mother's feeding, the upstairs cleaning—

"Get 'er out of here."

The voice bounced off the laundry room walls. Mary tried to ignore it, as she always did. Yet the thick Irish brogue assailed her, conjuring lifelike images.

Moon-shaped faces stared at Mary across the round oaken table, then guzzled tea. Stared. Guzzled.

"The little eejit. Get 'er out."

Mam screaming. Crashing. Cups and saucers flying. Tea splattering.

"Ye swine." Mam spat into Killian's face.

"She's got to go. Now."

"All right, she'll go. And ye be cursed, all of ye."

As quickly as the voices had come, they faded. And left Mary trembling, damp laundry chilling her hands.

Overhead, steps pounded across the planked floor. It was Claire, banging her fist against the balustrade as she had for the past ten years, then thundering downstairs.

Mary dropped the laundry and bustled back to the kitchen. "Breakfast's ready, honey." She cracked some eggs, beat them until they foamed, and poured them in the skillet. *If only the voices could be handled so efficiently.*

Claire whooshed into the kitchen, bringing life and light and the smell of green apples and hair mousse. "Morning, Mom." At five foot ten, Claire towered over everyone in the family but her daddy. Her younger sister, Chloe, dubbed her a red tornado, not just for her mane of hair but for her temper.

Cabinets banged and the refrigerator door creaked. "Where's the jelly?"

"Over there, dear." Mary slid her arm around Claire and managed to hug her.

Claire offered a cheek, then grabbed a bowl of granola, plucked a scone off the rack, and slid onto a bench seat. "Don't forget, I've got Key Club tonight. I'll just grab something after practice."

Mary nodded, then turned back to Paul's eggs, which were seconds away from being just the consistency he liked them. "Paul?" she called to the figure clattering about in the front room. "Your breakfast is—ooh! Quit it!"

A scratchy beard chafed the nape of Mary's neck, yet she didn't really want him to stop. If only she could hop with him into that rickety truck, patter about the barn with their goats and wooly-backed sheep, then meet for lunch under their sycamore tree . . .

"Mom? Where's my blue jacket?" Unnoticed, Chloe had crept down the stairs, gotten her cereal, and squeezed onto the bench.

"In the utility room. Pressed and ready."

"Thanks, Mom."

Mary smiled, both at the love in Claire's voice and at the way sunlight chose this moment to filter through the window and blush her daughters' cheeks. This was the way she'd planned it. She backed out of Paul's grasp, dished eggs onto a plate, and beelined back toward the laundry room to finish what she'd started.

"Whoa, girls. Let's bless the food." Paul grabbed the sash of Mary's apron, pinched her tantalizingly close to her back pocket, then led her toward the table. "That means you too," he said, kissing her on her ear this time.

"Oh, Daddy." The girls' giggles and rolling eyes suggested they'd witnessed their father's middle-aged shenanigans. But there was pride in their tone—and love.

"I'll just get another load—"

"This comes first." Paul had always been lean, but years of farming had hardened spare muscles into steel. He pulled Mary onto the bench across from their girls, and they all joined hands. "Heavenly Father," he began, "thank You for this food. Watch over my girls today. Thank You for—"

"Where are ye?"

Mary blinked, then cut a glance at the girls and again bowed her head. Couldn't Mother give them five minutes of peace? Five minutes for the four of them? As Paul kept praying, she clenched her jaw, willing her mother back to sleep.

"Jesus, Mary, and Joseph! I swear—" Mother's screech shook the room.

"Why can't she just shut up?" Claire jumped to her feet, tossed her napkin down, and shook bangs out of her eyes. "She ruins everything."

Mary felt heat rising to her face. She wished she could blurt out exactly what she felt, like her daughters did. But what kind of example would that be? She struggled to get her thoughts together, to make the best of the time they had left. "Claire, she's your grandmother. And I'll not have you saying that about her."

"Why not?" Chloe dabbed at her lips, which managed to stay Hot Hot Pink or whatever the name of her latest lip gloss was. "It's true." As usual, Chloe never shouted. Yet the words cut into Mary as if she'd yelled louder than the woman in the next room. "Besides, she's not really our grandmother," Chloe added, the napkin now a wad by her plate.

Mary looked long and hard at her daughters, seeing her nose in Chloe, her eyes in Claire, and her resentment of Mother in both of them. Claire and Chloe felt free to spill their feelings all over this well-set table. She, with the Lord's help, had been able to keep hers bottled up. But pressure was building.

Paul smoothed out his napkin and laid it by now-cold eggs. "Of course she is. And we're gonna honor her like we did Gran. It's our way."

"Why?" Some of the sting had left Claire's voice.

"Because it's His way."

"I'll have yer head for this, I will!" Mother's tirade had risen to a feverish pitch.

A glint entered Chloe's eyes. "I'll have yours first."

Claire's spoon clattered to the table. "Just shut up, Chloe!"

The sisters glared at each other, faces red.

"Not another word, either of you!" With a jerk, Mary untied her apron and tossed it onto the island cluttered with the remains of what she'd so hoped would be a special breakfast. Soon they would leave, and she'd be alone with Anne Harris, the eighty-three-year-old who was and wasn't her mother.

✢ ✢ ✢

"Get in here, girl."

A breeze tickled slatted blinds and carried the scent of Irish roses into the room, but the heady fragrance didn't still Mary's trembling hands or calm her thumping heart. She was still *girl*, not *daughter* or *dear*, words she'd waited a lifetime to hear. All the sacrifices they'd made for Mother—even moving into town when she couldn't manage out on the farm—didn't seem to matter. Mary flipped on the light switch in a vain attempt to brighten her thoughts. *But no matter what she calls me, Anne Harris is the only mother I've got now.* "I'm here, Mother." Somehow Mary managed to put a lilt in her voice.

"Girl?" The voice came from a huddle of quilts, only a stubborn jaw jutting above cotton and satin bedding.

"I'm Mary. Your daughter." Mary said it to herself as much as to the woman on the bed.

Mother's mouth twisted into a bitter smile. "You're not my daughter. Not really."

For just an instant, Mary longed to hurl some of Mother's bile back in her face, then stomp to the phone and reserve one of the "spacious suites" that the new assisted-living center was touting as the latest in "modern adult community." Let them clean her linens and change her diapers and puree her food and bathe her and listen to her. Most of all, let them listen to her.

"I'm off, honey!"

Mary whirled about. Paul stood at the threshold of Mother's room. She flew into his arms.

"What's this about?" He somehow managed to run one hand through her hair and pull her close with the other.

"N-nothing."

"It'll be okay," he assured her, nuzzling about her neck.

Mary breathed deeply of wood smoke and damp wool until her heart resumed its normal beat. It would be okay . . . wouldn't it? She willed Paul to forget about the calf with the gimpy leg, the trees that needed grafting, and stay home today. But she knew he couldn't. The farm was his lifeblood, and hers too. If not for Mother, she'd be out there by his side.

Too soon, Paul pulled away. After good-byes and air kisses, the girls pattered down the hall, right behind their daddy. The front door slammed, then clicked. She and Mother were locked in. Safe, but not necessarily sound.

Her heart heavy, Mary sunk to the plush carpet on her mother's floor. "Forgive me," she prayed. "I do love her, or at least I try to. And give me a friend, Lord. Someone to help me get through this loneliness."

She rose to see something akin to a smile softening her mother's withered face, the set jaw. That hint of a smile carried Mary through the diaper-changing, dressing, and resettling back into the old iron bed. She would be a daughter, regardless of what she was or wasn't called. "I'll be back with your breakfast, Mother," she announced as she hurried down the hall. The second breakfast shift was about to begin.

"*I'm the last of the Irish Rovers, bathed in a bed o' clover,*" she sang as she stirred the oatmeal, which was mushy, just like Mother liked it. Or used to, when Mother still expressed likes and dislikes. Still singing, Mary buttered toast, poured tea, squeezed juice, sliced fruit, and set it, along with the vase of asters, on a tray. "A good diet," the doctor had told Mary over a decade ago. "Plenty of love." Her hands gripped the tray a bit tighter, certain she'd succeeded at the first of his orders. But the second gave her cause to shake her head. *Lord, I've done my best. You know I've done my best.*

"Good morning." Mary smoothed back a shock of her mother's white hair. "Here's your breakfast."

Mother's mouth opened and closed like a baby sparrow's, yet there was no recognition in the filmy blue eyes.

Mary propped up her mother with pillows and pulled a stool near the side of the bed. She fed her a spoonful of oats, a smidgen of toast, prattling about anything she could think of, as emptiness edged in until she felt its cold fingers about her throat.

When the pale lips clamped shut and the papery thin eyelids closed, Mary dabbed crumbs off her mother's mouth, then carefully folded the napkin and set it down.

A blessed quiet filled the room. Mary stepped to the casement window and let the wind soothe away the tightness about her throat, her shoulders. A few brave rose blossoms remained amongst a tangle of stems and leaves in a futile gesture to stave off the approaching fall. Their scent permeated every corner of the room, from the mahogany wardrobe to the antique chest, transporting Mary to another place, another time . . . *'Tis the last rose of summer, lass, left bloomin' all alone. All her lovely companions, faded now and gone.*

For a moment, she was back on the cliffs, breathing deeply of salty spray, the smoke from a turf fire in her hair . . .

Mary jumped, then sighed. It was Mother, thrashing about in her sheets. She hurried to her side. *"Tura, lura, lura,"* she sang, stroking the wrinkled cheek.

Perhaps the eyes brightened for an instant. Then the bony limbs resumed their thrashing. "There, there," she kept saying, in between the gasps and grunts and heaves it took to get Mother into the rocker and in front of the television.

"You're the next contestant . . ."

The raucous laughter grated at Mary. They'd never wanted a television, never needed a television. Out on the farm, they'd survived just fine without it. She sighed as blue-haired grannies shrieked their way down the aisle. Yet the boob tube settled Mother as nothing else did, and for that, Mary was grateful.

"Come on down!"

Mary surged about the bedroom-bathroom suite, determined to let busyness still the nerves set on edge by the TV. She plumped cushions, straightened orthopedic shoes and slippers, and was washing out her mother's hosiery when the phone rang.

She let the answering machine get it. "Pick up, Mary." It was the voice of Sue, a family friend and the doctor who'd delivered her girls. "I need you."

Mary wrung out the stockings and hung them over a towel rack, hurried into the study, and picked up the phone. "Sue. What's going on?"

"Hey, Mary. Listen, could you sub today?"

Mary hesitated. Mother'd be okay by herself for as long as it took to play a couple of sets, or she could call Dora, who always wanted more hours. "Who's playing?"

"Mona and JoAnn and some new lady. She's pretty good, I hear."

Mary frowned. Two hours with Mona and JoAnn could last a lifetime, not to mention some stranger. "What's her name?"

"All I know is she's from the South. Listen, Mary, I don't have time for twenty questions. A patient's in the ER, and you're the only one I've gotten through to. It's just for a couple of hours. How about it?"

"Well, there's Mother . . ."

"Take my word for it, Mary. She's fine. Besides, she isn't going anywhere."

Mary bit her lip. It was true; Mother hadn't taken a step unassisted in five years. She'd call Dora. Besides, what else was there to do? The house had been scrubbed and oiled and waxed until it glistened. The garden had been winterized. Her summer clothes had been pressed and hung in garment bags. "No problem, Sue," Mary said. "I'll do it."

"You won't regret it, Mary. I promise."

For a moment, Mary stared at the phone. What did Sue mean by that? She'd been subbing for Sue on a regular basis since Sue opened her own clinic. And it helped Mary get in more practice, which she definitely could use to compete in the A League. But Sue's tone had hinted at something mysterious. Something hopeful. She picked up the phone and called Dora, the strange comment still ringing in her ears.

CHAPTER 2

Mary angled into a parking spot, jumped out of her car, and cut across still-dewy grass. She stopped short near a flower bed, held captive by the last of the asters and black-eyed Susans. It was a spot of beauty in a town whose Chamber of Commerce had the gall to brag about an odiferous tar mill and paper plant. Mary breathed deeply, then coughed. She'd give a fortune for ten minutes on the cliffs of her homeland.

"Mary. Get over here."

Biting back a nasty retort, Mary bounded onto the court.

"There you are." JoAnn, hands on hips, stood with Mona near the net.

"Sorry I'm late." Fumbling in her bag, Mary looked for a can of balls.

"I can't speak for them, but it doesn't bother me a bit. Of course, I operate on Central Late Time." From the shadows of sycamore trees stepped a chunky woman whose hair had been streaked so many times, Mary couldn't tell if it were brown, blond, or gray. She grabbed Mary's hand and shook it. "I'm Sally Stevens. Happy to meet you."

"Mary Freeman."

"Your hair's gorgeous. There's two things I always wanted—red hair and a skinny rear." She threw back her head and laughed.

Neither JoAnn nor Mona joined in the chuckles.

Mary didn't either; in fact, she stepped back. "Uh, thanks. So you're new here?"

"We'd never even been north of old Mason-Dixon; then we up and move here." Sally finally let go of Mary's hand. "I was born in Texas, but we moved to Louisiana when I was twelve. It was hard, but—"

"Hey"—Mona cut into the monologue, pointing to the next court—"we'll be over there. Waiting."

Sally smiled but didn't budge. "—Everything fell into place for my folks." She continued talking as if she'd never been stopped. "Kinda like it did for us when Sam's department chair found a house in our price range on the nicest cul-de-sac."

Mary arched her eyebrows. What kind of woman would spill out her socio-economic status two minutes after they'd met? Yet something about Sally's voice drew her in, and she wanted to know more. "And Sam is . . . ?"

"My husband. We met in college. I was standing in the dorm lobby and—"

The harrumphs from JoAnn and Mona drowned out the rustling of leaves overhead. But not the drawly syllables, which kept up their assault until Mary pointed Sally toward the next court. "Uh, we need to get moving."

Her lip quivering, Sally nodded and grabbed her bag.

"They get a little edgy," Mary whispered.

Sally's face dimpled into a huge smile. "You want backhand or forehand?"

Mary smiled. She hadn't been offered her choice of side in ages, certainly not since she'd joined the A League. This woman had manners, something Mary had heard about Southerners. And with every passing minute, her smile seemed more genuine. "You choose, Sally," she said. "I'm equally bad at both."

While Sally unsheathed her racquet from its cover and continued her barrage of words, Mary analyzed her appearance, a habit she'd gotten from Mother. Her tank top? At least two sizes too small. Wraparound skirt? Out of style since Chris Evert retired, and too short to hide cellulite. Still, her eyes were clear and bright, so what difference did it make what she wore? Squinting, Mary tried to see past the shadow that the trees cast over Sally's face to determine whether her eyes were blue or gray. As Sally squawked on, Mary decided that didn't really matter either. They radiated warmth, just like her smile.

"I know, sometimes I go on and on." Sally unwrapped two sticks of gum and stuck them in her mouth. "In fact, yesterday, I asked the produce man if they had any okra and ended up copying down Mama's gumbo recipe for him. I don't know how it happens." She blew a bubble until it popped. "Let's see. Where was I? Oh, Sam said . . ."

Mary surprised herself by laughing. *That crooked-tooth smile. The dimples again. She's . . . pretty.* "Hey, let's go before we get hit over the head." Mary picked up her bag, Sally followed suit, and they strolled toward the end court.

"It's about time," JoAnn said, manicured hands on slender hips.

Mary didn't like JoAnn's tone, but she had to agree. She hustled to the net to take some volleys, Sally trotting along beside her.

"You could fry an egg out here," JoAnn grumbled, trying to adjust her visor and hit the ball at the same time.

"Y'all don't know what real heat is. A gush of sweat soakin' right through to your bra." As if to demonstrate, Sally popped her strap. "That's Southern heat."

Mary giggled, taking her eye off the ball. A swing and a miss. She didn't look across the net, avoiding what she was sure were deadly glares.

As they stepped to the baseline, Sally gabbed on. "Back home, I've opened a frozen can of Diet Coke—you know how you freeze them to get them all slushy—and it's lukewarm in ten minutes. Speaking of Diet Coke . . ." Sally hurried to her bag, pulled out a can, chugged some, and plunked it down.

"Hey, you two. Up here. Spin for serve."

Mary and Sally scurried to the net.

"Up or down?" With authority, Mona spun her racquet.

Mary didn't hesitate. "Up."

When the racquet fell onto the court, Mona picked it up, showing Mary and Sally the *W*. "Your serve."

Sally scooped up the balls and handed them to Mary. "You go first." Her voice became a whisper. "I'm a little nervous."

"Don't be." Mary smiled again. "We'll do fine."

Mary served. JoAnn sent a forehand return down the line. Somehow Sally, who'd been poaching, managed to get the frame of her racquet on the ball. It hit the top of the net and dinked over. It was a terrible-looking shot. But it won the point.

Mona rolled her eyes, then stomped back to receive serve.

"Oh, I'm sorry." Sally shrugged her shoulders, gave her opponents a huge smile, then craned her neck at Mary. They locked eyes. Sally winked.

Mary bounced the ball with a bit more authority as she prepared to serve to Mona. She'd never dreamed when she agreed to sub that she might have a crack at beating these two. This might be an interesting day.

For an hour, they battled one of the city's best women's teams. JoAnn and Mona, old high school partners, had played thirty years of serious doubles. The closer the score, the more Sally tightened her lips and her game. She had

17

an effective, if unorthodox, backhand and sensed the opponents' moves like a grizzled tomcat anticipating the lunges of the dog next door. Somehow, they broke JoAnn's serve to make it 6–6.

"Will we play it out?" Sally whispered.

Mary shook her head. "With their experience, they'll go for a tiebreaker."

Mona and JoAnn trudged up to the net.

After exchanging a glance, Mary and Sally hurried to join them.

"Gotta go. Good game." Mona nodded, her eyes hidden behind sunglasses.

"Me too," JoAnn said. "It's almost time, anyway."

The four women shook hands. Then JoAnn and Mona scurried off.

"Did my deodorant wear off?" Sally asked.

"Of course not," Mary managed between giggles. "They couldn't risk a newcomer beating them." Only years of being schooled in proper tennis decorum kept Mary from bellowing out their little triumph. *Who cares how it happened? We tied the league's top team.* She practically skipped toward her gear, Sally right behind her.

They stopped near the fence and set down their bags.

"No asking if we want to play a tiebreaker or anything? What kind of manners did their mothers teach them?" Sally's easy drawl was gone.

Mary shrugged. If she got started on JoAnn and Mona, she might never stop.

Sally sighed. "I'm sorry." Then she grinned. "We would've beaten them."

Mary shrugged again, yet her heart pounded a victory song.

"Whew. It's hotter up here than it looks." Sally flopped down, right on the court surface, and pulled a candy bar out of her bag. After unwrapping it, she popped half in her mouth. "You want some?"

"Heavens, no." Mary shifted her weight from one leg to the other. Just looking at the sticky glob caused her stomach to cramp.

"Do you have time to chat?" Sally asked, between chews.

Mary glanced at her watch. "I don't know. I need to get home."

"Oh, well," Sally smiled, her eyes stating otherwise, "perhaps another time."

Something about that smile made Mary get down on one knee. "Oh, why not?" The next thing she knew, she'd sprawled out on the court next to Sally. She pushed back a curl and sighed. It was comforting to be close to all this Southern sun; in human form, of course. "How do you like it here so far?"

"We just love y'all's cool temperatures." Sally had grabbed another Diet Coke out of her bag and guzzled it between sentences. "And when I registered my kids for school, folks were so efficient they reminded me of these Swiss watchmakers I met once in Dallas. They make a timepiece that runs on air or something."

"Atmos. They measure difference in air pressure." Mary scooted nearer to Sally, tugging on her skirt so it covered her knees. "Never mind the fancy clocks. How do you really like it?"

A gust of wind blew red leaves onto the court, and Sally spoke with a catch in her voice. "It's tough. I miss my porch swing. Chatty neighbors." She lowered her voice, which still was thick with syrup. "I'm a bit lonely."

Mary cleared her throat once, twice. Surprisingly, she longed to comfort this woman, to pour out the story of her mothers and fathers. But they'd only just met.

A warm hand grazed her shoulder. "I'm sorry. I didn't mean to be so whiny."

"You're not whiny at all." Mary smiled. "And they'll get used to you. They finally did me."

"When?"

"Before you die, I promise."

When the laughter died down, Mary pulled sunglasses from a leather case and put them on. "Tell me about your family, your kids . . ."

The women leaned closer, and the exchange of information began.

Sally had a husband named Sam. Two kids, a girl and a boy. Hundreds of wacky relatives. She read like a fiend, had worked as a teacher and a freelance writer, played tennis, suffered from a chocolate and coffee and diet soda addiction, and liked Southern and Chinese foods. Her dream? To write a novel.

Uncharacteristically, Mary held her own. She had a husband named Paul, two daughters, cared for her elderly mother, volunteered at a soup kitchen, had owned two businesses, was a vegetarian, loved to run and cook, and also was an avid reader.

Sally crumpled up her can. "Suzi's just turned ten. I'm a bit worried about how she'll react to the move. Ed's eight. And as long as there's sports up here, he'll be fine." She rolled her eyes. "But how about your girls?"

"Claire's a senior. She's in the Key Club, on the tennis team . . . and practically everything else. Chloe's on the tennis team too, over at the junior high. They're both active in youth group, and Chloe sings in the choir."

"So y'all are Christians too?"

Mary nodded, a warmth spreading through her that had nothing to do with the sun. She'd thought it, hoped it, but to have it confirmed was . . . it was an answer to prayer.

"Do you have pictures of them?" Sally's eyes, definitely blue, danced now. "I'll bet they look just like you."

Mary drew away, her spine stiffening to a posture produced by years of tapping rulers. "I should say not." She grabbed her purse. "I'll show you." As she flipped past credit cards, carefully organized receipts, and membership credentials, she glanced at her watch, then almost dropped her billfold. Eleven forty? How had this happened? She leapt to her feet. "Hey, I've gotta run." Her face burned with the realization that she'd let down the drawbridge into her private life and Sally had tromped right over the moat. With staccato movements, she jumbled everything into her bag, then headed to her car.

Sally's face fell, but she nodded and bobbed alongside Mary. "Can we play again soon? I'm not that good, but it'd be great exercise. I jog too, once in a blue moon, and—"

"Uh, with my mother at home, the soup kitchen and all . . ."

The quiver made it to Sally's cheeks this time.

Mary longed to explain her standoffishness, which often seemed to come out of nowhere when she felt people getting close to the images, the words, the questions that were burning holes in her gut. But something besides their common faith seemed to be pulling the two of them together. She darted a glance at Sally's big blue eyes. She'd just met this woman who bubbled and fizzed like a shaken can of soda. What if she spilled Mary's life just as indiscriminately?

The quiver continued, yet it was joined by a smile.

Mary compromised by writing down her phone number. Sally seemed . . . different. And hadn't she been praying for another friend since the girls got so busy? She handed Sally the slip of paper. "How about next week? Call me, okay?"

Sally crammed the deposit slip in her pocket. "That's great. I can't wait to tell my peeps that I've got a friend."

"Your peeps?"

"My family. My people."

The words sent a knife through Mary. Sure she had the girls, she had Paul, she had Mother. But her *people*? She hadn't heard from her *people* in years. Unless she counted the voices.

CHAPTER 3

Erin, I hear ye calling, though years have stretched their length between.
Do you behold me listening? Longing to see your hills so green?
—Charles Marshall, "I Hear You Calling Me"

Morning sunbeams poured through the study's lead-glass windows and transformed ordinary dust motes into glitter. Mary set down her dust rag and checked her watch. It had been a good morning. Mother had eaten most of her breakfast and settled in, leaving Mary plenty of time to finish dusting, change clothes, and pick up Sally before the ministry opened at ten. All fall, they'd played tennis, had coffee, but this was their first time to volunteer together, and Mary wanted to be on time, get things off to a good start.

When bric-a-brac and wood turnings of the jeweled fireplace began to gleam, Mary turned her attention to shelves of cookbooks, novels, *Farmer's Almanacs*, and westerns. She sneezed as she stretched to reach the top shelf, then came face to face with the cluster of Freeman photographs on the mantel. Daguerreotypes and color portraits had captured images of hearty folk, men dressed in dark suits and starched shirts, women in high-collared, no-nonsense dresses. Sturdy German stock that had dug into the rich Midwestern soil and made a life for themselves and their children.

Mary tried to swallow the lump in her throat. Where were *her* folk, the ones whose rollicking faces and captivating brogue played peek-a-boo with increasing frequency in her fantasies? In spite of all that had happened, she longed for pictures of O'Briens, her mother's clan. Pictures of Mother, when she'd been young and, according to Daddy, looked like she knew all the secrets in the world. An image came to mind, a snarling face that made Mary want to spit, the taste in her mouth was so bitter. But no pictures of Killian. No, never.

The phone startled her. She rubbed her shoulders, trying to get rid of the tightness. Then she set down the rag and answered the phone.

"Hey, Mary, it's JoAnn."

"Oh, hi." Mary tried to keep her tone light but wished she'd let the answering machine pick up like she usually did.

"I'll get right to the point."

Mary stifled another sneeze. *When don't you?*

"We need a permanent sub, with Sue always bailing out on us. Any suggestions?"

Mary arched her eyebrows. She hoped a doctor would put her patients before tennis. And since when did the captain of the A League ask her opinion? Of course, she'd played for more than a decade, had come in third place once, won the sportsmanship award four times. But in their catty tennis circle, was that saying very much? Now, if Sally joined the league . . . "How about Sally?" Mary tapped her foot. She wasn't one to ramble on. Besides, she needed to get moving.

"Huh . . . Well . . ."

It was hard to keep still with the clock ticking, ticking toward soup-kitchen time. JoAnn usually flashed and jabbed her tongue with the skill of a professional fencer, so Mary was unaccustomed to all this fumbling and bumbling. "So what about Sally?" she asked.

"Well, she's not quite up to our level, you know."

Mary's scalp prickled, a slow burn crawling from the roots of her hair to her forehead, then her face. *No, I don't know. And she's more fun than the whole coven of you.* She bit her tongue just in time. "I think she's perfect." She hoped the next comment sounded matter-of-fact. "And come to think of it, I'm not sure I have time. The soup kitchen's always looking for someone to take on more hours. In fact, that's where we're off to in about five minutes. Sally and I, that is."

"For heaven's sake, Mary." JoAnn screeched. "You've just met her. How can you possibly think she's up to it?"

Mary visualized Sally's dimples, the warm embrace that had eased away the pokes and prods of several mundane mornings. Relaxing her grip on the phone, she remembered once again her prayer for a friend. "I've known her all my life," she said. "It's just that I recently met her."

The doorbell rang, Dora's arrival providing the perfect exit for Mary.

"Gotta go, JoAnn." Mary struggled to keep smugness out of her voice. "I'm glad you agree that Sally's up to it too."

✠ ✠ ✠

"So you give out food?" Sally tried to keep the waver out of her voice, but it wasn't easy, considering the passenger-window view of ravaged warehouses, abandoned homes, and burned-out cars.

Mary nodded without taking her eyes off the road. "It's about half soup kitchen, half food pantry, I guess you'd say. Prayers if they'll let us. The occasional cot on the floor. We aren't a full-blown shelter. At least not yet."

"Your church runs it?"

"Nope, God does." The sun found every bit of red in Mary's hair. "We just try to manage what He sends our way." Mary angled up a gravel driveway and parked the car. "Here we are."

"Should I lock the door?" Sally asked, her attention fixed on a couple of aimless-looking teens, baseball caps cocked sideways, pants drooping off thin hips, beater shirts adding definition to slouched shoulders.

Mary turned off the engine and stuck her keys in a pants pocket. "You don't need to. Come on. I'll show you around." They made their way to the front door.

Paint peeled off a shotgun-style frame. The front porch sagged dangerously. The whole block looked like it could benefit from an inspection team and a dozen bulldozers. It was definitely the wrong side of the tracks, which, to Sally's Southern way of thinking, meant Colored Town. A place where whites didn't set foot unless they were lost.

"Well, if it ain't Mary quite contrary. You get yo'self over here right this minute!" The voice came from a supersized woman who sat with some children at a picnic table shaded by towering oaks. With one hand, the woman shooed away flies; with the other, she stuffed something into her mouth. Yet elaborately made-up eyes and well-coiffed red-hued hair indicated that this woman cared about her appearance.

"Bertha!" Mary broke into a wide grin and grabbed Sally's arm.

Even though Sally allowed her friend to pull her forward, she had to force a grimace off her face as every crunch on a groundcover of leaves brought them closer to potential trouble. What if someone pulled a knife? A handgun?

"This is my friend Sally," Mary said. After the children hopped up and sprinted to a run-down swing set, Mary slid next to Bertha, not bothering to wipe what looked like bread crumbs off the seat. "Sally, this is Bertha, one of our clients."

"Nice to meet you." Bertha grabbed Sally's hand.

Sally winced, both at the leathery texture and at the power manifested in those pudgy, almost dwarflike digits. "You too."

For a moment, Bertha scrutinized Sally with indifferent eyes. Then she picked up a fork, jabbed it into a container of greens, and chewed carefully, like a judge in a cooking contest.

"How are you?" Mary asked Bertha, who had set down the fork and now rummaged through a sack of what Sally determined to be pork rinds.

"Done come down with the shingles again. You want some?" She extended the container of greens toward Mary.

The pale Irish skin turned even paler. "Uh, no, but thanks, anyway."

"Aw, take a bite," Bertha coaxed. "Great Mama done brought it by. Cooked 'em up with some neck bones and onions and pepper sauce. Course they'd be better hot."

"Your mother brought them over? How sweet." Mary continued to eye the concoction.

"She know we be comin' by here for food. And she know the place we be stayin' ain't got no stove."

Laughing, the two girls dashed back toward the table.

"Yes. Well, I'm sure it's delicious."

All eyes zeroed in on Mary, who now had the two girls climbing all over her as if she were a jungle gym.

Her face still pale, Mary shrugged. Something like a smile flirted with her lips. "I am a little hungry," she said. She took the fork proffered by Bertha, speared a mouthful of greens, and set to chewing like a Hereford. She even slipped a slender hand into the bag and grabbed a couple of pork rinds.

Sally struggled to keep quiet. One of Mary's favorite soapboxes was the state of American food, yet here she was, a vegetarian no less, acting as if she actually wanted to eat the horrible-looking pieces of pig flesh that had been folded, fried, salted, and preserved to be sold as one of the cheapest, least nutritious of fast foods.

"M-m-m." Mary wiped her hand across her mouth. "You tell your mama that sure is good."

"Yes, ma'am." In the midst of a belly laugh, Bertha set to scratching like she had fleas.

Mary scooted so close her curls brushed Bertha's cheek. "I use that Amish balm for chiggers. It cures about everything but bad breath."

Somehow, Bertha managed to shake her head and roar at the same time.

"I think I've got some out in the car. If not . . ." Mary's forehead crinkled. "I'll drop it by later. Are you all still staying in the trailer park?"

Bertha nodded.

"Let me get things going, and then I'll look." Mary jumped off the bench, hugged everyone, then practically sprinted up the front porch steps.

With a fraction of Mary's speed and enthusiasm, Sally tried to catch up with her friend, eager to get a couple of things straight. "They don't have a stove?" she asked when she was out of the black woman's earshot.

"More likely, the gas got turned off." Mary tripped up the last step, curls bouncing wildly. "It's a way for her to save face; don't you see?"

Sally certainly didn't see, but she moved on to the next question anyway.

Mary turned, her face shining like the Spirit was upon her. "I *am* a vegetarian, Sally. Just not here."

For the first time since Sally had met her, Mary looked . . . happy.

✠ ✠ ✠

Sally used a knife to open another crate of canned green beans, her chatty nature silenced by the angst oozing from the clients who'd slumped into this place all morning. "Call them friends," Mary had insisted as they served lunch to nearly three dozen men, women, and children. "And if you can't do that, call them clients. At least give them their self-respect."

Now that the meal was over, Sally, along with two other women, had been relegated to the storeroom. When she leaned past a shelf of dried pasta, she could watch the people trickle in—red, yellow, black, white, and everything in between—all lighting up when they saw Mary's curly red hair and periwinkle blue eyes. They were mainly women. Mainly unattractive. Unkempt. Unhealthy. Every one of them with a burden. Every one of them wanting to talk to Mary. And from all indications, Mary wanted to talk to them.

"It's not that I don't like her." One of the other stockers, a baby-boomer type with professionally streaked hair, darted a look at Sally. "But she's just so . . . bossy."

"Oh, right, right," agreed a well-dressed, matronly looking woman whom Sally guessed to be in her early sixties. "I mean, you can't fault her motives."

"But does she have to be so chummy with them?"

"It affects her witness." Bushy gray eyebrows became accent marks on a plump face. "She stood right over there, listening to a rap CD with some . . . hoodlum." She nodded toward the front room. "Then she gave him a ride home."

"She got in the car with one of the clients?"

It was a little off-putting for these women to blubber on about Mary with no clue that she and Mary were friends, so Sally pretended to be deaf and clunked aluminum cans onto dusty shelves as if it were her lifelong passion. Two months in the Midwest had taught her that introductions seemed to be beyond even the most civil of these folks; per the status quo, Mary had forgotten or chosen not to introduce her.

Another glance at the flapping jaws told Sally that it just might be the latter. Yet this banter might help her sort out the complexities of this new friend whose temperament ran the gamut from zealous to indifferent in the span of thirty minutes. Sure, Mary cloaked her emotions behind a model-perfect figure and designer clothes, which she'd left in her closet today. It was the occasional stare out the window, the burst of intimacy followed by a too-long pause that clued Sally in to the fact that something was going on. One day—hopefully soon—Sally could, with God's help, pull off the disguise that concealed who and what Mary really was.

"Why, Mildred overheard Pete saying that Reverend Pierce said she refused to be on the board. Said it removed her from her people."

"She is different. Lois told me that someone from Chicago said her father killed himself."

"No?"

Sally thumped some cans up on a shelf. This had really gone too far. Nonetheless, she perked up her ears and inched closer.

"I'm just telling you so we can pray for her. I wouldn't dream of . . ."

Even though Sally closed her eyes and willed her ears to catch the whispers, the voices faded into incomprehensible puffs of wind.

"I need some more toilet paper. Another box of pasta." With her bounding gait, Mary had energized the room. And stopped the whispers cold.

The blond craned her neck past Mary, apparently affording herself a view of the front room. "Is it for Esther? She's already been in this week. And the rules say one roll of toilet paper and one box of—"

It wasn't that Mary doubled up her fists or anything; she didn't even move. Yet the temperature in the stuffy room seemed to rise another five degrees, probably because of the lasers that shot out of her eyes. "The rules don't pertain to a half-blind, all-deaf eighty-year-old who's had five great-grandkids dumped in her lap." A tic worked in Mary's cheek, and her hands formed a steeple. "Now, are you going to bag them up, Martha, or do you want me to?"

Martha huffed and puffed until her face turned red.

"And while you're at it," Mary added, as she strode toward the door, "put in one of those tracts. The one about God's grace."

✢ ✢ ✢

"I'm starting a book discussion group." Sally stirred more sugar into a drink that was sure to already contain five hundred calories.

I knew she was up to something. Mary's stomach tightened as it had two months ago when she and Sally had met and she'd almost blurted out the whole dysfunctional story of her past. It was strange how a couple of kind words or sympathetic glances could crumble the most carefully erected barrier. Was Sally really trustworthy, or was she all smiles and silly conversation? It was too soon to tell. "A book discussion group," Mary echoed. "What does that have to do with me?"

"Ten women have signed up already." Sally's voice had a catch in it, yet her eyes kept their brightness. "And I was hoping you would too."

"Who?"

Sally seemed perplexed by the question. "Oh, let's see. A couple of girls from my neighborhood. Darlene—"

"Who's that?"

"Sam's secretary. Let's see. Who else? A few women from tennis. The widow down the street. I've got a list started." She scooted her chair closer to the table. "Anyway, I thought you'd be interested."

"I don't think so."

"Why not? You're always talking about books."

An image of buzzing schoolmates edged in, shutting out Sally's friendly face. "Could you quit stirring that?" Mary practically screamed. "I'm sure it's dissolved."

Sally's spoon rattled as she set it down, but her lip didn't quiver at all. "What's the problem, Mary?" she asked, her eyes begging for an answer.

The gentle eyes did it. Mary leaned across the table, wanting to be closer to Sally. Needing to be closer. "I dropped out of college."

Sally expelled her breath like she'd been punched. "You've got to be kidding."

"No, I'm not." Mary slumped, just for a second. So she'd been right to question Sally's motives. At least she hadn't gone too far and exposed her secrets. Her back stiffened, and so did her resentment of this newcomer. However, when she glared at Sally, a sharp retort loaded, aimed, and ready to fire, she continued to see nothing in the blue eyes except compassion. Her anger sapped, Mary set her nearly full mug down. "Oh, Sally," she explained, "I didn't even make it a semester."

"I can't believe you think that matters to me or anyone else. You like to read, don't you?"

Did she like to read? The words scalded Mary, and her hands and her voice shook. *Ye stupid Irish girl, ain't got the brains o' a turnip.* She was always "the stupid Irish girl," no matter how hard she tried to educate herself. And this woman wanted to expose that to a whole group? When Mary shoved back from the table, coffee sloshed onto the tabletop.

Sally blotted the puddle with a napkin. "I'm sorry, Mary. But this is important." She peered across her steaming mug. "Do you like books or not?"

"I love them. It's not that. But talking about them with complete strangers seems idiotic."

"Well, Mary, they're not strangers. You know JoAnn and Mona from tennis."

"Exactly. Complete strangers."

"They're not that bad when you get to know them. And you know me, don't you?"

No. That's the problem. And you don't know me either. Mary stared at all the colors in Sally's hair. She'd noticed the gray, the blond, the brown, but now she saw glimmers of red and for some odd reason felt a glimmer of hope. She'd try it. For Sally's sake. "When is it?" she asked.

"Next Tuesday. Eleven o'clock."

Mary nodded. "As long as Mother's okay." Mary swiveled around and tossed her napkin into a garbage can. "Just this once. Now, I've gotta get going."

"I know," Sally sighed. "You can't leave your mother too long with Dora."

✞ ✞ ✞

Mary cracked a bedroom window, letting a smidgen of icicle-sharp night air into the room. She sat in her chair, opened *I Know Why the Caged Bird Sings*, closed it, and then opened it again. When the front door slammed, she slammed the book down.

"Where've you been?" Mary padded across the room to hug Paul, who smelled of manure and straw and blood.

"Calf wasn't turned right." Paul ran fingers through hair flecked with gray and stripped off jeans whose smells and stains testified to hours in the barn. "And thank God it's over."

"Why?"

"Blizzard's in the forecast." He motioned toward the book. "What's that?"

"What they're discussing tomorrow at book club. Without me."

Paul padded about the room, getting ready for bed. "I thought you liked that group."

"I did—do." Mary hugged her arms, prickly with the cold that seeped through the windows. How could she explain it so he'd understand? She didn't like it, she loved it. First she'd inhaled *Snow Falling on Cedars*. The next month, she'd checked out *East of Eden* from the library and finished it in two days. And Mitford? Claire and even Chloe, hair wrapped in a towel, had drifted in around bedtime, curious about the laughter pouring from the master suite. She'd never dreamed a book about an Episcopal priest could be both entertaining and inspirational. But she'd been wrong.

Paul picked up the book and rifled through it. "So what's the big deal?"

Mary bristled at his insensitivity and then chastised herself. How could he understand how she'd felt when she bought it—when she bought any new book, with the woodsy smell, the crisp promise of the virgin binding? Then she remembered the old ones with their yellowed pages, the faint smell of fermenting yeast, the bent spines. Books, new and old, had been her friends through those desperate years with her mothers and Daddy, but some, like this one, she couldn't handle. She willed away tears and looked at Paul. "I can't stand to read about what they did to her."

"What are you talking about?"

Mary pointed to the cover. "They abused her something awful."

Paul shot Mary a curious, though sympathetic, look. "That's life."

Mary grabbed the book from him and tossed it onto the floor, where it splayed awkwardly. Again, she hugged her arms, this time so she wouldn't slap him. Why did he have to be so matter-of-fact, so unemotional? She retreated to the bed. Of course, there were things she hadn't told him about her past. Things she hadn't told anybody.

"If you feel like that, then don't go." He dimmed the light from the wall sconces, climbed in bed, and pulled her close.

With his touch, most of the anger melted away. How could he, coming from a happy family, ever understand? "It's not that easy," she finally said, her voice as soft as his sighs.

"Why?"

"For one thing, I said I'd be there. And I'm supposed to give my report."

"On what?"

Mary pulled away from her husband, just far enough so she could think. For three months, she'd not only attended, she'd sat in the front row. And she'd answered all the discussion questions. It was Sally's leadership, as much as the books, that she loved. Somehow Sally managed to coax opinions from the more reticent while tactfully shutting down the motormouths. And then Sally had asked her, of all people, to research the bestsellers in the *New York Times* book section.

There was just enough light from the sconces for Mary to see the cover of this month's book, which was pitched like a tent on the Kilim rug. If she could just show up at Sally's, give her report, and then leave, it might be okay. But to hear this . . . travesty discussed, to have it probe at the deep, dark places—this story, so different than hers yet similar enough to chip away at the wall that she'd erected to keep in all the memories—for final confirmation, Mary studied Angelou's hoop earrings, her short Afro, before she rolled toward her husband. No. She'd rather be put in traction than go to the meeting.

Paul propped himself up on an elbow. "I asked you, what's your report on?"

"*New York Times* bestsellers."

"What's so hard about that?"

Mary kicked at him, then scooted as far away as she could get.

With one swoop of his muscular forearm, he pulled her close.

It was hard to distinguish the shivers from the cold and the shivers from his touch, and Mary didn't try to. In spite of what had happened to her, God had given her the girls, had given her this man, and it was enough. Oh, yes, it was enough.

After he turned out the lights, Paul pushed a curl from her forehead and outlined her lips with his finger before kissing them. "It'll be okay," he said. "You don't have to go, you know." Then he quit talking. They both did.

Later, Paul fell into the deep slumber of a man who'd worked long hours in harsh weather, but Mary tossed about until the sheets were tangled. When the wind's whistle became a howl, Mary remembered how it had assaulted that simple Irish cottage, remembered how her mother sang to her as they lay in that freezing room. *I was a-walking down by the sea shore, the wind it did whistle, the waves, they did roar. I heard a fair maid make a terrible sound, like the wind and the waves that did echo around.*

Mary reached for her husband, then drew back and curled into a ball. Why hadn't she told him the other thing bothering her? Tomorrow was *her* birthday, the other one who was and wasn't her mother.

She tapped on the front door and then tiptoed into the entryway without waiting for a response. She made sure to walk slowly, deliberately, to negate the trembling inside. She mouthed a hello, slid into the only empty seat in Sally's cozy den, and steeled herself to ignore the sighs and glares of more than a few women.

Sally set down that dreaded Angelou book and gave a big smile. "Hi, Mary. I'm sorry you had to miss the discussion. But I'm glad you took the time to drop by, in spite of your appointment."

Mary's mouth flew open. How could Sally have known what she was going through? How, though she'd arranged for Dora to stay all day, she'd dawdled for an hour, dreading the goggling eyes and gaping mouths, the probing questions that might pierce the skin and dig into bone? So Sally wasn't all smiles and silly conversation.

"And I'm sure you didn't have time to read the reviews, with your schedule and all. Could you do it next month?"

Mary heaved a sigh of relief. "Sure."

"Okay. Speaking of next month, any volunteers?" The women got quiet, and Mary felt everyone staring at her again. "Oh, well," Sally quickly added, "we'll figure it out later. I'll call y'all." A couple of women tried to clear dishes off assorted tables, but the room was so stuffed with bodies, it was almost impossible to budge.

A tiny woman, her skin the color of toffee, a woman Mary had admired from afar at the last meeting, tapped Mary's shoulder. "You're Mary?" she asked.

Mary nodded, somehow glad to have someone to talk to, yet still tense. It was the crowd, the weather, the past, all pushing in.

"I'm Aruna." She smoothed a bejeweled hand across the pleats of a gorgeous silk sari. "I just wanted to say how much I've loved your reviews." Dark eyes danced to match a trill like tinkling glass. "When you mimicked that highbrow who bashed *The Christmas Box*, I snorted so hard, punch came out of my nose."

Mary's eyes got wide. The Indian women she'd been introduced to, mostly doctors' and engineers' wives, had been educated in England and never talked like this . . . did they? "Why, thanks," she managed after quite a pause. "I don't know how I missed that."

Aruna laughed. "I'm glad you did." She curved her arms in a sinuous way, jangling a dozen bracelets. Mary longed to ask how she managed to wrap herself up in that sari, longed to ask several things, as a matter of fact. Like where she had met Sally. She scanned the cramped room, not exactly jealous, yet wondering how, in six months, Sally'd made more friends than she'd made in over twenty years. Of course, for much of that time, they'd been out on the farm. And Mother and the girls had kept her busy since they'd moved into town.

Aruna and Mary chatted, and so did everyone else. The noise level swelled, talcum and deodorant and perfume mingling all the while, until Mary's airways constricted and she got dizzy. Then the lengthy Midwestern rebundling process commenced, women donning coats, scarves, gloves, hats, and even blankets, all in Sally's entryway. The door opened and shut like an accordion, letting in an occasional icy blast that opened Mary's bronchial tubes so she could breathe again. Finally the crowd thinned. Mary darted about, pretending to be absorbed with cleanup.

Sally hugged the last straggler, then collapsed onto the couch. "Wow, I'm beat."

"No wonder." Mary nodded toward a side table groaning with biscuits, grits casserole, barbecued wings, and sweet potato pie, then picked up a wadded napkin someone had left on the bookcase. Sally must've cooked all night. Of course, elaborate eats were integral, indeed, the very essence of the meetings because Sally tied the food to the book's themes. In January, Bonny Gray had prepared every dish mentioned in *At Home in Mitford*, right down to Esther Bolick's Orange Marmalade Cake.

"You want to take some home?" Sally asked.

Mary shook her head, her stomach cramping at the thought. "Hey, I'm sorry I was so late."

"It's okay. How's your mother? The girls?"

"Okay." She gestured toward the tables. "Let me help you with this stuff."

Sally waved her arms and shook her head, setting off a fierce jiggle. "Heavens, no. Let's chat a bit." She motioned for Mary to sit down.

Mary lowered herself onto the mushy couch and tried to get comfortable. A truffle disappeared into Sally's mouth. "How about one of these?"

Mary looked out the front window. "I don't touch the stuff." A few snow-flakes wafted in on a westerly wind that came out of nowhere.

"I didn't realize you were that strict about it. Never, as in not ever?"

Mary nodded.

"For how long?"

"Over twenty years."

Sally's mouth dropped open. "You're kidding."

"It goes back to The Health Food Shoppe."

"What's that?"

"It's a long story."

"I knew you were into health food, but no chocolate?" When Mary didn't answer, Sally pushed on. "You don't drink either, do you?"

"Not anymore." Before Sally could ask another question, she continued, "That's another long story, too long."

Sally's voice took on a falsetto ring. "You missed the announcement about our next book, *Angela's Ashes*. It's a bestseller about Ireland and—"

"McCourt's book?"

"So you've read it?"

Mary turned away from Sally and pretended to study the paint on the wall, which seemed to have darkened from rose to crimson. "All hell's about to break loose out there," she said without even a glance toward the window. "I'd better be off."

"Hey, you're from Ireland, aren't you? Maybe you could have it at your place."

Mary clenched and unclenched her hands. *Stop it. Now.*

Sally talked faster, louder. "You'd be perfect, from Ireland and all."

The wind shook the north side of the house, rattling every loose piece of siding. Mary felt her body go rigid. What would it take to get Sally to drop the subject of that beautiful and sorrowful and hated and beloved land?

"From what McCourt said, all they had was potatoes and lots of tea. Of course, they guzzled beer and whiskey, but we won't do that. I'll help you make a potato casserole or something. In *Southern Living* there are all kinds of recipes for—"

When Mary leapt from the couch, she almost knocked over a floor lamp. "To answer all your questions, yes, I'm from Ireland, and no, I'm not from Ireland." Her voice rang out. "I hate potatoes and haven't touched a drop of tea for decades. And do you really think I need your help to host one of these meetings?"

Sally's mouth fell open, but she composed herself. "What do you mean you are and you aren't from Ireland?" she asked, her voice gentle.

"I just am." Mary paced back and forth and then sat down, a little farther away from Sally. Her voice lowered in volume but not in intensity. "What's your first memory?"

"Why?"

"Just tell me."

Sally looked closely at her friend. "I don't know. I've never thought about it."

"How pretty, not to have to think of it. My first memory cuts so deep into me, how could I not think of it?" Her eyes settled on the window as the snow fell with heightened fury. "It's a round oaken table, surrounded by moon-shaped faces guzzling cup after cup of tea. Asking what's to be done with the little eejit. That's my first memory. I'm five years old, and a roomful of adults discuss my fate as if I'm not there." She tossed her hair, growing more agitated. "It's been over forty years, and I can't drink tea to this day. Can't stand the smell of it."

"I didn't know tea had a smell."

"Can you keep quiet for once and just listen?" Mary glared with such intensity that Sally only nodded. Mary didn't stop talking for hours, words and memories spewing all over the room.

CHAPTER 4

One, two, three, four, five, Hunt the hare and turn her
Down the rocky road, dear girl, another way to Dublin
Whack fol-laddie-ah!
—"The Rocky Road to Dublin," traditional Irish folk song

Dublin, Fall 1947

Sixteen-year-old Kathleen O'Brien had thrown off all attempts to disguise the bulge that made her flee the village of Cree. In the same way, she'd extinguished the flicker of hope that the streetcars, electric lamps, and even an occasional plane had ignited in her. Sights she'd never dreamed of seeing in the village were commonplace here, yet the poor of Dublin were no better off than the poor back on the cliffs; in fact, they had it worse. In the crowded tenements, she had no stars to wish on, no salt spray to wash the coal dust from blackened faces. And the hope instilled by the shiny new things had tarnished her soul, leaving it dark and dull.

It was hard to drag on, but drag on she must, for it had been three days since she'd eaten. When she'd first approached the shops in search of a job, her face had been bright, her smile hopeful, but the city folk had taken care of the shred of dignity she'd had left after Johnny abandoned her. Often when she knocked on doors, no one answered, just peered at her from sooty windows. Still, she knocked until her knuckles ached.

The door flew open so abruptly, she gasped. "Have ye any work?" she managed.

Contempt etched into his face, the shopkeeper glared at her. "Up the pole, ye are. 'Tisn't the likes of ye we'll be needing in Dublin." The door slammed, but not before a wad of spittle found its mark. Kathleen wiped phlegm and tobacco from her cheek and tried to wipe the stain of yet another rejection from her mind.

Kathleen's prayer—that Dublin would provide anonymity and be a refuge from catcalls and brazen stares—had gone unanswered. Her questions remained unanswered as well: When would the baby come? How would she feed it? Where would she sleep tonight? She slumped listlessly through numbing drizzle.

"Ye brasser." The woman edged away from her, fluffing up her collar.

Kathleen tried to hold her head high, but the load of what they called "her sin" weighed so heavily her chin fell to her chest. She minced through congested streets toward the docks, where there were fewer noisy vehicles, fewer people, yet more whistles and wheedles. More men.

Without meaning to, she bumped into a stringy figure.

"D'ya fancy a leg-over, luv?" Leering, he grabbed at her sleeve.

Kathleen shuddered away from pock-marked arms and clothes reeking of rotgut.

"Aye, burnt yer coal and didn't warm yerself?" Spit flew from between broken teeth. "May the devil take yer runt."

She whirled, prepared to vent pent-up steam. Then she saw his hungry eyes. The rage that filled every inch of her, right down to her scuffed boots, drained out. She limped away from the salt-bleached piers where women sold the only thing they had to men desperate to fill the void in their souls, the ache in their loins. A seagull's cry split the dread silence, sending a shiver up her back. She straightened and tried to brush off dust and ash. Thank the Virgin Mary she wasn't reduced to that. Not yet.

The sun fell, the sky turned dusky blue, and by the time Kathleen trudged back to the posh district, the moon beamed its strongest light upon the fine homes of Dublin. The gate of the first house was locked, so she jiggled the second. When it clanked open, she made her way up the walk and pushed the bell.

A portly gentleman answered the door, then tried to shut it.

Kathleen wedged her foot inside. "Please," she begged. "Have pity on me. A cup o' milk or broth or—"

When the door slammed on her, she collapsed in a heap. Rubbing her ankle, she didn't try to stop a flood of tears. It was no use. She'd have to go back to the village, where at least she could eat. Then she remembered the priest and her mother waggling their fingers, threatening to send her to the Magdalenes where, if that old widow woman was right, she'd disappear forever, along with her baby. She clenched her fists, then made the sign of the cross. *They won't lay a hand on either o' us. As God be my witness.*

With fresh resolve, she tried to get up, but the ankle could not bear her weight. She fell onto cold cobbles, a spasm gripping her. Warm liquid flooded her skirt, and she screamed so loud, the sound echoed in her ears. "Holy Mother o' God, help me . . ."

✠ ✠ ✠

The cold metal table bit at her; bright lights hurt her eyes. What was happening? Where was she? Then she forgot everything but blinding pain, a brief respite, pain, rest—all thoughts retreated as she combated the cyclic assault on her body. Then it was over.

A man with twinkling blue eyes and curly hair peered down at her and laid a warm bundle on her throbbing middle. "I'm James Coughlin, lass. Ye got a girl, a lovely one at that. Flamin' hair around a moon face. Born on the night o' the full moon."

Kathleen struggled to get words out. "Sweet Jesus, is she sound?"

"She's a wee thin, but you'll take care o' that, soon enough, ye will."

As if in response, the infant howled and flailed sticklike arms and legs.

"Aye, full o' spit and fire," the doctor continued. "Fighting for life just like her mam, from what the priest said. Practically dead, ye were, when he brought ye in." He caressed the baby's head. "Has she a name?"

"Mary Elizabeth. After my best friend. Mary, she'll be." She tried to sit up. "But how'd he get me here?"

"Ne'er ye mind the details. You're safe and sound." The doctor gestured toward the corridor. "Bridget, she needs a bath. And tell Meg to prepare a bed."

A sallow-skinned ward maid leaned a mop against the wall and peered into the delivery room. "Another runner. How's he allowing it? There's no room for proper girls, much less the likes o' her."

Laughter echoed down the hall. "Get a bed for the queen and her brat."

"You mean a throne?"

"Queen Elizabeth, she is, straight from the gutter."

"Long live the queen."

The doctor cleared his throat. "Put an end to it, ye two."

The ward maids grew quiet; so did the baby. The only sound was swishing mops.

Kathleen pulled the blanket off the baby's face like a new husband pulling back his wife's veil, her tears christening the tiny forehead with love and hope. The sapphire eyes of her daughter drew her in, making all her pain, all her worry melt under their intensity. Drawing her daughter to her breast, she was further rewarded with noisy suckling sounds.

The doctor patted Kathleen's arm. "Do ye hear that? She's a survivor."

Tears mingled with sobs. "It's little hope I have for her. I can't even feed myself."

As if sensing her mother's angst, the baby shrieked.

"Hush, there," Kathleen whispered, gently guiding the perfect baby lips back to her breast. "*The currachs are sailin', way out on the blue.*" She trilled a cradle song, one remembered from her childhood. "*Laden with herring of silvery hue. Silver the herring, silver the sea. Soon there'll be silver for baby and me.*"

The doctor drew out a stethoscope and listened to Kathleen's heart. Then he searched, and found, her gaze. "'Tis a job for ye, in our house." He touched her arm with slender yet strong fingers. "You'll be a maid for the missus."

Kathleen tried to sit up, but a stab of pain forced her to lie back. She thought of the leers of the men on the street, the betrayal at the hand of the boy who swore he'd love her until the moon dropped from the sky, and jerked from the doctor's touch. "If ye think—"

"Upon my song, a housekeeper." The room seemed to sigh as the doctor made the sign of the cross over the infant's head. "A housekeeper indeed."

✠ ✠ ✠

"Shush, now!" Kathleen set her rag on the hall tree in the Coughlin entryway and smoothed flaming curls from three-year-old Mary's face. But it was too late.

Mrs. Coughlin put her hands on her hips and glared at Kathleen. "Get her out."

"Yes, missus." Kathleen picked up Mary, then gripped the rail of the curved staircase. Even now, pains shot through her abdomen when she carried a heavy load.

"Then get to yer cleaning."

Missus's imperious airs made Kathleen's blood boil. Still, she waited until the jangle of bracelets and the swish of skirts signaled that Missus had carried her tirade to the cook. "Scour this, scrub this," she railed to Mary. "It's impossible. Murder."

The child waggled her tongue, like Missus had. "Get to yer cleanin.'"

Despite her pain, Kathleen smiled. *She's got fire, she has.* With a spring in her step, she carried Mary up to their room, which held a single bed, a chamber pot, and a weathered dresser. "Right here you'll stay." She set Mary on the floor.

"No." Mary punctuated her word by a stomp of her foot.

Kathleen scooped up Mary and held her close, longing to make the embrace good enough, long enough, to last for a day. "*Who are ye, my pretty fair maid?*" she sang. "*Who are ye, my honey? Too-ry-ay, fol-de-diddle-day, I am me mother's darling.*"

Mary rammed her head into her mother's body, leaving Kathleen no choice but to slap her. The child didn't say a word but broadcast a baleful glare.

Tears sprang to Kathleen's eyes. "So hard already ye are, yet such blue eyes you've got. Just like yer pap's." *Where are your eyes that were so mild, hurroo, hurroo? Why did ye run from me and the child? Oh, Johnny, I hardly knew ye.* For a moment, Kathleen was back on the cliffs with her blue-eyed Johnny. Had he known even then, as he'd sung her that old folk song, what he'd do to her? To his daughter?

As Kathleen memorized every tint and hue of her child's face, the wind rattled the windowpane, mocking their hopes, their dreams, even their very existence. She gripped Mary's arm, avoiding the eyes that begged for things Kathleen could not give, and shoved her toward the bed. "Don't ye stir," she ordered.

The child swiveled her head toward the birch rod on the dresser and obeyed.

Her heart heavy, Kathleen tiptoed down the stairs, careful not to tinkle the crystals of the table lamp in the entryway with her movements.

"The child doesn't fit in now, James." The bracelets jangled. Silk rustled.

"She's not just 'the child.' She has a name."

Kathleen had to strain to hear the doctor's voice.

"Aye, she doesn't. And that's the problem. They've got to go."

Kathleen's hands flew to cover her ears. It took no effort to hear Missus.

"And where to? They'll just send her to the Magdalenes. She'll lose the babbie."

"But what of it?"

"Ye can't mean it, Rose. Think o' your own."

With no effort, Kathleen could envision the sneer on her mistress's face.

"How can ye compare that trollop to our daughters, off at school and so good?"

"It'll be worse if we don't help her."

"You've a notion about her, don't ye?"

When she heard the scrape of a chair, Kathleen, her breast heaving, rushed into the dining room.

Her mistress gaped at her, then pointed to plates of nearly untouched food. "Off wi' them," she ordered.

The doctor rushed past Kathleen and into the entryway. After jerking his hat off the hall tree, he paused, one hand on the front door. "We'll manage," he finally said. The movement of his head was so slight it could barely be called a nod. "All of us."

♱ ♱ ♱

"Get down here, lazy one."

Kathleen flinched but quickly recovered. She'd been called worse than *lazy one* by Missus lately.

As she reached the bottom stair, a basket was thrust at her. More mending. More wash. She rubbed her back, longing to pull off the shoes that so pained her swollen feet. Instead, she stiffened her spine—and her resolve. She wouldn't cry, wouldn't give Missus another reason to rail about her to the doctor. With a nod, she took the basket of silks and wool and taffeta.

Four-year-old Mary tripped down the stairs, adding light and life to the entryway. She leapt toward the shimmering crystals, which painted rainbows on the paneled wall. With a crash and a thud, the lamp crashed to the floor.

It wasn't clear to Kathleen whether Mary or the Missus screamed first.

Missus flew to Mary and slapped her face.

When Kathleen leapt forward, the clothes basket flew out of her hands. Fabrics mingled their textures and colors with those of an oriental rug. In a rage of reds and blues and greens, Kathleen jerked Mary off the floor.

The child didn't whimper, nor did she move.

Kathleen didn't blink, nor did she step back. "Don't ye touch my child."

Missus, her eyes bulging, raised her hand again.

Kathleen moved a step closer. *How could he love her?* She stared at the gray eyes, the jowled face and, for the first time, knew raw hate.

The missus stared back.

Kathleen steeled herself to stare for as long as it took, fists coiled, preparing to strike. Finally, Missus looked away.

The small victory lessened Kathleen's rage and allowed a bit of reason to step in. She longed to attack Missus with her words, her fists, but feared what might happen if she dared. For nights, she'd tossed about, a dozen scenarios racing through her mind. Scenarios all ending at the same place. They had nowhere to go, no one to depend on. But now Missus had slapped Mary, had crossed an invisible line that had kept the house from erupting into chaos. It was one thing for Missus to hate her—in some ways, Kathleen didn't blame her for that—but now the horrid woman had slapped her child. She had to strike back, didn't she?

Missus stormed down the hall, taking most of Kathleen's anger with her. No. They had to stay here. No matter what Missus did, the answer was still no.

Kathleen's respite was brief; the Missus stalked back in, waving a paper. She stared and glared and waited, hands on her hips.

"'Tis sorry, I am." Kathleen choked on each word and swallowed the curses she longed to utter. "It won't happen again."

Missus's eyes gleamed as she held out the list. "It's market day. Now scram."

"But the mendin'?"

The eyes triumphed total control. "You've got nothin' else to do with yer nights, now, do ye?"

Kathleen didn't bother to reply. She grabbed a basket and Mary, strode under the arched door, and pattered down the steps. "She's a wretched thing, she is," she shot at the closed door.

Mary studied her face, then squinted and tilted her head in such a comical way that Kathleen's anger evaporated, laughter and song rolling in.

"*In Dublin's fair city, where maids are so pretty, 'twas there I first met my sweet Molly Malone.*" Kathleen clanked the gates shut, hoping the words of the old song would close out lingering memories of Missus. "*She was a fishmonger, but sure 'twas no wonder . . .*"

With Kathleen still singing, they meandered through a maze of alleys that led to the bustling market. Before they melted into the throng of shoppers, Kathleen studied the list. *Fish. Meat.* She shuddered. *Sweet Jesus, not the butcher's son. Last, it'll be. And have him on an errand, dear God, please.*

Sounds, sights, and smells coursed through the cobbled streets, and the mother and child skipped, singing, "*Cockles and mussels, alive, alive-o.*" Life for Kathleen was reduced to the wonder mirrored in her child's face. Mary, crinkling her nose in response to the pungent odors of the fishmonger's stall. Mary, her nose buried in the rosebud proffered by a red-cheeked flower vendor. Even the battle for fresh produce became child's play with Mary near.

The last purchase seemed heavy as Kathleen tucked it into the basket. They had to get back. "*Cockles and mussels*"—she tried to revive their earlier gaiety—"*alive . . .*"

A man stepped toward them, grizzled eyebrows giving him a stern look.

The song died on Kathleen's lips. *He's starin' like he knows us.* With suddenly numb arms, she managed to pull Mary into the folds of her skirt and still hold the basket.

"Jesus, Mary, and Joseph! Kathleen O'Brien!"

The gravelly voice sent a chill up Kathleen. Images of the village pushed in. She whisked Mary into her arms, took off running. Faster, faster. Dare she look back? Almost as if she had no control of it, her head swiveled about. She had to see. Had to know.

His eyes were wide, his mouth open, but it came to Kathleen almost at once. *The village postmaster, 'tis, here in Dublin.* Every muscle in her body tensed. *Of all the bloody coincidence, that he'd find me here. Another minute, hour, day . . .*

The man pressed forward. Before she could vanish into the crowd, he grabbed her by the shoulder and spun her around to face him.

"'Tis really you." He pulled down his spectacles to peer at her with rheumy eyes. "You've worried yer mam to the grave and back." Like he was shooing off pesky flies, he waved his arms. "Where're ye stayin' in this jungle o' humanity? How can ye care for her here?" When Kathleen didn't answer, he grabbed her arm. "Talk, for heaven's sake, girl. Talk." He reached for her arm. "Need I call the guards?"

Kathleen stiffened like a dying carp; she spat out a name, an address, before she considered the consequences. Then she tore from his grasp and sliced through the crowd, careening off shawl-clad women. *Alive, alive.* She pressed Mary so close to her breast their hearts beat as one. *Oh, oh.* Perspiration mingled with chilling rain as Kathleen flew, her breath escaping in pants, her heart clopping like horse hooves. When she reached the gate, she threw open the latch and tried to shut out the reminder of her old life.

✠ ✠ ✠

February 20, 1953

Dear Daughter,

    The postmaster reports you are in Dublin. Kathleen, we are your blood and bone. For the love of family, will you come back to County Clare with the child? We've found a match for you, Killian McNamara, who will bring you back to where you should be. He lives with his sisters on the rocky cliffs near Glascloune. We'll be sending twenty pounds for carriage.

Mam

Crimson sparks echoed the burning in her soul as Kathleen balled up the letter and threw it into the parlor fire. "They cast us out, they did. Now they want us back?"

The child laughed at the popping and hissing of the wood.

"Ye think it's a sport, do ye?" To ease the tension that gripped her, she stroked Mary's hair, which the flames had tinged with gold. Could this be what she'd prayed for? She envisioned being with another man besides the lanky six-footer who could outrun every lad on the bog, but it repulsed her. She'd loved Johnny, had given herself to him . . .

Missus's footsteps, clacking nearer, nearer, reminded her that she might have no choice. She wiped sweaty palms on her apron. And how about the doctor? Where did he fit into the chaos that was her life? Did she imagine the softening in his eyes when he looked at her? She didn't think so. But was it pity? Or something else?

Charred remains of the letter floated up the chimney. She forced herself to again consider this Killian McNamara. Did he have hands like the doctor's, strong yet gentle? Or were they like those clublike digits of the butcher's son, ripping up carcasses as if he enjoyed it? And which, by prayers to the Holy Mother, she'd thus far avoided. But for how long? The fire flamed, her letter now ashes. And though the parlor was warm, Kathleen shivered.

☦ ☦ ☦

When she tilted her head and peeked into his study, she could just see him. And it made harder the thing that she had to do. The last of the sun's warmth radiated through the window, illuminating the formal posture that belied a heart she knew to be tender. She slipped past the hat rack and stepped for only the third time into the room that housed shelf after shelf of thick medical books detailing the travails of the human body. The first time she'd touched spines boasting words she couldn't even pronounce—words like *pathology*, *embryology*, *histology*—a chill shivered up her. The next time, while she pretended to dust, Missus had insisted she leave, saying she might interfere with his work. She clasped and unclasped clammy hands. Would this third visit be the last? After crossing herself, she stepped toward the massive rolltop desk.

"The missus said ye had an offer." He stared toward the window, seeming to inspect the patterned velvet that shut out the twilighting of the spring sky.

"She read my letter? How dare she?" Remembering the loose seal on the thin envelope, Kathleen surged toward him like a rogue wave, boiling and out of control. *Of course. Before she'd set it on my dresser, she'd have taken in every word of it.*

"It's no good." He studied a file on his desk before he wounded her with swollen, red-tinged eyes. "God help me, 'tis too much for a soul to bear."

"Ye haven't a clue what a soul can bear." Hate made her voice hard; at this instant, she hated him. She threw herself across the desk and dug her nails into his smooth hands, knocking off a paperweight. The tic near his left cheek let her know what this was doing to him, but that was the only sign. Limp hands deflected her passion, and she longed to get the paperweight and hurl it at him. Was his a complicit betrayal, or had Missus worn him down with her endless nagging? Like a marksman, she searched for his eyes, vowing to destroy him with a furious glare. Unexpectedly, the pools of blue, with flecks of brown about the pupils, took her captive. She turned and slumped out the door. As Missus had said countless times, she had to go.

✠ ✠ ✠

The Cliffs near Glascloune, Spring 1953

Kathleen crawled about in the arc of light created by a sputtering kerosene lamp, her sweat dripping onto the floor of the front room in the McNamara house. For weeks, she'd tried to scrub years of neglect from stones so filthy they blackened her knees as she crawled about. No running water, no electricity—so different from Dublin, especially in a posh home. Yet it was better to scrub this floor, stay busy; avoid thinking about what awaited as the moon rose along with his insatiable appetite.

A thud from the back room sent a shudder through her. *Not a lamp, Dear God, she'll burn this heap down.* When a crash followed soon after, she sprang into action, her heart pounding.

"Get out, ye bloody tinker."

Kathleen flew into the room. There was Mary, a heap at the feet of Killian.

"Get 'er out." Words slurred out of a mouth slack from too much drink. He glared at her, meanness concentrated in dark pinpoints of light that passed for eyes.

Kathleen slung Mary over her shoulder and stormed out, sloshing through barnyard muck as rank as her thoughts. When they reached the bare open space where the slate and sea and soil whirled in a desolate mist, where even potatoes struggled to take root, where on a clear day, you could see the faint outlines of mysterious isles, she set Mary down.

In spite of the reddening swell on her cheek, Mary shielded her eyes with her hand and pointed across the great water. "Mam, look!"

A flock of puffins swooped near, striking black-and-white markings visible by the light of the full moon.

Kathleen followed their pattern of flight. Dare she too take wing from this cursed place? She had suspected what he was the first time he had grabbed her, but now she knew why three prospects had rejected him just last year. She tried to massage some feeling into hands numb from carrying her five-year-old, but it was no use. Her feelings for everything were disappearing fast, much like those birds.

"Where are they off to, Mam?"

"Only God knows, lass." With pride, Kathleen studied her child, who held her head high in spite of the torn dress, thin arms, bruised face. If it weren't for Mary, she would—

She tried to shut off her thoughts, steady her trembling limbs, steel herself to face another night.

A pair of crows cawed, harsh like the sisters' voices. Kathleen longed to hurl a rock at them. The old-maid sisters were the blow she hadn't expected. Did they hate her because her womb hadn't dried up, her breasts were supple? Her heart grew heavy from the burden of it all, especially how they piled the most demeaning tasks onto her shoulders, her back, her limbs.

The crash of an unexpected wave jolted her to the truth. Neither the sisters nor the work pushed her closer to the jagged edge. It was the nights that she detested most—when he jarred open the door of the room where she huddled with Mary, when he sprang onto the bed until it creaked. After he left, she'd lie spent by the cumulative assaults and endure a final rebuke by the whining and wailing wind. Clinging to Mary, she pondered the things she'd done and the price she was paying for them. Then she wept.

"Look, Mam!" The light in Mary's eyes accentuated the swollen red lid, another evidence of Killian's wrath.

Tears flowed faster; Kathleen did not try to check them. How long could Mary keep her spirit while pummeled with thick hands? Cursed with blasphemous words?

A lone puffin broke away from a knot of feathers and beaks, as if in direct defiance. Without even so much as a flick of its wing, it sailed across the horizon, distancing itself from the flock. Kathleen memorized its every move, then lurched forward and almost fell. When she regained her equilibrium, she wheeled from the cliffs, Mary in tow. It had to be done. The question was no longer *if*, but *when*.

✝ ✝ ✝

Mary fell silent. Huddled into the corner of the couch, she looked like a lost child.

Sally prodded gently. "Then they decided to send you away?"

"My first memory . . . They just sat there, around that table, spilling tea and words all over my future." Her mouth shut, then opened, but no words came out.

Sally moved closer and put an arm around her. "Then how did you learn what happened before that, in Dublin?"

"My grandmother told me years later." Mary talked as if she'd been drugged. "And she gave me Mam's old letters." She rubbed her hands together as if she were washing them. "It's surrounded me, become a part of me. It's almost like . . ."

"You feel like you were there?"

Mary leapt off the couch and paced in front of the window. "It's like God allowed me to experience it somehow. I seem to know what she looked like, what he smelled like . . ." Turning back, Mary met Sally's eyes. "You understand, don't you?"

Sally held her gaze. "I want to understand. Very much."

Tears threatened then. "Sally, I don't know what came over me. Biting your head off when you asked me about Ireland. It's just that I've never told anyone except Paul." Mary looked out the window. Snow fell softly, blanketing Sally's lawn. "I wasn't even going to come today, but I promised. Then it started snowing and—" Mary laughed and cried at the same time. "I'm not sure why I'm telling you. Except . . ." She bit her tongue. *The loneliness. The voices. The past closing in.*

Sally grabbed Mary's hands, cradling them in hers. "Tell me the rest of it. Now."

Slowly, Mary nodded. "For weeks after they decided to send me away, I monitored Mam's behavior like a weatherman." She spoke with careful enunciation, as if she were reporting the six o'clock news. "When nothing happened, I relaxed a little. I had no idea God planned a hurricane to blow my way."

CHAPTER 5

A poor little lamb has lost its way. Baa! Baa! Baa!
Poor little black sheep, gone astray. Baa! Baa! Baa!
—Meade Minnegerode, "The Whiffenpoof Song"

Out on the cliffs, five-year-old Mary measured time by the changes that nature announced. From the big boulder at cliff's edge, if she leaned over, she could see the setting sun streaking the water with pink, orange, and red and watch for changes. Sometimes seabirds flapped of a coming storm or the wind whispered before high tide, but tonight, there was nothing. Her body relaxed, freed from worry about *Chicago* and *Harris*, words she didn't really understand, anyway.

The sun melted into the sea, highlighting the shimmering surface with its last embers and bringing the expected evening chill. Shivering, Mary dashed through the field, angled away from the barn, and, with a whoosh of breath, jumped onto the creaky porch. When a dandelion peeked through a rotted board, a smile wreathed her face. Mam had shown her how to pluck the feathery blooms, make a wish, and scatter them with a puff. She picked the flower, then sat on the top step. Breathing in the scent of the damp earth that lay under the shaky foundation, Mary squeezed her eyes shut and made a wish.

An answering clatter in the barn informed her that it had not come true. Killian had not been plucked up and eaten by a sea serpent. Mary clenched her fists. Killian's curled-up lips, narrowed eyes broadcast the fact that he hated her. But she hated him more. His hand, rough as sandpaper. His face, red with drink. She closed her eyes and wished again.

"Sup's on. Set the table." It was Ma, her voice raspy as the puffins' cry.

Hope for food propelled Mary into a room that had a table, a fireplace with a pot hanging over it, and chairs. Last night, Killian had sopped up every mouthful of soup. Even though it had been thin with only wilted shreds of cabbage floating on top, Mary would have fought him like a dog fighting for a bone if she'd had any chance at it. Of course, she hadn't. She grabbed spoons, scattered them across the table, hoping tonight would be different.

When Killian banged in the door, the whole house shook. "Off wi' ye, slish!"

Mary scampered away and cowered by the bubbling pot, peeking around the crusted, cast-iron rim to watch Killian cram bread and ladle soup into his mouth.

Sneering, he tossed a spoon toward her. "As you're there, give it a stir."

Mary darted to the spoon, grabbed it, and stuck it in the pot. When it wobbled, she steadied it, but heat seared her fingers. The spoon skittered across stone.

"Leave it be," Mam ordered.

Mary froze. Should she obey Mam or Killian? Her legs tensed like a lamb wary of a new scent. The tightness of Killian's mouth, the death grip he had on his spoon, provided the answer. As she stirred, she closed her eyes and let the aroma wash over her. If she couldn't eat it, smelling it was second best.

Killian bolted his food, kicked the door open, and lumbered to the barn.

It was as if Mary had been set free. She scurried to the table, slurped soup from Mam's bowl, then waited, her heart fluttering. She could hear the music, feel the music . . .

Sure enough, Mam curled by the fire and pulled Mary close. *"Black's the color o' my true love's hair. Lips like wild Irish roses fair."* Flames lit her eyes, her smile.

The music lifted Mary's spirits, and so did the fact that she had been right about what would happen. She jumped and twirled about the room, the familiar chorus making her heart swell like it did when the doves cooed and the cows mooed.

"Come here, ye dear one. I'll brush yer hair."

Mary ran to Mam's side, warmed by the attention. It was a good night so far. She'd eaten. And there had been music.

"Mother o' Jesus. Get 'er out." The door banged a second time.

There was no decision to make. Mary flew into the back room and threw herself on the bed. She clenched her toes, her hands, her lips, even her heart, and wished again.

The wind howled a warning, pricking Mary's ears. *Cold blows the winter air. Soon, child, soon.* Even if the message was bad, it was better to know. Yet she could not understand exactly what the wind was trying to say to her.

Later, Mam, mewling like a hungry kitten, slid into bed and pulled her close.

Mary patted Mam's wet face and stroked her back. Why did Mam cry so much?

"'Tis got to change, it does." Her head bowed, Mam made the sign of the cross. "A sign. 'Tis all I ask, dear Jesus."

Mary brushed a curl from Mam's face and, with the moon's help, studied it. What was the change that was making Mam cry?

"I will take you back, Kathleen." Mam's eyes got soft, and since she was singing, she could not cry.

Mary's head fell on Mam's chest, and she quit worrying about changes.

"When the fields are fresh and green, I'll take you to your home again . . ."

As Mary's heart found the rhythm of Mam's heart, the two beat as one. A gentle rain joined the chorus, and then Mary herself echoed the words. Right before she drifted off, she smiled at the splendor of the night music.

✠ ✠ ✠

"Will ye ever hurry up?"

Mam didn't need to say it twice; Mary ran in circles like a dog trying to catch its tail. She dashed out the door and skipped ahead but made sure to look back from time to time to ensure that Mam and the sisters were following. Especially Mam.

"Morning." Farmer O'Loughlin set down his pitchfork. "Where are ye off to?"

"Kilkee." Mam smiled. "'Tis a fine day for work, sir."

"Aye, but no time to tarry." He turned back to the pile of hay, pitchfork in hand. "'Twas a red sky this morning."

Mary turned to Mam, afraid not of the wisps of clouds in the sky but of the clouds in the farmer's face. "What's it about?" she asked.

Either Mam didn't hear her or she pretended not to. It was enough to make Mary slow her step. She had to stay close to Mam.

Mrs. O'Loughlin, the farmer's wife, waved, and the sun seemed to shine brighter. "'Tis a bully day, Kathleen." Flour dusted her cheeks, nose, apron, even her hair.

"Aye, Abigail, 'tis. Bakin', ye are?"

Mary's stomach growled, her mouth watered, just thinking of the yeasty slabs. And butter thick as paste. She walked backward, her eyes frozen on Abigail.

Something honked like a goose.

Mary spun around, then slipped and fell on the gravelly road, yet she barely noticed the scraped hands and knees for the new sight. "What's this about?"

"Ye stupid twit. Ye—" Jean started to say something else, but Mam cursed with such force that even Jean fell silent.

"'Tis a road for the rich folk and their fancy cars. Now, up with ye." While Mary stared at the noisy sight, Mam yanked her up. They trudged on, the sisters trailing even farther behind.

Images of the shiny cars swirled in Mary's head, and for the first time, she thought that changes might be good. Then the road curved to reveal a sandy beach and waves caressing the feet of dancing children. Mary's heart leapt to join them; so did her feet, her hands, her—

"Mary Elizabeth, stop!"

The tone of Mam's voice halted her. Mary fought the bounce in her step, the song in her heart, and trudged back toward Mam, who was coming fast and flinging her arms. *And saying my whole name, which means a whipping if I don't take heed.*

"'Tis for Kilkee we're bound. Now come on!"

Mary turned for a final look, her arms extended, her hands opening and closing, as if she could grasp a bit of the happiness and pull it near. But she knew without Mam having to say a word that the children's happiness was not for her.

The four of them walked slower. Mam kept smoothing down her dress. As they walked down the street, a man approached them, swaying and weaving. "Filthy bogsiders," he hissed. "Ye breed like flies."

Mam spat horrible words at him, then yanked Mary close and practically dragged her into a store. Mam's steps slowed, and she waved the sisters toward a table piled with clothes.

What's this about? Mary cowered behind Mam, petrified of the intensity in the women's eyes as they dug through the fabrics. Another change was coming, sure as the sun sank in the sea at day's end. Mary knew they didn't have a tuppence to spare, yet here they were in a store. She cleared her throat, the questions unable to stay inside. "What's this about?"

"Hush." Mam's eyes were glued to the table. "'Tis too many questions yer asking."

The women sorted clothes as if it was wash day. Jean handed dresses to Mam, but she pushed them away. She seemed to forget Mary was there, so intent was she on her work. Then she turned and faced her daughter, as if to include Mary in the task. "Lass, it's yer choice," Mam said, her eyes bright. "Lass?"

Mary shrank back. Why would she want an eejit to choose? *What's happening?*

Mam smiled with her lips but not her eyes.

She wanted to make Mam happy. Needed to make Mam happy. She inched closer.

"Be quick about it. Which three?" When Mary still didn't speak, Mam pointed at Jean. "You'll leave it to Jean, then?"

Mary shook her head, then tried to let all the colors, the patterns take away the fear. Pink like a piglet's belly. Blue like the sky that very day. White. Red. Her head spinning, she grabbed the pink and blue dresses.

"Get away now, you'll wrinkle 'em!" Mam glared at Mary, then seemed to soften. "One more, lass."

The incredible riches overwhelmed Mary; she shook her head and stepped away.

Mam chose the white one, swirl after swirl of lace bound at the waist with a satin ribbon thicker than Mary's arm, then pointed Mary toward another aisle. "Shoes, it'll be."

Cold crept into Mary's fingers, then her arms, and spread over her body. Something was terribly wrong; she'd never worn shoes.

Everything paid for, they left the store, Mary at Mam's heels like a loyal dog. Jean led the way into another building.

A man behind a counter nodded as if he knew them. Dark eyes studied all of them, especially Mam. He fumbled through a pile of letters, then handed one to Jean.

Whatever she saw on the letter lit up Jean's face. She clutched it in shaking hands.

Mam lunged at Jean, her bosom heaving, her arms waving.

Jean swatted Mam away, then tore into the thin envelope. "'Tis more than we hoped," she gasped, her eyes gleaming like new tuppence.

"It's the Harrises, is it?" A frown tightened the skin around Mam's eyes.

Harris. The word dug into Mary. Wasn't that what they'd said around the table? And was this the sign? Kicking and yelling, she threw herself on the floor. This change wouldn't take her easily. She'd fight it, she would, she'd—

Mam jerked her up.

Mary glared, stuck out her hip, and waited for the usual slap. Instead, Mam twisted her mouth into—not a frown, but not a smile, either. Mary just stood, watching the three women. Before she could decide what to do, another change occurred.

"Come on, and I'll buy ye something nice." Mam guided Mary out the door and into another building. "A treat."

Colors took over again, as they had tried to do in the store. Mary felt her eyes get wide at rows and rows of blue and pink and red and white candies waiting so patiently in clear-lidded jars. She stepped forward, then hesitated. How could one pick between so many lovely things? Without a second glance, she hurried past the ones holding sweets whose secrets were hidden behind paper. *No unknown things, not for me.*

Mam traipsed with Mary along the candy counter, the lines about her mouth gone. She pointed to a jar filled with strange black ropes. "I once took a liking to licorice."

The shopkeeper smiled at both of them. "It will last 'til the sun sets."

Those words sealed Mary's decision. While Mam paid, Mary pulled a twisted strand of licorice from a jar and bit into it. Her lips puckered up in surprise, unsure about the strange mix of sweet and bitter. After a second taste, she clung to it like a prized toy.

As she walked home, Mary nipped tiny bites off the candy and chewed as slowly as she could, her mind on the dresses, the shoes, the letter. But the sun on her shoulders and the breeze in her hair buoyed her hopes that nothing would happen. She skipped ahead, singing. In her excitement, she dropped the candy into a puddle, then frantically dug through mud and manure to find it.

With lightning speed Kathleen yanked Mary from the road. "You've mucked it up, ye wretched child."

The growling in Mary's stomach, the watering of her mouth grew, and she found herself walking faster, hunger propelling her farther ahead of the women, through trampled grass that marked the path past the O'Loughlins'. Dare she ask the missus for a piece of her bread, warm and moist and full of oats and wheat and salt? Mary could almost taste it, somehow crunchy and soft at the same time.

"One a penny, two a penny, hot cross buns." Girls clad in navy jumpers whirled from around a bend. One balanced a book on her head; the others clutched them to their chests. They pointed and laughed and hurried toward a white-steepled building.

Mary's heart ached with a feeling she didn't understand. They were so pretty, so neat, their hair pulled back from shiny faces. She touched her ragged shift and stared at her dusty feet. As they tripped into the building, it enticed her like a secret cave filled with untold riches. She yearned to fall in behind them and let them lead her.

Mary ran toward the familiarity of the O'Loughlin barn. "Where are they off to?" she asked the farmer.

"School." Farmer O'Loughlin set down a hoe, sweat pouring off his face. The lines around his eyes relaxed as he pulled Mary onto his knee.

She looked up at his face. "What's it about?"

"Ye learn to write and read, Lass."

"Can I go too?"

He stared off at a thin line of clouds forming over calm water. "Ask yer mam."

Mary jumped up and ran to Mam with such eagerness she almost knocked her down. "Can I go to school? The farmer says—"

"No, ye can't." The lines had returned to Mam's mouth. "Who's he to plant such a farfetched notion in yer mind? School 'tisn't for the likes o' ye." She handed Mary the package of dresses. "Here. Take 'em and begone."

Mary burst into tears. Why couldn't she be like the schoolgirls? She flung the bundle on the ground and kicked at it.

With a sigh, Mam picked it up and handed it back, then tried to wipe Mary's sticky face. "Put on yer favorite one, and get that rag of a doll. 'Tis a tea party we'll have while all the proper ones rot in the stinkin' school."

Mary clutched the bundle to her chest once more and hurried home, the schoolgirls a dim memory. To play with Mam! They hadn't had a chance since—since they'd come here. She sped into the house, ripped open the bundle, and pulled out the pink dress. Whoosh, it was over her head. Grabbing her rag doll, she posed for the mirror, twirling round and round. Fancy, she was now, and ready for a party. She tried to walk tall and proud like the schoolgirls did as she took her doll to the table.

When Mam came in, Mary bounced up and down, and so did the doll. "Can we have sugar, Mam? Please?"

Mam poured the tea, then plopped a cube into Mary's cup.

Mary pointed to her doll. "She wants one too."

When Mam giggled, her face glowed like those of the schoolgirls. She patted the doll on its mop of yarn. "How do ye know what she wants?" she asked Mary.

"Because she's like me." Mary said, then bit her tongue. She wasn't like the doll anymore, now that she had nice clothes, but she'd pretend. She dipped her finger into the cup, then smeared tea across its face. "Can ye sing, Mam?" she asked, wanting the music to join them.

Mam shook her head but didn't say no.

"Please, Mam." The doll bounced up and down along with Mary.

Minutes later, they were both secure in Mam's lap. "*The water is wide*," Mam sang. "*I can't get o'er. And neither have I wings to fly.*"

Mary leaned her head against Mam and relaxed her grip. If only they could do this every day . . .

"*Give me a boat that can carry two. And both shall row, my love and—*"

Boots tromped into the room. "Fetch me water, ye doxie." It was Killian, followed by his sisters.

Mary threw her doll down and crumpled next to it. Killian had even managed to spoil their party. Tears spilled onto the scarred floor.

The slosh of water and the plunk of the pail startled Mary. Before she could protest, Mam jerked her up, yanked the sash free of its bow, and pulled the new dress over her head. "Now, off with ye. Get to the bog where ye belong."

Mary burst from the house and raced to the cliffs. "Why don't they want me?" she shouted. A stiff gust shoved Mary's words back at her with such force even the sheep scooted away. It was enough to quiet Mary. The sheep were her friends, and she didn't want to scare them. Sniffling, she tiptoed toward a lone lamb that lay near a mound of stones. As she got close, she held her breath so she wouldn't startle it. The lamb tensed as if it too would scamper off, but then relaxed and let Mary pet it. Together they watched the sun sink into frothing waters and disappear into the deep.

✟ ✟ ✟

"You're telling this like it happened yesterday."

Mary nodded. "I still have one of those dresses packed in the basement. I thought it meant happier times." She shook her head. "What a fool I was."

"You didn't know." Sally kept her voice calm, but she wanted to scream. What mother would let a child pick out her going-away clothes? "You were, what, only five?"

"Almost six. I sensed another change, and there was nothing I could do to stop it."

CHAPTER 6

I leave thee in sorrow, no more—nevermore—thy rich vales to behold. The stormy
Atlantic shall bear me to-morrow and dash its cold spray on a bosom as cold.
— "The Exile's Farewell," traditional Irish folk song

Mam?" Thunder crashed; rain splattered against the window. Mary bolted for
the door, not bothering to warm herself by the fire. "Mam?" Her heart plummeted
when she saw the trunk sitting strangely by the table. Change. A big one.

The door creaked open. Jean and Isabella stood before her. "There ye be."

"Where—where's Mam?" Mary asked, her hands a knot.

"She's not here." Jean grabbed Mary's wrist. "Come with me. Now."

Flailing her arms, Mary jerked away. She had to find Mam. She slept with
Mam, ate with Mam, sang with Mam—

"Be a nice one, and come on," Jean coaxed and wheedled. "We mustn't
be late."

Isabella stepped close and took Mary's hand. "Come, come. We'll find yer
Mam." She led Mary to the bedroom and picked up her favorite new dress, her
new shoes. "There. It'll look lovely on ye, it will."

Mary stepped into the dress, careful not to flatten the skirt. *Maybe we're*
having another tea party. But where is she off to? As Isabella buttoned her up,
Mary weighed the evidence. Good change? Bad change? That was the problem.
She didn't know.

"There's a good lass." Isabella pulled a comb through her hair and tied
a ribbon.

A honk. A car.

"Come along," Isabella said, her voice hard.

Mary shook her head until the ribbon fell out. The new clothes had been
good, she'd been sure of it before. But she had been wrong.

Isabella kicked it aside. "You'll see yer Mam, I swear it." In a too-sweet voice, she added, "And you'll get yer first ride."

Mary's heart raced like the engines of the cars that chugged to Kilkee. Would Mam get to ride too? She let Isabella lead her outside. They got into the car, the sisters like sheep dogs by the windows, Mary herded into the middle.

The engine sprang to life. As they bumped down the lane, Mary's favorite lamb skittered toward them. "No!" She kicked at the seat. "No ! Stop!"

The car swerved toward the lamb. There was a thud. A bump. A horrible strangling cry.

Mary screamed and beat the back of the seat. She hadn't seen the lamb get hit, but she knew that her little lamb friend was hurt. Or worse.

"Shut up, ye little bugger." All Mary could see of Killian were hunched shoulders. But she heard him; oh, she heard the words that spewed from him like a poison gas.

Mary flung herself onto Isabella. She bit her lip and clenched her fists from the questions that would not stop. Why did he run over her lamb? Would he kill her too? Questions churned in her stomach.

They streaked past endless lines of stones, hedgerows, sheep—were they taking her to Mam, as Isabella had said? Or was it Chicago and Harris?

The car stopped. Jean tried to straighten Mary's hair. They all got out and went into a building, Killian lugging the trunk.

They were greeted by men and women dressed in crisp green uniforms, with such smiling, white teeth. Mary felt sure Mam would be here. She tried to put the lamb sounds far, far away, and it was easy in such a bright place.

One of the new people led her to a huge window and explained about airplanes. Then they stepped back to where Killian and the sisters stood. Mary watched the airplanes creep along like wasps drunken on nectar. When they gained speed and, with stiff wings, lifted into the air, her heart soared. If she ran through the field and stretched out her body, could she lift off the ground? Surely then she could find her mam.

Isabella touched her shoulder. "Yer things are in the trunk. Bye, Lass."

Mary mustered every instinct, every lesson she had learned, and studied Isabella. *Crying, she is? Has something happened to her? To Mam?* Fear rumbled, shaking her.

One of the uniformed women, still smiling, knelt by Mary. She smelled of talcum powder and had a sweet voice like the buntings.

When Mary glanced back, the sisters and Killian were gone. Mary took the nice lady's hand, and they walked through more doors. All the while, the lady talked to Mary in a voice so soft, Mary longed to do everything this nice lady wanted. The fear hadn't gone away, but it was still and small, a little ball lodged deep inside.

Then came steps, more than Mary could count. Up, up, up, into one of those planes she'd spotted from inside the building. Then between rows of seats until they came to where she was to sit. The lady fastened a belt around Mary, talking, talking. "'Tis okay, lass. Just settle in."

Mary tried to do that, and her mind did slow a bit. She watched people open and close doors and take their seats almost as if she weren't there.

The plane trembled like it might explode. Mary clutched her arms, sobs mixed with ragged breathing. The plane rolled slowly, then faster, faster. Her insides shook as if she'd been grabbed by the shoulders and shaken. She remembered handling her rag doll like this, and she longed to dig it out of her trunk and hold it tight.

Finally, the plane stopped shaking. The lady came back to Mary's seat, leaned over, and pulled back a curtain, uncovering a small window, right near Mary's face. "Look out there now, will ye?" The lady pointed out the window.

Mary pressed her face against the glass. Down below was so much water it must be the tears cried by all the people in the whole wide world. She looked up. A sky that reached to God Himself. "We're a bird?" she asked, her voice a mix of wonder and fear.

The lady laughed and nodded, then sat down next to Mary.

When the plane quit climbing, Mary scooted closer to the nice lady and thought of the words she would say, the words that could change everything. She practiced them until they seemed perfect, then tugged on the lady's sleeve. "Please, ma'am, I don't mean to trouble ye, but I need to find me mam."

The lady looked past her and out the window. "Not now, lass." She put her arm around Mary in a gentle way—not strong and firm, like Mam would, but still good.

Mary fell asleep, then startled awake. The lady gave her food. Mary gobbled it down. She gave her more. They talked, but not about Mam.

When the jet clanked onto the ground, the lady, who Mary now thought was beautiful with her soft brown eyes and shiny smile, pinned silver wings on her dress. Mary's arms felt light again. Was this the sign to help her find Mam?

All the people on the plane stood up, but the nice woman led Mary into the aisle before any of them. They edged toward a man in the same blue uniform as the others, who saluted Mary. She gasped. He wore wings like she did! It must be a good change. She rushed toward him, but he ducked under a low door and then shut it.

The nice lady turned toward another door and pointed at steep steps. "Go ahead, dear," the woman coaxed when Mary balked.

From the top step, Mary stared at another airport, just like the other one except much bigger. A flock of geese honked a harsh message from overhead, black-and-white heads bobbing against the wind, and Mary winced to hear Mam's voice somehow intermingled with the geese's cry. *The wild goose calls, and I must follow, even though it brings me sorrow.* "Ye can't come!" they seemed to honk. "Stay away!"

"Mary Elizabeth?"

Mary stared down at a vast stretch of pavement where men swarmed like hornets.

Near the bottom stair stood two people waving, it seemed, at her. Her hands still gripping the rail, Mary looked over her shoulder at the jet. Where was the nice woman?

As if she understood, the nice woman appeared at the top of the stairs. Passengers crowded about her, pushing and waving.

"Go ahead, dear. It's fine." Over and over the woman nodded and smiled.

Mary moved first one foot, then the other, stepping down the stairs as if they were slippery, all the while clinging to the rail, her dress billowing in the wind.

"Good morning, Mary Elizabeth. I'm Anne." The woman called Anne wore a silky blue dress. Her brown hair was pulled back into a tight bun, and she hugged her arms to her chest. She didn't smile or frown but squinted as if the sun was in her eyes.

How'd she know my name? Did Mam send her?

Anne held out a gloved hand. "I'm your new mother. This is your new father."

Mary could not have leapt backward faster if the woman had thrown boiling water in her face. *Mam* was her mother! They were lying. The fear that had been kept at bay roiled in her, and she crouched, ready to spring away.

The man got down on one knee and looked at her with calm brown eyes. "Hello, Mary Elizabeth. I'm Edmond." He wore a suit with wooly material like the farmer's cap. "It's nice to meet you."

Mary stared at his lips, which seemed to chop off the words. A pounding in her head dulled her thoughts. These people smiled like the lady on the plane. Were they Mam's friends? She tried to figure it out, but she couldn't. If this was her mother, who was Mam? Where had she gone? Her eyes darted about. Planes. Carts. Crowds of people. She tensed her legs, intent on fleeing.

Edmond moved closer yet never took his eyes off her. "Here, child." He spoke calmly like the farmer speaking to a skittish lamb. When he took her hand, she jumped. Would he hit her? His hands were big like Killian's, but the inside part that touched her palm was soft, and he didn't hold too tight. She let her tightness melt into his warm hand, and she tried to match his large steps.

Anne walked in front but turned around occasionally to make clucking noises like the hen did to her chicks.

They stood in line for a long time. Then Edmond stuck fingers in his mouth and whistled. A man appeared and hustled her trunk into a shiny black car. As they drove, Anne rambled on. Mary had trouble understanding her scratchy voice. But what she heard convinced her that Mam was not here. And she knew, with every bit of knowledge she'd gathered from the wind and the birds and the sky, not to ask about Mam.

Edmond peered at Mary from a small mirror which also made him look small. "Welcome to Illinois," he said.

"The Heartland," Anne added.

Mary pressed her face against a window. The first car ride had taken her by rustling green grass. Now she sped past a flat, bare land that looked like all the grass had been burned off. And where was the ocean? The hills?

"What do you think of your new home?"

Mary kept silent. What did they want her to say? That it was ugly and she was scared and she didn't like them? Mam had taught her about that kind of question.

"We're close to Chicago, one of the world's greatest—"

A sob slipped from Mary. *Chicago*. An ugly name for an ugly place. And the ugly things they said had been true. They said she had to go; she had. But why? Tears filled her eyes. It hurt not to know any answers. She slumped against the window and shut her eyes, not only to avoid the ugly scenery, but to avoid ugly thoughts. Shutting her eyes didn't help.

"Here we are."

Edmond pulled into a driveway. "Welcome to Lisle," he said. "Home."

Mary stared at the clipped grass and the huge tree with red and orange leaves. "Is the tree on fire, sir?" she asked before she really thought about whether it was a good or bad thing to ask.

Edward laughed. "You might say that."

Encouraged, Mary pointed to a white house with black shutters. "Is it new?"

"Pretty new." The man turned to Anne. "Isn't she smart?"

Anne smiled as if her questions were a good thing, then nudged Mary toward steps and a door. She showed Mary how to wipe her feet, pulled a key from her purse, unlocked the door, then ushered Mary to a couch. "Sit down," she commanded, her eyes glittering like sunlight on wet leaves.

The room took Mary's breath away with its beauty. Not throbbing with life like the cliffs, but still beautiful. She noticed shiny lamps and tables, a scent of lemon somehow coming from all the furniture, and strange flowers pouring from a glass vase.

Edmond stepped into the room. "Why don't we let her rest a bit, take this all in?" He put his arm around Anne.

Anne pulled away and straightened her sleeve. "Let me handle this."

Edmond nodded and left.

"We'll have lunch," Anne continued, "after we unpack and go over the rules."

Mary understood rules. The hen squawked at its chicks when they got too close to the goat. The bitch growled at its puppies when they nipped her tail. Her mam had given Mary one big rule: stay away from Killian. She looked around the new place, her stomach a coiled spring. *What are the rules here?*

Anne snapped her fingers. "Come on, dear," she said, her words clipped and hard. "Let's unpack."

Mary followed Anne down a long hall. She touched the clean walls, the framed pictures. She craned her neck, hoping to see into the back room. Were there aunts back there? It seemed too big for just two people—three, now.

Mary followed Anne into a room, careful not to get too close, like a dog avoiding the horse's hooves. She gasped. More wonders. A frilly blue spread covered a huge bed. The sun streamed through lacy curtains.

"I sleep with ye, do I?"

Anne sniffed. "Don't be ridiculous. This isn't Ireland."

So many changes caused a swirl of thoughts. *'Tis a good thing, not to sleep with her, 'tisn't it? Aye, but I've never slept alone.*

Anne swept her hand across the airy space. "It's all yours. We're in the other bedroom. Now let's get to work." She unfolded clothes from the trunk that Edmond had set in the room, shook out wrinkles, and put them in a dresser.

A doll was perched high on a shelf. Mary stretched to touch its curly hair.

"Be careful. That's a Madame Alexander." Anne smiled, her eyes dreamy. "It was given to me when I came here."

"Can I play with it?"

Anne snapped to attention. "No. It might break."

Mary pointed to a bright-colored box. "How about that?"

"You can play later." Anne moved about the room in a jerky way, her lips set in a tight line. So different from Mam, who seemed to flow about the house as she worked, laughing and singing if Killian weren't around. With the same sharp movements, Anne hung up one dress in the closet but put the others back in the trunk. She set Mary's doll on the shelf. It looked so sad and tired next to the fancy doll with its matching dress and bonnet. For a moment, Anne studied the dolls; her smile faded like Mary's doll. Then she moved on, motioning for Mary to follow. "We'll eat now."

As if it could hear, Mary's stomach growled, the hunger ache pushing out all the other aches she'd stored inside. She stepped, tentative at first, down the hall, into a spotless kitchen. A bowl of apples rosier than Mam's cheeks and grapes bigger than sea pebbles sat on the table, but when Mary poked the grapes, they were rubbery, like galoshes.

Anne motioned her to a chair.

In a flash, Edmond entered the room and sat down across from her, studying her like Farmer O'Loughlin did the new lambs. "Do you like your room?" he asked.

Mary covered her eyes with her hands, then peeked at him through her fingers. He seemed to be nothing like Killian; still, she had to be careful.

Anne set a plate on a mat in front of Edmond. "Ketchup, dear?"

Edmond nodded.

When Anne opened a closet, Mary gasped. Rows and rows of shiny cans, more in that one place than all the people in Kilkee could eat. Then Anne put a plate before her.

Mary shoveled lumps of potato into her mouth. She darted a glance at Edmond, but he didn't seem interested in taking her food. The potatoes melted in her mouth like butter; she didn't even chew. She didn't chew the juicy hunks of meat, either.

"Stop this instant." Anne flew across the room and wiped off Mary's hands. "Here." She gave Mary a fork and thrust a napkin in her lap. "And no elbows on the table, please."

Edmond excused himself and left the room.

Mary scraped every bite of food from her plate, yet her eyes kept darting to Anne. She didn't know these rules. What was she supposed to do with her elbows?

While Anne stood at the sink and scrubbed dishes in a quick circular motion, all Mary could think about was how different she was from Mam, who sang and banged the pots like they were drums. Mary longed to show Mam all the food and ask her about the funny grapes. The last bite of rich food seemed to stick in Mary's throat. Hadn't Isabella and the nice lady said she'd see Mam soon? When was soon? Or was it a lie?

After eating, Mary went to her room and played with her new toys, but the ache for Mam clouded out all the shininess of the new things. She wanted to be held. She wanted Mam.

Anne came in, Edmond trailing her. She laid out Mary's pajamas and explained about the light and about bedtime. Then they left, shutting the door behind them.

A void spread through Mary as if she'd been abandoned on a black cliff. Her heart plummeted over the edge, and she began to cry. Through her tears, she spied a girl in the mirror, with well-mannered curls, a moon-shaped face sprinkled with freckles, and red-rimmed blue eyes. She was dressed in a pink gown with tiny red roses dotting the fabric. A girl who looked more like one of those schoolgirls than a filthy bogsider.

She watched her eyes widen like the unblinking stares of the dolls, then rubbed the silky red-gold hairs on her arms. Who was she? The room that had seemed so pretty closed in on her. She turned out the light, jumped into the bed, pulled up the blinds, then choked back a scream. There were no stars. A black void engulfed everything. She put her forehead against the cool glass and squinted, barely able to make out dark branches and leaves. There, behind the tallest tree, was the tiniest sliver of a moon.

All of Mam's songs jumbled in Mary's head, and Mary mixed her own words with some of Mam's and sang to the rising moon. "*So red and rosy were her cheeks,*" she whispered, "*how scarlet was her hair. How costly was the dress that the blue-eyed girl did wear. Tears came rolling down her cheeks, how mournful she did cry. My Mam has up and left me, and surely I will die.*"

⚜ ⚜ ⚜

"Time for school."

Mary rubbed her eyes and sat up. The warm tingling from a dream of Mam vanished when she looked about the new room. "Wha . . . where . . . ?"

Anne thrust something at her. "You're going to school. Here's your uniform."

Mary jumped out of bed and grabbed the skirt and blouse and white knee socks.

"For heaven's sake, don't wrinkle it. Now hurry up."

Mary pulled up the socks, all the while thinking of the schoolgirls. Anne had given so many answers about school her head had spun. Only one question, however, played over and over in Mary's mind: *Would she, could she, be like them?*

With stiff fingers, Mary buttoned up the starched blouse, its whiteness reminding her of the scrubbing and sweeping she'd done all week. She'd trailed after Anne, intent to pass her cleaning course. In no time at all, she expertly read Anne's unspoken language. Hands on the hips meant another mistake. Pursed lips meant go to her bedroom. Mary watched what was going on like an eager dog wanting to please an indifferent master, but after a time, her mind and her heart would creep back to the unkempt house on the cliff that held the mother she loved. The mother who had disappeared.

Anne stood at the door, hands on her hips. "Hurry up, dear." She pattered through breakfast, then nudged Mary into the car. "Sit straight," she continued as she pulled onto the street. "Raise your hand before you speak." The turn signal clicked in response to Anne's command. "Since Edmond's mayor, we have to act a certain way. Don't bolt your food. Or slouch. You'll look common." She turned to Mary. "Do you hear me?"

Mary sat as straight as she could against the soft leather seat. "Yes, ma'am."

Rules were fired so rapidly that, after a time, Mary quit listening and focused on noisy machines which scooped up dirt and dumped it into a pile. Her face crumpled in spite of her resolve. The ugly land was getting even uglier. She choked on the dust and smoke that somehow seeped into the car and imagined the grassy smell of turf fires, the salty scent of ocean breezes. It seemed so real, her fingers itched to touch the foamy spray. "Not too close, now!" Farmer O'Loughlin would yell as he hoed a row of potato plants. A tear rolled down her face and onto the blouse. When could she go home? When would she see her real mother?

"... right this minute. Do you hear me?"

"Yes, ma'am. Sorry, ma'am."

Anne stopped the car in front of a brick building. They got out and walked past a large statue. Then Anne pushed Mary through a heavy door and nudged her toward a woman swathed in black from head to toe. "Sister Christine, this is Mary Elizabeth."

"Hello, child." Sister Christine's face seemed to shine like it was lit from within.

Mary swallowed the bitter taste that rose into her throat. *Changes, rising up.*

"You'll start her in first grade? She is six." Anne handed the sister a paper.

"Today, if I'm reading her birth certificate correctly." She smiled at Mary. "Happy birthday, dear child."

Mary studied the faces of both of the women. Was a birthday another change?

"I'll be at the office if you need me." Anne walked to the door. "At three o'clock, I'll pick you up out there." She pointed to the courtyard. "By that statue."

A weeping woman, made of white stone, held a badly hurt man, also stone. Still looking at the statue, Mary clutched at her stomach. Who was this man who looked like he hurt a thousand times more than she ever did, even when Killian hit her?

"Mary Elizabeth. Welcome to St. Joan of Arc." In contrast to the stark black robe, the sister's smile was alive and inviting.

Mary ducked her head, swallowing down the bad taste that swirled close to her lips. To keep it down, she focused on little specks of black in the green floor tiles.

With her hand on Mary's shoulder, Sister guided her down the hall and into a room, then bent close. "God bless you, child," she whispered, her breath tickling a curl about Mary's ear. Then she turned to another woman, also dressed in black. "Sister Joanna, this is Mary Elizabeth," she explained, in a much louder voice. When Sister Christine left the room, the buzzing began.

Mary stood, her back to a chalkboard, and stared at rows of children wearing the same blue and white uniform that she wore. Her heart pattered a warning for her to run from the changes, and energy surged through her limbs, but when she started for the door, her legs had frozen. She opened her mouth, then clamped it shut.

"Let's tell Mary Elizabeth hello."

"Hello, Mary Elizabeth." The buzzing students stopped long enough to drone her name in a single chorus.

Mary ground her teeth and tried to clamp her lips together, but it was no use. The changes, the loneliness, the bitter taste, the homesickness, all poured out, and she vomited all over the bright green tiles.

✠ ✠ ✠

"Not like that, dear." Sister swished to Mary's desk, flipped open the writing pad, and pointed to the letters Mary had tried so hard to copy, the letters that were still, after two months, as foreign to her as the games played at recess. Firmly, yet gently, Sister placed the pencil in her hand and helped her form the letters. The students giggled as they had when she'd thrown up that first day, but Mary pretended she didn't hear them. This was too important to let them distract her. The writing seemed to take forever, and Mary's palm became slick with sweat, but she didn't care about that, either.

Sister's eyes became as luminous as the moon. "Look. Your name." She spelled out each letter, slowly, as if it was important. "Mary. Elizabeth. The mothers of Jesus and St. John the Baptist."

The power of what she had done spread through Mary's whole body. She jumped up and marched in place, just like the schoolgirls in Ireland had done.

So many children giggled that the room convulsed in one big titter.

"Dumb as an Irishman."

"Ain't got the brains of a turnip."

The words sliced through Mary, and she slid into her chair and laid her forehead against the cool desktop.

Sister whirled around, her skirt brushing Mary's uniform. She marched to her desk, then rapped on it three times. Finally, the titters stopped.

Later, with slumped shoulders and a lump in her throat, Mary packed her supplies and went to the statue. When Anne honked, Mary hurried into the car.

"How was it?"

The eager look on Anne's face sucked the last bit of air from Mary. Every day, Anne asked the same question. Dared Mary tell how the tittering stabbed at her, how she struggled to read even the simple words, how—

"Well, dear?" Anne asked, her hands gripping the wheel.

"It was fine." Mary tried to smile as best she could.

Anne chattered as she started the car.

In a way, Mary was glad Anne didn't notice her sorrow. Anne got sad when Mary couldn't tell her good things, and it made the day much worse. It was better just to smile and try to keep her sorrow inside. She studied the statue of Jesus, the Son of God the nuns had told her about. He hurt too, so badly His mother had to hold Him.

Anne pulled onto the street. "Do you have homework?"

Mary shook her head, unable to talk.

"Good. When we get home, we need to wash that uniform—how does it wrinkle so? If you'll pull it down before . . ." Anne kept talking, but Mary wasn't listening. She bowed her head and tried to pray to the Jesus of the statue. At the end, she made the cross sign carefully as the nuns had taught her—maybe that would help Him hear her.

☦ ☦ ☦

Sally's shoulders sagged, as did her spirits. "So Mam did send you away."

"They settled my future around that table. Anne, Killian's older sister, emigrated from Ireland, then married Edmond. When they couldn't have children, they agreed to adopt me." Mary studied her fingernails. "Of course, I didn't know that until years later."

For a moment, Sally saw herself standing red-faced in a classroom in Monroe, Louisiana. A new student, she'd been late that very important first day of school. She shuddered as she remembered what had made her late . . . and what had happened two months later. Sally rubbed her arms, willing the smells, the sounds, to leave. "We moved too, when I was in sixth grade," she said, her voice sounding tinny and small.

"Then you know what it's like. Sitting alone at lunch. Being the last one chosen."

Sally shook her head. "I have no idea what it would feel like to be torn from my birth mother and country." She touched Mary's sleeve. "I don't know how you did it."

Mary shrugged. "Every day, I started out full of hope—for Lisle to be home, to find a friend. Then jabs and sticks deflated me, and I got weaker and weaker."

Sally fidgeted on the couch, Mary's pain transferred to her. How could they do that to a little girl? The poor thing didn't even know about birthdays. At least Sally had remained in the comforting bosom of the South for those childhood moves. Drawly greetings, neighborly visits . . . She shook her head. And her beloved family. Always there to infuse love into her.

She glanced at Mary, who was rubbing the tips of her fingers. *No wonder she gets nervous around strangers. You just can't escape those early memories . . .* She cut off those thoughts. That wasn't biblical. God could change anything, make things better. "Did it ever get better?" she asked, praying for a good response.

Mary's nod came slowly. "For a while. With Daddy, anyway."

CHAPTER 7

Some voice whispered o'er me, as the threshold I crossed.
There was ruin before me. If I loved, I was lost.

—Thomas Moore, "Desmond's Song"

The door slammed, and even before Edmond took off his coat and settled in his living room chair, Mary sprinted down the hall and flew into his arms.

"I love you," he said between chuckles.

A part of Mary that had been closed since she left Ireland opened up. She had known he loved her even before he'd said it. And she loved him back. It wasn't the same love she had for Mam, but still, it was love. Everybody said he was an important man, but she didn't love him for that. She loved him because he loved her first. He hugged her tight, studying her with soft eyes as if memorizing every inch of her, making her forget those third graders' chants of "freckle-face."

"You're my Lizzie." He took off his coat and hat and sat down, then waved her back into his arms.

She jumped on his lap, tilting her head toward his. "Lizzie? What's that?"

"A tin lizzie. Ford's little workhorse."

"I'm a horse?"

His laugh reddened his cheeks. "No. It's a car. A reliable little car."

"What's 'reliable'?"

"A good worker." He tickled her belly. "Like you."

Mary's heart swelled so she had to share it. She threw her arms around him, hugged his thick middle, bowled her head into his chest. "I like my nickname."

"I'm glad. And now I'd like you to call me something."

"What?" So eager was Mary to keep sharing, she almost bounced off his lap.

"I want you to call me Daddy."

The bouncing stopped. "Was Killian my daddy?"

Something dark went across Edmund's face.

Had she asked a bad question? Mary held her breath and lay so still, she felt his heartbeat through his starchy shirt. She'd made the mistake of asking Anne bad questions, and she didn't want to do that with Edmond.

"No, Mary. He was never your daddy."

Mary let out her breath, and the worry, and snuggled in close. "Daddy," she said, loving the sound of it, "I love you too." And she did love him. It wasn't just words she said because she had to, like some of the prayers at school. She loved everything about him, even his big nose and stomach. But it was his eyes that captivated her. They captured the light from every shiny thing in the room—the brass lamps, the television screen—and radiated that energy onto her.

"Aren't you going to look?" Daddy asked, resuming their nightly ritual.

Mary clawed at the satiny lining of one pocket. Nothing but jangling keys and his billfold. She dug into the other pocket. Nothing. She bit her lips, trying not to let her new daddy see how she wanted, needed, the nightly surprise.

One night it'd been a cute little plastic burro that Edmond called a Mexican Democrat. She hadn't known what that meant, but she'd laughed, anyway. The surprises had varied, but for months, the routine hadn't. Hugs, surprises, and then stories. She didn't want that to change.

"Hop up a minute."

She climbed off his lap reluctantly.

Daddy moved to the couch, picked up a bag, and pulled out something shiny and smooth. "Have a look."

Perplexed, she turned it over and over in her hands. Looking at Daddy, she rewarded him with a tiny smile. A bad surprise sure beat another change.

Daddy burst out laughing and got down on the floor. The lamp shone on his bald head. He grabbed the tube from her, tilted it up, then held it to her eye. With his other hand, he fiddled with the end of the tube. "Right there," he practically shouted. "Look in there!"

Mary wanted the surprise to be good, but the metal edge poked her in the eye. What was Daddy so excited about?

"Can you see?" he kept saying over and over, leaning against her shoulders, the smell of cigar on his breath.

Rosy hexagons bordered with violet triangles. Swirls of color. Mary gasped. Circles and rectangles—shapes which kept changing with every breath she took.

"How does it work? Are there jewels in there? Can I—"

If possible, Daddy laughed harder than ever. If possible, he loved the surprise even more than she did.

"It's not jewels, Lizzie. Just a bunch of broken glass. It's all in how they tumble about, fit into a pattern. Then the light takes them, and—presto." He held it up to her eye again and showed her how to turn it. "It's a kaleidoscope. You can play with this a zillion times, and you'll never get the same pattern."

The shapes and colors sent shivers through her.

Finally Daddy shooed her toward her room, threatening to skip tonight's story if she didn't get ready for bed.

She quickly brushed her teeth, washed her face, put on her pajamas, still thinking about all the broken little pieces that someone had transformed into the most magical thing she'd ever seen.

Racing back to the living room, Mary jumped into Daddy's lap, making his rocker creak.

Daddy tickled her. "Hey, careful, or you'll break it."

"The old eyesore." Mary mimicked Anne's complaints of its Old Spice and cigar smell by holding her nose and trying to talk all nasally, like Anne.

"The chair or Mother?" Even though they giggled, Mary cut her eyes toward the kitchen. The last thing she wanted to do now was upset Anne.

"What story do you want, Lizzie?" Daddy asked in a more serious voice.

Mary scrunched up her forehead. The best stories started with questions. She liked to know why things happened the way they did, and Daddy seemed to know all the answers. "Why don't you have hair?"

Daddy smiled. "You've got a touch of the Irish bold, do you?"

"Is that bad, Daddy?"

"Of course not."

"Tell me, Daddy. Tell me."

He leaned against the doily Anne had arranged on the chair back. "When I was twenty, I had an awful bout with rheumatic fever."

"What's that?"

"A terrible disease. Fever so high, the thermometer burst."

"Really?"

"I promise. Little silver balls of mercury rolled out. They were impossible to pick up, which was a good thing."

Mary glued her face on his bright eyes. "Why?"

"Poison," he yelled, tickling her until she begged him to quit. "For six days I fought those fevers. On the seventh morning, I woke up, bald as an egg."

Mary put her hands on his shiny head. "No," she protested.

"Brown clumps scattered all around my pillow like some wild Delilah had crept in and cut my hair in the middle of the night. It never grew back."

"Who's Dinah?"

"Delilah. She tricked a man into giving up all his power."

"Tell me that one too." Mary kicked at his pants leg. "Please."

"Tomorrow," he promised. "Now give me a kiss, and off you go. Tomorrow's another day in the trenches."

"What are the trenches?"

He laughed so hard his belly shook. "That's another story." Mary kissed him on both cheeks, like she had kissed Mam. Her new daddy, her first daddy, pulled her close, hugged her, then turned on the television. Their time was up.

✤ ✤ ✤

"Can I play outside?"

Anne parked the car and put the keys in her purse. When she turned to Mary, lines formed around her mouth. "Where?"

Mary pointed to the house next door.

"The Nelson boys?" Anne shook her head. "It's out of the question."

Every afternoon, neighborhood kids played at the Nelsons'. The girls skipped ropes and played jacks. The boys straddled the street and arced balls over passing cars. Their bicycles huddled in the driveway, a community of rubber and chrome. Mary longed to be pulled into their laughter, their games, even their fights. They were alive. They were part of something. "Why not?" Mary asked, a frown on her face.

"Your father's mayor. Certain things we just don't do." Anne marched into the house, Mary following behind. "Now get on your homework."

Mary stuck out her lip, the distance to her room stretching as she plodded down the hall. Those kids had each other; all she had were the silly old dolls that just sat up there—she glanced twice, to make sure. Her rag doll was gone.

Her heart pounding, she looked under the bed. In the closet. She yanked open drawers. Nothing. She stood in the middle of her room, then ran to the trunk and pried it open. There it was. Mary picked it up, surprised to find it damp. She ran her finger across the lips, which had once been stained with tea. A prick started inside and began to spread. Anne was the only one who could've done this. But why had she done it? Didn't she know those weren't stains but memories of her real mother?

Sucking in her breath, Mary marched into the living room. "Why did you do it?" She flung the doll toward Anne. When it plopped onto the floor, a seam split open, and stuffing poked out.

Anne didn't look up from her paperwork. "The thing was filthy."

Mary stomped her foot. "It's not a thing; it's my doll. And don't touch her."

"I could dump her in the trash. Now go do your homework."

"I don't have any."

Anne's eyes glittered. "I'll tell Edmond if you don't behave."

Mary opened her mouth, but Anne's iron gaze erected a wall between them that her words could not cross. Somehow, Daddy was fenced in with her, yet the thought did not comfort her at all. She stormed back to her room, desperate to get out of the fence or to at least put something else in. She grabbed the china doll, which looked so like Anne with its fine-boned features, and slung it into the chest, then set the rag doll up on the shelf. Yet the fenced-in feeling grew. And the rag doll just stared, its arm ripped, its smile faded. It seemed to signal that there was more pain, more loneliness to come.

✛   ✛   ✛

She'd gotten ready for bed, amused herself with the kaleidoscope, yet the knot in her stomach tightened with every tick of the clock. What if Daddy had been killed in one of the wrecks the newsman reported in his matter-of-fact voice?

Anne turned off the TV and reached for her sewing bag.

Mary scooted near, wanting, needing for her to say something. About Daddy.

"You're in my light. And besides, it's way past your bedtime." Anne folded her arms across her chest and fixed her eyes upon Mary, then began her sewing.

The tightness got worse. Anne had seemed worried too, but now Mary wasn't sure. It was always worse when she didn't know what Anne was thinking. And it wasn't just that. The whole night routine had changed. No rocking. No story. No Daddy.

She climbed into bed, unable to push away thoughts of the other big change, when Mam had disappeared. Would that happen to Daddy? She curled into a ball and took deep breaths. Sleep did not come. Neither did Daddy.

Mother creaked down the hall. An owl hooted. Cars drove by. *Click.*

Mary sat up. The door shut. She jumped out of bed and tore into the living room. "Daddy! I didn't know . . . are you okay? Did you . . . Daddy! What happened?"

He scooped her into his arms and held her close.

She sank into the comforting tobacco smell. But another smell like incense made her sneeze. She patted his flushed face. "Daddy. What's wrong?"

"It's a jungle out there." His voice slurred, and Mary imagined lions and tigers clawing at his car as he fought his way home. Stumbling, he carried her down the hall, then tucked her in her bed. "Good night," he mumbled.

Mary's face fell. She didn't mind not having the surprises, but she wanted, needed, a story. She studied his bleary face, unsure how to ask.

He turned to leave.

"I need a story," she blurted out.

He put his hand on her door. "It has to be short, or your Mother'll kill me."

She thought of the two of them, just for a moment. "How did you meet Anne?"

He looked past Mary, toward the window. "That's not a short one."

"Please." Mary sat as still as she could. Sometimes it helped him decide.

"We met at a golf club," he finally said. "I was a young whippersnapper, itching to challenge the old bucks. And to get my hands on their money." He chuckled. "I had a darn good short game."

She stared in disbelief at him. "Anne played golf?"

"No." Laughing, he smoothed the sheet about her shoulders. "She did housekeeping for the family that managed the club."

Mary sat up so fast the sheet slid off. "She was a maid?"

Daddy nodded. "The prettiest thing I'd ever seen."

"She was?"

He didn't answer, and Mary was about to ask him how Anne, with her severe hair style, the tight lines across her forehead, her pinched mouth, could be pretty.

Then Daddy started, slow and halting. "Wavy brown hair that she twisted at the back of her neck. Long, slender hands always helping someone with this or that. A gaze so determined you knew she'd make something of herself. And of you, too."

"Did she, Daddy? Make something of you?"

He ignored her, pulling out his wallet instead. Right in the front was Anne's picture. Mary studied it carefully. She wasn't convinced Anne was pretty, but in this picture she did seem to know the world's secrets. Not in a bossy way. In a safe way. She looked safe.

Daddy kept talking as if Mary wasn't there anymore. "We met in the late '20s, a time when folks threw caution to the wind. Until the crash, that is."

Mary wondered what the crash was but didn't want to interrupt.

His voice got quiet as if the most important part was about to come. "We worked hard, two capitalists glued together at the hip. A real team."

They were a team? How could that be? Mary looked at Daddy. That glue must have worked really well.

"Then Uncle Sam called me."

Mary nodded. She'd learned about this in social studies.

"Your mother, right in the middle of the war, opened not one but two businesses. Every day she wrote me when she finished up at the diner. Those letters, full of her latest entrepreneurial strategies, kept me alive over there in Europe."

"Entre-what?"

He smiled and patted Mary's head. "It means business."

"I didn't know ladies could run businesses by themselves."

"Oh, you'd better believe it. She ran a diner, bussed trays from dawn until dark if the help didn't show. Then she jumpstarted our first taxi service in her spare time."

Mary's hand flew to her mouth. "Anne drove a cab?"

"Kept the books, drove the cars. Whatever it took." The bed creaked as he shifted his bulk and moved closer to Mary. "All women. The men were off at war."

Something stirred near the door; Mary saw Anne's shadow. She snuggled closer to Daddy, praying Anne wouldn't send her to sleep yet.

"While us men were off fighting Krauts, your mother drove the womenfolk everywhere they needed to go. The hospital, their relatives', the grocer's. And she didn't charge a dime if they couldn't afford it. You see, most women couldn't drive then."

"Will I drive one day?"

"Of course you will."

The shadow coalesced into Anne, who stood just inside the door, blowing her nose with a Kleenex.

"She saved every dime. It was quite a nest egg."

"What's a nest egg?"

"A pile of money. When I got home, she met me at the airport with the biggest hug you can imagine and a thick file of papers showing what she'd done for me. For us."

Anne cleared her throat, but Daddy didn't seem to hear.

"That started Harris Realty. Next was the insurance company. Those vets had to protect their American dreams, you know."

"And then you bought our house?"

His laugh shook the bed. "What a little capitalist you're turning out to be."

"Edmond, she needs to get to sleep now." Anne crept closer to the bed, talking softly, like Daddy when he told the story.

"You did all that?" Mary kept looking at Anne, trying to see some sign of the girl in the picture.

Anne joined Daddy at the bedside. She smiled her answer and bent toward the bed. "Good night, Elizabeth." She smoothed a curl out of Mary's eyes.

After they left, Mary lay awake for what seemed like hours. Anne came from Ireland, like she had? Was she from the cliffs too? *Am I a part of the American Dream, or is it just the two of them?* It sounded like they had been in love. Did you lose love, or did it just go away for a while? Mary snuggled into bed. Maybe the love had come back.

The moon shone bright as the hopes born this very night. She'd lost Mam, at least for now, but she had a daddy, and maybe soon, a new mother. Or would it be a second mother? Her eyes closed. She still longed for Mam and Ireland, all jumbled into one memory of cliffs and sheep and mist and ocean and hugs and mouth kisses and rustling grass. But for now, she'd keep it separate. Mam. Mother. That's how it would be.

✢ ✢ ✢

"Want to eat out tonight?" Daddy's eyes drew in the light, like usual.

Mary jumped out of bed, her head nodding so hard that it hurt. She loved going to restaurants, where she could order what she wanted. And Mother and Daddy smiled a lot, especially when people came up to their table.

Daddy's eyes sparkled, and Mary hoped Mother had seen them. "That's one advantage of my job—that big expense account. Politicians have to eat too, don't they?"

Mother walked into the room and handed Mary her school uniform. When Daddy tried to pull her close, she pushed him away.

Mary glared at her. Why was she warm one minute and cold the next? "Are you going too?" she asked Mother. In a way, Mary wanted her to, but in another way, she feared Mother would ruin the fun.

"I don't think so." She rummaged through the desk while Mary dressed. "What's this C about?" She held out a math paper.

Daddy yanked it out of her hands. "Not now," he said, in a flat tone.

"She needs to do her work, not gallivant with you."

"She can do it later."

"If her marks fall, don't blame me." She flung the paper on the desk and left.

Daddy let out a sigh. "I'll be home by six. Wear your new dress. We're going to the Drake."

"What's that?" she asked, jumping up and down.

"Only the best restaurant in Chicago. Crystal chandeliers. Doormen in tuxedos. You can get the works. Lobster, baked Alaska, whatever you want."

"What's baked Alaska?"

"You'll see." He kissed Mary on the forehead and left.

☦ ☦ ☦

When Mary got home, her blue velvet dress, a slip, and white tights had been laid on her bed. A shiver went through Mary. Did Mother understand how a dress could change everything as if a magic wand had been waved? She tried to picture Mother in an elegant gown, but all she could see was a suit, high-collared blouse, and sturdy shoes.

To make time go fast, Mary pretended she was racing as she vacuumed.

Then Mother came in the room, a half-smile on her face. "Go ahead and get ready." She paced about the room as if she were thinking of racing too.

Mary stood and watched her, paralyzed by fear of another change. Would Daddy be late? Would he not show up at all?

The cleaning finally pulled Mother away, and she left the room.

Mary sucked in her stomach, worked the tights up her legs and over her hips, then studied herself. The mirror confirmed all the things the school kids said about her. She smoothed back a curl and tried to push away the chants of "Carrot head" and "Chubby," but they rang in her ears. Reaching for the dress, she hoped it would work its magic.

Mother seemed to come out of nowhere. "Here. I'll zip it." She fastened the hook at the nape of Mary's neck and twirled her around. "You're beautiful. Just like a princess."

Like in the story. Of all the books on the shelf, Mary liked *Cinderella* best. Somehow, Mother knew it. She grabbed Mother's hand. "Why don't you come?"

Instead of answering, Mother shuffled out of the room.

Mary stared after her. There it was again—happy, then sad. She smoothed down the dress and resolved to quit trying to understand her mother, at least tonight.

Right on time, Daddy pulled into the driveway, honking the horn over and over.

"Get the umbrella." Mary had to strain to hear Mother as she called from her bedroom. "It's raining."

Mary grabbed it from the closet and hurried into the storm. Even the rain, the gusting wind, couldn't stop this special night with her daddy.

"Allow me." Daddy stepped around the car and opened her door.

Mary bounced on her seat in sync to the rhythm of the windshield wipers. The car wasn't a carriage, but her daddy was driving. That made it perfect.

Daddy told jokes, but Mary was busy envisioning the stairs of the palace, her velvet dress now a gown with a royal train.

At last they pulled in front of a green awning. Fur-swathed women glided out of long black cars. A man in a maroon uniform opened her door. He bowed low and swept a gloved hand toward her. "Welcome to the palace, little miss. Your kingdom awaits."

Mary almost stumbled as he took her arm. *How could he have known?* She stepped onto a red carpet.

The man drew himself up and then bowed. "Good evening, Mr. Harris."

"Evening, Jefferson. Can you see if our table is ready?"

"Yes, sir. Right away." Jefferson bustled to a telephone.

Daddy led Mary up the stairs, just like the footman who led Cinderella, and into a—she rubbed her arms—ballroom. Tiers of candles and chandeliers illuminated tables of glittering women and handsome men, starched and straight in white and black jackets. Music, somehow sad and happy at the same time, poured from a room off the main hall.

Mary tugged Daddy's arm. "What kind of music is that?"

"It's classical. A man named Rachmaninoff."

"Rock who?"

"A famous Russian composer." Daddy tucked her hand into his and led her to the doorway of the room that had the music. Flickering flames caught the sheen of brass instruments, and luminous bows shivered across violin strings. The fairy tale continued as they walked past equally splendid rooms, then went into one of them.

A waiter approached. "Street view, Mayor?"

"Of course."

The waiter led them to a booth.

Daddy pointed out the window. "There's Michigan Avenue."

"Where Mother shops?"

Daddy nodded.

While Daddy and the waiter talked, Mary looked out the window. People bustled by, their arms full of parcels. Taxis streaked past. A woman huddled against the side of a building. With her face buried in her hands, she looked like Mam used to when she cried.

"Is this suitable?" The waiter's sweeping bow recaptured Mary's attention.

"Of course."

"Should I bring you the usual?"

"Wonderful." The waiter lit a candle, careful to shield the match with his hands. Soon, another waiter brought a tiny glass.

"For my digestion," Daddy explained, downing it with one gulp.

The waiter brought another and another.

Daddy told Mary all about baked Alaska, how big the real Alaska was, what it looked like, how he was going to take her there one day. Waiters kept asking if they were ready to order, and every time, Daddy would say that they were talking business.

Mary's stomach growled. As much as she loved his stories, she was hungry. "Can we eat now?" she asked, when she finally managed to edge into Daddy's monologue.

"I'm pretty hungry myself." The husky voice came from a black-haired woman who sidled up to the booth and put her hand on Daddy's arm.

"Barb, this is Mary," Daddy managed, after a cough.

The woman nodded at Mary but kept her eyes on Daddy. She tried to smooth a tight skirt over her thighs as she slid into the booth. "I see you've got my seat warm."

"My secretary." He pulled a handkerchief from his pocket and mopped his brow. "We need her to take notes."

Barb scooted closer to him, but she didn't write anything down.

The table seemed to grow until it was a giant wall, Barb and Daddy on one side, Mary on the other. And it made the ache in her stomach grow.

Daddy snapped his fingers; a waiter appeared like a genie summoned out of a bottle. "Champagne, please." Daddy's words were sloppy now.

The waiter returned and uncorked the champagne. When he poured it, golden liquid bubbled onto the white tablecloth.

Mary shuddered. Maybe it was good Mother was not here. The knot in Mary's stomach got worse. "I'm hungry," she whined. "And I need to go to the bathroom."

"I'll take her." Barb slid out of the booth, grabbed Mary's hand, then pulled her past table after table and steered her into the ladies' room.

Women giggled and laughed as they adjusted their dresses and dabbed rouge onto their cheeks. A cloud of a hundred perfumes and powders condensed, then settled near the ceiling. Glowing red lamps stoked up the heat.

Sweat trickled down Mary's chest. Feeling faint, she hurried to the marble vanity.

Barb leaned one hip against the cabinet and cocked the other, then hiked up her skirt and pulled at a silky stocking. "It might be better if you stay home next time. Your daddy and I need to do our work." She opened a sequined purse and outlined her lips with a smear of red. "And don't mention this to your mother." There was no notebook in the purse. There was not even a pen.

Mary, her face burning, whirled to the sink. She turned on the water, splashed it on her face, and dried her hands with a towel proffered by a wide-eyed, dark-faced attendant. "I don't have to do what you say," she retorted. The towel fell to the floor.

Barb grabbed Mary and jerked her outside. "That's right." Her eyes were outlined like her lips, except her eyes were charcoal dark. "And I'll tell your daddy what a little brat you are. You wouldn't want that, would you?"

Mary's face stung as if she'd been slapped. She could not open her mouth.

Laughing, Barb swaggered toward the table.

Mary trailed behind, trying to sort it out. Daddy had lied about the notes. Barb had lied about the work. She slid into the booth, longing to lay her head down, but there was no room in the jumble of dishes. Tears filled Mary's eyes. The whole night was a lie.

Barb grabbed Daddy's arm and snuggled close.

Mary scanned the nearby tables, but no one else seemed to notice how Barb and Daddy were doing what Mother and Daddy should do. Now she understood why Mother absolutely positively could not come, and it drained her of everything except sadness.

"Here." Daddy offered Mary a basket filled with steaming rolls.

Mary pressed her face against the window. "I'm not hungry." Then it got dark outside, and all Mary saw in the window was the reflection of a girl who had tried, but failed, to look like a princess.

At last the waiter brought the check. Daddy dug a money clip out of his pocket and laid several bills down.

All the way home, Mary hugged the armrest in the roomy back seat until the car crunched into their driveway.

"Mary, I've got to take Barb home . . ."

Without waiting for him to finish, Mary jumped out and ran toward the house.

Mother opened the door before Mary reached the steps. "Get to bed, young lady," she said, her face looking pinched under the harsh porch light. She pulled her bathrobe about her, like a winter coat. "It's late." Her head down, Mother hurried into her room.

Mary ripped off her best dress and threw it on the floor. She hated it. She hated Daddy too. No story. No baked Alaska. Nothing. She kicked off her tights. She didn't really hate him, she loved him. Her mind was a jumble, and she tried her best to sort it out. Right now, she disliked Daddy very much. And she wanted to kill Barb.

✟ ✟ ✟

"You loved him and were starting to love her. And they both turned away from you." Sally found a tissue for her friend.

Mary nodded. "I thought they might love each other and we'd be happy. I thought Daddy's job kept him leaving early, returning late." Her voice dropped to a whisper. "Of course, that wasn't the reason. It was women. Lots of them."

Sally wanted to engulf Mary in a bear hug, but feared it might overwhelm her. The folks up here just weren't as affectionate as Southerners. But then Mary wasn't really a Midwesterner; she was Irish. And down South, there weren't any Irish, so Mary was a case study of one for Sally. Yet, remembering how Mary had thrown her arms about a bruised little boy at the ministry, she scooted closer and gave Mary a big hug.

Mary melted at Sally's touch, her eyes liquid with tears. "My poor mother," she whispered. "His betrayals stabbed me twice—for my own sake, and for Mother's. I didn't know all that back then, but I did know something was terribly wrong."

"Did y'all ever talk about it?"

"Of course not." Mary's jaw tightened. "We didn't talk about anything. Now it's too late."

CHAPTER 8

Does time with his cold wing wither each feeling that once was dear?
Then, child of misfortune, come hither, I'll weep with thee, tear for tear.
—Thomas Moore, "Has Sorrow Thy Young Days Shaded?"

As she did every day, Mary stood by the statue and watched best friends. Today it was Suzi and Carol, their hands clasped together like a knot. They giggled and whispered fifth-grade secrets as usual, but today Carol had a bag in her hand. Curiosity got the best of Mary. "Are you going on a trip?" she asked Carol.

Carol turned around, her nose high in the air. "I'm spending the night at Suzi's," she announced.

A longing started in Mary as she watched them get in a car. Would Mother let her have a friend over? And would anyone come, even if Mother allowed it? She leaned against the cold marble statue base, feeling more alone than ever. Everyone had a best friend to sit by at lunch and play with at recess. The blacktop at recess was nothing more than a cluster of best friends, except for Clara and Sarah and . . . Mary.

Mother pulled up and Mary got in the car.

"How was that test?" Mother gripped the steering wheel as if her life depended on Mary's answer.

"Okay, Mother. I think I made a B. Or an A."

Mother flashed a smile. "Wonderful. Set your goals high, dear."

Mary frowned. She had set her goals high, and nothing happened, unless she counted the perfect-attendance buttons. Four of them, stashed in one of Daddy's old cigar boxes. But schoolwork wasn't what concerned her; it was getting a friend.

Mother turned onto their street, a wistful look on her face. "What I would have given for a chance to study at university."

But Mary wasn't really listening. "Could I have a friend over?"

Mother frowned. "You interrupted me." She pulled into the driveway, jerking her purse off the seat as she got out. "As for having a playmate over, you've got too much to do." Even though Mother was halfway up the porch, Mary heard every syllable. "You're late on your correspondence as it is."

✢ ✢ ✢

Mary smoothed down the thin blue stationery. Here it was nearly bedtime, yet in spite of Mother's hounding, the page remained blank. What did she say to the woman she hadn't seen for five years? That was the other thing; was she Mam? Kathleen?

Mother, her hairnet in place, her robe on, stood at the door. "It's not finished?"

Mary shook her head. It was hard to explain, but with Mother's glare, she had to try. "I don't know what to say to her. I don't know who they are. I . . ." She swallowed the rest of the words. Nothing she'd said would make sense to her mother.

"She's your Irish family." Mother tightened the belt on her robe.

Questions swirled so, one more just had to come out. "Am I Irish or American?"

"No. Yes. Just write the letter, for goodness' sake." Mother thrust a pen at her. "I'll check it when you're done. We can't have those Irish thinking you're stupid."

Mary yearned for the Mam of her memories, yearned for the land that still was a part of her. Yet she'd learned in geography that it was five thousand miles away, so the chance of reunion with either of them seemed impossible. Uncapping the pen, she wrote what she thought Mother and Mam or Kathleen or whoever she was wanted to read:

October 15, 1957

Kathleen McNamara
Kilrush Post Office
County Clare, Ireland

Dear Kathleen,
    I hope you are doing well in Ireland. I am doing well in
Illinois. It is nice here. School's hard, but I like art. Do you

*have a job? Anne runs an office. Edmond is a mayor. We got a
new TV. Do you have one? I watch it sometimes after I do my
homework and chores. My favorite program is Howdy Doody.*

*Love,
Mary*

Mary reread it. There. She'd found the nerve to add *love* before her name,
the word she'd never written. Squeezing her eyes shut, she prayed God would
perform a miracle and let Mam see the thousands of things she meant by that
one word. Laughter and hugs and her hair and salt and songs and tea parties
and her smell and lying beside her in the lumpy bed, their legs entwined like the
vines on the wild roses, her dancing eyes. And while she was praying, she asked
for another miracle—a best friend.

"I can't do it anymore."

Mary's eyes flew open.

"You have to."

Something about the way Mother's voice boomed down the hall made
Mary get up from her chair. She tiptoed down the hall lined with photographs
of Daddy and important people, then crouched outside their bedroom door.

"I've had it. I've got to get some help."

"With what?"

"To fit it all in."

A prickle ran across Mary's scalp. Why didn't Mother just spit out that *she*
was the thing that needed fitting in? She stepped closer.

"What are you talking about?"

"You have no idea what it's like, being right in the middle of something
and having to rush to the school. Hurrying home, keeping her on task, putting
together dinner, plowing through the chores, poring over the ledgers."

"She's older now. Why can't she just stay with some of the neighbors?"

"Like who? Besides, you have no idea what she might pick up."

"Oh, it can't be all that bad."

"How could you possibly know?"

Mother's comments seared, leaving a white-hot scar on Mary's heart. *Mother
doesn't like me. I'm just in her way. And I don't like her, either.*

"Why don't you pay Maggie to watch her?"

Mary gasped. She rarely saw her cousin, since Mother couldn't stand Daddy's
only sister. Mary's only aunt. When she did, seventeen-year-old Maggie, a cross

between Miss Teenage America and a female Eddie Haskell, kept her in stitches with her imitations of Mother. She squeezed her eyes shut, another prayer on her lips. *Please, God, please. I'll do everything Mother says, I'll—*

"Maggie? That little hussie? Just like your sister, when—"

The tone of Mother's voice made Mary's heart sink.

"We're not talking about my sister here." Daddy began pacing, from the sound of it, his voice rising in volume to match his strides. "And you're the one that's got the problem; don't forget that."

Mary crossed her fingers. *Yes, Mother, don't forget that.*

"Well . . . what is she now? A senior?"

"She's a junior, I think." Daddy's pacing stopped. "Yeah, a junior."

"Well, see what your sister says." Mother talked as if she'd done Daddy a favor.

If Maggie gets to babysit, she's certainly done me a favor. As quietly as she could Mary hustled down the hall and back into her bedroom. So it was up to her cranky aunt . . . and Mother.

✝ ✝ ✝

"Wow. Can I play?"

"No, me. Pick me." Girls huddled around Mary for the first time ever.

From the edge of the school yard's cracked blacktop, Mary surveyed bobbing heads and waving arms, her chest swelling with the power she had, thanks to Maggie's Chinese jump rope. Before recess, Mary had tucked it in her waistband and walked past the nuns in what she'd hoped was a nonchalant way.

"You." She pointed to Suzi, Carol, and Linda.

The others turned away without changing expression, as if they'd known all along they'd never be picked.

Mary pulled the rope from its hiding place.

"I want to go first."

"No, me." Suzi smiled her biggest smile.

Mary bent over, carefully arranging the elastic bands around her ankles so Suzi could jump first.

Suzi pointed to Linda. "You hold the other end."

With a nod, Linda complied. They stretched the rope until it was taut.

"Step back." Suzi touched her toe over the band. "*Ching, ching Chinaman, chop chop suey . . .*" As she chanted, she motioned for Mary and Linda to raise it higher.

"My turn," Carol insisted.

"Not yet." Suzi glared at Carol, then smiled at Mary. "Where'd you get this?"

Mary smiled back. "From my cousin Maggie."

Carol arched her eyebrows. "Is she the Maggie that's a junior over at Sacred Heart?"

Mary nodded.

"My brother knows her." Carol's smile was smug. "He says she's fast."

The girls giggled, and Mary wondered if being fast was good.

"Hey, it's my turn," Carol continued, her voice whiny now.

Mary wanted to shout at them all. *How about* me? *It's my cousin's rope.*

"Not yet." Suzi's voice rang with authority. "I'm almost done, though."

"Psst." Carol pointed toward the door.

Her eyes wide, Linda tugged on the thin elastic at the same time Suzi stepped on it. The band snapped, then plopped, limp and useless, on the asphalt.

Something snapped in Mary too, as she picked up the shriveled-looking remains of Maggie's rope. No matter what she did, Suzi and Carol would never like her. And Maggie wouldn't, either, when she learned what had happened to her rope.

✢ ✢ ✢

Her eyes downcast, Mary didn't even watch all the best friends. She slumped against the statue, wondering if there was anything she could say to Maggie that would make up for the broken rope.

Mother pulled up, right on time. "Get on in here, will you?" she called out the rolled-down window.

Mary sighed. She could tell Mother had had a bad day by the way she spat out words. As quickly as she could, Mary slid into the back seat, next to Maggie.

"I've got a filing to get off, and Maggie wasn't ready . . ." Mother gripped the steering wheel and continued her tirade.

Maggie made a sign with her middle finger, a sign shielded by the back of Mother's seat, but Mary didn't giggle. She cleared her throat once, twice. It was a perfect time to tell Maggie about the rope. Mother's presence might keep Maggie from getting too mad, and if she whispered, her mother might not even hear about it. "I . . . I broke your rope," she whispered. "But I'll give you some money and you can—"

Her cousin shrugged.

"You're . . . not mad at me?" Mary bounced on the seat, rid of the burden that had weighed her down since recess.

"Of course not. It's just a stupid rope." She leaned so close to Mary a strand of her blond hair brushed Mary's cheek. "But this . . . this is special." She slipped a necklace out from under her blouse.

"What is it?"

"A locket from my best friend."

The words cut into Mary and hurt, strangely enough, almost as badly as the rebuffs of the popular girls. She leaned against the window. *So I can't be her best friend.*

A blackbird fluttered by, and Mary wondered if it were as lonely as she was. It didn't look lonely as it soared higher, higher . . . When it was out of sight, Mary smiled at her cousin, trying to hide her disappointment. "It's cool," she said.

Maggie shook bangs out of her eyes. "It's got a lock of her hair in it. We're best friends forever."

Mary nodded, though she longed to ask Maggie how to get a best friend.

Sleet pinged against the car as the two girls rode in silence. Then Mother pulled into the drive. "No games," she said as Mary got out of the car, "just homework."

"Mother—"

She shook her head. "Not until those grades improve." She pulled away.

A frown on her face, Mary hurried inside to change out of her uniform, expecting Maggie to do the same, but when Mary came out of her bedroom, Maggie was sprawled across the living-room floor, setting up the game of *Life*.

Mary plopped down next to Maggie. "She said no games."

"Who cares?" Maggie sucked in her breath until her cheekbones stood out and her face looked gaunt, like Mother's. "It's not a game. It's *Life*."

Mary giggled. "Okay, then. What color should I be?"

"Orange, like your hair." Maggie handed Mary the orange car and a pink peg. They took turns spinning the noisy wheel.

Maggie scooted her car to the "Stop. Go to College" space. "I can't wait," she said, tossing her hair about. "Boys, booze, and no parents." She pulled gum from her purse and offered Mary a piece.

"I can't," Mary said. "Mother won't let me."

Maggie sniffed. "*I* won't tell."

After Mary stuffed the gum in her mouth, she spun the wheel. Even though she rolled a ten, she stopped on the red space to get married, like the rules said.

"It's so stupid." Maggie tossed Mary a blue peg. "Who wants to get married?"

Mary spun for the wedding gifts. "You have to."

Maggie set down her money. "No, you don't. You can be with a guy without it."

"How?"

Maggie sidled closer and lowered her voice. "You meet someone cool, then you get to know him. You know."

Mary looked out the window. Snow was falling, thick white flakes transforming the barren brown yard into a mysterious place. Unknown. How could she admit to her cool cousin that she didn't know anything? "That's not what the nuns said."

Maggie spat out her words. "Like they could even get a husband."

Mary thought of the sisters, then herself. "I want a husband," she said.

"I bet you want kids too." Maggie rolled her eyes. "If I land on the "Baby" spaces, I'll sell you mine. A hundred bucks each."

It was hard not to smile at her crazy cousin, so Mary did. But the thought of selling children, even plastic ones, wasn't funny.

All afternoon, *Life* went on. Mary bought insurance; Maggie didn't. Mary got the highest salary. Maggie got fired. Mary stuffed so many blue and pink pegs into her convertible, a baby boy fell out of the car and onto a plastic bridge. Gritting her teeth, she scooped him off the game board and laid him across the other pegs in her car. When she had children, she wouldn't let anything happen to them. And no man would talk her into giving them away, as Killian must've done with Mam. She bit back a question, then squared her shoulders and looked her cousin in the eyes. "Do you have a boyfriend?"

Maggie nodded. "But you'd better not tell. Mother would kill me. And Daddy . . ." Maggie leaned toward Mary, knocking money out of the bank. "I have to sneak out to meet him." Maggie's eyelashes fluttered like the wings of a moth. "He's so fine. And a Prod too."

"What's that?"

"A Protestant. Daddy would die."

Maggie talked and talked, and Mary listened. Neither one of them heard the key turn in the lock. When the door flew open, it was too late.

☦ ☦ ☦

"Why do you always interfere when I do something like this?"

Rising voices, then pauses so long Mary's toes cramped from trying to be still. It was getting old, sneaking down the hall to eavesdrop. Still, it was the best way—the only way—to get information.

"Anne, I'm not trying to argue with you. I just wonder if it's best."

"After she flat-out defied me?"

"They're just children."

"If you could have seen the look on her face. Sheer willfulness."

"I'm just thinking of Lizzie."

"Why do you insist on calling her that?"

"Now, Anne, that's beside the point."

"It's precisely the point."

Mary's heart slowed a bit. If Mother had heard the talk about the boy, she wouldn't waste her breath on such an unimportant thing as her nickname.

Mother gave an exasperated sigh. "I'm just trying to protect her."

"From her cousin?"

"She's a bad influence."

"She's her only friend."

Mary flinched at his unintentional stab. Was it that obvious she had no friends?

"I don't see what that has to do with this."

"It has everything to do with everything. She likes Maggie."

"As though *that's* important."

"I think it is."

"You just don't understand, do you?"

"What?"

"You live your life like before, never thinking about the burden of . . ."

Of me. It cut into Mary so deeply she had to lean against the wall.

"That's why you got Maggie, isn't it? To help with the burden of—"

"I just don't think she's a good influence."

"But what does Mary think?"

"What do her feelings have to do with this?"

"Well, I just thought—"

"You thought. That's part of the problem. You don't do anything; you just think."

"Fine. I don't want to get into a big stew over this."

"Then Maggie's got to go."

She had to stop it. Had to. Mary burst into the room, all rules forgotten. When she bounded onto her parents' bed, Daddy's drink sloshed all over the sheets.

"Look what you've done!" Mother jumped up, then scurried into the bathroom, returning with a towel.

Still sitting on the bed, Daddy pulled Mary close. "Why are you yelling at her? It was an accident."

"That's easy for you to say. You don't have to clean this place."

Mary threw her arms around Daddy. "Don't make her go away." She begged him with her eyes, her arms, even her toes, which she tried to curl around his legs.

Daddy seemed to take a long time to decide. He looked at a wedding picture in an ornate silver frame. He looked at his lap. Finally he looked straight at Mother. "Maggie will stay." He set Mary on the floor. "Now go to bed."

Mother just stood there.

The cold from Mother, from Daddy, from their whole house, spread to Mary. She'd hurt Mother just by wanting Maggie to stay. But something else sent a shiver through her. Even though she loved Maggie, she knew that they'd never be best friends.

✚ ✚ ✚

September 10, 1958

Dear Diary,

Sixth grade is even worse than fifth grade. The boys like the popular girls but hate the rest of us more than ever. I'm mad at Daddy for giving in to Mother like he always does. I think it's because of his girlfriend. I'm not supposed to know about that, but the lipstick and the perfume make it pretty obvious. Mother hasn't spoken to Aunt Andrea since the Maggie incident, and of course, it's my fault. I don't know why I can't stay by myself. I keep praying for a friend, but it hasn't happened yet.

After recess, a novice handed her a note: *Frank will pick you up today in the usual spot.*

Mary wadded up the paper into a tight ball. Where was Mother? What was wrong? Changes, even small ones, were something to worry about.

Frank, Daddy's business associate, was waiting in the parking lot. Tall and slender in a dark suit, with slick-backed hair, he stood by the car, his arms crossed. Mary got into the back seat and several times opened her mouth to ask him what had happened, but his cool gaze warded off questions. They drove home without a word.

When Mary saw Mother's car in the drive, her heart lightened. *The car's broken down, that's all. Or she has an appointment.* She thanked Frank, then stepped into the ripe apple fragrance of a fall day. Leaves floated, up down, up down, until they streaked the lawn with red and yellow and brown. Nature's fall message reminded Mary change could be good.

Mary bent to pull the key from under the doormat, then stiffened. Scraping sounds were coming from inside the house. Fingers suddenly frantic, she fumbled with the lock. It wouldn't budge.

Then Mother screamed.

Mary's mouth went dry. "Are you okay? Mother? Mother!" Over and over she jiggled the handle. "Somebody, help us!"

The door yanked open.

Mary stepped back. After her eyes adjusted to the darkness inside, she stared and stared. Her table. Her chair. Her trunk. Dragged into the entryway. Her diary, lock ripped open, pages bent, secrets spilled onto the wooden planks.

Mother paced like a caged lion, pausing now and then to shove something across the floor.

Mary's hands flew to her mouth. "Mother, stop."

"How dare you?" Mother's eyes tore into Mary, sending a message of rage.

"What happened?" Trembling, Mary reached for Mother.

She shoved Mary away. "How dare you leave such a mess?" Saliva sprayed out of her mouth. "And then to write about me like that?"

It was Mother thrashing about, not an intruder. Shaking her head, Mary took a step back. But why? What was Mother doing? Better yet, what had *she* done?

Mother kicked at the diary. "I'll pack you up, send you back to that Irish filth."

Something happened in Mary when she heard the word *filth*. She was Irish; was she filthy too? After all she did to clean . . . Mary clenched her fists but couldn't stop black thoughts from amassing. Had a few wrinkles on the spread caused this? A half-shut dresser drawer? Mary made her glare hard. Cold. It was no use to pretend that they could get along. Mother hated her, and it was time for Mary to accept it. And hate her back. "You wouldn't send me back there. You'd lose your maid."

"That's right," Mother sneered. "A bloody nasty tongue. Just like the Irish."

Mary turned toward her mother, hands on her hips. "I thought I wasn't Irish."

A whirling dust devil of gray and flesh and white spun across the room. Mother slapped Mary so hard she fell against the doorjamb. Then she shoved Mary over the threshold. The door slammed.

Mary rubbed her cheek. The slap had hurt, but not as much as all the little things. The innuendos. The shrugs and sighs and glances and withdrawals. *Welcome. The Harrises.* The etching on the brass door knocker mocked Mary as she rubbed her cheek. Was she a Harris? She'd thought so, but now she wasn't sure.

Mary streaked across the street, toward the pinks and purples in the neighbor's flower bed. When her eyes focused, she spotted Mrs. Novak, the one neighbor she knew, crouched among the last of her beloved asters.

"Lovey?" Mrs. Novak wiped dirty hands on her apron before she enveloped Mary in her thin arms.

"She slapped me." Mary clutched at the birdlike woman, her breath coming in huge gulps. "She never did want me."

"Now, now," she cooed. "Come in. I've got just the thing. Fresh *kolaches*."

Everything came into focus, and Mary stepped back. "I'm not supposed to."

"Oh, just this once." She waved Mary inside and down steep basement stairs. "Here, dear. Can't eat too many of 'em, not with your figure."

Sliding onto a stool, Mary stuffed pastry after pastry in her mouth. *Tart and sweet and gooey, they are, and if I eat enough of them, maybe they'll fill the ache in me.* She didn't even chew the pieces of apricot.

"Here." Mrs. Novak took the empty plate and set a cup of coffee in its place.

Mary's eyes got big. She couldn't break another rule. Could she? "I'm not supposed to," she managed.

"Oh, rot. What'll one cup do?" Mrs. Novak grabbed cream and sugar and dumped in several spoonfuls of each. "There. It's not coffee." She rattled on in a guttural accent.

Mary managed a thin smile and took a sip. The coffee and Mrs. Novak's ramblings, half of which she didn't get, soothed her ragged spirits. *Is this how some people live? Coffee and sweets and hugs and ragged clothes and dirt on your face?*

A cuckoo clock startled Mary; she almost knocked over the stool in her haste to get up. "I've got to go." She wiped her face with a napkin. "Thank you, ma'am."

Mrs. Novak dabbed her eyes with her apron skirt. "Come back any time, dear."

Buoyed by the words she did understand, which translated to friendship, Mary hugged Mrs. Novak, then sprinted up the basement stairs, out of the house, and across grass glazed gold by the autumn sun. Near her front door, she screeched to a halt, cupped her ear, and listened. Nothing. Holding her breath, she pushed open the door. What if something was wrong with Mother?

The entryway gleamed as if it had been waxed, yet Mary dared not exhale until she checked her room. The spindly-legged antiques were back in their customary places as if nothing had happened. She let out hot, quick breaths, yet her hands were cold as ice. Her emotions ran hot and cold as well. She hated Mother—no, she didn't. Loved her? Again, no. But she didn't want anything bad to happen to her, either. She sat on her bed and pulled back the drapes from her window.

Scalloped clouds marched across a blue expanse, sending a shiver through Mary. Another change was on the way. Would Mother send her back after all these years, like she'd threatened? A part of her wanted to reunite with Mam, or at least the idea of Mam. Mam had to love her more than Mother did. When the white clouds swelled until there was only a patch of blue in the sky, Mary let go of the lacy drapes and slid onto her bed.

Mother stepped in the room, all smiles. "Time to eat."

Her body drained of energy, her mind numbed by fluctuating emotions, Mary followed Mother into the kitchen. The lights had been dimmed. Candles glowed as if for a celebration. They had their usual silent dinner. But while Mary scraped the last of the peas and onions off the plate, she felt Mother's gaze on her. She looked up and almost dropped her fork to see Mother's sad, empty eyes.

"What do you want from me, Mary Elizabeth?" Mother spoke with such a soft voice Mary had to strain to hear. "What is it you need here?"

"I want"—Mary barely thought as words tumbled out—"a best friend."

When tears flooded Mother's eyes, the mystery continued. *Why is Mother crying? I'm the one who needs the friend, not her.*

Mary did the dishes as usual, but tonight, Mother helped her dry them and put them away. Eventually Mary's heart quit pounding, and her breathing returned to normal. Mother wasn't mad enough to send her away. But was that a good or a bad thing?

That night as Mary curled into bed, she pulled her pillow close and tucked the sheet under her chin. Sister Brigid said Jesus listened to your prayers. She'd tried it, and it hadn't worked, but she'd try again. She squeezed her eyes shut and prayed. *Jesus, it doesn't have to be a best friend. Could it just be something like it?*

✞ ✞ ✞

For a long time, Sally avoided Mary's gaze and instead looked out the window. The snowfall had abated, and the scene reminded Sally of one of those snow globes. Beautiful, but not something you could touch or cozy up with. Like this whole part of the country. Ice crept into her veins too. This part of Mary's story touched at a part of Sally that nobody knew about except her own parents. After that move, when she'd struggled to find someone. She paused, remembering just one of the things He'd done for her. *God . . . thanks for Ella. That first friend.* Turning to her new friend, so striking in profile—fire-and-ice coloring, chiseled cheekbones—she longed to hear good news. "You found someone . . . didn't you?"

Mary dabbed at her eyes. "No. Yes. Well, kind of."

CHAPTER 9

First storm of winter blew high, blew high.
Red leaves scattering to a gloomy sky.
—Alice Milligan, "Life of Wolfe Tone"

High school was no better than junior high. It was a different school, even had a different statue—of Jesus holding out His arms as if to embrace the whole world—but the isolation Mary felt within the school walls was as bad as ever. At least she had found a family. She lived for the afternoons when she could see them.

At precisely three thirty, Mother pulled into the drive. The whole way home, she and Mary never spoke. Before Mother even got inside, Mary was in her bedroom, changing clothes. As fast as she was moving, the walls still closed in on her, so she tied her sneakers on the run and intercepted Mother at the door. "Can I go out?" she asked, wincing at the little-girl sound of her voice.

Mother's face darkened like a night sky. "To that Mason girl's? I've told you, time and time again—"

"No, Mother. The Novaks.'"

"Those ... refugees?" Her eyebrows arched. "Well, okay. But be home on time."

Her hand on the door, she stared at Mother. Weren't she and Mother refuges too, same as their Czech neighbors? A cool breeze swirled about Mary as she dashed across the street. After being cooped up in school, being at the Novaks'—whatever others thought of them—seemed like heaven.

Mrs. Novak opened the door before Mary knocked. She ushered Mary in, then bustled about the room, a dust rag in her hand. "Is your mother home?"

"Yeah—I mean yes, ma'am."

"Do you think she'd like something?" She pointed to a decanter and little glasses on a tray by the door.

"Uh, she's busy cleaning," Mary said, avoiding Mrs. Novak's hopeful eyes. Mother wouldn't be caught dead in "those people's house." And for that, Mary was glad.

Mrs. Novak swatted Mary with the rag as she pattered down the hall. "Okay, Lovey. Scoot on down. Soup's a'boiling. Beef heart."

Wonderful smells and laughter wafted up from the basement, and Mary's heart lightened. She clattered down the stairs, pulling off her sweater. *Home, at last.*

"Mary." Mr. Novak rested in a recliner, his grandchildren Vincent and Katie tussling at his feet. "Get us some soup." He sighed, as if he could already taste it.

"Mary!" His face glowing, Vincent leapt into her arms.

She rubbed his frizzy hair. "Hey, hold on." She hoisted him on her hip and carried him into the kitchen. He wasn't her brother, not really, but she could pretend.

She set Vincent down, grabbed a potholder caked with old stains, and lifted the lid. The soup, thick and bubbly, with a peppery aroma, made Mary's mouth water. After she served Mr. Novak, she sat cross-legged on the floor and spooned soup into her mouth. She closed her eyes, concentrating on each flavor: cayenne, tomatoes, and . . . something else. Running her tongue along the spoon rim, she savored the exotic spice. Mother would never dream of cooking this way, of eating this way—whenever you felt like it and not at six o'clock sharp. And the Novaks didn't mind if soup spilled on the rug. She took another bite, the soup warming her like the glow of candles on a winter night.

Vincent tugged Mary's sleeve. "Play ball."

"Then bring it here." She rolled her eyes and clucked as if she was calling a pet. And wasn't he a pet, with his big brown eyes, his chubby cheeks?

With speed surprising for a toddler, Vincent flashed across frayed carpet. After grunts and an elaborate windup, he somehow bounced the ball off his head.

Mr. Novak, Mary, and Katie doubled up, howling like hyenas. Mary wanted to grab this moment, just a little thing, really, yet it made all the difference between belonging and being an outsider.

Vincent threw the ball again. This time it hit Mary in the arm.

"Uh-oh." Vincent covered his face yet peeked out between splayed fingers.

Mary laughed away the sting, but it touched a place inside of her. Why couldn't she have a family like this?

All too soon, Mrs. Novak appeared at the top of the stairs. "Lovey, it's time," she said, tapping on the face of her watch.

Mary groaned. "Already?"

"Now, now, don't be late, dear."

Mary set her bowl in the sink, then blew kisses to her sometime brother and sister. She trudged out of the house, the exotic spice smell clinging to her clothes.

Mother met her at the door. "You're late again. And what's that dreadful smell?"

"I'm not late," she managed, the words slipping between gritted teeth.

"Yes, you are. Now, go wash your hands, Mary Elizabeth. It's time to eat."

They ate in silence as usual. When she looked at Mother, she longed to see Mrs. Novak's rosy smile. While she cleared the dishes, she thought of Mr. Novak rocking away in his tattered chair, Vincent and Katie at his feet. Was it her fault Daddy never came home to eat? It couldn't help that Mother and she didn't get along. Mary grabbed a rag and scrubbed the countertops until her knuckles ached. She'd do better, help out more. And she'd tell Daddy she missed him.

✤ ✤ ✤

Suzi, Carol, and Evelyn huddled like conspirators in the cloakroom. "It's because she's pregnant," Suzi said, her cheeks flushed, her eyes bright.

Mary shivered. It was the season's first serious storm, and the temperature had plummeted. But it wasn't the chill in the room that made her shake. All signs pointed to juicy gossip, gossip that frequently targeted her. To be as unobtrusive as possible, she ducked under a rack of coats and began to take off her boots and coat.

"Who did it?" Carol asked.

"Sammy's the father, according to my brother."

"He's messing with a sophomore?"

"Yeah, can you believe it? A slut like her?" Several girls giggled.

"What'll happen now? She can't come back here."

Mary focused on stuffing gloves into her pocket. Someone was pregnant, and she hadn't even noticed? Wouldn't her stomach stick out? Wouldn't—When Mary's fingers went slack, a glove fell on the floor. It had to be Clara. She inched closer to the three girls but kept her back to them.

"How do you know all this?" Evelyn's whine sent another shiver down Mary.

"Mrs. Jones told my mother."

The room got quiet for a moment. Too quiet. Mary shot a look over her shoulder.

"Look at that hair!" The girls tittered and pointed. Mary was the new target.

Mary burned all over. Would it never end? Mary knew the answer. With Clara gone, who else would they have to talk about?

The girls continued to laugh as Mary left the cloakroom and slid into her seat. Then the bell rang, more students tromped in, and the girls in the cloakroom hurried to their places.

Sister Martha rapped on her desk. "Class, I have an announcement."

The girls continued to titter.

"Clara won't be with us anymore."

The room was silent except for the clicking of sleet against the window.

Mary craned her neck enough to look behind her. Sure enough, Clara was gone. Mary scribbled Xs in her notebook, purging years of questions. So that was what happened to Mam. But who was her father? Daddy had told her the truth. It was not Killian. But it wasn't Daddy, either.

"Why?" Mary's voice cut through the rustle in the room. Sleet fell harder.

Sister, her hand poised to open a book, froze. "Excuse me?"

Mary scribbled so hard now, she ripped the paper. "Why did she leave?"

"That'll be enough, uh, Mary." Sister Martha continued to stammer, her eyes locked on her desk. "Now, it's high time we began on algebra. Open your books to . . ."

Everything came into focus—the pinks and blues of the world map, the whorls of the carnation on Sister's desk—as if Mary had put on glasses. So Mam had been knocked up, and Mary was the result of that "knocking." They'd kept it from her all this time, but now she knew. And the knowledge made her feel even more different. And angry.

The day wore on. The storm intensified. Sister made them stay inside after lunch. Suzi and her group played a geography game while Mary struggled with algebra. Others pretended to do homework as they chatted with their study partner. A couple went to the library.

"She's not so bad. Not so chubby anymore."

Evelyn nodded. "Her hair's not so kinky."

"Her dad's the mayor, you know."

"Did you see Sister's face when she asked about Clara?"

The lead in Mary's pencil snapped right in the middle of a long equation. How dare they talk about her as if she was deaf? She stomped to the pencil sharpener.

"Want to play?" It was Suzi, her tone wheedling, her eyes wide.

Weaving a bit, Mary stepped back.

"Come on," Suzi urged. "We need one more."

Five heads bobbed.

Mary glanced at, then past, the window reflection of her round face, her mussed-up hair. How many times had she longed to be asked to join their little group? Now it had happened. As snow blurred the view, Mary visualized Clara huddled at the wall, sitting out yet another gym class, her face against the bricks. "Balloon breasts," they had taunted. "Pimple face. Uglier than Mary." Mary's vehement shake seemed to hush the room. For once, the popular girls were silent.

✦ ✦ ✦

"How was your test?"

"Mother, I told you. I don't feel like talking." Mary wiped snow off her face and settled into the front seat. While Mother veered past stalled cars and a snowplow, Mary thought about Clara. Her Irish mother. Her real father, whoever he was.

As soon as they got home, they started their daily cleaning. Mary vacuumed while Mother dusted artificial flower arrangements of too-purple pansies, too-red roses, and stiff sprigs of heather, surreal on gleaming furniture.

"How was your test?" Mother again asked. "You never answered me."

"How do I know?" An image of Clara and all the laughing girls refused to leave her mind's eye. "I just took it."

"How dare you talk to me like that? I'm your mother. It's bad enough that you—"

"That I'm what? Finish it." Mary jerked the vacuum cleaner plug out of the outlet and stalked near her mother. "That I'm illegitimate? I know what that is now. That I don't really have a father?" Words tumbled out before Mary took time to weigh the consequences. "I'm not your real daughter. You don't even want me. Only Daddy does."

"Daddy." Mother's eyes were filled with a weary redness. "He wants you so much; that's why he's always gone."

"How dare you?" Mary was in Mother's face now, the fact that what Mother said was true only making it worse. "If it weren't for him, I'd leave."

"And where would you go? Back to the bog?" Even though her eyes narrowed, Mother talked in a conversational tone as if discussing the weather.

"I've had it with you." Mary lunged toward a coffee table and knocked off a vase of roses, then leapt toward an end table and swept off an urn of heather. The crash, the shattering glass, made Mother wince, but not Mary. "You're sterile, just like these things." Mary strode to Mother's desk and raked her hand across the surface, spilling pansies from a china cup. "Do you hear me? I'm sick of it all." Coatless, she streaked out of the house and across the street.

Mrs. Novak opened after the first knock. "Dearie, get in here right now." She wrapped her shawl around Mary and guided her to the chair nearest the fire. "You're turning into a beauty, Mary." She pushed a curl off Mary's brow. "Bright as those flames. And so tall and dignified. Your mother must be proud." The only clue that Mrs. Novak knew something was wrong was the rapid-fire way she spoke.

Mary stared out the Novaks' picture window. Why couldn't she live here? She willed tears to return, anything but the deadness where her heart should be.

"I don't have a mother," she blurted out. As soon as the words materialized, Mary ducked her head, wishing she could take them back. How could Mrs. Novak understand?

"Now, now." Mrs. Novak's eyes darted about. "Go on down. Vincent's there."

Mary hurried downstairs, hoping the kitchen, the kids, would warm her heart.

As usual, Mr. Novak whistled and snored, tilted back in his chair.

Vincent ran to Mary, threw his arms around her, then pointed upstairs. "Ba-ba," he whined.

"You want your bottle? I'll get it."

Mary climbed the steps, opened the basement door—

"I don't know." Her back to Mary, Mrs. Novak twirled the phone cord about her finger. "Yah. Yah. She ran over here, saying she doesn't have a mother. You know the Irish. Uh-huh. That's right. Sure, I've got plenty of eggs. Okay. Bye." She hung up.

Snatches from other conversations and her own imaginings coursed through Mary's mind. *Sluts, they call them. Was my mother a slut? What does that make me?* A coldness sliced through Mary. This wasn't her family; she'd been a fool to think otherwise. "I've got to go," she said, her fists clinched, her back stiff. She stared at the white lace on the shawl she'd borrowed, then handed it to Mrs. Novak.

"Keep it till tomorrow. Please." Sickly pale, she patted Mary's shoulder.

Mary stiffened once again, then jerked away. "I can't." At the look on Mrs. Novak's face, she forced a tiny smile. "You know. Too much homework these days."

Mrs. Novak's eyes flickered, and some of her color returned. "I understand."

No, you don't. You don't understand anything. Mary opened the door, a blast of icy wind stinging her cheeks. "Oh, Vincent wants his bottle," she mumbled, turning her back to the home she thought she'd found. With a shiver, she sprinted across the street to the house where she lived.

Mother sat on the couch, a stack of mail in her lap. The floor had been swept, the flowers set back in their usual places. It was enough to make Mary scream. How could Mother just sit there and slit open letters like nothing had happened?

A blue envelope on the silver tray caught Mary's eye. Hugging it to her chest, she forgot all about Mother and the Novaks and the simpering girls. She slammed the door to her room, then ripped open the letter:

October 2, 1962

Mary Elizabeth Harris
507 Main Street
Lisle, Illinois
United States of America

Mary Elizabeth,
We received your note about your confirmation and catechism. I remember mine.
'Tis hard here. Two calves died last week, and without the money Anne sent for medicine, it would've been worse. Killian spent the rest on a hired hand. With the rains pouring down, the fields are a mire.
You asked about my family. Gerard—he's eight—favors his pa. Kelly's just a sprout, still tearing about the cliffs.

Sincerely,
Kathleen McNamara

Staring at the slanted black letters, Mary shivered over and over. Kathleen McNamara. Not Mam or Mother or even Kathleen. Signing her formal name like she was writing a letter to someone she barely knew. *Of course, she barely knows me.* She tried hard to remember Mam. Rich dark hair. A bright smile. She put her finger on each word, desperate to draw out more meaning. She counted the sentences and reread it. *I'm her child, even though I'm illegitimate. Doesn't that count for something? But if it did, why did she send me away?*

The wind rattled the window pane. Winter coming, and soon. Was it so in Ireland too? She glanced at the date on the letter, and her heart leapt in her chest. How had she missed it? Written on her fifteenth birthday. She tried to visualize Mam sitting in her house on the cliffs, writing the letter. Did she weep for the daughter she'd flung across the ocean? Did Kelly remind her of the daughter who'd also roamed the cliffs, before she'd been given away?

Mary slipped the letter between the pages of her diary. She wasn't positive why they sent her away, but it had something to do with being illegitimate. She longed to know why Mam did it, longed to know who her real father was, but more than anything else, she longed to go back to Ireland. As she slid her diary under the mattress, she promised herself one thing: one day, she would go back and get the questions answered.

☩ ☩ ☩

"So you quit going to the Novaks?"

Mary's let out an exasperated huff. "You don't understand, do you? Back then, it was a dreadful stigma to be illegitimate! You were unwanted. Unloved. Trapped."

Sally grabbed a lock of hair and twirled it, praying that Mary would calm down. She didn't dare put in her two cents about how pregnant girls were treated down South. Anyway, it didn't sound much different. She struggled to think of something positive to say. "Uh, how about . . ." *What did they call it?* She hadn't known many Catholics and was clueless about their lingo. "Your . . . confirmation, did that help?"

When Mary's face turned scarlet, Sally wondered if she'd pushed too far.

Finally, Mary spoke. "No. Not for a long, long time."

Snow fell like rain, whiting out the sounds of a world that lay outside these walls. When Mary wasn't looking, Sally glanced at her watch. Two hours! She squeezed her eyes tight, praying that Mary wouldn't stop now. Sally wanted to hear this story, needed to hear this story. And what's more, Mary needed to tell it.

CHAPTER 10

Faint not, nor fear,
His arms are near.
He changeth not, and thou art dear.
Only believe, and thou shalt see
That Christ is All in all to thee.

—John S. B. Monsell, "Fight the Good Fight with All Thy Might"

"Can you believe Father Bob?" Blond bangs falling into her eyes, Georgina gyrated around the cramped dorm room. "Too old to move, much less teach." Boas encircled her neck, and she'd hiked up her uniform skirt so short her underwear showed.

Nodding, Mary stretched out on Georgina's bed. "He's definitely senile."

Georgina plucked a feather and tossed it toward Mary, who caught it as it floated toward her, then stuck it in her hair. She loved being a part of things like this. Belonging.

Since last fall, Mary had gathered in the dorm room of Georgina, Fontine, and Marie while waiting for drama club practice. Mother had all but forced her to join "to overcome those bogsider roots." She didn't like to admit it, but Mother had been right. It had become a comfortable ritual, like wearing broken-in slippers. Mother would die if she knew the things they talked about—not just the usual tirades against Father Bob and the sisters, but really juicy stuff like the Beatles, the Vietnam War, and, of course, boys.

"He's better than that witch Marguerite." Fontine, glossy black hair gathered in a ponytail at the side of an angular face, flipped through a contraband *Seventeen* magazine.

Mary nodded. "She made me stay late yesterday."

"Why?" Marie, the top student in their junior class, slid next to Mary on the bed. With her flawless, almond-colored skin and mass of black curls, she looked like one of the wealthy girls, but rumor was she'd been abandoned on the steps of a Central American orphanage.

Mary hesitated. "She overheard my joke."

Dark eyes fixed onto Mary. "Tell us."

Mary adjusted the pillow she'd been leaning against. "I forget," she said. It embarrassed her now, that thing that had seemed so funny, about how God had changed Sister Marguerite into a frog, and then a prince killed himself rather than having to marry her.

"At least you didn't have to copy that stupid prayer."

Mary sighed, grateful that Georgina had changed the subject.

"Did she hit you with the ruler?"

They laughed, then got so quiet the only sound came from Marie turning the pages of her book.

"Her own uncle raped her." Georgina plopped onto the bed, apparently unwilling to drop the subject of Sister Marguerite. "That's why they put her in the convent."

Mary sat up straight. They all did. "Who told you that?" she asked.

"My mother heard it from Mrs. Farnsworth."

Fontine laughed harshly. "Serves her right."

Georgina also laughed, though not as loudly.

Marie didn't move a muscle and buried a very red face in her book.

Mary shuddered, then darted glances at the girls, trying to think of a way to stop this. But of course it was too late. Why didn't she have the guts to speak up when the talk turned nasty? After Clara had left, she'd been made the butt of all the classroom jokes. She of all people ought to know better than to spread malicious gossip. Yet she sat here wringing her hands. Doing nothing.

"Are you leaving town?" Fontine asked, her gaze fixed on Mary.

"We're staying here," Mary said, glad to tuck away her embarrassment into the talk of spring break.

"Must be nice." Fontine ripped open a candy bar and tossed the wrapper into her sheets. "My folks are off to Paris. Again."

"You're complaining about Paris?" Mary envisioned the Eiffel Tower and French boys.

Fontine shrugged. "It's no place to be by yourself. Between Daddy's embassy meetings and Mumsey's parties, I barely saw them."

And that was a bad thing? "How about you?" Mary asked Georgina, eager to steer the talk away from parents. "Switzerland again?"

Georgina shook her head. "I'll miss my ski instructor." She sighed, then brightened. "*Pero los chicos* will be lining up before my plane lands."

Mary stared at her. "You can date?"

"Only with chaperones since I snuck out the last time I was home."

"You did?"

Georgina's eyes got big. "Daddy even hired a bodyguard."

"The guys were that dangerous?"

"No. I was."

A pillow fight erupted, Mary starting it. She couldn't get enough of these stories, even though half were probably lies. So much seemed to happen to the other girls, and Mary wanted things to happen to her too. Especially if it had to do with boys. Of this group, only Marie seemed uninterested in the opposite sex.

When things got quiet, Mary scooted closer to Marie, who hadn't said a word since they'd talked about Marguerite. "What are you doing?"

"Staying here." Marie brushed off her hands and got up. "It's time for practice, you guys. And spit out your gum."

Rising to her feet, Mary wanted to kick herself. Of course Marie would stay here. Where else could she go? She thought of inviting Marie to their house for the week, but Mother would never allow it.

Groaning, the girls pulled themselves off beds littered with clothes and trash. With Mary at the back of the group of four, they made their way to the main stairwell.

"Girls . . ."

Mary froze, then looked up. Why was Sister Helen standing at the head of the stairs? With ashen face and black habit, she looked eerily like a statue of the Virgin Mary.

"Girls," Sister repeated, her voice shaking. "We're not having practice." She clutched at the railing as if she would tumble over any minute.

Sister would never cancel practice. She loved them, she loved . . . somehow Mary found a voice in her tight throat. "Why?"

"Our president's dead." Sister spoke haltingly. "Assassinated."

Our president? Mary remained motionless, her hand on the rail.

"What's going to happen? What—"

"Heavens above!"

"Holy Mother, help us," Sister Helen prayed.

Voices ricocheting off the walls in the enclosed space slammed into Mary.

Georgina's breath came out in irregular gasps, her skin a sickly gray-white. Both she and Fontine stood trembling by the door. Marie collapsed into a pile on the floor, her head in her hands.

For an instant, Mary battled the old sick feeling that another change was coming. But the cries of the other girls shut out the worries and fears about what would happen. She led Georgina and Fontine to the bottom stair and got them to sit down. She made her way to Marie and draped her arm about shaking shoulders.

Mary's actions seemed to energize Sister. She flowed down the steps, habit trailing behind her. She took Marie in her arms and led her to the other girls, then turned to Mary. "They've killed our first Catholic president," she said, her pale face crumpling.

For a moment, Sister and Mary embraced. Then Sister straightened, the blush back in her cheeks. She answered each girl's questions as best she could. She told them it had happened in Dallas. She told them the government would take care of everything. She got Marie and Fontine and Georgina to their feet. "Come on." Her tone was almost conversational. "I'll make you tea."

Mary gasped. Another change. Weren't the sisters' quarters off-limits?

Their bodies cast ghostly shadows as Sister led them down a corridor lit only by wall sconces. Silence, the near-darkness, and the knowledge of the tragedy transformed the sacred space into a dungeon.

Sister stopped in front of a wooden door adorned with a gold crucifix.

"Come on in." She led them into a room so spartan Mary wondered how anyone could live in it. "Make yourself comfortable," she continued.

Mary hesitated, not knowing how to do that, since the space was claustrophobic with a bed, end table, kitchen table, and a lamp. Where would four sets of gangly limbs go?

As if she understood, Sister pointed to the bed. "Just plop down there." While the girls complied, she rattled around in a cabinet.

"What are you doing?" Fontine asked, her voice uncharacteristically timid.

Sister set out marshmallows and graham crackers. "Have you heard of s'mores?"

All the girls except Marie nodded.

"I'll melt them a bit over the hot plate," Sister continued, humming quietly as she set water to boil. Mary felt the tide of darkness ebb, almost supernaturally.

"I had those once when I went camping." Georgina leaned back, as if the tragedy had lessened its grip on her as well.

"Me too," Sister said.

"You've been camping?" Marie and Mary asked Sister at the same time.

"I loved it." Sister's voice bubbled like a brook. "I knocked through the woods with my brothers, catching fireflies, frogs—whatever was out there." She pulled out plates and cups and served the tea and snacks.

Mary raised the cup to her face, drawing in the pungent smell of grass and lemon, then took a sip. "This is good."

"Chamomile. My aunt sends it at Christmas. It reminds me of home."

The room hushed, the girls seeming to remember what brought them here.

Georgina broke the silence. "Why did you leave?"

Mary's nostrils flared. How dare Georgina ask such a personal thing? She itched to understand it herself, but weren't there things you just didn't talk about?

Sister's voice got soft. "Our church had a painting above the altar of Jesus on the cross." The glow of her skin transformed plain features into a beautiful face. "When I was about your age," she continued, "I'd sit on the pew and stare at it." She talked slowly, savoring every detail. "He gave me so much that one day I asked what I could give to Him." Her voice got louder until it seemed a chorus of angels had joined Sister as she shared her story. "It was glorious how He showed me a little at a time. To bear daily burdens. To love the unlovable. To leave the world I knew."

A rustling presence stirred in Mary's soul, something she'd never encountered before—not during her catechism, not during the receiving of the Host.

"But why did you have to leave home?" Georgina asked.

"It was the path He chose for me," Sister said, her voice unwavering.

Smoothing out her habit, Sister knelt beside them. "It all started there." She pointed to a crucifix that hung over her bed. "Jesus taking on my sins."

Sins. Mary bowed her head. How could she have earlier ridiculed poor Sister Marguerite, forced into the convent by circumstances she couldn't control? *How could I have been so ugly?* With begging eyes, she glanced at the crucifix. He seemed so vulnerable. Could He really forgive sins? She bowed her head and prayed, just in case.

Sister Helen made the sign of the cross and rose from the floor.

When Fontine lifted her nearly empty cup in a toast, Mary accidentally knocked it out of her hand.

"Oh, dear." Sister frowned, then erupted in laughter. "A job for Father Bob."

The girls collapsed into the covers.

Suddenly all business, Sister collected their dishes. "Mary, your mother's probably on her way. And you"—she nodded at the boarding students—"it's time to wash up for dinner."

"Potatoes and cutlets?"

"I'll put my money on roast."

"Now, girls, let's don't bet."

Giggles and smiles, the girls whooshed out; only Mary remained.

"Thanks for . . . everything." She longed to remain in the glowing warmth of this room. She again glanced at the crucifix. Even if a war were raging outside, there was a peace in here that she'd never experienced.

Mary hugged Sister and left the room. She ran toward the heavy doors, pushed them open, and let the snow powder puff her face. Then she remembered the dead president, and fear gripped her nearly as hard as it had when she'd first heard the news. Shivering, she craned her neck, desperate for Mother to come.

Headlights blinded her, and for a moment, she couldn't see. Then Daddy's sleek Lincoln pulled to the curb. She jumped in. "Where's Mother?" she asked.

"A headache." Daddy reached over and patted her hand. "How's my best girl?"

Her normal resentment of Daddy, brought on by his philandering, was put on hold. She was glad to see him, to feel his touch. She sank into the seat. "I'm scared. Oh, Daddy, what's going to happen?"

"You already know?"

She strained to see his expression, finally illuminated when the headlights of an approaching car beamed into the front seat. "Of course, Daddy. They told us." A sob convulsed in her throat. "What's going to happen?"

"Nothing." He peered past whizzing wipers. "We're better off without him."

Mary gasped. "Daddy! How can you say that?"

"He almost got us all blown up."

"Sister didn't feel like that. She was so upset she canceled practice."

"What do you expect? The church got him elected." Not a trace of sadness was on Daddy's face. "That and the jigs and the Commies. Not to mention the bribes."

Mary drew her hand away from Daddy, his bigotry and coldness both frightening and angering her. No matter what Daddy said, John F. Kennedy had been the president. And he had been Catholic. That was enough reason to respect him. She stared out the window. The streets were deserted as if everyone had withdrawn into the safest place they could find.

"Here you go, Mary." He pulled into the drive, then shifted into reverse.

Mary reached across the seat and touched his sleeve. "Daddy, please," she begged. "Can't you eat with us?" She tried to let him see her fear by widening her eyes. Regardless of how he acted, she wanted, needed him to stay home.

Not a muscle moved on his face. "I've got a meeting."

Mary jumped out and then glared at the car until its taillights disappeared, as if that would lessen her anger. Finally she ran, shivering, into the house, almost slipping on glazed front steps.

As soon as Mary stepped inside, Mother called out from somewhere in the back of the house. "Be careful. Your feet are wet."

Mary pulled off her shoes and padded to her room, her anger sucked out and replaced with emptiness. She wanted to talk to someone, to ask questions, to try to understand what had happened. Should they have built that bomb shelter, like Mother wanted? Was it really the Communists' fault?

She heard a rap on her bedroom door. It opened.

The woman who stood at the threshold, her hair sticking up like pins in a pincushion, her shirtwaist dress wrinkled and beltless, looked like a poor relation of her impeccable mother. "Time for dinner," she said.

The toneless voice brought tears to Mary's eyes. She rushed across the room and threw her arms around her mother, who stood limp, as if she hadn't the energy to embrace her or to push her away. "It's okay, Mother." She kept talking in soothing tones to her mother, expecting Mother to jerk away and ask about her homework. But she didn't.

Finally, Mother pulled away. "Let's eat in there." She pointed to the front room.

The two of them, their dinners on trays, sat mesmerized by the television coverage of what had happened earlier that day. Soldiers placing a flag-draped casket into a jet. Mrs. Kennedy, boarding the same jet, her head held high in spite of spatters of blood on her suit.

"Poor woman," Mother kept saying. She didn't eat a bite, just huddled on the couch, clutching a pillow to her chest like a life preserver. When they showed the same images a fourth time, Mother switched off the TV and shuffled and mumbled her way down the hall. She seemed to forget about Mary. The bedroom door clicked shut.

Tightness gripped Mary. When had Mother's hair turned so gray? When had her face gotten so drawn, so tired-looking? She longed to burst into that cold bedroom, to tell Mother that everything would be okay. Her breath came in shallow gasps. But would it?

Ha. You. Mary froze on the couch. She glanced toward the television, but it was turned off. *And what do you think you could do?*

With a gasp, Mary bounded into her room. What was it? Was it real? The voice left, but haphazard thoughts tagged close behind her shivering body. She hurried to the window, as she often did when she was sad and confused.

Gusts tore at the house. She pressed her palms against the window pane, desperate for the internal and external storms to be stilled. "Oh, God, please help poor Mrs. Kennedy and Daddy and Mother . . . Mother. Have mercy on us all."

☦ ☦ ☦

"I remember it like it happened yesterday." Years tumbled away for Sally. "I was in sixth grade in Monroe, Louisiana, and thought the world was ending." She didn't mention to Mary the terrible thing that had happened to her on that very day, a thing she had tried to block out for nearly thirty years.

Mary nodded. "It marked a turning point, at least for me." She twisted and turned a gold band on her finger. "But there was much more disillusionment to come."

The room darkened, and Sally, shivering, wondered where the sun had gone. Everything up here was so dark, so dreary . . . With a big smile, she brightened her voice. "Did those friends help?"

Mary laughed. "Better put, acquaintances." She sighed. "They were just enough to keep the inevitable at bay."

"The inevitable?" Sally's mind jumped ahead, anticipating the next twist and turn. Southerners could tell stories, but this Irishwoman . . . She glanced at Mary, whose expression squeezed at her heart. This wasn't some tall tale. It was her friend's life.

"You'll hear about it by and by. But it was more of the same. Questions with no answers."

CHAPTER 11

This life is all chequered with pleasures and woes that chase one another
Like waves of the deep. Each brightly or darkly, as onward it flows.
—Thomas Moore, "This Life Is All Chequered with Pleasures and Woes"

Mother's roast. Mother's sighs. This was getting worse by the minute. Mary gritted her teeth as forks scraped against plates. There must have been a reason Daddy came home, Mother had used the good china. What was it? Why didn't they get on with it?

"Pass it to your father," Mother ordered, pointing at the roast. "Now, while we're all here . . ." She grabbed a stack of college pamphlets and fanned them across the table.

Mary grimaced. Of course. More college talk. She didn't know what she wanted to do next year except get out of here as soon as she could. She cut her eyes to the stack of pamphlets. Of course, there had been that one from Marquette, but she didn't dare act too interested.

"We need to get to the bottom of this." Mother continued the pattern that had started when the first bulky catalogue plunked through the mail slot. It was nauseating, the way Mother ripped the plastic off the slick view books and, dabbing her forefinger to her tongue, flipped through the pages, almost as if she were the one going to college.

Mary shoved away every brochure except one. "I'm not ready," she said.

"Then you need to get ready."

"At least look through them, Lizzie." Daddy's rare appearance, his cajoling like she was an undecided voter, only served to irritate Mary further.

Mother rifled through the brochures, setting several, including the one Mary had in mind, in the middle of the table. "These seem feasible."

Mary glared at her. "What do you mean *feasible?*"

Daddy fidgeted in his chair. "The ones we feel are appropriate."

"And what does that mean?"

He smoothed out his napkin and his voice. "Let's start over. Where would you like to go, Lizzie?"

"So it's a given that I'm going, that—"

"And why on earth wouldn't you go? When I was your age, I would have—"

Mary tried to shut out the ambition that gleamed in Mother's eyes. "That's just the point. You're not my age. You're not me. *You're* not going to school."

"What about this one?" It was so skillful how Daddy transitioned right out of the argument, but Mary resented his approach, as if he were dealing with bickering council members instead of his daughter. If he cared so much, why wasn't he ever home? She put down her fork, the steak's gristle, the gray bone, making her queasy. If she didn't go to college, what would she do? They'd made it clear that nothing else was good enough for their daughter.

Mother nodded, then scooted her chair closer to Mary. "Look at this."

The smiling St. Mary's coeds in the glossy photograph, their arms linked together in some secret collegiate bond, mocked Mary. Could a mixed-up red-head fit in there? She doubted it. Besides, it was an all-girls school. She cut a look at Daddy. Of course she wouldn't mention that.

"Your father knows one of the lay trustees, and I'll bet—"

Mary tossed down her napkin. "You think they care about the daughter of a small-town politician?"

Mother slammed down the catalogue, but oddly, Daddy seemed unperturbed, almost calm. "What do *you* want, Lizzie?" he asked.

Mary bit her lip. The concern in his voice unnerved her enough to quash the next nasty comment. She flipped through the stack and found the Columbia catalogue. It was time to implement her plan. "How about this one?" she asked. "Sister thinks they have a strong arts program."

"Too far."

"Oh, Mother." Mary forced out a sigh. "It's just New York."

"With the Black Panthers and all?" Ever since Kennedy's death, Mother had been consumed by the anarchy erupting all over the country, portrayed in living color on their new television. Students stomping on the flag, then setting it afire with cigarette lighters. Blacks and women's libbers, with their cries for social upheaval, seemed to agitate her the most.

"Mother, the Black Panthers aren't even in New York."

"Well, if they're not, someone else is."

When Mary quit laughing, she made another suggestion. "How about U of I?"

"It's out of the question."

Daddy shook his head. "Not a state school."

"Why?"

"Too dangerous."

Mary tossed her hair until it hid her eyes. "You don't want me to go anywhere."

When Mother handed her another folder, Mary shoved it away. "Not DePaul." *Not when it's practically in our back yard.*

While she and Mother argued, Daddy leafed very slowly through the stack. "Well, now, how about this one?" he asked, when it finally got quiet.

It was hard to act disinterested with her heart pounding such hope. Mary took the Marquette brochure, the one she'd practically memorized. "Oh, I don't know. It looks too hard." She looked at both her parents with half-mast eyes. "And a bit too big."

✟ ✟ ✟

"You're supposed to curtsy. Now." It was trademark Sister Marguerite, a black scowl on her face, venom in her voice. But Mary didn't care. She was almost free.

All twenty-five graduates, elegant in full-length satin and chiffon gowns, lined the shimmery reflecting pond on Sacred Heart's lawn. Across the sparkling water stood junior girls awaiting the symbolic passing over of long-stemmed white roses from the seniors. And from the looks of the fire in their eyes, the bounce in their gait, this younger class had as much impertinence, as much spunk as Mary's class.

The sisters, their habits billowing in a gusty spring breeze, closed in like guards sensing a prison riot. Fontine had spiked the water with bubble bath, and now it foamed and threatened to spill out of the concrete retaining wall.

"Your turn, Mary." If possible, Sister Marguerite's frown deepened.

Mary reached across the pond, then tripped on her hem and fell. Amid a contagion of laughter, her rose plopped into the water. When Mary bent over for it, her bouffant unraveled like a poorly sewn seam. "Your turn now," she hissed at Georgina.

Georgina's phony coughing spell didn't cover up her trademark guffaws. "With this rose, I bequeath—" In an ad lib of the script, she clenched the rose between her teeth like a flamenco dancer and splashed water on the unsuspecting junior.

Sister Marguerite tried to jerk the flower out of Georgina's mouth, then winced. "*Ay. Valgame sur juana inez de la cruz,*" she screamed.

Another sister hurried to her side. "What happened?"

"A thorn." Spanish streamed from her mouth as she wrung her finger.

The sister lunged toward Georgina, who, in an effort to keep from falling, grabbed Marie's gown. Something ripped.

Marie shrieked, then shoved Georgina. "I hate you!" Her voice boomed over the thrashings of the sisters, who were trying to fish Georgina out of the water. "You've ruined everything." Holding up the torn part of her skirt, she stormed away.

Mary's laughter died in her throat. Since that day in Sister's room, Marie had become even more introverted, refusing to take part in their little rebellions like sliding down the fire escape, slathering on eye shadow, sassing the nuns. She had no doubt that, upon graduation, Marie would initiate the process to join an order. Now they'd trampled on something sacred not only to Marie, but perhaps to others. What kind of example was that for the younger girls? Mary stared first at the convent's ornate front doors, behind which Marie had disappeared, then at the white petals swirling in the pond. She could never be a nun. Did that mean Jesus didn't love her? But then again, why should He?

✠ ✠ ✠

May 30, 1965

Dear Kathleen,

I graduated from Sacred Heart today and am going to Marquette, a Catholic school in Milwaukee, Wisconsin. I plan to study communications or maybe psychology. We drove up there for a visit last month. Wisconsin's beautiful, lots of dairy farms and rolling green hills. I wonder if it looks like County Clare. It's not by the ocean, but there are lakes everywhere.

How are you? Busy with Gerard and Kelly, I'll bet. When I get my address, I'll send it to you. Mother, could I maybe come for a visit? Some day?

Love,
Your daughter Mary

114

✠ ✠ ✠

She couldn't believe it was happening, but all she had to do was look in the back seat for confirmation. The car had been packed nearly to the ceiling. A Marquette decal had been plastered on the bumper. In a rare gesture, Daddy had taken off from work so he could drive her to campus. Mother claimed a headache and stayed at home. Mary swallowed once or twice. She didn't feel well, either. She nodded at Daddy's awful jokes and tried to settle her nerves and her jumble of thoughts. *It'll be good to get away. It's what I wanted, to finally be free. But . . . what if I can't do it?*

Later that day, Daddy veered into the parking lot near the dormitory they'd visited during orientation. The cream and red bricks flushed with pride, an art deco motif softening the facade only slightly. Mary got out, leaned against the car fender, arched her head back, and counted sixteen stories, her heart plummeting. *I don't belong here. I can't do this.*

A couple of boys dressed in frayed blue jeans and work shirts rushed over and introduced themselves as Ben and Nate. Ben offered a limp hand first to Mary, then Daddy, who refused to shake it, snorting at the jumble of shoulder-length hair, unshaven face, and wrinkled jeans.

Mary's skin prickled as she admired Ben's tan, his white teeth. Was Daddy just being a drag, or was he trying to protect her, though that was the last thing she wanted?

Ben shrugged off Daddy's behavior as if it was what he expected from the uncool older generation. His eyes fixed on Mary. "Need a hand?"

"My daughter and I can handle it."

"That'd be great," Mary said simultaneously. She handed them tote bags and boxes, hoping Daddy hadn't scared them off.

Two hours later, Mary's things were piled on the floor of Room 709. When she'd arrived, no one had been in the room, but a pink blanket, teddy bear, and study pillow covered the bottom bunk. One of two identical desks was crammed with framed pictures.

When Daddy went for a final load, Ben lit a cigarette. "When's your old man leaving?" He inhaled deeply, then blew smoke in her face.

Mary coughed, partly from the smell, partly from the shock of what Ben had done. She flew to the hall, looked both ways, then hurried back. "You can do that here?"

He shrugged, the smoke from his cigarette curling toward the ceiling in loopy circles. "It's not against the rules. Unless you're in bed." His leer made Mary cringe, yet her heart raced. If Daddy disapproved, wasn't that enough reason to hang out with them? She'd chafed to break free not only from Sacred Heart's rules, but also from Mother's and Daddy's. These guys were just the beginning. She smiled at Ben, then Nate in what she hoped was a hip way, yet nerves cramped her stomach. Could they somehow sense that she'd never talked to a boy before?

Nate fussed with the beads around his neck, then picked up a picture from one of the desks and whistled. "Is that your roommate?"

The image epitomized the reams of brochures that had so fascinated Mother. Lots of curves. Thick blond hair. Beauty-queen smile. "I guess so." Mary touched a stray curl. Why hadn't she let Fontine straighten her hair last week?

Ben nearly ran into Mary in his eagerness to see the picture. "What a fox. What's her name?"

Mary shrugged, even though she'd known her roommate's name for six weeks.

There was an uncomfortable silence. Then Daddy, his keys jingling, came in, Mary's last things a heap in his arms. He put them on the top bunk, his eyes darting about as if he was lost. He mumbled something to Mary and kissed her on her cheek.

The look on his face so confused Mary that she had to bite back a sob. Wasn't this what she wanted? What she needed? "Bye, Daddy," she finally managed.

He turned to leave, then whirled back. "Excuse us, you two." Crossing his arms, he glared until the boys scurried into the hall. "I love you, Lizzie," he said, his voice husky.

"You too, Daddy." Tears flowed, and she couldn't help but remember when Daddy had given her a nickname and first told her he loved her. She collapsed into his arms, longing to tell him she felt like a child lost in a department store.

The familiar scent, Old Spice and tobacco, comforted her, but before she could snuggle in and lose her fears in the strength of Daddy, he pulled away and slumped down the hall.

✢ ✢ ✢

"It sounds like you got off to a good start."

Mary eyed Sally suspiciously. "Are you kidding? I'll bet you were one of those cheerleader types, just like my roommate."

Sally plastered on that special smile that those closest to her knew wasn't really a smile at all. Inside, she fumed. It was so stereotypical, thinking a bubbly personality meant you were a bubble-head, no-name blond defined by big hair and a big chest. "Didn't she have a name?" If she dropped a hint like this, would Mary realize how depersonalizing her comments were?

"If she did, I've forgotten it."

"I'll bet she hasn't forgotten you."

"Now there's a scary thought." Mary drummed her fingers on the coffee table. "Anyway, you didn't answer my question."

"I wasn't a cheerleader, but I was on a drill team. We were kind of like the Rangerettes."

"Really."

Sally grabbed a truffle off the candy plate on the end table and popped it in her mouth. Mary's tone was a dead giveaway for what she was thinking: with those trunks for legs, that midriff? It was time for a bigger grin. "Haven't you heard of them?"

"Can't say that I have."

"The Rangerettes wore—still do—little pleated skirts and vests and white cowgirl hats and—Oh, dear, you don't care about them, do you?"

"Well, sure. I mean, who wouldn't want to hear about a Texas dance team?"

Of course Sally noticed the sarcasm oozing from Mary's words, but she smiled even brighter. "We had a 126-kick torture routine. And we performed in the Cotton Bowl Parade in Dallas."

"Is that where you met the clock makers?"

"No, silly. That was years later—Hey, what am I doing? This is your story, not mine." Sally grabbed another truffle and finished it off in one bite.

Mary turned to face Sally. "You know, that's one of the things I love about you. How you feel free to talk about almost anything, from your bra size to your aunt's cancer."

Sally tried to pull down her top to meet her pants, her laugh becoming brittle. Sometimes Mary carried things a little too far.

"I'm just kidding. You ought to know that by now." Mary checked her watch, then grabbed her handbag. "I really need to see about Mother." But she leaned back against the couch as if she wanted Sally to coax her into staying.

"I thought you said Dora was staying all day."

"She is."

Sally folded her arms across her chest. "Well, then, it's settled. Besides, you can't leave now that you've caught me, hook, line, and sinker."

Mary fiddled with her purse. "I don't know, Sally. The worst thing you've heard so far is that I was selfish and rude and confused and lonely and had issues with my parents."

Sally's heart opened wide to this woman who'd opened the door to a past so dark, so lonely, that it grabbed at Sally in ways she couldn't explain. "Look." She caught Mary's gaze and spoke with what she hoped was a strident voice. "You're a fellow believer, a loving mother, wife, and daughter. You cook for half the invalids in the church, not to mention the hours at the soup kitchen. You welcomed me to this grimy little town before anyone else." She didn't try to wipe the tears from her eyes. "You're brave enough to tell me this. And you're my friend."

CHAPTER 12

*Musha rig um du rum da. Whack fol the daddy o
Whack fol the daddy o. There's whiskey in the jar.*
—"Whiskey in the Jar," traditional Irish folk song

Ben leaned so close to Mary she could smell the smoke on his breath. He and Nate seemed to take over the tiny dorm space with their loud humming, their constant clicking of cigarette lighters. "Where did you say you're from?"

Mary stifled a cough and tried to do the same with the tension that gripped her stomach. She'd get used to the new smells. Wouldn't she? "Lisle."

"Where's that?"

"Chicago." She didn't want to explain about her little town, her Catholic school. Why should she?

"We're from Detroit." Ben drummed against Mary's desk until she thought her eardrums would burst. Finally, he jumped to his feet. "How about a beer?"

Mary hesitated. Then the room closed in on her, as it must be doing to the boys. Nodding, she grabbed her bag and tripped down the stairwell, taking the steps two at a time to keep up. Ben motioned her into a beat-up Mustang; she had to shove crushed beer cans onto the floor so she could sit down.

It was no less stifling in the car than it had been in the dorm. Mary rolled down the window, letting in a breeze, which tangled her hair into a wild mess.

Screeching tires, jarring chords that crackled through a busted speaker, and screaming lyrics competed with the boys' chatter. Mary tried to understand the words, to groove along with Ben and Nate as they dipped and jerked to the beat, but she felt stiff and awkward like a baby bird on its first flight.

"You dig Hendrix?" Nate pulled a fibrous square of paper out of his pocket and rolled it into a stubby cigarette.

Mary's lips got dry, her palms sweaty. "I haven't, uh, heard his stuff."

"Who, then?"

"Uh, the Beatles. The . . ." She racked her brain. What were those records of Fontine's? The Beatles, the Stones were all she could think of.

"Want a toke?"

Mary accepted the homemade cigarette as if it were a loaded gun. For an instant, she thought about asking Ben to take her back to the dorm. How had she gone, in just one day, from schoolgirl pranks to smoking what she was sure was marijuana? She'd wanted a new life, but did she want this? She barely knew these boys, and she hadn't unpacked or met her roommate or done any of the things she was supposed to do.

The red-yellow ash of the reefer glowed a different message, and with the wind wildly whipping her hair, her body settling into the beat of the music, it was an easy decision. She'd been bottled up for eighteen years, and it was time to let it out. She inhaled the sweet grassy smoke; it burned her throat, and she coughed.

Ben patted her on the thigh. "Your first time, right?"

Mary nodded, the last of her inhibitions melting away. They understood her and would help her get used to things. "Yeah," she said. "I'm a novice, all right."

Minutes later, Mary was sitting between the two of them at a bar, soaking up beer and new experiences. Pulsating strobe lights. Lascivious looks. Music. Laughter. When Ben grabbed her hand and dragged her to the dance floor, she ground her hips and gyrated about the crowded space. *It's started! The cork's out of the bottle.*

In synchronization with a strobe light, the night flashed in fragments. Like the patterns in her old kaleidoscope, the wheel being rotated at a dizzying speed. Mary didn't know if it was the marijuana or the alcohol, but somehow she escaped linear time and saw both the present and the past. She closed her eyes and let it flow . . . right on, sister, Mother, a whirling dervish of laughter, kissing Ben, bitter-tasting beer, blowing foam at strangers, Daddy, an argument, older guys, doors slamming, a lonely cliff, kissing Nate, a hundred flights of stairs, right on, sister, retching into a flowerbed of spectacular yellow mums, Mam, right on, sister . . .

When Mary woke the next morning, the room was empty. She glanced about, wondering where her roommate was, what she was doing, then sank back into the bed. She rubbed her temples, trying her best to think past the pounding. *Did we meet last night, or am I just remembering her picture?* The blankness of her mind made her tremble, and she opened the door as if to prove to herself that she was really at college.

The noisy chatter of girls in the hall reminded Mary where she was and what she was supposed to be doing. She slumped out of bed, picked up the orientation packet—placement tests, picnics, receptions, registrations—studied it, then laid it back on the dresser, shocked at how much she'd already missed. The roommate's photo seemed to mock her, and Mary resisted an urge to smash the carefully framed image. She'd be there, with all the rest of the freshmen, eager to make a good first impression.

And why not? Mary's skin prickled, and so did her conscience. Hadn't Sister Helen devoted a whole day to helping her with the application? She thought of Daddy's hopeful smile, of Mother's ambitious eyes, and again picked up the packet.

It was easy to find her schedule and the map, since Mother had stapled and clipped everything together. After she read it, she dug through the pocket of her jean jacket for her keys and a pen. That was when she found Ben's phone number on a scrap of paper. Twenty minutes later, she was shooting pool a few miles from campus, the orientation, the roommate, tucked away in a tiny corner of her mind.

From time to time, Mary attended classes, but her main teachers were in bars with names like Whiskey a Go Go and Someplace Else. Soon Ben and Nate faded away, replaced by John and Jeff, and a few weeks later, Melanie and Joe. Then Rick. She determined her companions by their bent on rebellion, how well they drank, and if they pretended to have a good time. If they did all that and had wheels too, they were perfect.

☩ ☩ ☩

"Are you sure he didn't call?" Mary hoped she kept the longing from her voice.

Her roommate nodded, then refocused her energy on polishing her toes.

The two girls had settled into a system that seemed to work for two people with nothing in common; they only spoke when absolutely necessary. "You'll get the key?" A nod. "He called?" A shake. If more was needed, they composed terse notes. *Call the registrar. Lab canceled.* They arranged their schedule like children on a seesaw. When she was out, Mary was in. When Mary was in, she was out.

Mary paced the floor and stared at the phone, wondering if she could will it to ring. When it finally did, she grabbed it before her roommate could. "Rick?"

"Happy Halloween, babe."

Mary's heart thumped against her work shirt. A month ago, she'd met Rick at a bar, and was drawn to his passion for political causes. But when he looked at her with narrowed green eyes, she felt a different kind of passion. "Where are you?" she screeched, then winced at the sound of her voice.

"Whoa. Chill out."

Mary wanted to slam down the phone. How dare he tell her to chill after she'd waited for hours? Half the time, he didn't even seem to care if she was there.

"I'm down here, babe. Ready when you are."

At the endearing term, her resistance melted. So he did care. "I'll be right there." She grabbed her jacket and purse, determined to ignore her room-mate's glare.

Mary hurried into the elevator, a closet of mirrors reeking of cheap perfume. Not wanting to see the reflection of the girl with bruised-looking eyelids, she stared at the Down button, trying to ignore her growling stomach. When had she last eaten?

The elevator opened. Mary walked into a lobby made festive by bored switchboard operators. Paper goblins with devilish smiles hung from the lights and fluttered accordionlike limbs. A pumpkin, its zigzag smile flickering yellow and black in response to the sputtering candle in its carved-out center, grinned evilly.

"Hey." Rick leaned against a wall of house phones.

When he moved toward her, hips swaying, honing in on her as if she was prey, she struggled to get words out. "Hey, yourself," she finally said.

Rick pulled her so close she felt the steel hardness of his belt buckle. His lips curved into a lazy smile that accentuated an aquiline nose and chiseled cheekbones. The graduate student on duty glared; as if to spite her, Rick gave Mary a long, deep kiss.

Mary clung to him, not caring what the Goody Two-shoes thought. She was an adult now, and she could kiss her boyfriend whenever she wanted. When Rick ran his finger along the swell of her breast, however, she pulled away. "I'm hungry," she said. And it was true. But for what, she wasn't sure.

Using both hands, Rick shoved back wheat-colored hair that had slipped out of a ponytail. "You can just grab a burger at the bar."

Mary nodded but inwardly fumed. So much for their stance on animal rights. She cast a sidelong glance at him. Did he care about anything that she did?

Rick shoved her toward the parking lot. "Come on," he said, an unusual tightness about his eyes. "We're late."

Make Love, Not War. Groovy, Baby. Drop Seeds, Not Bombs. Flower Power. Rick's car was so plastered with stickers, it was a cinch to find in the crowded lot. As Mary got in, she wondered if he believed in half the causes he espoused. "You got a meeting?" she asked, swallowing back other questions.

Rick throttled the gear shift.

Mary tried to squelch a squeamish feeling. Despite his grandiose vision of equality, he treated her like trash. "Come on," she cooed, oddly drawn to his silence, "talk to me." As soon as the words came out, she cringed. She sounded just like Mother.

The silent treatment continued. Rick parked. They went in the bar. The bench-style tables were full, but Rick's friends—the antiwar group—had saved them seats. John and Joe and several rough-looking guys seemed to be arguing. Smoke from their cigarettes amassed into a hazy cloud and stalled like a storm front over the table.

"It's too early, man."

Mary bit her lip. It was the same thing every time. Rick and Joe wanted to make a big statement to protest American involvement in Vietnam—kidnap the Marquette president, burn down the student union. John and the others balked, wanting grassroots support to swell at the traditionally conservative Catholic school before they acted.

"You're wrong." Cursing, Joe tamped cigarette ash into an empty pitcher. "It's way overdue."

Rick stepped over the bench seat and sat down. Mary squeezed in next to him.

"Speaking of overdue," Joe said, his lip curled into a sneer, "it's about time you showed up."

Rick put his arm around Mary. "I've got an old lady. You know."

Mary nestled closer, warmed by Rick's term of endearment, but she fixed her eyes on the bubbles that hurried to the surface of a half-full pitcher. Who were all these people? And what, really, was going on?

The bubbly brew, promising to ease the tightness, called to her, and Mary was happy to answer. She picked up the pitcher, pulled a mug from the middle of the table, drank. Poured, drank.

"Here they are. Hot off the press." Someone thrust a pile of papers at Rick.

He glanced at them and shoved them onto a floor littered with peanut husks. "You expect me to wait three months?"

John slammed his fist against the table. "Like I said about six times now, they're not ready."

"Then we'll get them ready."

"If the SDS can't do it, you think you can?"

As if the cops had walked in, a hush came over them, and that, as much as the words, sent a chill down Mary's spine. She knew the SDS advocated violence. What was Rick—what were all of them—flirting with?

Rick's eyes blazed. "It's time." His flailing arms knocked over a mug of beer. "You seen the news? The lumps in the body bags?"

Mary, desperate to busy her hands now that the pitcher was empty, tried to wipe it up, yet she wasn't sure why since no one else seemed to have noticed the amber stream trickling onto the floor.

Rick's voice took on a higher pitch. "It's time to crash their party."

"What kind of trip are you on?"

Rick flew around the table. His hand a hook, he grabbed John's shirt and yanked him to his feet. "Don't you dare talk to me like that." His lips thinned into a snarl.

If Mary could have moved farther from him, she would have, but she was on the edge of the seat already. Scanning the crowd, she sought a familiar face but saw none. Doubts assailed her. Was it too late to get out of here? She could say she was sick—

Joe grabbed Rick and shoved him away. "Hey, man, cool it."

Rick let go but continued to stand menacingly close to John.

"Only sixteen thousand at the rally." John kept up his glare but stepped backward.

"That's a fact. And that's in DC." Others Mary didn't know grumbled and mumbled their agreement.

"They ain't ready, man." John seemed to have regained control. He sat back down, grabbed another pitcher, and slopped more beer into his mug. "Not on this campus. Just face it."

Rick kicked at the bench, which made him lose his balance. "Then they're pigs too." After steadying himself, he grabbed Mary's arm and yanked her toward the door.

She winced as he tightened his grip on her but didn't say anything.

Minutes later, they peeled out of the parking lot, expletives streaming from Rick's mouth, along with wild rants about the Weathermen and social justice.

Mary's heart raced as she clung to the dashboard. *Do I dare ask him to slow down? To take me home?*

When Rick stomped on the accelerator, the motor whined with increased shrillness. They zigzagged past lanes that dead-ended at the reservoir, past abandoned warehouses and lots littered with rusted-out cars. At the corner of

Seventh and Maple, a black cat streaked in front of them. It arched its back, its tail stiff like a sail full of wind.

A twisted smile on his face, Rick veered toward it. Then there was a sickening crunch of bone meeting rubber.

Images of Killian and her lamb flashed before Mary. She threw her body against the door. "Stop! Let me out!" she screamed. Her sweaty hands tugged at the handle, but it wouldn't budge. Seconds later, Mary felt Rick jerk the gear shaft into park. When the car lurched to a stop, her head banged on the steering wheel. She screamed again.

Rick lunged at her, grabbed her shirt, and yanked her toward him.

She flailed feebly. The thud of her heart echoed that horrid sound of cat and tire. Too late, she understood the meaning of Rick's shifty jaw, the way his teeth ground together when something got in his way.

Ice-cold fingers gripped her, spreading chills down into her groin.

"No." Her voice was a whimper.

Rick used his forearm to shove her head against the seat, then tore her shirt open.

Mary flinched at the rip of the fabric and screamed, "How dare you?" She tried to fix her shirt, then shoved away from him, her body one concerted convulsion of disgust.

Sweat poured off Rick's forehead. He grabbed one of Mary's breasts, his fingernails raking sensitive skin, then squeezed it.

She flailed against him, kicking and screaming with all her might now that she knew beyond doubt his intent. "How dare you? Stop it. Stop!"

Rick responded by grabbing her hair, then yanking so hard, he grunted.

The rip Mary heard this time was not fabric, but her hair. Seconds later, her eyes clouded over from the agonizing pain at her scalp, she retched. When she could focus, she stared at the pool of vomit on the seat, her limbs locked.

"See what happens, you little slut?" Rick held up the clump of curls like a trophy.

Mary's eyes narrowed, and her body swelled with a hate more intense than she had ever felt. She summoned every reserve of strength, coiling against the seat like a cornered rattler. He shouldn't have called her that. He'd gone too far.

When he grabbed her again, she was ready. The first slap, with her palm, stunned him. He rubbed his jaw, a blankness clouding his features. His pause gave Mary the time she needed to make a tight fist, created from the built-up fury that added power to each knuckle, each sinew. Her second blow slammed his skull into the driver's window.

She kicked at the door. It finally opened. She ran as if his heavy breath, his raging eyes followed. Past trees whispering of the coming cold. Past deserted intersections, the traffic lights swaying eerily in response to the bitter breeze. Up and down graveled drainage ditches like a rabid dog in the final throes of disease.

A horn honked. Another. She fell, scraped her knees. When she got up, the twin Gothic spires of Gesu cathedral loomed before her, the stony frame solid and silent but sure.

"Oh, God. Oh, God." Pent-up words poured out. Her pace slowing, she stumbled up the dorm steps. Coeds in the last stages of passionate goodnights clustered about the doors. With her shoulders slumped, her head ducked, she darted past them and ran to the elevator. She dragged herself to her room and jiggled the knob, but the door was locked. She fumbled for keys. Banged on the door. "Let me in," she called. "I'm locked out." There was no answer.

She moved down the hall and knocked on more doors. Finally, a girl answered.

"What's the room of the wing-ding?" Mary paused to gag, feeling the bile rise again, and leaned on the wall for support. If she could just get behind her door, hide . . .

"701." The girl slammed the door.

Mary peered down the hall, her vision blurred. "705, 703 . . ." As she limped along, she squinted to read the numbers.

She knocked, or at least she thought she did.

The door cracked open. "What is it?"

"My roommate's locked me out."

The floor director, her hair wrapped around an orange juice can and then bobby-pinned atop her head, peeked out, then looked Mary up and down. "Are you Mary? 709?"

Mary hesitated before she nodded.

"Hold on." She grabbed keys and a notebook. "I need to talk to you anyway."

As Mary followed the floor director, the fog that had shrouded her brain lifted a bit, and she felt her senses come back to life. The floor director wore the pinkest, furriest house shoes, which squeaked as she marched down the hall. The door groaned when she unlocked Mary's door. The light switch clicked when she flipped it on.

Mary blinked. No framed photos. The sheets had been removed from her roommate's mattress. Just a whiff of perfume remained. Her head again spinning, Mary leaned against the door. "We're in the wrong room. I must be—"

"No. This is it, all right." The director sat at the empty desk. "Sit down."

Mary collapsed onto the empty bunk. "Where is she? What's going on?"

The floor director looked Mary up and down, sniffed, then averted her face.

Mary stared at her torn shirt, her fingernails, dirty, jagged and bitten, and balled her hands into a tight fist. Was that vomit on her shirt? No wonder this girl was so disgusted. For the first time in quite a while, Mary saw herself through the eyes of her roommate. What she saw made her want to sink to her knees and cry.

"She requested a transfer," the floor director explained, as if she could read Mary's mind. "She just couldn't take it anymore, you tumbling in here at all hours, blowing smoke in her face." She thumbed through papers. "You've been campused twice. And if I'm reading this right, you have four demerits right now."

Mary leapt to her feet, the room, the director's stare closing in on her. "I hate it here," she shrieked. "But you'd never understand."

The director leveled a gaze at her. "Try me."

It was as if cold water had been thrown at Mary. She opened her mouth, then closed it, stepped back to her bunk, and sat down. How could she explain that in spite of her affected disdain, she'd wanted her roommate's approval? That she'd love nothing more than a fresh start? She buried her face in her hands, longing to hide from them all, longing to hide from herself.

"We need to call your parents."

An alarm went off in her brain. Mary sprang from the bed, hands waving, sobs in her throat. "Don't call them. I'm okay. Really, I am." All she could think about was her parents' faces. What would this do to them? She reached for the director, her hands trembling. "Please, don't tell them. Please. I just had a rough night."

The director pulled away. "You need counseling," she said, "yesterday."

Mary tensed, her eyes glued to the director's face. "Okay." She mouthed the words, desperate to accept any terms. *Just don't tell Mother. Or Daddy. No, no, no. Not Daddy's little girl, sugar and spice and everything nice.* She trembled. Was it too late? Would she call them?

The director seemed to consider her options, then stood. "If you'll agree to counseling, I'll let you off with a warning." She picked up her keys. "Next time will be a different story." She walked to the door. "You know where I am if you need me."

Mary heard her pad down the hall.

As the tension melted off Mary, imminent danger past, a suffocating blackness moved in and took its place. She unlatched the window and gulped cold night air. The icy wind slapped her, and her breath came in rasps. What could she do now? She stared past the roof of the law school toward some distant road. Vehicles, their headlights flashing, hurtled toward destinations unknown.

With all the presence of mind she could gather after almost being raped, after being rightfully deserted by her roommate, she considered her options. Fast forward, stop, play, rewind, play. The insistent honking of a trucker's air horn pierced the early morning stillness. Mary shook all over, hitting rewind again and then play. Play. Play. Play. Stop.

She turned from the window. She'd head for the freeway, littered with jagged bottles and fast-food wrappers, dart into onrushing traffic, and scour away the despair, the meaninglessness, the chasing of the wind.

On the way out, she grabbed her coat, then froze. What was that sound ... that cackling voice?

You won't need that where you're going. You are nothing. It is all nothing.

Mary tore at her hair, imploring her mind not to listen.

A clearer voice stepped in with such resolve, such surety that she looked toward the door half-expecting someone to step in. *You can hold on. You can make it, for I am with you always.*

The power in the words seemed to shove back the darkness. She shuddered into her jacket but didn't take another step. What caused the voices? Was it the drinking? The pills she'd tried ... when was it? She closed her eyes and tried to concentrate on what Rick had said about them. Nothing. Just another scramble of jagged memories.

Feeling dizzy, she half folded, half collapsed onto the floor, using her purse as a pillow. As best she could with a pounding headache and waves of nausea, she considered her options. The abyss. Another roommate. A job in some other city. She thought of the crazed look in Rick's eyes, of her shiftless, purposeless life, and she wept.

The first hint of dawn illuminated the picture on her desk and Mother's careful notation—*Graduation Day. Mother. Daddy. Mary Elizabeth.* She pulled herself from the floor, grabbed the photograph, yanked her quilt from the bed, and curled under the window. As the campus roused for another day of academia, the chapel chimes ringing, ringing, Mary's eyes closed. She was going back to Lisle, going back to home, or at least the closest semblance to it that she could find.

CHAPTER 13

But if I should return, O! T'will be in the spring.
I will show you how the flowers grow, make the nightingale sing.
—"The Grenadier and the Lady," traditional English ballad

The light blinded Mary. She pulled a blanket over her face.

"Get up."

Of course. It was Mother. "I'm sleeping," she mumbled.

"I said, get up."

Mary's head pounded from last night's excesses, the same laughter and deep discussions. Draft dodging. The legalization of dope. Then hugs and kisses and names and numbers written on torn napkins. She'd dropped out of Marquette just in time for Mother's dry stuffing and turkey. She'd lived at home for a year and a half now, yet there was little difference between how things had been last fall and how things were now.

With effort, Mary sat up. "Says who?"

"This is my house. You follow my rules when you live here."

Mary tried to swallow the cottony taste in her mouth. "What is it now?"

"We've heard from the school again."

Mother's tone snapped Mary to attention. "Marquette?"

"No." Mother's lips curled into a sneer. "Your little drama school." She thrust an envelope toward Mary, who didn't have to open it to know what it said.

"And?" Mary played along, though she really didn't know why.

"Your grades aren't acceptable."

"To you or to me?"

Mother tapped the floor with her pump. "How can you make Cs at a drama school, for heaven's sake?" She picked up Mary's quilt and began smoothing it over the bed.

Mary stared at the jumble of stitched memories, stifling an urge to yank it from Mother and hide under it. Why had she come back here? New bad memories piled on top of old bad memories. And Mother trying to solve everything with a basting stitch or two. "Why do you try to fix everything?" she asked.

Mother's scowl contorted her face. "Because you need fixing."

Mary flung back the covers. "How do you know what I need?"

"Half the time, you don't even go to class."

"How would you know? You're always at work."

Mother tapped her shoe, louder now. "We're not talking about me, young lady." She clicked to the door. "It's gone on too long. If things don't change, I'm throwing you out." She slammed the door, rattling the china doll.

Mary went back to sleep. When she woke up, she struggled for a moment to remember where she was. Streetlights had come on, yet the drapes only allowed a faint glow into her room. Rising, she roamed about, touching familiar objects and new trinkets. The china doll, Mother's first gift. A peace symbol on a rawhide string, last month's rally. A children's book, Daddy's Christmas present. A string of Mardi Gras beads, another happy hour. She picked up her kaleidoscope, but its patterns were lifeless in the dimly lit room.

Tiredness enveloped Mary, her arms heavy, her energy sapped. She ran her finger along the spines of books hemmed in by brass bookends. How could she stop the madness? She felt trapped in her current lifestyle, a revolving door of substance abuse and causes she wasn't even sure she believed in. It spun about with such a whirl that she couldn't escape, even if she wanted to. Just getting up and getting dressed were monumental efforts. How could she make any real changes?

Absentmindedly she pulled *Treasures of Ireland* off the shelf. What did she want? College? A job? Roosevelt was a fine school, not the farce that Mother made it out to be. But it fit her no better than her jeans, which hung on her emaciated frame. She opened the book and almost cried at the inscription. *From your real Daddy, Christmas 1957.*

Who was her real daddy? Her eyes burned, a hot, indignant flame. Dared she ask Mother? Daddy? Did they even know? Should she pen a plaintive letter to Kathleen, begging for the truth?

Her mind racing, she flipped through the pages. Hearty islanders leapt to greet her, as did sheep grazing on rolling hills. She flipped another page, another—then stared at black and orange birds huddled in crevices of craggy rocks. All of a sudden, Mary could hear Mam shouting, "Get back! The sea'll take ye." Waves crashed, and she scampered to Mam, shielded from the shroud of fog, the ocean spray. As she stared at the puffins, the quote under the picture expressed what her heart sang of. *Long be my heart with memories filled. Like the vase in which roses once were distilled. You may break, may shatter the vase, if you will. But the scent of roses will hang 'round it still.*

Her home. Ireland. It still touched her in a deep place. Carefully, she shut the book. A thin sheet of paper fluttered to the floor. Blue. Airmail. Ireland.

October 2, 1965

Dear Mary Elizabeth,
Jesus, Mary, and Joseph, a daughter at university. Who'd dream a lass from the cliffs could go so far? I thank you for the letter and the graduation picture.

Mam

She flung the book down and grabbed her coat with one hand, Mam's letter in the other. The room seemed to lighten as she read it over and over. Mam was proud of her. She was bound to relish a visit. Her spirits soaring, Mary ran into the front room.

Mother set down a magazine, frowning. "Where are you going?"

"Out." Mary flung a scarf about her neck, her fingers shaking.

"You need to stay in this house, young lady, and—"

"How could you keep her letter from me?" she screamed. Not waiting for a response, she slammed out of the house and sprinted to the El. Her anger evaporated as she boarded the train, studied the passengers, an odd mix of late-shift workers, students, and partygoers. She'd go back. Make a fresh start with her real mother. By the time they'd pulled into Union Station, her mind sped like the train had as it raced through the suburbs. When it screeched to a stop, she jumped off and hurried into a bar.

A handsome gentleman smiled at her. Mary smiled back. The tinkling of ice in his glass, the amber glow of his drink beckoned her to join in the cheer. She slid onto a bar stool. Why not? She had something to celebrate. She was going home!

By midnight, it all blurred together in the sickening sameness. To fight the dizziness, the nausea, Mary lowered her head onto the cold, wet counter of the bar.

"Mary! How on earth are you?"

She startled upright. The voice sounded familiar, but the face . . . she couldn't see.

"Are you okay?"

When she stared hard, he came into focus. She jumped off the bar stool and hugged him. "Michael, it's you." Giggling, she staggered, knocking his trench coat askew. It was Michael O'Looney, a boy she'd met in the Marquette dining hall. A popular senior who'd gravitated toward a different crowd, one that studied and went to class and mass.

He took her arm. "Let's get you home."

Smiling, she staggered toward him. "I don't have a home."

His tone was patient, as was his expression. "Come on. How far is it?"

"Five thousand miles."

Mary awoke on a lumpy coach, her head pounding its resentment of last night's drink. *I have to stop this . . . Where am I?* She rubbed her eyes and tried to keep from heaving. All she could remember was something about Ireland. And the bluest eyes. She hurried into the next room, a breakfast nook furnished with a table and two stools. Then she smiled. There he was, dimples, white straight teeth, and those eyes. Suddenly she remembered last night, or at least parts of it. The parts that included him.

Sighing, she slid onto a stool. "Thank God for you, Michael O'Looney."

"Have you slept it off?" He ran fingers through hair the color of cinnamon sticks.

She tried to ignore her headache and scrutinized his appearance. Not exactly her type: clean-shaven, pressed khakis, oxford shirt, navy blazer. But still a handsome man.

"You ought to know, being Irish too." They laughed in the familiar way of college acquaintances. "What're you doing here in Chicago?"

"I live here now. I'm an economist for a brokerage house."

A dove fluttered onto the balcony ledge, catching Mary off guard. She stared out the sliding glass door. How had she managed to get up to this floor and not even remember? She swallowed, then gestured toward the door. "Pretty high for a lad born in Ireland, wouldn't you say?"

Michael studied her for a moment. "That's because I stop after a drink or two." He smiled, as if aware that his Irish tongue was sharp as ever.

"Touché." But it was three or four, if she remembered. She smiled, determined to keep her tone light. If she irritated him, he might reject the plan solidifying in her mind.

"You were wasted," he continued, not letting go. "Still pulling college stuff?"

"Remember, I didn't graduate. And I didn't ask for you to get involved."
Mary bit her tongue, scolding herself. All he'd done was help, at considerable
trouble, she imagined. So why was she snapping at him?

Michael's eyes pierced into hers. "What's going on? Last night you poured
out some tale about cliffs and an auburn-haired woman."

Mary squirmed. She wasn't about to dump her whole dysfunctional history
on anyone, much less Michael. Of course, he'd probably heard rumors of why
she'd dropped out of school. She needed to explain that too, but now wasn't the
time to overwhelm him. She shrugged her shoulders. "Just some Irish folk tale."
Once again, she tried to keep her tone light. "Michael, I need to go back."

"To Marquette?"

"No. To Ireland. A long-lost relative type thing. Will you take me?" The
pretense disappeared; words gushed like a busted hydrant. "I know it might
seem ludicrous, but I was reading about it last night. And spring break's coming
up and then I saw you and . . ."

He looked her up and down, making a clucking noise with his tongue. "It
must be in the stars? Not the best way to make decisions."

Mary caught a glimpse of her reflection in the sliding glass door. Flushed
face. Bloodshot eyes. What she saw made her sick to her stomach. She had to
stop this. Soon.

Michael grabbed a notebook off the table and flipped it open. "Believe it
or not, I need to go home too. A business deal, both for me and the firm." He
described the tax advantages of buying a new car in Dublin, then shipping it
to the States.

Mary only half listened. What she wanted to do was jump up and down,
fling open the door, and shout from the balcony. This was God's answer. She'd
prayed for a way out of the revolving door. She wasn't walking out of it; she was
flying . . . to Ireland. And while she was there, she planned to find her mother.
Her family.

"I promised Ma I'd visit." With a misty look in his eyes, Michael stared
at the conglomeration of steel and brick and mortar. "I miss it. The land. The
people."

"It's time to go home," Mary blurted out.

"Where are your folk?" he asked, looking at her curiously.

"County Clare," Mary said without hesitation.

"'Tisn't far at all."

A bit more chat, mixed with laughter, and by the time Michael called her a
cab, it was settled with a handshake and a peck on the cheek.

Mary raced toward Lisle after one stop. When the taxi driver crunched into the driveway, she saw Mother peering out the window, and she braced for another argument.

"Where have you been, you little—" Mother didn't wait for Mary to unbundle before unleashing her wrath.

Mary chuckled to cover up the spasm that gripped her stomach. "My, my, aren't we extreme this morning?"

"Mary Elizabeth, your father and I waited up for you."

"I've told you not to do that."

"We were worried sick." Mother's eyes were puffy, her skin, chalky white.

Mary met Mother's gaze. "If he's so worried, where is he?"

"How dare you do this to us after all we've done for you?"

"Well, you won't have to worry about me much longer. I'm leaving."

"Where are you going?"

"Back to Ireland."

"We won't give you a dime for that."

"You don't have to," she said, a bit more smugly than she had planned. "I stopped at the bank. Emptied my savings."

"You did, did you?"

"It'll just cover the ticket and expenses."

Mother paled more than Mary thought possible. "Edmond? Edmond!"

Daddy came out of the back bedroom, his face sagging, a gray pallor to his skin. "What's this about Ireland?" His voice sounded defeated as he motioned for Mary to sit.

"I want to find Mam—Kathleen."

He glanced at Mother. "We don't think it's a good idea."

Mary jumped off her seat. "I don't care what you think." Memories of a thousand little indignities coursed through her mind. "After everything you've done." She stared at Mother. "And then, for you to hide her letter. It's—"

"It was me, Lizzie." Daddy's voice dropped to a whisper. "I hid it."

Mary grabbed her coat and flew toward the door.

Mother wrung her hands and stared first at Mary, then her father.

"Don't go."

His words made her take her hand off the cold brass knob. Even though she'd pretended not to care, the lines on her parents' faces cut into her. Only God knew what her latest shenanigans had cost them.

"What I did was wrong," Daddy mumbled. "I just wanted to protect you."

She could feel his presence, and a part of her longed to melt into his embrace. But she'd been hurt by his own set of shenanigans. She turned and looked him in the eye. It was time for a change.

It was as if Daddy knew her thoughts, the way he spread out his hands in a conciliatory gesture. "You have our blessing," he said, his lips pressed together.

Around midnight, Mary's thoughts turned to God as they often did on moonless, black nights. She tried to pray, remembering how a presence had shoved away that other voice on that awful night at Marquette. Was it God, or was it the karma some of her friends believed in, a jumble of Hinduism and Buddhism that sounded convincing after a couple of joints?

She tossed and turned and finally groped about in the dark until she found Mam's letter. Here was something in black and white. Mam was ready to let a grown daughter back in her life. And she would step right in and begin again. As if to confirm her decision, an old song echoed in her ears, as did the image of a woman. *Last night as I lay dreamin' of pleasant days gone by, my mind bein' bent on ramblin', to Ireland I did fly.* Mary smiled, comforted a bit by the old words. But when she tried to see the woman's face, everything went black.

✛ ✛ ✛

"Were you afraid?" Sally asked.

"No. I was so sure it was the answer. As far as I was concerned, it was all I had left to do." Mary took a deep breath before she continued her story.

CHAPTER 14

Erin, oh, Erin, thy winter is past.
And the hope in my heart shall blossom at last.

—Thomas Moore, "Erin, Oh, Erin"

For days, she barely slept, the book's images mingling with her first memories and stirring her soul. On a crisp spring day, she met Michael at the airport. Check-in went smoothly, as did boarding. Michael stowed their bags, then folded his lanky frame into the seat. "Pap's picking us up," he explained. "Then I'll take you to your folks."

Mary's smile was cautious. "Or I can get a cab."

He shook his head. "We Irish take care o' our own." Then he buried his nose in an economics treatise as thick as a dictionary.

Mary was thankful not to make small talk. The gentle surge of the plane, pulling her closer, closer to her homeland, made her eyes heavy, her breathing slow . . .

Someone shook her shoulder gently, then with more urgency.

Mary's eyes fluttered open, then got wide. A man was leaning close, a paper cup in one hand, a steaming towel in the other. She smiled. It was Michael.

"We're here," he said, then pointed to the window. Crinkly lines around his eyes once again drew her to how blue they were.

For just a moment, Michael's smile penetrated the barrier of ice Mary had erected around her heart, and she smiled back. But when he touched her hand, the coldness returned. Vowing to keep her sights off romance, she pulled back the ruffled curtain that covered the plane window and got her first glimpse of Ireland in fourteen years. White dots pranced in a field of grass so green it looked artificial. As they got closer, Mary could make out ewes and their lambs huddled in pairs in the lush valley. The pilot zeroed in on the slick runway.

Mary's heart flip-flopped, but it wasn't from a fear of flying. What if Mam didn't want her? What if this was all a mistake? By the end of a week, she'd know the answer.

✛ ✛ ✛

"Look a' this muck." Holding a dilapidated umbrella, Michael did his best to both shield them from the rain and carry his bag. Mary, her things crammed into a bag and a backpack, bobbed next to him and tried to stay dry.

A wino staggered past, then paused to vomit on pavement already slick with rain.

The familiar sound of retching made Mary shudder; she vowed, in the land of Guinness, to stay dry. When a raindrop plopped into her eye, she giggled nervously. Maybe not that kind of dry, but no booze. No drugs.

Michael slapped her on the back. "Where's a pub when you need one?"

Was he serious? Mary checked her watch, which she'd adjusted for the time change. "It's nine in the morning, for heaven's sake."

A few rogue raindrops splashed onto Michael's smiling face. "'Tis always time for a Guinness over here." He leaned his shoulder into Mary. "We wouldn't be Irish, would we, if we didn't make a welcoming toast?"

With each drip of rain, Mary's predicament became a bit more complicated. How could Michael ever understand what she was going through? After all, they'd reconnected in a bar, and now she was going to tell him that she couldn't drink?

A rattling Peugeot saved Mary from an answer; she wiped her brow, then jumped back, the driver apparently oblivious to the fact that he was spraying water all over them.

"Aye, Michael?" An arm appeared from the driver's window and waved wildly at them. The idling car set off a riot of honking horns, squealing brakes, and cursing, the airport boulevard a sudden quagmire of vehicles.

Michael shoved the umbrella at Mary, dropped his bags, vaulted off the curb, into the street, and flew toward the car, yelling, "Pap. Me pap."

A grizzled head popped out of the driver's window.

"Me pap," Michael kept saying. He cradled his father's head in his arms, kissing him over and over, apparently heedless of the drenching rain. Then he ran around the car and followed the same routine with a woman whom Mary assumed was his mother.

Doubt about her journey washed away. *This is how it'll be with her.*

138

Michael ran back to Mary, grabbed the suitcases, and motioned for her to jump in. Amid a cacophony of honks and curses, they sped away.

"This is Mary, Ma. Pap."

A woman, her smile rosy, threw her arms across the seat. "Aye, welcome."

"A red-haired Yank." Still driving, Pap blew a kiss. "'Tis a sight for sore eyes."

"Thanks." In spite of the time difference, Mary was wide awake. She was home.

When traffic piled up at a roundabout, Mary's enthusiasm dimmed. Her rain-streaked window didn't hide garbage piled along cobblestone streets. Sludge meandered like a poisonous stream between dingy tenements. Yet as pedestrians slumped along the alleys and byways, Mary searched for the auburn hair, brilliant smile, and dimpled cheeks she'd come to see. Now she was closer than ever.

A child, his face smudged with what looked like soot and ash, darted at their car. He cupped his hand, then pointed at them as if he were begging.

"Is it . . . always like this?" Mary asked, wondering where the green fields had gone.

"Aye." Michael somehow managed to be heard over Ma's and Pap's chatter. "Or worse. At least here in Dublin."

Then Pap told jokes, and Michael gave a discourse on how the boom after World War II had eluded the Irish. Although Mary nodded and asked the occasional question, she longed for Mam and the wild, open spaces she remembered from her childhood.

A woman swathed in wool hustled by. *She'll be about that age.*

"We've lost three million people to emigration since the mid-1800s."

"Really? I had no idea." *Will her hair be long or short, like that woman's?*

"The rural folks"—Michael pointed to Ma and Pap—"live hand to mouth, just like they did a hundred years ago."

Had the rugged farm life out there on the cliffs kept her young or aged her?

Michael lowered his voice, even though Pap was so engrossed in another tale, Ma was giggling so, it was unlikely they heard. "They still use a chamber pot too."

Mary sat up straight. "You're kidding."

"Two years ago, not a soul in their village had a phone. I bought them one for a sack full of shillings. Now it's the most prosperous business in the neighborhood."

Mary's brow furrowed. "What do you mean?"

"They charge five shillings a call, unless the folks talk a blue streak. Then Pap ups it to ten."

Even though Mary chuckled along with him, the differences in her and Mam's lifestyle began to seep in like the wind that whistled through the cracked car window. What would await her out there on the cliffs? And could she handle it?

✢ ✢ ✢

It took a good hour for Pap to maneuver them out of Dublin, headed to their village. Ma chattered like a magpie but trailed off when the green hills rose up to greet them, as if she understood the reason behind Mary's monosyllabic answers, her wide eyes. "You've fallen for us, have ye?" she asked, her voice full of pride.

All Mary could do was nod.

The countryside was just as she'd pictured it, both from her book and memory. Shades of green were everywhere: Kelly green on hills, sage green on buildings, yellow-green of new growth. Even the water and sky were green. She'd expected the greens, but what captivated her were the whites. White green legs of the sheep, like knees on a child's jeans. White gray stone walls crumbling from years of relentless exposure. White gold wisps of wool that clung tenaciously to barbed wire. White white of lambs' backs. White brown of rams' backs.

The scent of earth and salt and rain kept Mary speechless. Near Lisdoon-varna, fog surrounded the car and trapped them in a netherworld of rain and sky. She wanted to tug Michael's sleeve and shout: *I'm home!* Instead she listened to the mournful minor key of an Irish ballad, sung by birds Pap identified as dippers and dunnocks.

"Here we are. Welcome home." Pap pulled the car in front of a bungalow of stucco and wood, and they hurried out of the chill.

"You'll stay wi' us, ye will," Ma begged as she led Mary to a seat by the fire. "'Tis too late to head off. We'll just sit ye here, by a roarin' turf fire—"

"What kind of tree is that?"

"Ye split my side, lass," Pap said, when he came up for air. "It's peat, lass, cut from the very core of our earth. Burns day and night, summer and winter. 'Tis the worst of luck, lass, to let it die out. '*Oh, the rattlin' bog . . .*'" With a quickness that belied his age, he leapt to the hearth, clicking his heels and dancing what he called a turf jig.

Mary guffawed with them until she cried, letting tears cleanse years of feeling unloved. It was so tempting to take them up on their offer, to let this earthy yet sweet smell wash over her. She had made it. This was her country. These were her people.

"O-ro, the rattlin' bog, the bog down in the valley-o . . ."

Ma clicked her heels and joined Pap, then grabbed Mary's hand and drew her into the cramped space by the fire. The jig led to talk, which led to tea and biscuits, then more talk, which Mary would've treasured in other circumstances. But when the fire sputtered, Mary shifted in her seat, thinking of another fire, another mother, another home.

After Mary poked Michael, then eyed the door, he got the not-so-subtle hint. Yawning, he rose to his feet. "I've got to run Mary to her Mam's."

Ma O'Looney grabbed Mary's hands. "Aye, ye miss her, do ye?"

Tears she hadn't expected filled her eyes, and her heart leapt to her throat so that she struggled to speak. "Aye. It's been a while." *Fourteen-and-a-half years.*

Thankfully, Michael cut off further questions, leading Mary to the car. As they pulled away, Ma and Pap waved and blew kisses as if they were launching to the moon.

✢ ✢ ✢

"It's better off this way. Trust me." While the car idled in a gravelly place in front of a dingy-looking store, Mary mustered every bit of resolve she possessed. "We need . . . some time to catch up." She tried but failed to smile at Michael.

Through the rolling greens of rural Ireland, Michael had sung and laughed and done his best to ease the tightness on her face. He'd talked of a stop at the Cliffs of Moher, a stop at a pub or two. If he'd had his way, they'd be listening to some fiddler in a cozy spot. But as the chalky limestone of the rugged coast began to dominate the scenery and rocky patches yawned out the lush valleys, fear gripped Mary—fear of what Killian might say; fear of what Gerard and Kelly might do; most of all, fear of how Mam might feel. As they'd gotten closer to the Glascloune store, the agreed-upon drop-off point, Mary had bitten her tongue more than once, knowing it was irrational that Michael's carefree mood should irritate her. And no matter how long Michael argued in favor of taking her to the cliffs, Mary knew that this was something she had to do by herself.

The passive side of Michael's personality made a rare appearance. He cocked his head, continued to study her, jumped out, came around, and opened the door for her.

Mary grabbed her things, then shut the door and turned to face him. "Thanks so much. I . . ." Her voice broke, and she couldn't continue.

Michael pulled her close, the world reduced to the blue of his eyes. She tried to move back, but he stepped closer, the scent of turf and musk clouding her determination to keep him at a distance. She stood on her tiptoes and stretched to kiss him on the cheek.

In an instant, she was pulled into an embrace so tight the air whooshed out of her.

"Michael, I've got to go," she managed, while struggling to pull away. She could feel his gaze seeking to understand her, to know her, and she winced under the scrutiny.

"Okay." The hand he rested on her collarbone burned through her blouse. With his other hand, he cupped her face toward his. "But promise you'll call if you need anything." He pointed to the store. "They'll have a phone, even if your mother doesn't."

More questions were in his face, in his words, but Mary turned away, not allowing herself to meet the gaze she was sure was still on her. She stepped toward the store. Her shoulders and neck tensed. Her resistance waning, a nagging thought found a foothold: had this all been a mistake? Not until she heard Michael's car putter away did she set down her bags, retie a hair ribbon, pick up her bags, hurdle a shaggy dog that blocked the store entrance, and clatter inside.

Three women sat around a blazing fire. A man stood behind a counter. As the women cackled, Mary wished she could decipher the brogue and get in on the joke.

When she approached, they fell silent. One woman, who had pink foam curlers arranged across her head, eyed her with suspicion. At last, the man stepped from behind the counter, wiping his hands on a bloody apron. "Can I help ye, miss?"

"I'm . . . I'm looking for the McNamaras," Mary stammered.

The Glasclouners froze in place.

"Aren't they . . . don't they live around here? I came from America to—"

The one with the curlers finally spoke. "They do and they don't."

"If you can call it living," one of them muttered.

"Shush!" yelled the one with curlers. "That tongue o' yours will clip a hedge."

Mary held her breath. What did that mean?

"They're two miles down the coast, on a rocky spit that's a Dubliner's dream."

The air whooshed out. A beautiful place. Those first memories were just Killian's hotheadedness, his eagerness to have his new bride all to himself. Now that he'd had his own family, things had changed for the better. "Oh? And why's that?" Mary asked.

"Miss, it's a rare thing indeed to have one glorious body of water as yer footstool. The McNamara land's the crown o' the west, overlooking both the mouth o' the mighty Shannon and the Great Ocean. But ye better—"

"Ask me arse!" bellowed the man. "The priest'll have yer tongue. 'Tis half a county to the Shannon. And it would take a man standin' on the Tower o' London to spot it."

A black-haired woman spoke for the first time. "Forgive her, dear. The spinnin' and weavin's got the best o' her." They all cackled like crows.

Mary's skin crawled. "Yes. I best be getting on." Something was not right about either these folks or the McNamaras, and she was certain it was the former. Her hand on the door frame, she turned and, in a small voice, double-checked the directions she'd coaxed from Mother before leaving Chicago.

The black-haired woman spoke up. "Just a stone's throw on. Gee right at the next building. 'Tis about three kilo, past two white barns. The next house ye see, o'er the crest o' the hill, t'will be the McNamaras'."

Ignoring the gaping mouths and bulbous eyes, Mary swung open the screen door and, in her haste to leave, popped the dog right in his chest with her suitcase. He didn't move, a symbol of this somnolent town on the edge of civilization.

☦ ☦ ☦

"Hey, I gotta go." Mary knocked over her bag as she jumped off the couch.

"Not now," Sally protested. "You can't leave in the middle of it." When she stood, her legs wobbled, as if she'd been on a very long car trip with no bathroom breaks.

Mary shook her head. She got her keys, hung her purse on her shoulder. "I've got to. It's been eons since I've left Mother like this."

"Which mother?"

When Mary didn't answer, Sally wished she hadn't tried to make light of Mary's story. For four hours, it had gripped her and shaken her, and she couldn't wait to let it pull her in again. "Let's get together. Tomorrow."

Mary paused, then nodded. "All right," she said. "Ten o'clock."

CHAPTER 15

Take a view o'er the mountains, fine sights you'll see there.
You'll see the high rocky mountains o'er the west coast of Clare.

—"The Cliffs of Doneen," traditional Irish folk song

Another shout. Another curse. Another morning with Mother.

Chloe set down her fork. "I wish she'd shut up."

It was hard for Mary not to cry, looking at the stony face of her daughter, seeing the same resentment she'd displayed toward Mother for years. Had those feelings been transferred to Chloe as some kind of penance which must be repaid to God? She hoped, she prayed, not. "Just go on and eat, Dear, before it gets cold." Darting glances at her daughter, she hummed an old folk tune, hoping to change Chloe's mood. Chloe's mind. Chloe's heart.

"How can I eat, with all that racket?" Her bottom lip puffing up, Chloe made a face at a plate full of perfectly fluffy eggs. Perfectly buttered toast. Food which Mary feared would go uneaten.

"She's not feeling so well these days." Mary worked to keep the edge out of her voice as she set some perishables back in the refrigerator. The last thing she wanted, or needed, was another tangle with Chloe. "In fact, I'd better check on her now."

Keeping her step as light as her tone, she made her way down the hall. By the time she entered Mother's room, the shouts had become horrid whistling moans.

A sound eerily like Mother's moan escaped Mary's lips. She hurried to the bed, fell on her knees, and clasped a hand reduced to nothing but bones and a stretch of skin. "Now, now," she cooed.

The horrid sound continued, and seemed to rattle the very rafters of the room.

"I wish she'd just die." The voice came from behind her.

How could Chloe, her baby sister, say that? Think that? Without meaning to, Mary squeezed her mother's hand, a defensive counter to the hate in Chloe's voice. Still holding tight, she straightened, then pivoted, very slowly, away from the sunken eyes, the stiffened limbs which were getting harder and harder to rouse from the bed, the face hued now with green and yellow and—*dear God, no*—perhaps a touch of black.

"It looks like you'll be getting your wish." Mary's jaw locked, her eyes burned, until even a sassy, nasty eighth grader had to blink.

✝ ✝ ✝

"It's about time." Sally took Mary's coat and ushered her into the den.

"Where's my grits? My glass of sweet tea? And how's Sam? The kids?" Mary called on humor to mask her emotions still frayed from this morning's incident. This story seemed to mean so much to Sally; she had to get through it.

A hand flew to Sally's mouth. "Oh, gosh! I didn't even think to offer you anything."

"It's okay. I ate with Chloe," Mary lied, her voice breaking just a smidgeon. "And you know how I feel about tea." She laughed, hoping it would cover up any evidence that Sally could pounce onto and drudge up.

A quizzical look came over Sally's face, but she didn't say anything. Taking Mary's arm, she pulled her to the couch, curled next to her as if she planned to stay a while, and looked at her expectantly.

✝ ✝ ✝

Walking north on this odyssey that incorporated travel by plane, car, and now foot, Mary locked her eyes on the next rise in the road, then the next, intent on reaching the house that held her real mother. It seemed like an eternity since their plane had touched down. Yet a glance at her watch told her it had only been seven hours. Seven hours she'd spent in the land where she belonged.

Tucked into her backpack were Mam's letter and Daddy's old cigar box, full of keepsakes to share. It lightened Mary's step to envision fireside chats like at the O'Looneys', spontaneous but simple. Then she'd call Michael, tell him she was staying. The length of her stride increased as she raced ahead with plans for next month, next year, perhaps even a lifetime. She'd be safe here on these cliffs, safe from the demons that dogged her.

Mary conquered landmark after landmark—the postmaster's, the barns, the hill—just as the woman had described them. The winds whipped up her skirt, and she kept setting down her bag and smoothing it out. She wanted to look her best in—a thrill ran along her spine—a few minutes.

A strong gust knocked her off the path; when she righted herself, she spotted fuchsia-colored flowers and wild thyme growing like weeds. Pulling the ribbon from her hair, she fashioned a bouquet, determined to present it to her mother.

All landmarks had been found except for that last one. Mary stepped toward the house, smoothing down her skirt for a thousandth time. There was no sign of life—no sheep dogs or barn cats running up to greet her. She listened more intently, worried that she'd trudged out here for nothing. She walked slowly, as if giving her mother time to arrive—inane thoughts, nervous thoughts. Halfway between the barn and the door of the cottage, her breath caught in her throat, and she stood still as stone.

An aproned figure peered at her from the side yard. She was bathed in a beam of light that had just broken through a mass of clouds. Mary couldn't see her features, just the triangles formed by the one hand on her hip and the other on her brow. She stepped toward Mary, her bare feet trampling what little grass remained about the front porch.

A transfixed Mary watched her step closer. She was a hefty woman, kind of a female Paul Bunyan, and the hand that shielded her eyes held a still-lit cigarette. Mary tried to move but found that she couldn't. Her heart beat the question, but she couldn't get the words out. *Are you Kathleen O'Brien McNamara? Are you my mam?*

She bore no resemblance to the auburn-haired Kathleen with the dimpled cheeks and dancing eyes with whom Mary remembered playing dolls. Of course, she would have added a few wrinkles, and maybe her hair would no longer be the color of roan horses' flanks. But this woman didn't look anything like the picture Mary's mind had saved all those years. Except for the eyes.

Something about the eyes gave it away—a slant, a certain shade of hazel. But their dancing days were long past; dullness had set in deep, which spread to Mary and blanketed her earlier excitement.

"Who ye be?" her mother rasped. That voice—years of chain-smoking? The roughness of her skin—harsh winds? Swollen hands and feet—grueling labor?

"Mary Elizabeth," was all Mary could manage. She willed her body to remain motionless, like a car stuck in neutral, fearful of the knowledge that her future hung on the next few moments.

"How did ye get here?"

"I walked."

When Kathleen looked her up and down, years rolled away. Mary once again became the girl in the dirty shift, the little eejit they'd sent away.

"Mother, I've so missed you. I wonder, could we—"

Kathleen's stony expression froze Mary's desperate plea. "Ye be coming in for a cup of tea," she said, her voice so harsh Mary winced. "But then ye be leaving, and we won't tell Gerard and Kelly who ye be."

The wind grabbed her mother's words, then slammed them into Mary's face.

Her mother slumped toward the door. Step by step, Mary played follow the leader with her mother across the threshold of the house where she'd been slapped and beaten and cursed, all the while processing what had been said. About the time she spied the scarred old table, the cruelty of it all hit her full force: she'd traveled five thousand miles for tea in a cup that was probably cracked.

Each frame of action knifed deeper into Mary. The rigidity of her mother's turned back. The screaming silence.

From her vantage point in the middle of the room, Mary memorized every detail. Sofa. Upholstered chair. Four wooden chairs. Table. Fireplace. Basket of turf. A raggedy girl and boy, whom she assumed to be Kelly and Gerard, sprawled around a table covered with greasy newspapers. Gerard looked to be a teenager; Kelly, several years younger. They wore filthy clothes and had stained teeth.

"Kelly?" Her back still to Mary, Kathleen motioned to the girl. "Set the water to boil."

When Kelly ignored her, Kathleen shuffled to the fire.

With growing bewilderment, Mary studied her. Bruised arms and legs. Torn hem. Her hands shook, her chest heaved as she removed the pot that was roasting what smelled like potatoes and replaced it with a teakettle.

She pointed a thick finger at Mary. "'Tis a Yank friend o' Anne. Pap's sister."

Their mother's explanation of a dinner guest who'd traveled from the other side of the world didn't even evoke a raised eyebrow from Gerard or Kelly. Her stepbrother. Stepsister. It did, however, seem to set off some old rivalry as a scuffle began.

Gerard kicked at Kelly. "Ye cheeky git."

"Hump off."

The jostling, the kicking caused Mary to shudder, not just at their nasty sibling struggles, but at Kathleen's indifference. What had happened to reduce the dancing eyes, the smiling mouth, to the defeated woman in front of her?

With a ponderous sigh, Kathleen lumbered to the table, a cup in one hand, a teapot in the other.

Uninvited, Mary slid into a chair.

When Kathleen tried to pour the tea, it slopped all over the table. "Fetch a cloth," she muttered, her tone conveying little hope that anyone would comply.

Kelly responded by kicking Gerard.

Mary tried but failed to keep her lips from curling at the wretched shabbiness around her. Last year's calendar of the flora and fauna of Ireland. Rips and stains on the chair. Yellowing paper shades shielding what was supposed to be a magnificent coastline. The human beings sitting before her—any civility they'd had, dried up and gone.

Kathleen slid into the last chair, a surprising fluidity in a body long on muscle and bone. When she leaned over her tea, her dress slipped off her shoulder, revealing dingy brassiere straps.

Something about that simple exposure made Mary reach toward her, yearning to transform the dullness in her eyes. This was her mam, after all. She studied the contours of her cheeks. There was a slight resemblance, wasn't there? "Mam . . . Kathleen . . ."

Kathleen looked her over like she was a cheap cut of meat, every second of silence suffocating the spark of affection, yet igniting a fire of another kind.

Isn't she going to say anything? Ask about college? What's wrong with her? With me? Mary felt the same adrenaline rush she'd felt when she hit Rick, and she made an effort to breathe in a measured way. She'd stripped naked her feelings just by coming across the ocean, and with one look, Kathleen had slain her with the grimy truth.

"It's a lovely spot." Somehow Mary found her voice, sitting there at the same table where she'd heard her fate nearly a decade and a half ago. Now Mary also drank tea, or pretended to, with a different cast of characters, but she shuddered from the same revulsion as before. "And brilliant tea." Her words seemed to come out of someone else's mouth, and their inanity astonished her.

Kelly's and Gerard's sniveling continued until Mary longed to slap them. *Why doesn't she do something, anything, to shut them up?* Neither Anne nor Edmond would have stood for it, and Mary thanked God for one good thing about being raised a Harris.

Mary couldn't reconcile this woman with the one she'd imagined for so long, the one for whom she'd lugged the box of memories across the Atlantic. One special item, worse for wear after a decade, was a Valentine, foil hearts pasted onto a picture cut out of one of Anne's old *Good Housekeepings*. Mary had labeled the creation My Real Mom. One look at the bleary eyes across the table told Mary that the picture had been a lie.

The smell of tea brought back conflicting memories, as well. Of course, the worst memory was around this very table. But had she imagined the tea parties, the songs by the fire, the caresses through the coldest of nights? Had they been lies too?

Sudden scraping noises made Mary jump.

The sniveling continued as Gerard chased Kelly out the door.

With shaking hands, Mary pulled out that last letter, seizing what might be the only chance for them to be alone. "In your letter—" The words froze in her throat as she set it near those thick, stained fingers.

For a moment, the eyes softened to the color Mary remembered, years of hard living perhaps sweetened by some brief memory. Then, her chair scraping, she rose heavily to her feet. "'Tis late," she said, her eyes darting toward the door.

Matching her mother's motion, Mary jumped to her feet, then shoved the already wilting flowers across the table and snatched the letter from under her nose. "Yes, it is. And thanks for the tea. I've got to go."

"Wait." When Kathleen flung out her arm, it brushed against Mary. As if it pained her, her mother limped to the part of the house that Mary remembered, where it was warm and safe, with the night music pouring in . . .

"Here." Startling Mary, Kathleen rumbled in from the back room, waving a paper, which she thrust into Mary's face. "Now, off with ye," she rasped, her eyes on the door.

Mary wadded the note into a ball, stuffed it in her pocket, staggered outside, and sliced through stony fields to the cliffs' edge. She stared at the churning sea, her heart ripped open by her mother's words; her stares; most of all, her indifference. A cry slipped from her lips, and the sea hurled it back at her. She thought of all the lies, mainly her own. *Killian forced her to do it. Or maybe his sisters. The lure in the last letter, a lie, too, and you grabbed it like a starving trout and pulled it all the way across the Atlantic.*

Mary fell on her knees. "How dare you?" Tears mingled with foamy spray as she reached into her backpack and pulled out the memory box. Hanging over the jagged rock, she slung it as far as she could, then watched the worthless memories scatter into roiling white water. Her movement scared a lone puffin from its perch on a nearby rock, and it wailed an eerie cry that chilled her soul. Mary answered with wails she'd suppressed since Kathleen had refused to acknowledge her in front of her half-blooded brethren.

She clawed at the rocks; they clawed back, tearing the skin of her hands. She screamed again. A gust of wind pushed back her voice, and the madding sea had its own response. "You are nothing," it seemed to say with each crashing wave. "Nothing."

When Mary lost her footing and fell, something snapped. A decision made. The button pushed. Just like at Marquette. To let go, to follow her memories over the edge of the slippery cliff. To stop the pain, once and for all. To never be shut out again. The slippery shale urged her to become one with it. The salty spray begged to purify her for a final time. On her hands and knees, she moved, closer, closer . . .

Get up. Jump. It is finished. A nasty cackle, a fiend's voice. She crawled to the edge, the raging cauldron beckoning her to lose herself in its furious energy. *Closer, closer*, the voice coaxed, until her head hung over the chasm.

White lased through the clouds, so dazzling, so blinding, Mary blinked. *You are mine. I am with you always.* The clouds shifted so rapidly the sky seemed to spin. Mary once again clawed at the rock, this time with the intent to hang on.

For what seemed an eternity, Mary lay there, her eyes closed, until every trace of the beckoning blackness had passed. When she lifted her head, she was aware of a not unpleasant emptiness, as if a battle had been waged and won, but at high cost.

She lay numb with cold, until she quit trembling. Then she stumbled and staggered, getting as far away from the white green foam as she could.

A figure stood by the front door, almost obscured by the shadow of the eaves, but Mary turned away from it, too. When she reached the path, she brushed off, then heaved the backpack onto her shoulder. Lugging her suitcase, she trudged south.

It was still light enough so she could see the narrow lane. She plodded on, numb and empty. "Have mercy on me. God, have mercy on my soul," she prayed, in cadence with every step. She shivered, water dripping from drenched clothes, but she kept going, trancelike in her determination.

She couldn't think beyond what had happened on the cliffs and played it over and over in her head. She'd come a few inches from ending her life, had faced evil, she was sure of it. Without God's help, she would have died. Sweat dripped into her eyes. She wiped it away. It had been Him, hadn't it?

Then there was the other voice, the voice that still made her shiver, the voice full of hate and despair. Black and evil, just like at Marquette, daring her to end it all.

"God, save me." A shiver. A stab. "Save me. Help me." The jagged rocks along the cliff had cut Mary's hands and legs, and she wiped blood onto her sleeve. She limped from blisters on both feet. The miles she'd walked earlier with such anticipation now seemed an impossible distance. She noticed every shabby farmhouse, felt every stone that pocked the dusty path.

When Mary saw the post office, she broke into a run, slow at first, then faster, faster, until everything blurred. Her arms ached from carrying the bags, and every step knifed pain into her feet. Finally the faded sign came into view: Glascloune, 250 Strong.

She slowed as she approached the lit store, the ladies cackling even louder than before. Mary limped past the still-sleeping dog.

"Lass, what happened?" The women gaped and gasped. "Ye cut yer face."

"Ye look a sight."

"Have a seat." The black-haired woman walked behind the counter and returned with a steaming cup of tea and a cold rag. "Here."

A tear rolled down Mary's face in response to this small kindness.

"I didn't introduce myself properly, Lass. My dead mother'll speak ill o' me to Saint Peter. I'm Martha McCullough. 'Tis my husband, Frank."

Mary could only nod at the woman with pink curlers.

"My sisters, Kaitlin and Katherine."

The women craned their necks to have a closer look.

"Do you ... have ... a hotel?" Between gasps, Mary dabbed at her face with the rag.

"Nary a one."

"Or a room to let?"

Martha shook her head. "T'would be in Kilkee, about seven kilos west."

She couldn't walk another step. She didn't bother to control the tears but wiped them off with her sleeve, with the rag, with anything she could find.

"Ye best be stayin' put."

The words served to calm Mary's sobs. She lifted her head and tried to smile. "Oh, no, ma'am, I couldn't do that, but could I use your phone?"

They nodded toward Frank, who still whacked, whacked, whacked at the meat. He pointed behind the cash register. Mary found Michael's number. After the third time, her trembling fingers managed to find the right holes in the dial of the phone.

"It's Mary."

"Where are you?"

"In Glascloune. The store. Can you come get me? She didn't ... it didn't work out." She glanced at the sisters and lowered her voice. "And there's nothing here."

"I'll leave right now."

Mary hung up, a prayer on her lips.

Martha beckoned her close with the crook of her finger. "What happened, miss?"

Mary staggered back to the table and sat down, shaking hands barely able to hold the cup. The rejection hurt so, she longed to unload her story. "I came from Illinois—"

"'Tis a long way."

"To see them," she sniffed, "and they didn't even ask me to stay."

"Ye don't say." The sisters leaned forward to catch every snippet.

"Terrible."

"All they gave me was a cold cup of tea."

"They're not worth a lump o' coal, those McNamaras."

"What do ye expect from pigs but grunts?"

"And how would a Yank know them?"

Four sets of goggling eyes bored into Mary's face.

The room spun for a moment, and then everything became clear, very clear. Her back straight, Mary rose from the table. "Thanks for your hospitality," she managed. Despite what Kathleen had done, despite the pain of being abandoned a second time, she wasn't going to throw her mother to these gossips.

That plan got Mary out the door; she collapsed on the stoop and buried her face in her hands. She wanted a drink to fill up the void, then bubble over the ugly truth that she hadn't asked the right questions: *Why did you do it? Can I come back? Who is my father?* Her head slumped almost to her lap. Why couldn't she get it right?

The dog came alive and nosed her in the side. Mary couldn't help but stroke his mangy fur and scratch behind his ears. Should I force the issue? Push into her life and not move until she deals with me? What would she have done if I had insisted on staying? Mary thought of the strong arms, the solid bone. Would she have bodily thrown me out?

When the dog nosed Mary again, this time rustling the paper in her pocket, she remembered the note and smoothed it out.

Ellen O'Brien. Your grandmother. Cree.

No explanation. No sentiment. Tears stung like thistles. *Why did You do this? Give me another golden thread to follow, another one that will surely unravel?* Blackness closed in, its old familiar pressure forcing Mary into action. She dug in her backpack and yanked out her travel guide, desperate to occupy her mind. Something, anything . . . A picture, a paragraph caught her attention.

Every year in April, the puffins arrive on the western cliffs of County Clare to perform their mating rites. Their eerie, grating cry attracts the curious spectator. However, they find warmer waters of the South Atlantic and are gone by summer.

Mary slammed the book shut. Why did she come to a place so foreboding even puffins wouldn't stay? Should she try to meet her grandmother and risk being tossed out again? Her mind whirling, she put the book up.

The Peugeot's rattles set off a fresh round of sobs as she sprinted to the car.

Michael jumped out, ran toward her, and took her into his arms. "Mary . . . What happened?" He dabbed her eyes with a handkerchief.

The words, the emotions practically strangled her, but how could she begin to explain the ugly truth: that she'd been given away by her birth mother, not once, but twice? "I . . . Michael, thank you so, so much." She handed back the handkerchief. "But I . . . can't talk about it right now." When she opened the car door, the wind whooshed, whipping her skirt above her waist, but she didn't bother to smooth it down.

Michael tossed her bags into the wagon and started the engine.

As they pulled onto the highway, Mary looked back at the store. The four old settlers stood under the sign, craning their necks to get a good view of the knight who rescued the distressed lady. Very bored, very nosy old settlers.

After negotiating a curve, which made Mary slide into Michael, he downshifted, then hummed a folk song as he stroked her hair. She felt her eyes get heavy and let her head fall against his shoulder.

"How could she do that?"

Mary shrugged. "I don't know, but I do know this. It still cuts like a knife."

Sally looked at Mary for a long time before she spoke. "It's not about you. It wasn't your fault that she rejected you."

Mary shook her head, careful not to snap at Sally. How can she understand? *She moves to town and has more friends in six months than I've amassed in decades.* And with her oodles and oodles of kin . . . Mary looked away, but when she looked back, Sally's eyes were wet with tears. Her own eyes misty, Mary grabbed Sally and hugged her. "You precious dear. Not everyone did."

Sally breathed a sigh of relief. "Your grandmother took you in?"

"Yes. No. Oh, you'll just have to hear about it."

CHAPTER 16

And now that I'm going back again to dear old Erin's isle,
My friends will meet me on the pier and greet me with a smile.
—Steve Graham, "Dear Old Donegal"

Mary awoke. She was in a car whose windshield wipers were fighting a losing battle.

The door opened. "Mary. We're here." The voice came from far away.

"What? Where?" Her eyes seemed to have weights on them, yet she stirred enough to recognize Michael's house through sheets of rain. Then she remembered where she had been and what had happened.

"You're at my place." Michael bustled bags out of the car. "And I've checked with Ma. You're stayin'. She insists."

Moving as if drugged, Mary made her way to the fire. Her legs buckled; if Ma hadn't guided her down the hall and into a bedroom, she might have collapsed.

"Don't say a word. Ye need rest. The pot's under the bed, and may Saint Patrick himself watch over ye." Ma made the sign of the cross, then turned for the door.

"But—"

"Shush, shush, now. You'll stay as long as ye want. Goodnight, lass."

After changing, Mary cocooned under cotton and wool and slept.

When she awoke the next day, the sun beamed warmth, and hope, through the window. Even though the memory of Mam's rejection stung, the hospitality of Michael's family lessened Mary's pain. That, and the rolling green hills, the blue sky, which she could see from her perch on the bed.

Delicious baking aromas lured Mary into the kitchen. Ma, off to the market according to her note, had left homemade bread, fruit, and a still-warm pot of tea. An additional note was propped up on the counter. *Off to Dublin. Ma says help yourself. Michael.*

Nibbling on soda bread, Mary padded to the fire, attempting to warm goose-pimpled arms and legs. The mantle was crowded with framed pictures of laughing eyes and dimpled faces. Family. A chill ran through Mary. There might be another welcoming hearth like this at her grandmother's, but dared she risk another rejection? She pictured the note she'd stuck in her bag. *Ellen O'Brien. Your grandmother. Cree.* She'd memorized the words; now she tried to decode them. Was her mother passing her around like an Irish hot potato? Or was she orchestrating a meeting away from the scrutiny of her family? Hope surged through Mary as she slipped on her shoes. If Michael would take her, she determined to visit Cree.

✟ ✟ ✟

It had been a good idea to get out of the house, to collect her thoughts, her dreams. Mary walked faster, breaking into a skip as the day came alive before her. Now that she was out here in the open spaces of her land, things were definitely brighter. A postman clanked by on a rusty bicycle, the only sign of life besides birds, cows, and sheep. "Top o' the mornin'." He waved madly, then pedaled on, his voice booming over chirps and moos. *"Down by the Sally gardens, my love and I did meet . . ."*

Mary waved to his retreating figure. *The whole country sings, they do.*

Today the sun had declared victory over yesterday's dark sky by transforming the palette of greens to shimmering blues. The new canvas displayed a periwinkle horizon dotted with cottony cumulus clouds. Mary pulled off a sweater and tied it around her waist. She was safe here, far away from the unpredictable west coast.

A crumbling stone wall failed to prevent Mary's or nature's wild ramblings. She leapt into a blanket of green and pinks and golds and gathered flowers. *It's all right,* wild roses whispered. *Yes,* rustled the daisies and orchids and red clover. *She wasn't the one, but your grandmother is,* the bees buzzed.

Mary whirled around and around, the sky and grass and flowers and stone becoming a kaleidoscope of patterns that changed with every revolution of her body. Dizzy, she collapsed into the field's cushioning embrace, intoxicated by the flowery and grassy fragrances. *There's still a chance for me here. I just know it.*

✦ ✦ ✦

Smoke curled from the O'Looneys' chimney as Mary, brushing off curlicues of wool and cockleburs, skipped up the drive. A crowd of neighbors clustered about a screaming red Jaguar parked in the driveway. Remembering the goggling eyes at Glascloune, Mary bustled past them and into the house.

On three-legged stools, Michael and his parents clustered about the fire. They rested bowls of what looked like soup on their laps and somehow managed to talk and laugh and eat, all at the same time.

"Aye, Mary. There ye are. Ready for a bit o' stew?"

"Yes, ma'am." Mary tried not to grimace. This wasn't the time to launch into her vegetarian bent; Mother had taught her better. For the second time in as many days, she silently thanked her parents.

Ma hurried into the kitchen, chattering all the while. "Had a fine walk, now, did ye?" She handed Mary a steaming bowl of stew, then motioned for her to sit down.

Mary nodded. "Climbed right over that stone wall. I hope it was okay."

Laughter bubbled from Ma. "It's crumblin' like old bread. Been there a thousand years if I'm a day. It's just a testimony now. Of those who were here before."

The room got quiet except for the clanking of spoons. The fire and the legacy of her ancestors warmed Mary. Those very stones represented her people, who had made homes in this wild land.

They ate right there around the hearth, interspersing folk tales with bites of stew and thick black bread. Mary nodded and smiled, but her mind raced ahead. The O'Looneys had treated her like family; perhaps she was a surrogate for the three daughters who had grown up, married, and moved away. But to have a chance for a life here, Mary needed to find her own family, which had been reduced to a slip of paper: *Ellen O'Brien. Your grand-mother. Cree.*

✦ ✦ ✦

The room was empty except for Michael and Mary. Yet Mary struggled to breathe. And it wasn't just because of the smoke coming from the fireplace. Michael had pulled his stool so close to hers, she could smell his aftershave.

"Great car," she told him, as heat rose to her face.

"Thanks."

"Great family."

"Thanks again." He leaned closer, as if planning a kiss.

Mary tried to scoot the stool back. She needed all her faculties right now. "I need to go to Cree." She tried to keep her voice steady. "If you'll take me."

An eyebrow arched; blue eyes widened. "Cree? What's Cree? Not Paris or London?"

It was hard not to blink, but she managed, all the while scooting her stool farther from the fire—and from Michael. "No. Just Cree. Or I could catch a cab."

Guffaws from the back room told Mary that big ears had tuned in.

"Maybe we could draft Cousin Seamus, but there's no Yellow Cabs out here." Again Michael leaned close, cupping his hand to his mouth. "Anyway, what's in Cree?"

"My grandmother."

Michael tiptoed toward the door. "There ye be!" he bellowed, then dragged Pap into the room.

"Aye, just comin' to get the mail." His face flushed, Pap banged out of the house and came back seconds later, holding a stack of letters.

"Where the blue blazes is Cree?" Michael asked Pap.

With a plop, Pap sat down again. "'Tis a wee spit between Kilkee and Ennis." His eyes burned questions into Mary. "But why are ye goin' there?"

Why indeed? Mary shifted about her seat. How could she tell Pap something she didn't know the answer to herself?

Michael set his hand on Mary's shoulder. "She has someone she needs to see."

Pap opened his mouth, then shut it. He flipped through his mail as if suddenly absorbed with his affairs, then tossed several letters into the flames.

Michael blanched. "What are you doing? Yer not even opening them."

"Just bills, they are. We'll be hearin' from 'em again." When Pap stoked the fire, the unpaid bills, now ashes, flew up the chimney. He set down the poker and turned his attention to Mary. "Why don't you stay, lass? We'd love to have ye."

"Another time, Pap." Michael's smile was gentle; for the first time Mary saw a resemblance between the two, even though their fiscal approaches seemed vastly different. She wanted to hug and kiss them—Ma too—and let the sweet smell of turf and smoke wash over her. This was the Irish connection she'd prayed for, and if God was on her side, as He surely must be by now, it was only the start.

Before they were out of the village, Michael put his arm around her. "Are you sure about this?" he asked, all the while massaging her shoulders.

Warmth flowed over her, yet she pulled away. "Yes. Well, I . . . I think so."

Narrowed eyes darted a glance at Mary. "I don't know what's going on." The car jerked, then smoothed as Michael accelerated out of a curve.

"I don't, either."

Once again, Michael took his eyes off the road and studied her. "But I don't want to see you hurt."

Her hands became a knot in her lap. "Thanks," she mumbled. "But this is something I have to do."

Once again, Michael used the car to express his emotions, taking a curve at a speed that made Mary gasp. "Whatever it is, something tells me it's not good," he said, throttling the steering wheel. "I'm just trying to save you from making a big mistake."

"It's not your job to save me," Mary said, then wished she hadn't. For two days now, the light in his eyes, the warm touches had set off warning gongs in her heart. It was only yesterday when that same heart had been torn out, and if she wasn't careful, it might happen again. She cast a sidelong glance at Michael, taking in the strong arms, the glint of red in his hair. Particularly a man like Michael.

Michael threw on his brakes, veered into a bald spot in the field, roared backward, then turned at the crossroads he'd overshot. "Here 'tis." He flung his arms around her, momentarily letting the car steer itself.

Mary gripped the armrest, Michael's impetuous nature overwhelming her—and not just his driving. She wasn't ready for this, yet she'd set herself up for it by coming over here with him. She did care for him, but caring and loving had tangled up in Mary's mind like an old ball of yarn. It was going to take a long time to untangle if she wanted to make something out of it.

While Michael drove in cold silence, Mary took in the telltale signs of an Irish village, which unfolded like a well-planned tapestry. Quaint cottages. A market. A graveyard. A cathedral whitewashed and adorned with spring blooms.

"There." Mary pointed to a priest who was bending over a flower garden, pulling weeds. "Let's ask him where my grandmother lives."

Michael seemed to bite back a retort, then pulled over and parked.

Mary felt her face flush. This whole quest must seem irrational to him. Right now, it seemed irrational to her. "I'm sorry I snapped at you," she said. "You and your family, you've . . . you've been a godsend."

Michael reached out slowly and traced the line where her jaw and cheek met until it became a caress.

Mary pushed his hand away. "Michael . . ."

Tapping at the window made them both jump. A man with white hair and deep-set eyes peered down at them. A black robe belted with a cord accentuated a portly frame. "Top o' the morning," he boomed through the rolled-up windows. "And who may I be greeting?"

Mary tumbled out of the car. "Do . . . do you know where I can find Ellen O'Brien?" she asked.

Snowy eyebrows met on a lined forehead. "And who'd be wanting to know?"

"I'm her granddaughter from America."

"She's expecting ye, is she?"

"I don't know." Mary's eyes filled with tears, the garden now a blur of pinks, purples, and yellows. Had her mother somehow warned her grandmother? Would she be sent away again? With effort, Mary focused on the steepled cross, forcing herself to stand tall, as if the slightest slump would allow the memories of yesterday and the fear of today to reduce her to sobs and sniffles. *Please, God,* she prayed, *help me.*

"Sorry, miss. Surprised me, ye did." The priest knelt by a cluster of bearded irises, caressing them as if they were his pets. "I'm Father O'Malley. Welcome to Cree. And if yer looking for Ellen O'Brien, take this road for a kilo or so, then bear right at the first turn. 'Tis the second house." He scratched his head. "Tuesday, it is?"

When Mary hesitated for a moment, Michael answered. "Aye."

"She'll be washin' up a storm."

Once again, Mary was speechless.

"You'll see what I mean." Father's laugh softened the wrinkles across his forehead. "She's a gas character, she is. And works the teeth off a saw."

"Thank you." When Mary offered her hand, Father shook it with gusto.

"May God bless your time here in Cree, Miss—"

"Harris."

"Well, I do say that's a sight for an Irishman!" His business done with Mary, the priest had turned to Michael; more particularly, his car.

Michael beamed, a father proud of his new child. "Father, are ye right for a pint? I'll treat ye, if there's a local pub."

"Now, lad, would it be Ireland if there were no pub?"

Mary seized upon the sudden bonding of the two. "If you don't mind, I'll just walk." She shielded the sun out of her eyes. "'Tisn't far, is it, now?"

"Aye, yer grandmother manages it six days a week. And ye should see her, market day, on the road to Kilkee. She's an old dog for a hard road."

"Well, if you two wouldn't mind . . ."

"You get a start on your chinwag. I'll zip by later with your bag."

Mary smiled and waved as she headed down the lane with just her hopes and her backpack, but inwardly, she cringed. *What if it doesn't turn out? This is my last chance, isn't it?* Images of past failures flooded her mind. *One at a time,* she told herself. *Not too fast. And avoid all the sharp stones in the road.*

"Help me, God." She prayed every step of the way, in spite of her uncertainty that He listened. Her body still ached from yesterday's excruciating walk, and so did her heart, which now thumped in her chest just like it had as she had walked to Kathleen's. Once again, she adjusted her skirt, her hair with slick palms. Step by step down the lane, left, second house . . . stucco . . . slate . . . *Indistinct from a thousand others out here except that this one holds the only grandmother I'll ever have.* She knocked tentatively, then harder. "Please," she mouthed for the chirping birds and, hopefully, God in heaven to hear.

Steady footfalls from inside the house got louder, louder. Whoever was coming was no invalid. The door jerked open. At first, Mary thought a nun had answered; the woman was dressed in black from head to toe. A dark mantle didn't hide a silver braid that reached her waist.

The woman pierced Mary with her gray eyes. "*Failte isteach*—Welcome home, Mary Elizabeth."

"But how—did she tell you I was—"

A shadow seemed to fall over the woman's countenance. She made the sign of the cross, then looked to the sky. "Nobody told me anything, least of all, her. But I knew." She pulled Mary into the house with a hearty grasp, her forearms as muscular as Mam's. "I'm yer Grandmother Ellen. Seventy-four years I've stayed alive, just to see ye."

Mary's skin tingled where Grandmother touched her, years of restrained pats and limp handshakes forgotten. She dropped her bags and threw herself into a mountain range of a bosom. Arms massaged away the pain of yesterday—had it been yesterday? It seemed like years ago. Mary breathed in the sunlight and tobacco and spice scent that clung to Grandmother's clothes, and something broke free in her heart. There were no words spoken, but Mary knew it just the same. Her grandmother loved her. It was in the pull of Mary's head to her chest, the pressure of her kiss on Mary's hair.

A minute seemed a lifetime; how long they stood in the embrace, Mary didn't know. Finally, her grandmother pulled away. "The wash is waitin'," she said, smoothing down her dress. "'Tis a dirty bird that won't keep its nest clean." She turned and walked through a kitchen, out a back door, and into a yard.

Mary followed her, a smile on her face. *She may be leading me to an execution, but I'll still follow. I'm home. Home.*

Dozens of handkerchiefs, fluttering like kite tails in the wind, hung on a line strung between two rusted posts. Grandmother picked up a basket and got to work.

"Mrs.—Ellen, why?"

"Don't call me that. I'm yer grandmother. Always have been. Always will be."

"Grandmother," she said for the first time in her life, "do you have a cold?"

"Blarney. Where ye getting such a wild hair? Use 'em for snuff. When I had a bad dose, the doctor prescribed a pinch or two, and I've used it ever since."

"When did you see this so-called doctor?"

"Thirty years ago, it was. Nary a day have I ailed since."

Mary did her best to keep from staring. Were her teeth yellow? Were—

"Now, don't get yer knickers in a twist." A grin showed white teeth. "I daresay I'll outlive ye a good bit." She cackled as she handed Mary the basket.

Mary unclenched her fingers and pulled down handkerchiefs, sun-kissed and soft, their touch confirming the truth that she was loved, wanted . . . It was so natural, so right to follow the rhythms of Grandmother. Stretch. Unpin. Fold. Stretch . . .

"Come on, now, Ginger." Even though her knees creaked, Grandmother managed to duck under the empty line. "Yer great-aunt's awaitin.'"

Ginger? A great-aunt? Mary hurried after her grandmother. More Irish family.

They walked through the kitchen and into a tiny bedroom, where a tiny woman rocked rhythmically in a spindly chair.

"Mary Elizabeth, meet Mary Ellen, yer great-aunt." Grandmother's booming voice didn't seem to faze Mary Ellen in the least. She kept rocking, rocking . . .

Mary eyed first one sister, then the other, causing Grandmother to roar. "Me given name's Ellen. She's Mary Ellen. They didn't stray far for names back then."

Mary tiptoed to the side of the bed and took Mary Ellen's hand as if it were the hand of the queen herself. "Hello," she said.

Mary Ellen just stared with eyes hidden behind thick lenses. She wore a pink mohair sweater and skirt set that looked strangely familiar.

Grandmother seemed to read Mary's mind. "We got those from Anne. Yer Anne."

Mary's grip on her great-aunt's hand tightened. Why had she had to come across an ocean to learn about Mother's etiquette and generosity?

With Mary following, Grandmother shuffled to the kitchen, filled a glass with water, and took it into a bedroom. A dresser drawer opened, and a nightgown was laid on the bed.

Mary checked her watch. "Grandmother, it's just four o'clock."

"Ye mend yer nets afore ye fish, don't ye?" A study in constant motion, she bustled into the kitchen, filled a kettle, and set it on a fire grate. "Could've used ye yesterday with the cookin' and cleanin'."

Chatter streamed from her; laughter, too. Shortly, the kettle whistled, cheered by another tall tale. Grandmother's steady hand poured boiling water into china cups, and she heaped in several tablespoons of thick cream before Mary could protest. "Here's an Irish cuppa, not the watery bilge o' the British." With strong fingers, she pinched Mary's cheek. "Ye need a bit more to tweak, ye do, afore you'll fill anyone's door frame."

Someone rapped on the front door, but Grandmother didn't seem to hear.

"Yoo-hoo?" Father and Michael walked in, their gaits unsteady.

"Aye." Grandmother lunged toward Michael like a farmer's wife gathering a hen, clucking all the while. "Is this yer young man?"

Mary stared at the floor. "He's . . . a friend."

"'Tis a lonely washin' that has no man's shirt in it." Ignoring Mary's sputters, she pulled Michael close, then kissed him on both cheeks. "Handsome as my old beau, he is."

Father slapped his thighs. "Ellen, you've kept a secret from yer priest?"

"Aye, a storehouse o' them." Her hearty laughter, the shake of her head caused her braid to flop back and forth like a horse swatting flies with its tail. She bustled to the stove and lifted the kettle.

Father O'Malley shook his head. "Aye, none for me. I spent half the mornin' wi' the McAllisters. They drowned me in it, then stuffed me wi' biscuits."

Michael held up his hands. "No, thanks. I'm loaded wi' Guinness." The two men howled, the yeasty smell of beer oozing from their pores.

"When the drop's inside, the sense is outside, ye daft souls. Now sit!"

Both Michael and the priest sat down without another word. Biscuits were served, tea too, and all of them nibbled except Grandmother, who dunked three or four in her tea, then ate with gusto. During one of Father's rambling tales, Grandmother reached across the table and grabbed Mary's hand. Mary squeezed back, hard and sure. She was home.

When Father stood to leave, Michael did too. "Ready to head back?"

Before Mary could move, Grandmother jumped to her feet, thrusting out her hip, her chest. "Her feet ha'e brought her to where her heart is, and she's stayin' a spell." She narrowed her eyes and stared at Michael. "How long are ye here for?"

"Our flight leaves Dublin on Monday. I have to—"

"Are ye fey?" Her forefinger pointed into his chest. "Change it to Shannon, and leave the chick in the nest fer a spell. She'll fly away soon enough."

Mary held her breath. Her life seemed to hang on this decision. *Please, God. I want this, more than anything. If You'll let me stay, I'll go to mass. No more drinking. No more . . .* Her prayer went on and on, much like it had when she'd walked to this very house.

Grandmother tapped her shoe against the stone floor. "Young man, I won't take no for an answer. Our lease on life's short, ye know."

Michael shrugged. "It's up to Mary, of course."

Mary flashed him a smile, but she longed to jump on the table and dance a jig.

"And as long as I can change our tickets," Michael continued.

While Father and Grandmother cackled and babbled, Michael helped Mary get her bags, which seemed much lighter than they had earlier. Then she touched his arm, longing to find the words to tell him what this meant to her.

He looked down at her, his face flushed. "Call if you need me. The church will have a phone."

Mary nodded. "Michael, tell your parents thanks." She kissed him lightly on the cheek. "You don't know what this means."

He stepped closer and put his arms around her waist. "I think I'm beginning to understand. And if there's anything at all . . ."

The hug became an embrace; a brief kiss led to a more lingering one. But Mary's mind was on Grandmother and the new life God had in store for her. He was in control, and He was on her side.

✢ ✢ ✢

The room seemed warmer. Finally, family Sally could relate to. "I can see her now. That snowy hair, that tank of a body . . ."

Mary slipped off her shoes and leaned against the cushion, her shoulder touching Sally's. "I loved her so."

"She sounds like my Grandmother Hazel. And I have an aunt who would love those O'Looneys. On her Oklahoma homestead, they burned wagon wheels and tumbleweeds for heat . . ." Quite a bit later, Sally finally came to a stopping point. "So did you stay there?"

Mary nodded. "'Twas a blessed week."

CHAPTER 17

Come one and all, attend my call. Revel in pleasures that ne'er can cloy.
Come see rural felicity, which love and innocence ever enjoy.
— "Haste to the Wedding," traditional Irish folk song

The sun slipped below the horizon, ending the first day Mary had ever spent with her grandmother. They sat in the cozy kitchen, beams of gold illuminating a cross-stitched sampler, a crucifix, and one framed photograph. The dinner, boiled potatoes, black bread, and, of course, tea, had been simple but nourishing. For hours now, she and Grandmother had existed in their own world, memorizing each other's faces, listening for the tone behind the spoken words that revealed what was really meant. But so many questions remained. Who was her father? Where was her grandfather? Mary planned to tackle them one by one.

"More tea?"

Mary shook her head, keeping her gaze on the one framed photograph that proved her memory about Mam had been correct. "What was she like?" she asked. *Before those eyes got hard.*

Her grandmother's eyes became misty. She stared into her tea cup, never even glancing at the picture. "Ah, a tomboy, she was. Loved to race wi' the lads. Autumn 'twas her favorite, but school spoiled that. The nuns had to strap that one to the chair. Once, she walked to Kilkee to catch eels by the full moon." The chair scraped as Grandmother took dishes to the sink, her back to Mary.

As Mary looked at the picture, her mother seemed to come alive. She could see her running, laughing, with—Mary's voice caught as the picture seemed to fade right before her eyes. "Who's my father?" she asked.

Without answering, her grandmother shuffled out of the room.

Mary got up, unsure whether to follow or stay in the rapidly darkening kitchen. She ached to find out the truth of her past, yet tried to think of it from the old woman's perspective. After all, a granddaughter had just been thrown at her, and she'd need time to settle into things. Mary planned to give her all the time she needed.

✦ ✦ ✦

Moonlight bathed the grassy back yard. Roses that clung to the cottage walls perfumed the air. In Ireland, an outhouse trip was a sensory experience.

"*Oh, my lovely rose of Clare, so beautiful and fair. I will always love you, my lovely rose of Clare.*"

Grandmother's singing sweetened the night air, yet it pained Mary to hear the plaintive lyrics streaming out the window. Was she thinking of a lost love or her own daughter? Even though they were only steps apart, Mary was again reminded that people and places and things stood between them. She went inside, vowing to do all she could to break down the barriers.

Grandmother continued to sing as she sat before a dressing table, her hair a silvery shawl falling to her waist. "What is it, my dear?" She ran a brush through her hair, laughing as if she understood why Mary was staring. "God's numbered every one o' them, and I wouldn't think o' cuttin' it off."

"It's almost to your—"

"Don't wash it, neither. 'Tisn't good for ye."

This time, Mary didn't try to hide her laughter. Her grandmother was as odd of a creature as she'd ever met. She raised her eyebrows and made a face for the mirror and for Grandmother. At least she had an excuse now for her own quirks.

Rising, Grandmother set down the brush, full of cottony fluff. "May I live to see ye combin' yer own gray hair." The old knees creaked as she knelt beside the bed, bowed her head, pulled out her rosary, and made the sign of the cross. "In the name of the Father, and of the Son, conceived by the power of the Holy Spirit . . ."

As Mary changed clothes, she fought an urge to kneel as well, to say the words that, until now, held little meaning for her. She wanted to praise Him, to trust Him like her grandmother did. Perhaps, if she lived here with Grandmother, she would learn to pray. Just like this.

Ready for bed, Mary pulled back the cover, setting off a crunching sound as if a hundred people had wadded up candy wrappers. She shot a look at

Grandmother, who was still in earnest prayer. The noise got louder when she climbed in bed.

"He ascended into heaven . . ."

Bouncing seemed to exacerbate the noise. Mary rolled out of bed and, on her hands and knees, searched under it; she found nothing but twine-bound boxes and a clean-swept floor; no dust, hair wads, or sneezed-in tissues. Mary rolled her eyes. Grandmother would even pass the Harris criteria for housekeeping.

When Mary got back in the covers, the crackling continued but didn't drown out the prayers. Mary heard all kinds of Irish names. Some she'd never heard of, and some she had, like Kathleen and Kelly and Gerard.

"And the Holy Ghost. Amen."

More crackling. Mary cleared her throat. "What's that noise?"

"What noise?"

"That scratching. Hear it?"

"Maybe it's the dogs a' sniffin'."

Mary smiled. Even though Grandmother prided herself on an ageless head of hair, she wasn't blessed with acute hearing.

When Grandmother heaved her bulk into the bed, she set off such a cacophony of grunts and squeaks Mary couldn't keep quiet. "What's under here?" she asked.

"Not a thing but goose feathers and my horehound drops."

Horehound? For what she hoped was the last time, Mary hopped out of bed. After a few grunts of her own, she heaved up her side of the mattress. Dozens of individually wrapped brown tablets were heaped like reject Halloween candy.

The bed groaned when Grandmother sat up. "My doctor, have mercy on his soul, said it would cure cough, consumption, a pain or an ache anywhere, thanks be to God."

"What in the world is in them?"

"'Tis a plant o' the mint family, Ginger. Nothin' more, nothin' less."

The lamp clicked off. Grandmother creaked and rumbled as she settled back in and then fell silent. But the silence didn't last.

Mary failed to reach REM or any other level of sleep that night in the horehound-stuffed bed. If the noisy wrappers weren't enough, there was Grandmother's wheezy snoring, which rose and fell like the tides. Mary huddled near the edge, not used to having a sweaty body bump into her all night. For unlike Mary, Grandmother didn't seem perturbed by sharing her bed and twisted her boulder-like frame every which way.

A thud. A whoosh. Covers were pulled back, window shades thrown open. "Ye lazy girl! Get yer arse up. Lose an hour in the mornin', and you'll look for it all day."

Mary rolled over and groaned. "It's still dark."

"What's bred in the bone will out."

The vitality in Grandmother's voice rallied Mary to a sitting position. "What?"

"Flesh and blood, ye are. Now get up."

Bed couldn't compete with this woman. Mary shoved back the covers, Grandmother's words acting as a miracle tonic. *I'm with kin. And I can stay.* She closed her eyes and thanked God.

Still groggy, Mary stumbled into the kitchen, then broke out into a sweat from the smells and the heat. By the look of it, her grandmother had been up for hours. The teapot whistled and food sizzled as she cooked over a stove.

Grandmother whirled about the tiny space, scrambling, mixing, stirring at a dizzying pace. She piled a platter full of sausages, eggs, potatoes, tomatoes, and biscuits. A chunky mixture was poured into a gravy boat. It looked like enough to serve the whole parish.

Before she sat down, Mary hugged her grandmother. "It looks wonderful," she said, as she slid into her seat. She picked up her fork and, battling queasiness, determined to find a way to eat.

The sharp eyes honed into her. "Ginger, don't ye bless yer food?"

Mary set down her fork. "Why do you call me Ginger?"

"Haven't ye seen the red o' the ginger plant? Tasted the tang o' the root?" She harrumphed and settled a napkin in her lap. "Yer Ginger; that's all there is to it."

Mary smiled. Fourteen years ago, Daddy had called her Lizzie for the first time; now she'd gotten another nickname from someone she loved. She reached across the table and grabbed her grandmother's hand, feeling each callous, each rough spot. *Home.*

The prayer flowed out from Grandmother like a river to the ocean. Natural and smooth, interlaced with Grandmother's life, and Mary let it lead her along. *This is how it feels, God. Yes. Yes.* At the end, Mary prayed too, or at least she tried to.

After Grandmother made the sign of the cross, she was all business. Before Mary could say a word, she heaped food on both plates. "Here ye go. Eat hearty, lass, or yer legs will give out halfway to Kilkee." She went after her food as if it were her last meal. "Aye, I've got to get the dole. And the garden's full o' weeds." She chewed and talked and poured down tea, somehow all at once.

Mary smiled and nodded. When the keen gray eyes were on her, she took tiny bites, trying to ignore the grease, the gamey aftertaste. She swallowed, then cringed. How could she best choke down this culinary demonstration of love without gagging?

"Here I've gone on, Ginger." Grandmother soaked up the last bit of gravy with a biscuit. "Tell me, what are ye up to today?"

Mary put down her fork. What she was up to was learning about her father. But it wasn't going to be that easy to blurt it out. "I want to—"

"Aye, yer mouth's full." Grandmother rose from the table. "Get on wi' it. I'll see to Mary Ellen."

Sweat beaded Mary's forehead, and she wiped it off with a clammy hand. "Who's my father?" she asked, before Grandmother could leave the room.

It was as if her grandmother had been slapped. Her face reddened, and she jerked back. She stared first at Kathleen's picture, then at Mary. Something she saw seemed to defeat her, and she suddenly looked old and tired. "I can't help ye there, Ginger." Her voice trailed off, and she walked out of the room hunched over like her back hurt.

It took one last look at the bloody sausage for Mary to step, gagging, out the back door. She hurried to the garden and hurled the remainder of her breakfast into a crop of weeds. Questions rose up, along with nausea and bile. Was the truth so painful that her grandmother could not bring herself to tell? Or did she feel she could not trust Mary?

Tiny chartreuse shoots peeked out from among the dried stalks of last year's crop, already clamoring for the sunlight that a cloudless day guaranteed. Mary thought of how Grandmother had allowed their relationship to take root. The last thing she wanted to do was cut off tender shoots too soon. She wiped her mouth and went back inside.

When Grandmother came back into the kitchen, Mary was sitting at the table, scraping her empty plate, pretending she'd just polished off the last bite of sausage.

"Aye, Ginger. Did ye like the puddin'?" The sparkling eyes, the bustling step had returned, almost as if by magic.

Mary folded her hands in her lap. This was a game she'd played countless times with Mother; the blow-up, the facade of cheer. And with fourteen years of experience, she considered herself a professional. "It was all . . . amazing."

"It's Father's favorite. Got the pulse o' the farm in it, the best of County Clare, if I do say so. Pig's blood and liver and . . ."

Mary prayed for the bitter taste to go away and for Grandmother to be quiet. But neither thing happened.

"Ye mash lard into a paste, mix in breadcrumbs and oats." She described it carefully, a cook sharing a cherished recipe. "If you've a hankering for it, I'll teach ye."

Mary gulped a couple of times. "Oh . . . I couldn't. But thanks."

Grandmother shrugged but didn't seem offended. "Well, enough o' the talk. The floor's cryin' to be cleaned." She banged outside and came back with a mop.

Mary jumped from the table, glad to be off the topic of food. The other topic—her father—would have to be dealt with later. She took the mop and got to work.

No sooner had she started, than Grandmother stopped her. "Aye, ye got a cherry for yer brain?" With grunts and moans, she picked up the chairs and set them atop the table. While Mary mopped, Grandmother studied her every move, her eyes darting around to make sure she got the last stray crumb.

Mary chuckled, once again thinking of her mother. Little did Grandmother know that Mother was a seasoned veteran in the war against dirt. As she mopped, another question burned at her—had Grandmother known her mother Anne? After all, Anne was Killian's sister. Yet one look at those sharp eyes caused Mary to tuck away another unanswered question. Perhaps one day she could ask, but it wasn't going to be now.

✛ ✛ ✛

"*Oh, the summertime is comin'. Will ye go, Lassie, go?*" Grandmother walked several paces in front of Mary on the dusty road, swinging a cloth bag and humming to herself.

"How far did you say it was?"

"Twelve kilo to Kilkee. But Paddy'll be along fer us."

Mary froze, then cast a glance at Grandmother, who shot on ahead, singing another of her folk songs. Mary wanted to sling down her bag and collapse. She was going to retrace those steps she'd tread so gaily as a five-year-old, not knowing Mam and Killian's sisters were buying her going-away clothes.

The imposing figure turned and in a flash was at Mary's side. She laid her hand on Mary's shoulder. "Come on, Ginger." Her voice was soft. "Set it aside now. Come on."

There was power in the bent of the grizzled head, the swish of the thick braid, power and love. Somehow Grandmother knew. And cared. Mary nodded and, without another word, picked up her bag.

They trudged like pilgrims on the dusty road to the Promised Land, Mary managing to block out everything but the glorious day and being with flesh and blood. She found Grandmother's stride, then matched it. Her voice rose with Grandmother's, both of them soaring on the wind along with the songs of finches and warblers.

With her songs, prayers, and folk tales, Grandmother captured like a master painter the hues of County Clare: the butterflies that floated near; the starlings, which added their melodies to the finches' and thrushes'; the clouds that echoed the wooly texture of the grazing sheep. Hills did their part by adding perspective and depth, and stone walls framed the land with a sense of order and control.

At the crest of a ridge, brilliant gold flowers spread over the rolling green land like a quilt over a bed. "What is it?" Mary gasped, pausing to catch her breath.

"Gorse." Grandmother leaned her stout body, damp with sweat, against Mary. "Their blossoms spring from last year's thorns. Like Christ risen from the grave," she continued, her eyes on Mary. "'Tis the only way."

With a sinking feeling, Mary tore her gaze from the brilliant blooms. Would the pain, the agony of it all ever make sense to her? Would she ever accept the ways of God? She squeezed her eyes shut, praying as hard as she could.

"Well, if it's not Ellen O'Brien!"

A rusted-out pickup truck pulled beside them, and a man leaned toward the window, then unrolled it. "Thought ye'd sneak past me, ye did?"

Amid laughter, creaks, and groans, the two women climbed in the truck.

"Got a late start, I did. Glad I caught ye afore ye walked yer legs off." He beamed at Mary and held out a grubby hand. "Top o' the mornin', Mary Elizabeth. I'm Paddy McHenry. I catch her coming, going, or sometimes both."

Mary nodded at Paddy's familiarity with her. *So it goes in a small town. Just like home. No, Lisle's not home. This is.*

"Oh, it's no nay never," Grandmother sang.

"*No, nay never will I play the Irish rover,*" Paddy finished for her.

As they bounced down the dusty road, Paddy and Grandmother bursting with song, Mary let the lyrics and her heart make her decision. She was an Irishwoman. These were her people. She was staying in her country until they buried her in a pine box.

✛ ✛ ✛

For five blissful days, Mary shared Grandmother's life. With each hour that passed, she found new evidence to support the decision she'd made in Paddy's truck. They called on neighbors. Cooked and cleaned. Today, "in weather fit for na'e but baby ducks," they'd sloshed to mass. In the church nave, the Spirit had engulfed her, yawning out all doubts. Here in the kitchen, hours later, she could still smell the incense, hear the chants, envision the cross, bent heads, white silk chasuble, flickering candles, the cross, *ite missa est*, rosy-cheeked altar boys, prayer, veils, *deo gratias*, kneeling figures, the cross. All the rituals she'd learned in parochial school began to make sense. And so did God.

Grandmother chattered as she cooked, but Mary, in a nearby chair, barely listened, her eyes glued to the crucifix on the wall. He had died for her sins. He had forgiven her. And now He was letting her stay in her homeland.

"Are ye listening, lass?" In her usual pattern of keeping three things going at once, Grandmother admonished the dough to soften, the teapot to quit its clatter, and beat a dubious-looking mixture as if it were a naughty child.

Mary snapped out of her reverie and jumped to her side. She'd learned to beat soda bread batter until it foamed, to knead yeast dough until it glistened. And always, there was Grandmother, leaning close. It had been a blessed week. Every activity orchestrated from before dawn, when calloused toes hit the floor, to bedtime. Serving others. Constant prayer. If things went like Mary hoped, it would be a blessed life. But she needed to get things started by telling Grandmother of her plans. Now.

"Sabbath's over, and wi' it, our work begins." Grumbling, Grandmother handed Mary a food-laden tray. "Now, be quick about it."

Mary Ellen's room was quiet, as always, except for the clock, which admonished Mary with every tick. *Why don't you ask? Why are you scared?* Pulling up a footstool, she sat by her great-aunt, who rocked back and forth. Mary studied her vacuous face. Was it peaceful not to have to think about what had happened and what might happen yet?

Partly to quell her own anxiety, Mary prattled to Mary Ellen about Father's reading from Luke. Of the deluge that had soaked every cell of her body. Of kissing nearly every parishioner on both cheeks. Through the entirety of her ramblings, Mary Ellen never changed expression. After Mary exhausted the details of their afternoon tea, she folded her hands in her lap and just sat there, unable to think of another thing to say.

She blew on the stew, then held it up to Mary Ellen's lips. "There's a good little lamb," Mary coaxed, looking into filmy eyes.

Mary Ellen grasped Mary's hand and squeezed it tight. "My Mary."

For the briefest span of time, her gaze met Mary's in a look of recognition and love, filling Mary's eyes with tears. Another blood connection, one she hadn't expected. Then Mary Ellen faded into a place where Mary could not go, a land of mist and fog not unlike the view out the window. Mary threw her arms around fragile shoulders, longing to pull her back, then kissed her cheek, soft as a rose petal.

With a booming voice, Grandmother called Mary to dinner. The two of them bustled about, making final preparations, then sat side by side, as usual, and prayed.

"Mary Ellen seems better today," Mary said as she accepted the usual cup of tea.

"What makes ye say that?"

"She called me 'My Mary,' and I'd bet my life—"

"Don't bet at all. Let yes be yes and no be no. Anything else is the devil's fancy."

Mary cleared her throat. "Anyway, she seemed to know who I am."

Grandmother nodded. "Most days, she rocks and rocks, never losing that look o' the lamb that just banged its noggin' on a hedgerow. 'Tis a rare day—but still it happens—when, with all the sense o' King Solomon, she smiles and says, "'Tis a good mornin', Ellen.'" She passed Mary a plate, shaking her head all the while. "Only the Lord knows what's going on in that noggin' o' hers."

Cautiously, Mary tasted what was set before her. "Delicious. What is it?"

"A coddle. Ye just layer in leftovers—potatoes, veg, sausage—and heat it. 'Tis a good Sabbath dish."

"You're amazing, Grandmother."

"Aye, not me, child. 'Twas me mam that taught me. She learned from her mam, her mam—four generations we've spent right here in this house."

It was hard to keep from choking. "You've never left this village?"

For once, Grandmother stopped chewing. She set down her fork, her eyes misty. "Only once, long ago. I made a pilgrimage to Croagh Patrick."

"A pilgrimage?"

"A penance of sorts. We Irish ha'e done it for centuries. They flocked there like geese during the bloody Famine."

"The Famine?"

"Jesus, Mary, and Joseph." Her fork hovered about her mouth. "An Irish lass ignorant o' the Famine? Hard times they were, wi' most o' the babbies, the weak ones, laid in their graves." The fork clanked onto a half-empty plate. "While we dropped like flies, the British shipped our beef to the queen and her merry subjects. My mother lost three siblings, retching and foaming great mouthfuls o' grass."

"But she lived?"

"If ye can call it that. Sick all her days, she was, begging me not to feed her *pratai*." Grandmother's chair scraped as she lumbered to the stove. "My husband planted them by a horse-drawn harrow," she continued, while stirring a bubbling pot, "'til the day he left."

Her husband? *My grandfather.* Mary couldn't help but envision another story, which she'd hear soon enough. Along with a million others. "When were you born?" she asked, hoping to lead into the other questions. After all, plans needed to be made . . .

"'Twas 1893, in the year of our Lord."

"What sights you've seen," Mary continued, glad the conversation was flowing.

"Thank God I didn't see my babbie wither up and die." Mary didn't miss the quick glance at the picture. "Other sorrows, but not that sorrow."

The old woman shuffled to the window, providing the opportunity Mary needed. She'd put it off, stepped around it, backed off of it. She cleared her throat. It was time. "Grandmother, I need to talk to you."

"We've talked enough." Grandmother turned to face Mary, her eyes bleary and red. "Jesus, Mary, and Joseph, how'd ye get me on the old sorrows? And us rising tomorrow afore the crack o' dawn."

"Uh, that's what I wanted to talk to you about, among other things."

With a harrumph, Grandmother plopped into the chair.

"First off, I want to know—I need to know about my father."

The chair scraped closer. Grandmother jutted bulging eyes and a flaming face to within a foot of Mary's. "And why do ye want to dig up the bloody bones? Tear at the rotten shrouds and stick yer nose in the smoldering stink o' something long buried?"

Mary raked her fingers through her hair and pulled, hard. "To know if that's where I got my curly hair." She thrust out her fist, then unclenched her fingers.

Grandmother seemed transfixed by the tiny curl laying in Mary's palm. Then her breath whooshed out as from a bellows. "And what 'o it? What will it help?" She continued before Mary could speak. "I'll tell ye what." She stormed from the room, raising her voice as she went. "Not a thing. Not a single bloody thing."

Mary knocked a chair askew as she followed Grandmother into the front room. "How can you keep this from me?" she asked, anger boiling out. "I've a right to know."

"You've no rights here," Grandmother said, moving toward the front door.

Mary angled after her, all the rehearsed words evaporating. "Yes, I do." Her resentments, pent-up emotions flew out, and she didn't stop them. "It's my country too."

Grandmother took one more step backward until she was up against the wall.

Mary relaxed, just a bit. Surely she understands. Surely . . .

Suddenly Grandmother surged toward Mary, grabbed her hand, and pulled it to her chest. "Go back. We O'Briens aren't worth a worry. Leave this doomed island. Live like we never existed."

Mary grabbed Grandmother's sleeve, a wave of cooking grease and tea and ginger assailing her. "But you do exist. And I'm your flesh and blood."

Grandmother's eyes narrowed. "Aye! Didn't I tell ye what's bred in the bone will out? Haven't I spent all my days, and won't I spend the rest o' them, praying for ye?"

Mary lurched back, but not in passive retreat. Grandmother's words forced her to regroup. And let anger build. "You're sending me off too?" Her hands clenched and unclenched, as if trying to gain control. "You're no better than her," she finally spat out.

Grandmother jerked away from Mary, stalked to the window, and stared at clouds cached with more rain. "I was there that day," she whispered.

Mary stepped closer to catch each ponderous syllable.

"Around that table, sending ye away."

For a moment Mary froze. Then bloodied words spurted out. "How . . . nice. A mother-and-daughter conspiracy. Did you two also agree on that little plan?"

Grandmother kept her back to Mary, her voice muffled. "Haven't seen her in fourteen years."

The missile found its mark, and Mary exploded. "What's wrong with you?" Now she was inches from Grandmother and barely aware of the words she screamed. "What's wrong with the whole lot of you?"

A muffled voice ignored the insult. "Go back. America's yer home."

Mary grabbed her grandmother by the arm and swung her around. "Tell me to my face. At least have guts enough to do that."

Grandmother didn't blink or change expression. "Trust in God. He'll be with ye."

What had she tried to do all these years? If Mary had been angry before, now she was livid. "God?" she screamed. "I hate Him. How could He do this?"

Grandmother grabbed Mary's shoulder, held her still, then slapped her, not once but twice. The first stung like a hornet's attack; the second stabbed like a knife. Mary's cheek throbbed, and she tasted blood. Grandmother opened and closed her mouth like a fish gulping great mouthfuls of air and staggered from the room.

Mary sat trembling from the violence of it all, and not just the slaps. How could this be happening? She drank in her surroundings as if it were her last look at life. This was her home. She belonged here. The rhythms of the land, the minor Celtic key that the birds sang. The wind blew, coursed through her veins. It fit her seamlessly, and now that she knew it, and it knew her, she never wanted to let go. But how could she stay if her kin didn't want her? How could she argue with an old woman whom she loved with a fiery passion? A sob escaped her. It had been decided. It was over.

She hobbled to the bedroom, stuffed clothes in her bag, got ready for bed, grasping at the mundane in a desperate form of self-preservation.

Grandmother sat at the mirror, using her brush to beat at the crimps loosed from her bun. Harder she pulled, as if she were hell-bent to straighten them into submission. The brush clattered to the floor. It was only then that she faced her granddaughter, using the mirror as a go-between. "I'm sorry, Ginger," she said.

Mary opened her mouth, prepared to release the torrent of hate and resentment that the slaps had unleashed. She took a good, long look at her grandmother, the wrinkles that hadn't been there an hour ago, the bags and sags of accumulated sorrows, the pallor of a much older woman. A woman who looked to be on the threshold of death.

With that one look, Mary's resolve collapsed. The battle over, she buried her face in her hands. She couldn't wound Grandmother with more words, not when she loved her more than she'd ever loved anyone.

She heard a thud and opened her eyes.

Grandmother pulled a sheaf of letters tied with an orange ribbon from a dresser drawer and shoved them toward her. "They're yours now. Yer mam wrote them to her best friend, Mary Elizabeth. Yer namesake."

Mary's heart skipped a beat. What could these letters tell her that she didn't already know—that none of them really wanted her? Still, they beckoned to her, and she clasped envelopes thin as onion skin to her bosom. She glanced at Grandmother's reflection, happy that some of the flush had returned to her cheeks, then set the bundle aside. With an affected cheeriness, she bustled about, acting busy, but in truth, waiting, waiting, waiting. She wanted to meet Mam in a place of solitude, just the two of them. Would she finally reconcile those old memories of Mam with the defeated woman who shooed her from that house?

Around midnight, Grandmother's snores settled into a sonorous rhythm.

As if to help her, Mary's old friend the moon beamed a golden gift through the window. *All the world is sleeping, love, your friend the moon, has star-watch keeping, love. Come, come.* She tiptoed across the room and crouched as close as she could to the moon's luminous light. Her hands trembling, she squinted to decipher the words:

M. E.,
    Sweet night wi' the wee sprout. Bold, she is, and wild
as a newborn colt. Flamin' ginger. Carriage like the queen o'
England.

Your Kathleen

Mary read on, the words carrying her to another time. Her skin prickled as if she'd seen it herself—the bustling markets, the lonely nights, the anguish of leaving Dublin, the fear of what she'd find on the cliffs. Mary pulled the page closer; the handwriting had smeared:

    She's got his red hair, old Mary, my love, and I fear she's
got his wildness too. I couldn't hold him, Mary, he's wedding
another. No, not all the king's horses nor all the king's men nor
all the pretty maids all in a row could hold the handsome Johnny
Kennedy o' Cree. Johnny Kennedy, no Johnny Kennedy, no
Johnny Kennedy o' Cree.

Tears flowed onto the paper; Mary made no effort to check them. Mam had loved and loved hard; her daughter, her lover, her best friend. In her imaginings, Mary lost all sense of place and time, mesmerized by the pages she would have sold her soul to keep. She read them until the moon withdrew and sank out of sight. By touch, not sight, she replaced the fragile sheets in envelopes and retied the ribbon. *She loved me; I know it now. The evidence is right here.* She closed her eyes and recalled the photo of a much younger, much happier Mam, still not knowing what had happened to change her.

She slid the precious bundle in her bag and climbed into bed, but with her heart proclaiming the new discoveries, sleep could not be found. She knew his name. He was handsome. She exulted with the knowledge, then went limp. *What does it matter now?* She couldn't stay, not with Grandmother's mandate to return.

Tossing and turning, she checked her watch. Three o'clock, and Michael would soon come and whisk her from Ireland and Grandmother, perhaps forever.

✝ ✝ ✝

Sally did not move. Even she had run out of words in the face of another rejection.

Mary interrupted the silence with a voice devoid of emotion. "Do you see how it was the best thing and the worst thing, all rolled into one? I loved Grandmother, and I felt that she loved me. But she sent me away from my homeland, and that tore out my heart."

"How did you cope this time?"

"It was Daddy again." She smiled in a nostalgic way. "And Mother too, though I didn't think so at the time."

CHAPTER 18

Think, when home returning, Bright we've seen it burning,
Oh! Oh! Thus remember me.

—Thomas Moore, "Go Where Glory Waits Thee"

Michael checked the luggage and the schedule, led Mary past stewardesses in green hot pants, and found their seats. The occurrences of the past days numbed her into a stupor, and she slept in a way that blotted out everything. Seven hours later, rubbing her eyes, she remembered. And tears fell once again.

"Now that we're home"—Michael struggled to be heard over the hustle and bustle of landing—"would you please tell me what's going on?"

Mary made a fist with her hands. *We're not home*, she longed to scream. *I've left my home, sent away again. All these years and still the same result.*

He drew her close and touched her split lip. "Tell me. I've waited forever."

"Michael, I can't talk about it." When she saw the hurt in his face, she softened a bit. "But thanks for caring."

He put his hands over hers. "It's like a game keeping up with you."

A game? She pulled back like he'd slapped her. "It isn't a game. It's my life."

Michael gripped her face and turned it toward his with such a quick motion that her breath caught. "I know it's not a game. And as for your life, I want to be a part of it." A woman across the aisle stared, and he lowered his voice. "Look, Mary. This is coming out all wrong. I wanted to skywrite it, send you a telegram in Gaelic, something besides this." Desire, affection leapt from his eyes. "I care about you, Mary. I—"

Mary stiffened and put out her hand to fend off more words. "Michael, stop," she said, much more loudly than she'd intended.

"No." The stubborn streak that Mary had seen when Pap tossed bills into the fire manifested itself in Michael. "It has to be said." He leaned close enough for Mary to see a nick on his cheek. "I don't know what went on with your family, but—"

"Michael, it's a closed chapter. I . . ."

He tapped on his ever-present economics book. "Then we'll rewrite it. They do it all the time."

Mary's heart fluttered, yet reason stepped in. *No, Mary. He's not the one.*

"Look at me. I want to know you. But when I try . . ." He reached for her again.

Again, she drew away. Every cell of her body affirmed that it was no use. Though they were linked through the leaves of the shamrock, there was nothing more. Still, the truth hurt. She, so familiar with rejection, was about to inflict it. She took a deep breath, determined to explain. "'You're a good friend, Michael, loyal and trustworthy and kind. But there can't be anything more. You—you understand, don't you?"

Jet engines roared as the flat Midwest leapt up to meet them. For a moment, Michael seemed stunned by her answer. When the plane thudded onto the runway, he unbuckled his seatbelt and tried to stand in the tight quarters of the plane. "You don't have to say anything more," he flung at her. "'Good friend' was enough."

As the captain admonished them to stay seated, guilt assailed Mary, and she longed to say something that would wipe the pain from Michael's face. But there was nothing more to say. He wasn't right for her. And if she tried to tell him, she was sure she'd muddle it up even worse than she already had.

They filed off the plane, avoiding each other, awkward like soldiers who don't know what to say after the battle's over. He gave her an impersonal hug in the O'Hare lobby, then disappeared into a knot of travelers. Right by the baggage claims, Mary whispered what she should have said to the man who had taken her home, had treated her like family. "You're a good man, Michael O'Looney. Smart, handsome, loving. A fine husband for some lucky woman. But not me." The weight of another loss made her stagger; she longed to drop her bags and cry.

A gentleman flailed his arms and knocked her with his briefcase, jolting Mary back to reality. *Welcome home,* she longed to yell. *I see nothing's changed.*

Home. Daddy. Mother. She whirled through revolving glass doors, aghast at her bedraggled reflection. Would her parents notice? If they asked, could she tell them about it?

The crowd pulled her along. Using her bags as anchors, she pushed back, just to keep from getting crushed. She couldn't collapse right here, not with

Daddy arriving any minute. In spite of her sadness over leaving Ireland, Mary tried to be thoughtful. At least *they* hadn't sent her away.

Cars clotted the street, the noise nearly deafening. When a taxi accelerated and swerved around an eighteen-wheeler, Mary's heart raced with it. *Just a step off the curb*—her hand trembled, then stiffened. Where had that come from? Was she still so close to the edge? She shoved back the black thought that tried to find a crack in her restless mind. No more. Twice was enough. God had clamped His hand over that.

A bus driver's honk, a cab driver's curse drew her attention to a car stalled in the middle of five lanes of steel and chrome and fumes.

"Lizzie!" Daddy hung out the car window, somehow managing to be heard over the cacophony of traffic stacked up behind him accordion-style. He popped out of the idling car and streaked across three lanes, then crushed her in his arms.

Mary clung to his jacket. "Daddy," she giggled, "that's illegal."

He kissed her hair, then mussed it with his hands. "I know the mayor," he said. He grabbed her bag, and they zigzagged past more honks and curses and jumped in the car.

"We missed you, Mary Elizabeth."

Was it . . . *Mother!* Mary whipped about, staring. Mother, who avoided the airport as if it were a war zone, had come to greet her. Something had changed.

When Mother leaned forward and managed a kiss over the top of the head-rest, Mary's mouth flew open. Mother must have kissed her before, but she couldn't remember when.

"I made your favorite, Mary Elizabeth. Apple pie."

Mary felt herself turn red. "Mother, thanks," she managed, a bit confused by their gushy manner. Had they thought she'd stay in County Clare? Did they long to be close, as she did? She felt tears coming, intermingled with hope.

"How was it, Mary?" asked Mother.

"What happened?" Daddy darted glances at her in spite of heavy traffic.

Mary bit her lip. How could she explain that she'd fallen for a land so different from this that it made her cry just to look out the window? At this point, nothing would be gained by the truth. "It was fine," she managed. "I'll tell you all about it. Later."

They inched along congested freeways, so different from her western Ireland, every garish billboard and strip mall and spewing factory seemed to mock her. Mary leaned back in the plush leather seat, her heart calling out to the land of misty moon surprises, far away but not forgotten. Never, never forgotten.

Evergreens stood as silent sentinels about their front door, but all Mary could see, could smell were Grandmother's roses. Ammonia and furniture polish emanated from the furniture rather than tobacco and mint. Drab walls did nothing for eyes used to cross-stitched samplers and Catholic icons. And what she wouldn't give to hear Grandmother's laugh, see her hearty bustle. Grandmother's kitchen. Grandmother. Grand. Mother.

Daddy carried her things to her room, then stood jingling the change in his pocket. "Mother's made your favorites. So come on, let's eat."

"Don't forget to wash your hands," Mother called.

They sat down at the table. All Mary could think about was a bowed white head, a two-hundred-year-old kitchen.

Mother passed around a glazed ham with a cherry on top. She pattered on about the special meal she'd made, apparently forgetting that Mary was a vegetarian.

"Well, Mary. The election's heating up." As if Daddy already felt the tension, he interspersed small talk with gulping bites. "Those liberals are at it again."

"Oh, dear." Mary tried to keep her voice light and reminded herself who hadn't disowned her, but the words slipped out anyway. "And you won't let them."

Daddy chewed faster, still talking. "I'll just ask you, Mary, the way I ask them. You really think taxpayers want their hard-earned money used for a homeless shelter?"

Mary cut off a wedge of pineapple, focusing on the golden fruit, the thick core, anything to take her mind off the fact that Mother didn't know her favorite food, her favorite . . . anything. "So . . . Mother, what's been going on with you?"

"It's been a most productive time. Maureen and I reorganized the insurance files. It's the best shape we've been in since—"

"Since a five-year-old was thrown at you?"

Mother tossed her napkin down. "Mary Elizabeth, we're just trying to have a pleasant dinner, for heaven's sake."

"And I'm just trying to make sense of my life."

They sat staring each other down like pistol-toting gunmen. Finally, Mother looked away. "Tell her, Edmond," she commanded, her fork poised over a bite of ham.

Mary looked first at Mother, then Daddy, the old resentments clouding her earlier resolve to start anew. The truth was that nothing had changed here. They weren't compatible and never would be. She could have predicted the way Daddy took a sip of his drink, gazing out the window as if to gather his thoughts.

"We need to talk to you," he said, focusing on Mary. "Get some things straight."

"I'm listening," Mary said, drumming her fingers against the table.

"We love you, and because of that, we want what's best for you." His voice smoothed out, like a race car hitting optimum speed after a jerky start-up. "We want this to be your home, and our home too. For us three to get along."

Tears filled Mary's eyes at the unexpected candor, the smidgen of love in his tone. "Oh, Daddy, I want that too," she said, wringing her hands in her fervor to explain how she felt. "But I don't know if we can. You see, it's—"

"Sure, we can," he assured her, the politician's smile firmly in place.

"But there'll be no more weaving in here in the middle of the night. Do you hear me?" It was classic Mother, her voice crisp, businesslike, devoid of even a tincture of warmth. "No more skipping class. No more sloppy room. And you'll get a job."

In a flash, Mary bristled, then flew out of her seat. "Or what?"

"Or you move out."

Mary bit back a retort. *You're pitching me out too? Lisle does need that homeless shelter, Daddy. For the mayor's daughter.* Though she resented the cold way Mother presented the plan, she'd do things their way for now. Her head bowed, she vowed never to step near the abyss again, clinging to the image of Grandmother's strong old body, her prayers, her words, which echoed in Mary's heart. *What's bred in the bone will out.*

"Do you hear me, Mary Elizabeth? You'll move out."

Mary nodded, desperate to curl up in her own bed and shut out Grandmother and Mother and Michael and Daddy. She mumbled something about jet lag and got up.

"Aren't you going to answer me, Mary Elizabeth?"

For just a moment, Mary leaned against the wall, doing her best to visualize Grandmother. What would she say? What would she do? Finally, she nodded. "I'll check the job board at school. And as for the other things, I'll do the best that I can." It took all the energy she had to get down the hall.

Moonlight illumined the beautiful room that her parents had provided for her when she'd had nowhere else to go. A crystal vase of Stargazers, Mary's favorites, had been set on her bedside table. Their fragrance, lush and sensual, overcame her, as did Mother's simple but symbolic gesture. *So she does know one of my favorites.* She couldn't stem the tears. "Oh, God, help me to love them," she pleaded. "They're all I have." She tried to find the passion that Grandmother infused in her prayers, but it was no use. With the next breath, she started the old prayer about Ireland, but it wilted too.

✟ ✟ ✟

"How's Dr. Sparks?" In the crowded hall of Roosevelt University, Daphne cut an imposing figure, six feet tall, her sinuous body draped in a flowery outfit which was a cross between a sari and a tribal robe. Hoop earrings jangled and dangled, but a frizzy Afro clung to her scalp, refusing to join her body's exuberant dance.

"As goofy as ever. I hope they don't commit him before the orals."

"With your Irish gift of gab, you'll breeze through that stuff."

Somehow, Mary managed to laugh and shake her head at the same time. She could always count on this new friend to revive her, and about now, she needed reviving. After classes, the dinner shift at the diner, and the subway ride home, Mary wanted to throw down her books and forget them. It had been two years since she'd left Ireland, but her Grandmother's declaration, her parents' warning had given her a stiff backbone. And she wasn't quitting now.

"Hey, come on, girl. You want a ride? We'll get some grub before we clock in."

For several months, Mary had waitressed at the diner owned by Daphne's uncle. As she'd promised Mother, she'd followed up on a posting, and after she'd passed Daphne's screening interview, the uncle's had been perfunctory. It was back-breaking work and hard on her pride. She learned to take complaints and insults with pressed lips and a grimace. But she enjoyed comforting customers with food and discovered a different type of pride—satisfaction after work well done. And if she saved enough money, she might be able to implement her latest plan.

"Thanks, but I need the exercise. And I'm not hungry."

"Girl, you crazy. I ain't missin' no free meal."

"Not as crazy as an Irishwoman and a black woman working together."

Daphne doubled over, setting her earrings into a wild spin.

"Plus all that grease . . ."

Daphne's smile faded. "I forget. You're Miss High-Class White Girl whose big daddy's the mayor."

Mary's smile faded too. *Right. We're one big, happy family, speaking an average of once a week, on such deep topics as how to manage the chores.* "You know it's not like that," she protested, touching Daphne's shoulder. "It's just the diet I'm on—"

"A rich girl's fad, for sure."

"I don't have two nickels to rub together, and you know it. But that's the point. I don't think it's right to kill animals just to—" Mary stopped short. Daphne didn't want, didn't need her soapbox speech about healthy food.

"Then you ain't been hungry enough," she snapped but her eyes resumed their exotic dance. "And you need you a little fat, girl. Ain't nothing to love on. That's why you ain't got no boyfriend." She pinched Mary's forearm, the smile back in place.

Mary laughed, but the barb stung. Of course she wanted a relationship, but it was too risky. In a ploy to distract her, she grabbed Daphne's arm and dragged her through a foyer crammed with students. Somehow, they managed to bump and apologize their way to the bulletin board, which was filled with room-to-let posts, for-sale items. "There."

Cordon Bleu Culinary School. If you have a dream of owning your own bakery, working for an executive chef, living in magnificent Paris while you receive the finest hands-on training in the time-honored French tradition . . .

Mary held her breath. Would Daphne be magnetized, like she'd been, by the glowing promises of the glossy brochure?

"Paris? What're you on, girl?"

Mary shrugged. It was farfetched, but the image of that lattice tower had kept her poring over the books for more late nights than she cared to count. That and the words of her grandmother.

The smile, which could be flipped on like a switch, was back. "Go for it, girl." Another list arrested Daphne. She stared and then screeched like a mynah bird. "You made the Dean's List? Since when you been cracking the books?"

She acted embarrassed, but Mary was glad Daphne had noticed. Her parents had been so embroiled in their own conflicts when grades arrived they hadn't said a word.

"Don't get too smart, now." Daphne clucked her tongue, her arms waving all the while. "Guys don't like brainy girls."

"Get outta here!"

Daphne's laugh shook her earrings. "Okay. Sure you don't want a ride?"

"I'm sure."

When the halls cleared a bit, Mary tripped down the steps of the school, then channeled her way into a Michigan Avenue teeming with humanity.

"Watch it." A bald-haired man who looked like Daddy knocked into her with his briefcase. Mary's earlier smile faded. After a tenuous détente, her family had slipped back into Cold War. As she pushed her way south, skyscrapers loomed all about her, silent and judging. She quickened her pace at the realization that she judged too—Daddy for his philandering and greed-oriented politics, Mother for her bitterness and obsessive-compulsiveness and the other things Mary had learned in Psychology 101. The three of them had reverted to living separate lives behind closed doors. Sure, she was getting by thanks to school and her job, but things at home were as bad as ever.

The streets grew shabbier with every step farther from the campus, yet a breeze that found coolness above the mysterious deep of Lake Michigan washed over the city's polluted air. Mary breathed deeply and got a pleasant surprise. The unmistakable aroma of browning flour and baking biscuits told her Brown's Diner was just around the corner.

Banging open the screen door, Mary was greeted by the sizzle of the fry station. Even though it was only four o'clock, patrons, who fanned menus to ward off pesky flies, pattered away their troubles at the dozen tables and short lunch counter. Without looking at the blackboard, Mary could recite the specials, not just because they were always the same, but because of the tantalizing aromas wafting from the kitchen: Catfish. Biscuits. Turnip greens. Yeast rolls.

"Where you been?" Jimmy, Daphne's uncle, burst through swinging doors. A full-length chef's apron covered a body pencil-thin from smoking too many cigarettes and working too much overtime.

Mary stepped away from the smell of grease and ash. "It's early."

With a sweaty hand, Jimmy shoved back a starched and spotless chef's beanie. "Huh-uh, girl. It's late. The cook didn't show, and I ain't got time for this crap."

The idea struck Mary like a sudden shock, and a shiver went through her in spite of the heat. She touched Jimmy's shoulder as he whirled back toward the doors that hid steam and sizzles, boning and pounding, washing and drying. "Let me," she begged.

Jimmy spun like he'd been stabbed. "What you think you gonna do back there?"

"Cook."

Gleaming teeth contrasted with a dark face. "Says who?"

"My grandmother."

"Her and what army?" He bent over close, hands on hips like he was about to dress Mary down, then straightened to beam at two power-broker types who sauntered in.

"Please," she pleaded. "I've been practicing at home."

A fit of laughter threatened to split Jimmy in two, and he didn't stop until the laughs set off a spasm of wheezes and coughs.

Mary stood as still as she could. The whole place hushed as if waiting for Jimmy's decision. Almost against her better judgment, she laid her hand on his shoulder. She was ready; she knew it. But did he?

The laughter returned. Jimmy untied the apron and plopped the chef's hat on her. "Have at it." In an odd barter, he pulled the order pad out of her hand, then flashed the Brown smile that Daphne had been fortunate enough to inherit. "Daphne warned me about you," he muttered before bouncing over to greet the two men.

Mary's heart swelled to match the size of her head, even with the addition of the hat. She plunged through the swinging doors and into the kitchen. With one hand, she yanked a spatula from a tray of cooling yeast rolls; with the other, she grabbed an oven mitt. When she'd clanked a pan of biscuits into the oven, she rubbed grease on the grill, and when it sizzled, she smiled. Things were heating up.

Putting aside for the moment her home troubles, Mary faced each challenge with gusto. A stubborn pilot light. Rancid grease. A sack of rotten potatoes. Time flew as she soaked in a hodgepodge of experiences. The acid smell of vinegar as she poured it over collard greens. The not unpleasant sourness of buttermilk biscuit dough. The ding of the timer, which told her the chicken should be lifted from the deep fat fryer and drained.

"Here."

"Ooh." Mary jumped at the sudden coldness on her neck. "What are you doin'?"

"It's just a piece of ice, silly." Using her apron skirt, Daphne wiped sweat off her brow. "Whew. It's gotta be a hundred and ten in here." She poured Mary a glass of water, then bent over and scrounged through the cooler. "There's no more biscuit batter," she called over her shoulder, "or fish." She slammed the door, then kicked it.

Water trickling down Mary's back did little to combat the heat. "How's the crowd?"

Daphne rolled her eyes. "Prayer meeting must've been canceled, and they all came here. We're scratching the bottom of the barrel."

"Any potatoes in there?"

Daphne opened the door, releasing a cloud of icy air into the room. "Cored and peeled and ready for tomorrow's potato salad."

Mary jerked to attention. "Forget the salad. How about onions? Bacon? Ham?"

Her hand on her hip, Daphne turned and watched Mary with the narrow-eyed, noncommittal gaze of a food inspector. "What you thinking about?" she asked.

"Our customers."

"Well, here, then." Daphne handed Mary salt, garlic powder, and Tabasco. "Put enough of that in, and they won't know the difference."

Mary dumped all the ingredients into the largest bowl she could find, hand tossed the mixture, spooned it onto the grill, and fried it.

Daphne eyed the concoction like it was scrambled calves' brains. "What's that?"

"Coddle."

"Huh-huh," Daphne said, her earrings swinging wildly. "They ain't gonna eat something in all those little pieces."

"It's either that or tell them we're out of food."

And so it was settled. Daphne ferried plates in and out. Mary was so busy frying, she didn't have time to ask how it was going. Around seven, she added eggs to the mix. At eight, she rummaged through the icebox, found leftover chipped beef and onions, and dumped it in. At eight thirty, she leaned, dizzy but giddy, against the cooler.

Daphne slumped in, the doors swatting her bottom. "Last customer just paid. Bet you a dime he don't leave a nickel, and I refilled that sweet tea glass at least six times."

"Speaking of tea . . ."

In spite of her harrumphs, Daphne packed crushed ice into one of the few clean tumblers and poured tea over the ice until it crackled and popped. She offered it to Mary.

With a couple of swigs, Mary downed the whole glass. Side by side, the two of them scraped dirty plates and dumped grease traps and filtered and shut off the fryers. Finally it was done. They piled two plates high with leftovers, hobbled into the eating area, and collapsed. For quite a spell, they didn't speak, just huddled over their plates and let Jimmy refill their glasses. Before Mary knew what hit her, she'd eaten two heaps of cobble and a piece of sweet potato pie.

Daphne pushed her plate away. "Good stuff," she said, licking her fingers.

"The cobble or the pie?"

"Actually, both."

Both women leaned back, then propped their feet on a chair. "What'd you think?" Daphne asked her uncle, who was sweeping the last bit of trash into a dustpan.

Jimmy shook his head so hard, his neck popped. "Wouldn't touch that stuff with a ten-foot pole," he said, smiling, "but they sure did."

Daphne slapped the table, and Mary joined in the fun, yet the hour was closing in on her. Though she longed to stay in this cozy place where she was wanted, needed, she had studying to do.

"Girl, you're some kind of something." They raised their glasses, then clinked them together, a diner-style toast.

"Does that mean you think I can do it?" Mary asked, when the laughter died down.

Daphne propped her elbows on the table. "Do what?"

"Cook."

"Why you want to be a chef?"

"I'm not sure I do, but something . . . own my own restaurant, maybe."

"What happened to Paris?"

Mary giggled. "We'll always have it. And with my bank account, I'd better start thinking a little closer to home."

Daphne threw back her head and howled. "Chicago will do?"

When they both quit laughing, Mary continued. "Yeah. Maybe . . . oh, I don't know. A little café."

"Ooh, girl." The earrings went wild, and so did Daphne, bouncing up and down.

It was just enough encouragement for Mary to open up that other dream she'd locked away. "Maybe a health food store," she added. "But what about you?"

Daphne didn't hesitate for even a second. "An actress."

"Hollywood and all that?"

"Maybe someday." She wiped condensation from the glasses off the table. "Right now, I'd settle for a part in community theater."

"I can say we flipped hash back when." Smiling, Mary lifted her empty glass.

"You mean coddle."

✢ ✢ ✢

She'd bounded in after midnight. The dishwasher had broken; they'd had to scrub everything by hand. She was cranky and desperate for a few hours of sleep before tomorrow's finals. She opened her door. There was Daddy, perched in her chair, the *Treasures of Ireland* in his lap.

"It's a little early for you, isn't it?" As soon as she said it, Mary bit her lip. The more time she spent with Daphne's family, the more she resented the dysfunction in her own household. Yet was that reason to attack Daddy when he did come home?

Daddy handed her the book as if he hadn't heard a word. There were puffy lines under his eyes. "Remember when you used to sit in my lap? This was one of your favorites."

Did she remember? She knelt by him, longing to feel his arms around her again.

The book slid to the floor. "Lizzie, whatever happened over there?" he asked, his voice husky. "You never told us."

"You never asked," she spat back, then crumpled to her knees. She wanted to trust him, needed to trust him . . .

Daddy gripped Mary's hands so tightly she squirmed. Yet he continued the pressure, both with his hands and with his gaze. "Tell me now," he commanded.

Her head bowed to her chin, curls blocking a view of his face. "They didn't want me," she whispered.

For a big man, he moved quickly. Somehow, they both ended up sitting on the floor. She snuggled into the safety of her daddy's arms and burst into tears.

"It's all right, Lizzie," he kept saying as he stroked her hair.

The pain of several years gushed out in wild ramblings about where she'd been, what she'd done. Daddy didn't say a word, didn't even raise an eyebrow. He just consoled her the way he'd done when she was a little girl.

"I just don't know what to do," Mary said, when the emotion was spent and she only had the energy to lean against his shirt. "It all seems meaningless when I turn on the news and hear of more GIs coming back from Vietnam in body bags."

"I felt like that once," Daddy said, his breath tickling Mary's cheek.

"When?"

"When I came back from the war."

"Tell me about it," she whispered.

His eyes got misty and seemed to take him far away. "We were on a beach in France, digging into sand like crabs. There was a flash of light. A hellish thunder. A rain of steel. Sand and salt pummeling my skin. Soldiers flailing shredded arms, running on bloody stumps toward the dunes." He didn't change expression but continued in a low monotone. "A hole where a face used to be. Brains lying on the beach like jellyfish."

Tears burned Mary's eyes. "It must've been awful," she whispered.

"No."

She jerked up from the comfortable nest of his arms. "What?"

"World War II was the best time of my life."

"You can't mean that."

"I'm sorry, but it's the truth. It was when I came back that I was lost."

"How can you support that kind of thing?" She sprayed saliva onto Daddy's cheek. "It's what's tearing up the country."

"Our generation knew what was worth fighting for."

"It's because of your generation that we're in this mess."

For a moment, they glared at each other. Then something broke in Daddy's face.

Mary folded her legs underneath her. "Daddy, I'm sorry," she said carefully, "but we're like three people living separate lives here. Neither you nor Mother has a clue about what I'm feeling. About my life. About our family. About the war."

"Don't you see? It was the same for me." Words came out carefully, as if measured with a metronome. "Friends strafed in two by machine guns. A beach littered with bloody pulps." He shuddered, his face pale. "Scooping pieces of friends into body bags. Then I came home to another kind of war. One inside me." His voice broke, but he kept on. "How could I explain that I missed it so? That it was the one time I felt alive?"

A wave of nausea gripped Mary. "How could you miss it?"

"I don't know. Oh, Lizzie, not the killing. Not that. Just being alive. Believing in something. We were saving the world. We cared about something bigger than ourselves."

They held each other, letting silence smooth the gap between them. Mary wasn't sure, but she thought she understood what he was trying to say. "Daddy?"

"Yes."

"I'm sorry."

"Me too, honey. If I could do it over . . . if there's anything . . ."

His eyes reflected the glint from the moon, which poured light into the dim room.

Mary brightened. "There might be something."

"What?"

"I want to open a store."

"Mary . . ."

"I know I'm clueless about business. But I'm a hard worker."

"Yes, but . . ."

"If you'll just hear me out." She leapt to her feet, her fist banging on the desk as if it were a podium. "I want to help people eat better. Teach them about organic produce. Maybe have a juice bar, a reading area . . ."

Daddy stood, his arms folded across his chest. "I think it's a great idea." The stern face broke into laughter.

Mary's mouth flew open, and she rushed into his hug. "You do?"

"We're realtors, Mary. At least I can help you get started."

"You rascal, you," she cried. "When I saw the look on your face . . ." She gave him another hug. "Oh, Daddy. I don't know what to say."

"So you'll withdraw from school."

"At the end of the semester." Her breath escaped in a slow sigh. "You don't care?"

"I never wanted you to be a theater nut." He collapsed in a fit of laughter.

"What's this about a theater nut?" Mother appeared at the door, her face gaunt without the makeup she applied with an increasingly heavy hand.

Whatever spark had been ignited in Daddy went out. His face averted, he nodded at Mary, then left.

Why had she butted in? Mary wanted to lash out at Mother for interrupting, but one look at Mother's eyes checked even the slightest twinge of resentment. "I'll tell you tomorrow, Mother." Mary kissed Mother's dry, cold forehead. "Sleep well."

"Daddy, I think this is it." The month had zipped by in a blur of phone calls, appointments with realtors, and scans of the classifieds. Mary stretched the telephone cord across the kitchen so she could sit at the kitchen table. "It's downtown. At Diversey and Clark."

"What size is it?"

"Pretty small, but doable." She didn't want to tell him it was twenty feet wide.

"I'll swing by. Give me an hour to get rid of the new councilwoman."

Mary's laugh faded, and she was tempted to slam down the phone. Why had she shared this with a philandering, scheming politician? With effort, she forced herself to focus on her dream; anyway, it was too late to back out now.

✤ ✤ ✤

A pudgy man, his hair slicked back with lots of pomade, hopped back and forth in front of a tiny brick storefront with a big picture window.

Daddy put his arm around Mary. "Good afternoon. I assume you're Mr. Heinz."

"Mr. Harris? This must be your daughter. Lovely."

Daddy snorted. "Thanks for meeting us on short notice."

Mr. Heinz pulled a ring of keys from his pocket. "After you."

They stepped into a dank room, cluttered with boxes and dented shopping carts.

"Who leased it last?" Daddy asked.

Mr. Heinz shrugged. "Some Ukrainian immigrant's American dream. But those mom and pop groceries can't compete with the chains."

"Hmm." Daddy tapped his foot against a loose baseboard.

Mary ignored him, flying to the window. "Look! It's a great spot for my herbs."

"It looks like a giant soda straw," Daddy countered.

"It's intimate."

"You'll need to put up one-way signs down this aisle."

Mary shrugged her shoulders. "The reading area's out."

Daddy stepped toward the door. "Look around. I'll scout out the neighborhood."

Already pretending, Mary stood at the counter. Her clients could share struggles over a smoothie. Celebrate with steaming bowls of soup. She could make a difference. She'd offer good food and a sympathetic ear. A family atmosphere, like the diner.

Within minutes, Daddy and Mr. Heinz were sitting about a rickety card table near the register, their heads nearly meeting.

Mary could only overhear snatches of the talk. She held her breath and waited.

Finally Mr. Heinz pulled out a manila folder and pushed it across the table.

Daddy pulled out reading glasses, then motioned for Mary to join them. "What do you think?" he asked, his face, a mask.

She gasped. The monthly rent was several hundred less than they'd anticipated.

They shook hands. "It's a deal."

✝ ✝ ✝

Sally scurried to the kitchen for another Diet Coke, not even bothering to ask Mary if she wanted anything. Her pulse quickened, and not just from the short sprint. That Michael sure sounded like a hunk, but something about him just hadn't been right. Could a man be too impetuous? Too romantic? She thought so.

She eyed the cookie jar and for once resisted. That diner story had sure set her on edge. Down South, a white person wouldn't set foot in a black person's restaurant, much less work there. Anyway, those not-so-subtle signs about reserving the right to refuse service had kept all but the boldest blacks out of their restaurants. Before she could stop it, her hand reached in and grabbed a cookie. Her family wasn't prejudiced at all, but still, it was better to keep some things separate. Sally sighed, the cookie chewed and swallowed. If only she had Mary's good eating habits. She trotted back to the couch. "So what happened with Daddy and the store?"

Mary shook her head.

Sally didn't try to contain her outrage. "What? He reneged on the lease?"

"Of course not. He'd never do that. He was a businessman."

"Another secretary?"

"It was much worse than that. I see now how God prepared me for it. But first, let me tell you about The Health Food Shoppe. And Paul."

CHAPTER 19

Here still is the smile, that no cloud can o'ercast,
And a heart and a hand all thy own to the last.
—Thomas Moore, "Come, Rest in This Bosom"

Mary, professional-looking in the monogrammed apron Daphne had given her, had chopped and baked for hours yet felt as vibrant as she had opening day of The Health Food Shoppe, nearly a year ago. Perched on a stool at the juice bar, her mouth watered as she flipped through a cookbook. Irish stew, lentil curry—there. Smoothing down the spice-stained page of the ratatouille recipe, she checked the list of ingredients. When she'd served it last week, her customers had drawn back like it had fish eyes in it, but after one taste, they'd scraped their plates clean. The homeless people, whom Mary had taken to feeding and letting sleep in the dock area, loved it. And Mary loved them.

A key turned in the lock. Heels clicked against the floor. "Yoo-hoo?"

"Good morning, Mrs. Appleby," Mary called out.

Impeccable in a linen coverlet, silk stockings, and designer pumps, Mrs. Appleby hurried to the register like she was opening a bank vault. "Mary, dear. How are you?"

"Just perfect. Except you were right about the gumbo."

Mrs. Appleby nodded. "You just can't make a good roux without Crisco." The first week of operation, Mrs. Appleby, her first customer and a retired home-economics teacher, had begged Mary to hire her. Her only caveat was that she'd come in late on Friday, when she volunteered at Charity Hospital.

Mary began making smoothies. Mrs. Appleby stocked the shelves.

"Ahem. Mary?" Mrs. Appleby waved. "Mary?"

Mary switched off the motor. "Sorry." Sometimes she had three professional-size blenders whirring at the same time, liquefying oranges, mangoes, pineapples, carrots, and whatever else she tossed in. There was so much horsepower in the machines that her body shook in sync with their nutritional hummings.

"We need to stock more vitamins. They're the moneymaker." Mrs. Appleby stooped to stack organic soup cans on the shelf, then straightened and headed to the cash register. "And how's that smoothie?"

Mary's face puckered after a taste. "Too sour." She dripped honey into the mixture. "My folks can't afford fancy pills. Besides, they need living foods." She ran the blender for a few more seconds.

"Why, just yesterday, that businessman was asking about vitamin C when one of your homeless folks scared him off." Mrs. Appleby tsked and tapped her expensive shoe. "He was the first employed person you'd had in here all day."

"Ugh." Mary dumped the contents of the blender into the sink after a second taste. "But the unemployed ones are the ones who really need us. You know that as well as I do."

Mrs. Appleby's diamond-studded ears sparkled in the morning sun. "Well, yes, dear," she began, "but if you don't turn a profit, you can't keep the doors open." Emphasizing her analysis, she dinged the cash register bell three times.

Her lips still puckered, Mary erased cranberry smoothie from the specials board. "All I know to do is feed them and let the other stuff work itself out."

It was hard to read the look in Mrs. Appleby's eyes. "Ah, well, I'll handle the money part. You're a natural at the rest of it. They adore you."

Heat rose to Mary's face. Mrs. Appleby treated her like . . . a daughter. And it was attention desperately needed, Mother caring not a whit about her shop, refusing to be seen in "that kind of place." She rinsed out the blender. Because of the demands of the store, she was spending more time than ever away from Lisle, and she didn't regret it at all.

The bells Mary had tied around the doorknob jingled as several customers came in. A beanpole-thin man clad in toga and sock hat scuffed to the counter. The flush across his nose and cheeks, his fidgety behavior made Mary recall her own flirtation with addiction. She tried to ignore his stench and focus on his eyes. Beautiful eyes, they were, colored with experiences and situations only God would understand. "Welcome to The Health Food Shoppe," she said, smiling. "What can I get you?"

"Stew, please." He mumbled something else Mary couldn't understand.

She ladled a steaming bowl of stew and set it down. "It's my grand-mother's recipe. Hope you like it." She handed him a spoon. "Do you live around here?"

He never looked up from his food, but when he jerked his head, using it for a pointer, soup dribbled down his chin. "That's my Dumpster out there."

"Here." She stuck several rolls and a few bananas in a bag. "Take these."

His grin, toothless as a baby's, warmed her like the simmering soup. Then he extended a filthy hand. "Ellis Dee's my name."

Before Mary could answer, a young man laid a Bible on the counter and sat down. "How many vegetables for a dime?" Clear eyes seemed to be digging deep into her.

"A lot. You want bread?"

When he nodded, Mary set two slices of bread on a plate heaped with as much eggplant curry as it could hold. By the time she set it in front of him, he'd buried himself in the pages of his book. With his trim beard, well-pressed shirt and slacks, he looked like a clean-cut version of the street evangelists that gathered at Michigan and Erie.

"Are you a preacher?"

"A seminary student."

Mary rolled her eyes. Of course. That Bible institute. What was it, Moody? She'd heard they were nothing but fanatics. Yet it was hard to ignore his shining face, hard not to ask what he found so intriguing on the onionskin pages he flipped through.

Again the bells jingled, customers parading in like colorful floats. And if Mary had her way, they'd soon be members of her growing family.

"Hello, doll." A short man with stubby legs strode to the bar. His overcoat was buttoned to his jaw line, his collar turned up to hide his thick neck. A gray fedora dipped down to conceal his left eye. He clenched a torpedo-shaped cigar in his right hand.

Mary tried not to laugh. "What can I get for you?"

He straddled a stool like he was mounting his steed. "Naw, sweet-ums, it's what can I do for you." His head dipped and he talked out of the corner of his mouth. "Undercover, you know." He spun the stool at the same frenetic pace that he spun a tale of his career as one of Chicago's finest. Saving citizens from the mob. Busting a burglary ring single-handedly. "Listen, angel face, it's a jungle out there."

"What did you say your name was?"

"Gio." He leaned close enough for Mary to smell tobacco and Brylcreem. "It's short for Giodarno. And I can help you," he continued.

Mary kept her tone light. "Then start by putting that out."

He spit on the glowing end of his cigar, pinched the still-smoldering ash between his fingers, and stuck it in his coat pocket. "What next?"

Mary glanced at his waistband. Sure enough, he carried a handgun. "We'll see." She patted his threadbare jacket sleeve, thrilled to have another regular firmly in place.

☙ ☙ ☙

"*Green grow the rushes, oh.*" Mary stood at the sink in the storeroom, hoping that if she scrubbed the scorched pot long enough, she'd get rid of the stains . . . and the memory of last night's argument about cleaning, no less. Nothing she did ever pleased Mother, no matter how hard she tried. Thanks to a Brillo pad and her fingernails, the pot began to shine, but her relationship with Mother was as dull as ever.

"*One is one and all alone and evermore shall be so. Green grow the—*"

The door that accessed the alley creaked open. Ellis slipped in, his hair a matted jumble, his eyes wild. "They're after me!" Screaming, he rushed at Mary.

The pot crashed onto the floor, soapy water splashing everywhere.

He slid and slipped, then managed to grab hold of her sleeve. When he fell, she fell. "Don't let them get me." His eyes, unblinking, scanned the room with lightning speed, apparently searching for his tormentors.

"Don't move." The voice came from behind. "Slowly, now. Get up!" The Italian accent told Mary it was Gio. The click told her he had his gun.

"I'll kill them! I swear it." Ellis tightened his grip with each manic raving. "Stop them!" He pulled Mary closer, into a stench of garbage and sweat and booze.

"It's okay." Even though Ellis probably thought she was speaking to him, Mary was really speaking to Gio. And his trigger finger. Her heart pounded a desperate prayer not just for herself, but also for the tormented man who had her in a headlock.

Neither man said a word.

"Ellis?" Mary tried to turn her head, but he'd pinned it against her chest. "Ellis?"

"Shh, Mary! I can't hear them."

Ellis's ravings, his viselike grip, made Mary wince, but she had to ignore it. "Listen," she said, loud enough so Gio could hear. "This guy's an agent. On our side."

Ellis went rigid.

"Ellis? Ellis!"

Still no answer.

"If you heard me, tap twice. On my back." Again, she made sure to speak loudly.

He complied.

"Now, if you'll let me up, I'll go fix us a nice bowl of stew. You like my stew, don't you, Ellis? Grandmother's stew? Remember? All those nice potatoes, those nice . . ."

The grip loosened; Mary could breathe without it hurting. "Gio?" Her voice still shook. "Call Mercy, okay? Our contact on the third floor?" She tried to whisper but fear added volume to her words.

Ellis whirled, his face a question mark.

"You know the one," Mary cooed, as she led Ellis to the bar, then hurried back to a stunned-looking Gio.

"Our contact on the third floor?" Gio's hand still hovered about the bulge in his coat.

"The psych ward, Gio." Mary somehow managed a smile. "Don't you have any contacts there?"

♰ ♰ ♰

Since the incident with Ellis, Mr. Giordano became The Health Food Shoppe's unofficial security officer. Every morning before opening, Mary blended carrot, pineapple, and chlorophyll juices with vanilla yogurt into the smoothie she'd named in Gio's honor, "The Private Eyes Have It." They discussed anything and everything. Gio won the argument about the gun; Mary won the argument about the shelter out back.

One morning, Mrs. Appleby hurried in, her face flushed, her hair wind-blown. "You won't believe what happened."

Gio yawned. "Something, I hope. It's dead as a doornail." Hitching up his pants, he climbed off the stool, then took a deep bow. "How can I help, sweetums?"

"Find the bum who stole my car."

He pulled a pad from his pocket. "Make?"

"Volvo."

"Model?"

"Oh, what's the—"

"Details, sweetums. That's how we'll catch them."

Mary couldn't keep a straight face. "Get a badge. You'll look more official."

Gio drew up to his full height of five foot five and saluted. "I'd thought of that," he said before he banged out the door, setting the bells to jingling.

A sudden storm of customers dominated the morning. They operated like a surrogate family, looking through catalogues, pointing out products. Spare moments had Mary chopping and cooking, Mrs. Appleby doing the books and stocking the shelves. And Mary thrived on the busyness. While filling people's stomachs and listening to their woes, she didn't have time to think of the dysfunction in her real family.

When business slowed for the first time all day, Mary checked her watch. With the late start, she still had vegetables to scrub, fruit to slice. She pulled produce from the cooler, tempted to shuttle the whole mess straight to the Dumpster, especially the strawberries, blanketed with mold. "What are we going to do about this?" she wailed.

From her perch at the register, Mrs. Appleby looked down bifocals at Mary. "Not fit for hog slop," she agreed. Still sniffing, she pulled a thin book from her bag. "Here." She jotted down a number. "I have just the person for you. Paul at Strube's Vegetables."

Mary was hanging up the phone when Mr. Giordano burst into the store, his eyes sparkling like an elf with Christmas surprises. He tossed Mrs. Appleby her keys.

Mrs. Appleby lost her composure. "Where was it? How'd you do it? I haven't even had time to call the police yet." She hopped about until a heel snapped off one of her designer pumps.

Mary threw her hands up and laughed, but Mr. Giordano narrowed his eyes and spoke in a gravelly voice. "Contacts, sweetums. You gotta have contacts."

"Then take care of my speeding ticket," Mary begged.

He dipped his fedora and squinted. "You gotta make me an offer I can't refuse."

✠ ✠ ✠

An intense-looking young man, dark, shaggy hair touching his collar, rolled a dolly into the store. "I'm with Strube's. Where do you want these?" He pulled an order slip out of a faded jeans pocket and laid it on the bar.

"Right there is fine."

Mrs. Appleby fluttered toward the man, apparently checking the order.

Mary ripped open the top crate, then gasped. As a Midwesterner, she was used to bruised apples, puckered oranges, but this man had delivered rosy mangoes, plump strawberries. On time. She rubbed her hands together. This could be the start of a good thing. "So you deliver every Tuesday, uh . . ." She searched for a name on the slip of paper.

"Oh, dear; what's come over me?" Mrs. Appleby motioned for the man to sit on a stool. "Paul Freeman, meet Mary Elizabeth Harris."

Mary darted a glance at first Mrs. Appleby, then Paul. "Hello," she managed, wondering what exactly was going on. This wasn't tea time. They had work to do.

"Paul's quite multifaceted. He loves to garden—he even has his own land, don't you? And he loves to read—kind of like you, Mary Elizabeth."

Mary turned away from them. So she'd been right about the matchmaking, and it miffed her, because she'd made it clear to both Mrs. Appleby and Gio that she wasn't interested. She hadn't gone out since Daphne had arranged a disastrous blind date.

Paul leaned across the bar, close enough so she smelled loam and lime and lemon. "What genre do you like?"

"What?"

Dark eyes pierced into her like he wanted to know all her secrets. "Books? What type?" A hint of a smile played with his lips. "Let me help you. Mysteries, romance—"

"I don't have time to read." He was all angles and hardness, a little too intense for her tastes, so she stepped away.

He shrugged his shoulders, did an about face, then hefted a carton onto his shoulders like it was weightless. "Here. I'll unload it for you."

While he stuffed produce into the cooler, Mary noted powerful shoulders—a swimmer? A lean torso—a runner? She felt a tug at her heart, then pulled out a cutting board and sharpened a paring knife. Huh-uh. Her life was full enough with work.

Mrs. Appleby hustled to the register yet kept glancing back at them.

Mary kept chopping. And listening for his footsteps.

"Hey, Betsy." From the sound of his voice, he was near the oven. "Maybe we could take in a movie or something."

It was hard to keep from gasping at his brazenness. "I've got paperwork piled to the ceiling," she said, not even turning around, "and it's Mary Elizabeth."

He stepped to the bar, picked up the receipt, and handed it to her. Their eyes met. "You look like a Betsy."

Mary grabbed an onion and plunked it onto the board. How dare he presume to ask her out? She'd hired him, hadn't she? And what did he mean by calling her Betsy? The only Betsy she could think of was Betsy Ross, loyal, hardworking . . . She snorted. And how would he know about that? She opened her mouth, prepared to make some sharp reply, but it was too late. Paul and his clunky cart had rolled out of the store.

"See you next week," Mrs. Appleby called after him.

Before he'd pulled out of the loading zone, Mrs. Appleby and her high heels clicked to the bar. "Why were you so rude? You don't know what's good for you."

"And you do?" Mary's voice rose to a screech, then sank like the thud in her heart. "I'm sorry. I know you're just trying to help. But me and relationships . . ." Mary handed her the produce receipt. "I just can't risk it. I'm not ready."

The heel-tapping intensified. "He's a nice young man. Hardworking. Honest."

The handle of the knife thudded against the cutting board. *That explains their hush-hush talk.* "H-mm. And how is it you know all that?"

"I've known his family for years."

"So this was a setup?"

"The Freemans are good people." Mrs. Appleby pulled out a compact and dabbed on powder. "And I want you to be happy."

"I am." Mary banged the blender into the cooler and strode into the back room.

☦ ☦ ☦

Sally nodded. "I think I'm gonna like this guy. Of course I know I will, having already met him."

Mary just smiled.

CHAPTER 20

Step we gaily, on we go, heel for heel and toe for toe.
Arm and arm and on we go, all for Mairi's wedding.
—"Mairi's Wedding," traditional Irish folk song

Lock up, doll." The fedora went on, and a muffler. "None of those back-door dinners for your guys. With this weather, they should be in their holes, anyway." With a tip of his hat, a move that sent a whiff of stale tobacco Mary's way, Gio was gone.

For months, Mary had used the back room as a residence, to avoid both her parents and the Chicago traffic. And now that winter winds were dumping snow and stalling traffic, she'd be sleeping here more often.

To keep her mind off the creaks and moans of the old building, she grabbed Daphne's copy of *Love Story* and curled onto a collapsible army cot, Gio's contribution to her back room. According to Gio, the CIA had used it in Central America, and while she'd laughed when he had told her that, tonight, the idea set her on edge. She tried to shove away a caged-in feeling, which crept in despite the pains she'd taken to make this place a home. Last week, she and Gio had painted the wall a lush rose. Mrs. Appleby had contributed a Klimt poster, which Mary tacked over the worst water stain. When Ellis threw in a pair of sconces he'd fished out of a Dumpster, Mary's nest had all the trappings of a Gold Coast loft apartment, at a fraction of the cost.

Something crashed against glass. Mary threw down the book she'd been pretending to read, flew to the front room, and flipped on the lights. The wind had bounced a trash can lid off her window, then sent it tumbling down the street.

She felt queasy and hungry at the same time, picked up the phone to call Gio, then set it down. Pacing the narrow aisles, she reviewed details like she always did when nervous. *Vitamins, well-stocked. Low on sauerkraut.* A siren—two of them—competed with the ruckus of the wind and set her teeth on edge. For the first time since she'd had the shop, she wanted a drink. Or something stronger.

As the chill from the storm began to permeate the walls of her store, she grabbed her mouton coat, thankful for the thick fur, and her purse. Ratso's, a couple of blocks away, specialized in mounds of brown rice and undercooked vegetables heaped onto army surplus plates. The last she'd checked, they stayed open until midnight.

She stepped into a snowy maelstrom that obscured all but the barest outline of the grand Chicago skyline. Wind roared down the asphalt swath as glass and steel watched helplessly and then creaked a response. One measured step at a time, like walking on a frozen pond, she negotiated the trip. When a gust knocked her off balance, she clutched at her coat and strode on.

When she shoved the door open, the wind whooshed in with her. A gloved hand flew to her mouth. There was Paul, perched on a lunch counter stool.

"Hello," she said, her heart pounding. How long had he been making his weekly visits, punctual as the tides? Four months? Five? Since she'd ignored his overture that first day, they'd barely spoken. Now she studied him anew.

Immediately, she knew what was different—he'd grown a beard, thick and bushy, heightening his aura of intrigue and mystery.

"Hello yourself." The eyes still pierced her, like they had that first day.

With barely a second glance at her, he turned back to the heaping plate of food like it was his lover and leaned over to capture every grain of rice.

Mary stepped back. How could he look so good with such a big mouthful of food? "Looks good," she continued, grinning at her little inside joke. Would he offer her a seat? She shook snow off her coat, then stepped closer. "This weather's piqued my appetite."

He didn't say a word.

Mary followed his rhythmic loading and unloading like a spectator at a tennis match. *There's something else . . . What is it?* The answer almost knocked her down like the wind had. He hadn't changed; she had. Before, she'd ignored him because somehow she'd sensed that this relationship could be different. Not just a relationship based on physical attraction, but mental. And perhaps spiritual. Her heart unfolded like a rosebud, and she leaned still closer. "You having the special?"

He continued the love affair with his food.

Mary managed to heft herself onto a stool. "Aren't you going to say anything?"

"You look like a giant carrot cake. What is that thing, anyway?"

She bristled. "It's a mouton," she sniffed. "Of course you wouldn't know about that."

He kept chewing.

"Greta Garbo wore one," she added, wanting to keep this going.

"Was that in *How Not to Dress*? Or was it *Anna Karenina*? I'd guess the latter, with the Russian themes of natural isolation. Their climate and all."

Mary's mouth flew open. "You've seen that? Then why didn't you . . ."

He swiveled his stool around and wiped a snowflake off the tip of her nose.

Just inches away, a pair of smoldering coals enflamed Mary in a way she'd never imagined. Suddenly, the room seemed suffocatingly hot, and if she hadn't been frozen to her seat, she would have pulled off her coat.

"You don't know much about me, but you're about to find out." He set down his fork, the love affair with his food over.

Hours later, they closed down Ratso's. The manager had to push them out the door.

✠ ✠ ✠

As a blast of north wind carried off their last customer of the day, Mary went to hang the "Closed" sign on the door. Then she returned to the cold reality of the ledger, which lay open on the bar. "It's there in black and white," her only paid worker had told her. "You can't keep giving away food." But the figures were just a jumble to her; after a few minutes, she slammed the book shut.

Paul, who'd come in after his last run, scraped out a last bite of chowder as if nothing was going on. She imagined by now he was used to what Gio called "Irish flares." For two months, she'd cooked, and they'd gotten closer; and he'd eaten, and they'd gotten closer; and he'd delivered produce, and she'd run the store, and they'd gotten closer. When she was with him, she was usually happy. When she wasn't, doubt visited. Sometimes Mary thought doubt was good and kept them from getting too close. But sometimes, like now, she wanted them to be close.

Finally, Paul seemed to notice her frustration. "Let me take a look."

"No." Mary slapped her palm down. How could she expose her financial ineptitude? That would be like opening her underwear drawer to a stranger.

Paul jumped off his stool, walked with measured strides to the coatrack, and grabbed his jacket. "Where's that crate you wanted me to pitch?" he asked, his voice as cold as the climate. "After all, I am the vegetable man."

"I didn't mean it like that."

"Then how did you mean it?" When she didn't answer, he continued. "Do you think I would cheat you?" When she still didn't answer, he glared at her. "I need to know."

Rooted to the spot, she clamped her mouth shut. Why couldn't they leave things alone for now? Everything was fine. What would happen when he found out about the dysfunction in her families? She'd met the Freemans, and they were thicker than chowder. What would he think when he entered the coldness of her parents' home?

The yawning silence engulfed the whole room.

"Okay." He pulled out his keys. "Have it your way."

About the time he passed the organic cake mixes, Mary, ledger in hand, ran from behind the bar, the sight of his back necessitating action. She caught up with him at the bulk foods. "So that's it? You're just going to walk out?"

When he did an about-face, it was in such a slow, unemotional manner that her blood boiled and she struggled to clamp down the tempest within.

"What do you want me to do?" he asked.

Mary blinked. Dare she tell him the truth? *Love me. Don't change or start drinking or abuse me or give me up or cheat on me or . . .* She stepped back. "Help me figure out how to keep this place open." She tried to keep her voice light, but when she handed him the ledger, her hands shook.

The room seemed to whirl, the predominant colors, black and blue and flesh.

"I don't think that's what you want." He grabbed her and yanked her toward him, papers slipping onto the floor with a sigh. He stroked her hair and kissed her as he never had. She couldn't catch her breath between kissing him and trying to control the whimper that slipped out every so often. He couldn't love her like this, could he? She kissed him again. *Could* he?

"It's okay, Betsy." He kissed her again.

Her wrists, her neck, virtually every pulse point throbbed. She wanted him to take her to the back room, but they'd talked about that. And decided it wasn't an option.

He kissed her a third time, then moved away a bit. "It's time for you to trust me. For me to meet them. For us to make plans."

"I do trust you. See?" She pointed to the pages strewn all over the floor.

"Is that what you want? An accountant?"

She shook her head. Of course, she didn't want that; couldn't he see it in her eyes? She wanted to be with him, for him to never leave. She looked into black onyx, and along with the fire, she saw rock-hard constancy. Something she needed.

Something Michael hadn't had. She tried to smile, but her lips failed her. "No. I want you to be . . . I trust you, Paul. Can we leave it there right now?"

He didn't smile that often, but he smiled at her then, and passion sliced through her that even Mrs. Appleby with all her intuition could not have predicted.

He took off his jacket and slid back onto the stool. So graceful yet powerful. She wanted him. The physical and mental and all of it. "Okay," he said in a businesslike way. "But I still want to meet them."

She wiped her mouth on her sleeve and stepped back behind the bar. It had been close, so close, a near mid-air collision. But she was safe. For now.

"Fine," she said. "But they're nothing like your family. We're not even talking."

"Then you need to start." Before she could respond, he slid the ledger toward her. "The rent hike's a problem. If it goes through, I don't know how you'll manage."

She threw up her hands. "Gio works for free, and Mrs. Appleby won't take more than minimum wage."

He chuckled. "You don't know who she is, Betsy, do you? Her father was Lloyd Appleby, the stockyard baron."

"No wonder she doesn't eat meat." Mary laughed, but her mind was on something else. "Paul?" Her voice became soft.

He seemed preoccupied with the numbers. "Huh?"

"Why do you call me Betsy?"

He grimaced.

She leaned closer to him, drawn by the musk and lime. "Tell me. I want to know."

Paul fidgeted first with the pocket of his shirt, then with his collar. About the time he blushed, Mary felt herself fidgeting too. Was there a rival for his affections?

"When I was in third grade, there was this girl."

"Betsy?"

He nodded. "I called her brother some name; she punched me so hard I felt my jaw snap. She was no bigger than a pencil, all sinew and scabbed kneecaps and braids."

"So you fell in love with her?"

He growled and grizzled his eyebrows, like a bear. "I was all of eight. The next day, she brought me a bouquet of goldenrod."

When the giggle started, deep in Mary, she couldn't stop. "Paul, really."

He clamped his hand over hers, and she gasped that his one hand could pin her to the bar. She didn't dare look in his face for fear of the passion she might detect.

"I've been looking for a Betsy ever since. Someone that plunges into a sweet-smelling bouquet, ends up with pollen for face powder, and doesn't care. Someone who empties petty cash out for the homeless. Someone who can dress up and dress down."

She wriggled, but he clamped harder, and with his other hand traced her lips.

"Someone who loves to read and loves to cook."

Now she did look in his eyes, and what she saw melted a dark pit in her, a place no one had ever touched.

He kissed her forehead. "Mrs. Appleby has kept me well informed about you."

Tears rolled down her face, but his expression didn't change. In fact, the more she looked at him, it seemed he was discussing the weather.

"That's why I called you Betsy. Any other questions?"

Her body went limp. For two months, he'd only hinted at wells of passion. Now that they had surfaced, it overwhelmed her.

He glanced at his watch. "Gotta go. Deliveries." He blew her a kiss, the drama of minutes ago checked like a gentleman's hat. He was out the door when she remembered he'd called her Betsy that first time they'd met, and her shriek rattled the front door.

✝ ✝ ✝

Later, when Mary collapsed on her cot, her mind, her heart roared like the Irish sea. She thought she loved him, but other relationships had never lasted, so why should this one? And she hadn't really known him that long, even though her heart told her she'd known him a lifetime.

She stared at watermarks on the ceiling. Mrs. Appleby told her to watch a man at work to know who he is. She'd done that, and she liked what she'd seen. Peaceful. Thoughtful. A man of integrity. Things had been so smooth, so safe since they'd met. But it wouldn't last. Look how good Daddy had been. Or take Grandmother. She'd grasped happiness in Ireland, yet it slipped out when her own flesh and blood insisted she leave.

With a thud, she rolled over, facing the brick wall. She'd never known such a life existed, full of glimmering kindnesses, glittering hope. Yet what would happen when storms returned, as they always did in her life? Paul had been wonderful, but it was only a matter of time. She scraped her finger along the *grout between the bricks. That was it. Get close but don't let the unexpected pretty things—the sand dollar, the starfish on the beach—trick you into thinking it'll last. He'll wash away with the first big wave.*

☦ ☦ ☦

Mary heard boots clomping down the middle aisle, and her heart skipped a beat. She knew it was Paul before he stepped into the back room.

"Are you there?"

She hurried into his embrace and let the smell of just-laundered clothes and citrus aftershave wash over her.

He had to push her away. "It's time."

She drew back like he'd struck her. "I think they're busy this weekend."

"You promised."

"I know, but . . ."

He locked eyes with her. "You promised. You either keep it or you don't."

She crossed her arms on her chest. Why was everything so black and white with him? Things weren't that clear in real life. She stared into his unblinking gaze but couldn't hold it. "Fine," she said. "But don't say I didn't tell you it was trouble."

For whatever reason, he didn't take the bait. "Tomorrow night, then. And how about mass on Sunday?"

She shook her head slowly. "Mother and Daddy. But not church."

☦ ☦ ☦

Mary tried to visualize her house through Paul's eyes, wondering if he could see the same dreariness she did. The same chrome Frigidaire. The same wall clock. The same artificial flowers, which Mother had combined into one astonishingly garish arrangement. Even though Mary had lived there for more than sixteen years, it still didn't seem like home.

She checked her watch, barely listening to Daddy's longwinded story, counting the minutes until this ordeal would be over and done with.

Paul's smile took some of her discomfort away. That one change softened his jaw and transformed him from an intriguing man into a heartthrob. She found herself, in spite of her nerves, smiling back, even managing a bite or two of food.

"Could I get you some more?" Mother, trim as ever in a tailor-made suit, had bustled about, lighting candles that hadn't seen a match since Mary's graduation.

Was Mother's veneer as transparent to Paul as it was to her? Mary cut a look at Paul.

"Yes, ma'am." He smiled as if he liked Mother. And the rock-hard roast.

Mary managed to turn a snort into a cough. She'd thought he might choke down one slice, but for a vegetarian to gobble down two platefuls of meat . . . and all for her parents. All for her.

When the scraping of forks and polite murmurs died down, Daddy settled back in his chair. "What does your family do?" he asked.

"We're in the produce business. Have been for years."

Daddy nodded. "I like a man who rolls up his sleeves, gets to the nitty gritty."

"Mr. Harris—"

"Call me Edmond."

"Edmond, I understand you're in politics."

Daddy leaned way back in his chair and propped his right foot up. "You could say that. Took a hiatus, but now I'm back at it."

"It must be a hard job."

"It's like being a jackass in a hailstorm. There's nothing to do but sit and take it."

"Daddy!" Mary's hands flew to her face. She was used to Daddy's jokes, but how would Paul react? She met Mother's gaze. For once, they agreed on something.

Paul slapped his thigh just like Daddy did at fundraisers. Rising from the table almost simultaneously, the two headed into the front room, guffawing like old cronies.

As if they were conspirators, Mother leaned toward Mary, her eyes gleaming. "Do you want to help me serve dessert?" she whispered.

Mary set out plates while Mother sliced the pie. "He seems like a nice young man. What church do they belong to?"

"They're Jewish," Mary said with a straight face.

The knife clattered against the tin pie plate.

Mary giggled. "Not really, Mother. He's Catholic."

Mother set her lips in a thin line. "Mary Elizabeth, how could you say that?"

"For heaven's sake, Mother, I was just kidding."

At first, Mother seemed unsure how to react. Then she broke into a grin that smoothed out the furrow between her brows.

Mary kissed Mother's cheek. "Thank you. Everything was wonderful."

✦ ✦ ✦

The summer closeout sale was starting in ten minutes, yet Paul, who didn't shop, was holding a basket; Mrs. Appleby, who was a nervous wreck before sales, seemed strangely relaxed.

Mary pointed to the cash register. "Aren't you going to open that thing up?"

The two of them seemed to telegraph a message with their eyebrows.

"You're not gonna be around for the sale." Paul took Mary's elbow and steered her toward the back of the store.

What?" Her heart thumped of change, yet she let Paul guide her into her room.

"It's all arranged. Grab your tennis shoes. And that crazy hat I bought you."

She grabbed the hat, plopped it on her head, and studied her reflection in the mirror. Who was that carefree girl? Certainly not her. But Paul liked it, and she liked—she tugged the brim down—she loved him. She'd even offered penance of various kinds if God would allow them to be together. Even thought about praying, then tossed out that idea like an old lottery ticket. Prayer hadn't worked before. Why should it work now?

✦ ✦ ✦

As they zipped south in Paul's old truck, Mary rolled down the passenger window, hoping the cool breeze would quell the tension that gripped her. It didn't. "Where are we going?" she finally asked.

"Remember that land I told you about?"

She nodded, both excited and disappointed. Years ago, Paul had bought some acreage through a government program to restore wetlands. And while she loved to tromp and hike as much as Paul did, she was hoping for something more—she cut a look at him. What did she want? Since he'd met her parents, he'd hinted about the future. But he wasn't willing to settle for moving in together, and neither was she. She studied her hands, ringless, the nails carefully clipped off. So what was left? Marriage. Forever. And that seemed like too big of a step for either of them.

"We're going there. A picnic. You need a break."

Mary tried to find his eyes, but he was concentrating on his driving. She hoped, yet didn't let herself hope too much. She tried to shake off an optimistic feeling that he was different. *That's it. Keep the pretty things at bay. They'll just disappoint.*

"The government pays me to plant trees." He kept one hand on the steering wheel and waved the other. "Near the house, there's a perfect spot for a garden—organic, of course. A barn for a goat or two . . ."

Mary closed her eyes and let her imagination carry his words a bit further. *To talk and hope and love. Maybe one day have children. Babies. To love and to hold and to never give up.* When she opened them, she realized it wasn't just her imagination but also her heart that was talking.

"Some sheep." They rolled by farms, Paul talking faster than she'd ever heard him. And saying all the things she'd ever dreamed of. Her hand flew to her mouth.

"What's wrong?" He grabbed her trembling hand. "Hey, it's okay. She'll handle the store."

She closed her eyes again. *The store's the last thing on my mind.*

Two hours later, they swerved onto a dirt road, then another and another.

Paul put on the brakes and pulled Mary nearer. "Shut your eyes." He clamped his hand across her face.

She waited. Waited. Waited. "Here it is," he finally said.

He'd parked under a cluster of trees. A crescent-shaped lake shimmered its promise of a cool swim. A Monopoly piece of a house peeked from the wood's edge.

"It's beautiful." Her hands shook as she stepped down from the truck.

"Let's go. I want you to see the river." They ran through the floodplain, acres and acres of plowed fields and clusters of plants and little rills tripping to the river. "Look." Paul pointed to a pair of drab-colored birds. "Thrushes. They're mating." He grabbed her hand and pulled her toward the swift water. A family of turtles sunned on a sand bar. "What do you think?"

"I told you. It's beautiful." *Can't he see in my eyes what I think? Doesn't he see that I daren't open my mouth for fear it will all fall apart?* She held his hand as if she was in danger of drowning and stared at the swift blue water, which was wide, but not like the turbulent sea crashing on those desolate Irish cliffs. She bowed her head. *God, if this is a mirage or a cruel joke, let the deep wide water pour over me and end it now, if living means being without him.*

He let go of her hand and stared at her. "You only said two words."

"'It's beautiful' says a lot."

He shook his head. "*Beautiful's* a sunset or a full moon. This is my life."

What she really meant clamored to come out, yet the side of her that hated change, the side of her that was afraid, stepped in. "And your job?"

"I'll farm. Find something else if I need the money."

"Won't you miss the city?"

"No way. Would you?"

She wouldn't meet his gaze, because then he would know. "I've never thought about it," she lied.

A frog plopped into the water and broke the uncomfortable silence. Paul had tested her, and she didn't know if she'd passed or not. She looked into eyes deeper than the river. And her very life depended on the grade of this one.

"Let's go back. Race you to the fence."

They sprinted toward his property. At the last minute, she streaked past him, pushing until she thought her lungs would burst.

Paul grabbed her by the nape of her neck and pulled her close. "Light and graceful, like a deer." He caught his breath, then kissed her. "You're beautiful when you run."

Her heart pounded. *But I'm tired of running, Paul Freeman. I'm so tired.*

He led her to a blanket spread out by the lake, and they ate.

"Those are the maples." They lay there on the grassy green, and she stared at the majestic canopy that towered overhead. A breeze stirred the leaves, and the native grasses along the banks of the lake rustled a message.

I'll sing you one, oh. Green grow the rushes, oh. What is your one, oh? One is one and all alone and . . . He is the one, my love.

A wave of elation spread over her, now that she had determined to let him pull her along in this swift current. If she drowned, so be it. *We. We We. No more of you, Miss Mary. You're diving in. Or rather, you're letting him pull you in.*

"That's walnut." He fed her grapes and pointed out each species of tree that clustered about the banks, like they were his best friends. "The black locusts are over there." The words flowed like nectar from his lips. "Locust. Ash. Tough little numbers."

Will the trees be our children? Or will we have our own dark-eyed, curly-haired lasses and laddies?

He pulled her to her feet. "Time to go. But first, I want to say something."

Her heart beat the answer before he asked the question.

"Betsy, I want to live here with you. Be your husband. Take care of you. Marry you." He pulled a gold band out of his pocket and slipped it on her finger.

She burst into tears.

He pulled her to him, so tightly she could barely breathe. His heart beat as rapidly as hers, though they'd had plenty of time to recover after the run. "It's okay. You haven't told me everything about your family, but it'll work out." His husky voice sent shivers up her spine. "And I promise you, Betsy, I'm not going to hurt you. I love you."

She clung to him, vapors of doubt and regret and despair condensed onto the front of his shirt. Every cell hungered and thirsted for him and propelled them into one.

He outlined her lips, nose, and brow with his finger. "One more thing, Betsy. No doubts. We're not looking back."

On Monday, she told Mrs. Appleby and Mr. Giordano that she wasn't re-newing her lease, which saddened them, and that she was marrying Paul, which Mrs. Appleby, of course, already knew.

A month later, after Mr. Giordano handed over the shop keys to Mr. Heinz in a ceremony akin to England's changing of the guard, Paul helped Mary load her things into his truck. They lashed down the back doors with old neckties so pots and pans and clothes wouldn't be scattered all over the Midwest.

They were married on the steps of the county courthouse in Sullivan, Indiana, both sets of parents present. Mary kissed Daddy and Mother good-bye and smiled at the man God had sent to save her.

Haste to the wedding, ye friends, ye neighbors. The lovers their bliss can no longer delay. Forget all your sorrows, your cares, your labors. Let every heart beat with rapture today.

✟ ✟ ✟

Sally plunked down an empty Diet Coke can. She'd seen Paul at a football game and sized him up from the way he took Mary's elbow and guided her up the bleachers. It was weird how a touch of the hand, a slant of the eyes, gave more information than an encyclopedia full of facts. "So that's how y'all met."

"And we're still in love."

Sally studied Mary, wondering if there was finally a respite from all the pain. "It makes a difference, doesn't it?"

"Yes, but I soon learned it wasn't the most important thing."

"More problems?"

Mary nodded. "The next part's hard."

Sally scooted closer. "From what I can tell, it's all been hard." An idea glim-mered in Sally's mind. That book she'd wanted to write . . . She pushed it away and sat still as a stone, waiting for Mary to resume her story.

CHAPTER 21

*"When will this end, ye Powers of Good?" She weeping asks forever
But only hears, from out that flood, the demon answer, "Never!"*

—Thomas Moore, "As Vanquished Never"

Mary pulled some gourds from thick vines and plucked the last of the raspberries from scraggly bushes. Five years ago, she and Paul had tilled the earth for this garden, planting choice heirloom seeds and starter plants. In some ways, it seemed like five days. Their marriage had borne fruit and ripened, thanks to Paul sowing seeds of trust and cooperation.

Here in her garden, she often thought of Grandmother, her work ethic, her prayers, her love. A cold wind whipped through withered corn stalks, which answered with a death rattle and sent a shiver through Mary. But Grandmother had been buried in the cold ground of Ireland two years ago, ending any chance of a reunion, at least on this earth.

Overhead, cirrus clouds, wispy and misleadingly white, warned of sudden change. Mary set down her basket and checked her watch, determined to push away an uneasy feeling. If she hurried, she could make a cobbler before her ten o'clock appointment.

To supplement their farm income, she'd started Wallpapering With Red, which advertised by flyers posted on utility poles and by word of mouth. Since they had no phone, clients called their closest neighbors, Stan and Luann Tyler. The older couple allowed their "adopted kids" to trade produce and Mary's homemade cobblers and pies for use of their phone.

The crunching of gravel told Mary she had a visitor before she saw anyone.

"Mary?"

"Out here." Something about Luann's tone sent another shiver through Mary.

"There's been an accident." Luann, still in her robe, stepped from a stand of trees which marked the beginning of the Freeman property.

"What—who?" Gourds and berries tumbled from the basket when Mary set it down.

Luann wore an inscrutable mask. "You need to call your mother."

Her skin prickling, Mary whirled past scarlet and gold trees. Mother almost never called; Daddy did. She ran ahead of Luann, up the Tylers' steep driveway and into the house. Her hands trembled as she called the number.

After one ring, Mother answered.

"Mother. You called?"

"Your father's dead," Mother said, her voice so devoid of emotion it sounded like she was reading from a script. "He killed himself."

Mary slumped into a nearby chair. "What? Mother? I didn't hear. Say it again."

"He's dead."

"Mother? *Mother?* How?"

"I don't want to talk about it on the phone."

"I'll . . . Mother, I'll . . . Paul . . . we'll leave right away."

The phone slipped from Mary's grasp and dangled by the cord. "My daddy," Mary cried. "He's dead. I . . . he's dead. No. He can't be." Blackness pushed in so that she saw nothing but the swinging cord, heard nothing but the finality of a dial tone. Dead.

Luann rushed in, pulled Mary to her feet, and gripping her shoulders, led her through the woods and back home.

The next thing Mary remembered, she and Paul were flying past fields of dying soybeans and corn. Headed to Lisle.

Mary studied the frayed knees of Paul's jeans as if they held the answers to her questions. *Why? How?* From time to time, words spilled out as they drove down the road they'd traveled so often. "I . . . don't believe it. How could it be? No."

Paul stroked her hair. "It'll be okay," he kept saying. "We'll get through it."

Every time he touched her, she closed her eyes and replayed the call, desperate to understand. Had she misheard? Did Mother mean he'd brought on a stroke by drinking? Overeating? Then she'd see Daddy's bright eyes, his shiny head, and have trouble believing he had died. By the time Paul reached the Lisle exit, Mary had almost convinced herself that it wasn't true.

Cars jammed the small space in their driveway. As Mary got out, she noted the license plates, the colors of each car as if she was a reporter. Paul helped her into the house, moving her past people she didn't know.

They found Mother sitting at the kitchen table, her back straight, her eyes lifeless.

A man in a dark suit stood up and introduced himself, then said something about the body and a release, but Mary comprehended little of his talk. She ran to Mother and tried to embrace her.

With a thin arm, Mother shoved her away, picked up a pen the man proffered, and scratched her signature next to a big, black X.

The blood seemed to drain from Mary as she stared at the single line on the white paper. Her knees buckled, and she slumped over. With steady arms, Paul caught her, but she pushed against him as if he, not death, were the enemy. Her brain screamed a message—*It's true. Daddy did it*—but no words came out.

She longed to break free from Paul's embrace and rip up all pretense of normalcy: the plastic flowers, the careful pile of mail. How could things look like they always had, when her Daddy was dead?

Paul seemed to sense her angst, pulling her so close she could barely breathe. As he'd done earlier, he stroked her hair, talked to her in low, gentle tones. His touch, his words eventually numbed her into a mechanical acceptance. With Paul guiding her, they moved into the family room. She sat in her father's old chair. Daddy's chair. Daddy.

"Are you Mary Elizabeth Freeman?" The same man who had gotten Mother to sign the paper stepped toward her.

Mary didn't answer and clung to the arms of the worn chair, which smelled of hair cream and aftershave and tobacco. Smelled of her daddy.

Paul nodded for her.

"I'm Chief Rogers."

Mary blinked, then nodded. One of Daddy's old cronies; one she'd never met.

"I just have a few questions." Dark eyes darted about the room. "Perhaps we'd be more comfortable . . . in your room."

Paul took her hand and led her down the hall. When she passed the pictures that captured Daddy's political successes, she stumbled; again, Paul kept her from falling.

Moans sprang from her throat and the same words, over and over. "Why, Daddy? Why did you do it?" Somehow Paul got her to sit on the bed.

The same old books formed a perfect line in the bookcase. The desk surface, smooth and dust-free. The dolls, oblivious to the family tragedy. Mary rubbed her eyes. How could it be so normal, when her father was dead?

The chief pulled a chair to the side of the bed. "First I want to tell you how sorry we are. And if there's anything we can do . . ." He pulled out a notepad and clicked open his pen. "Now we need to ask you a few questions."

"Why did he do it?" Mary asked.

The chief hesitated. "Why do you think he did it?"

Mary felt bile rise. "I'm asking you."

For a moment, the chief studied the report. "The note referred to another woman."

Mary leaned so close, she could see the report. "There's a note? He left a note?"

The chief blinked. "Your mother turned it over to us."

The words slapped Mary. "My *mother* found it?" She thought of Mother's face, worn from years of misery, and her heart wrenched. "Daddy, how could you do it?" She clenched and unclenched her fists, as if prepared to strike something.

Paul rubbed her back, tucked curls behind her ears. "It's okay, Mary."

She shook her head, not caring that saliva streamed from her mouth. "No, it's not."

When Paul didn't respond, she pushed away from him. "How?" She jumped off the bed, screaming now. "How did he do it?"

"Slit his wrists. Then . . . carbon monoxide."

The chief's quiet voice, his bowed head, took a bite out of her anger. It wasn't his fault; it was Daddy's. And God's. She buried her face in her hands, sobs trickling out even though she willed them to stop. *How could you sit in that car and wait for death? You didn't even like to bandage a little scrape.* Her head still bent, she tried to make sense of Daddy's slide over the edge. Perhaps more than anyone, she understood the hopelessness. She'd been there, not once but twice. But for God's help, the same thing might have happened to her. The floodgates opened again. *But why, God? Why didn't You help my daddy like You did me?* Raw grief rushed out.

Paul stroked and talked and touched and prayed with her. When she could talk again, the chief quietly questioned her. Then she, too, signed her name next to an *X*.

✢ ✢ ✢

She'd woken slowly, feeling numbed, as if she'd taken a sleeping pill. From her perch in bed, she sat up on her knees and stared out the window into a black night. Black. Dark. Death. She checked her watch. Nine thirty? When had she . . . what had . . .

The door creaked. Mary whirled about, setting off a rustle of sheets.

Paul stood, beams from the hall light illuminating his face. "She's finally alone. Tidying up a bit in her room."

The harsh reality of what Daddy had done swept over her, and she leapt from bed. She had to reach out to Mother now. She'd been wrong all these years to pretend everything was okay. But now Daddy had forced their dysfunction, their isolation, into the open, and they had to talk about it. In a rush, she was at the door.

Paul threw his arms about her. "Stay put, Mary. You're about done in."

She pushed past him. "I've got to see her."

"I really don't think it's the time. Let's deal with it in the morning."

In spite of his protests, Mary darted past him and knocked on the door of the bedroom her parents used to share.

"I'm busy," said Mother, her voice laced with anger.

"Mother, we need to talk." Just for a moment, Mary leaned against the wall, the unanswered questions whirling. Then she opened the door. It had to be done.

With mechanical motions, Mother was gathering Daddy's clothes, then tossing them in a pile. The old robe swallowed her thin frame. A hairnet flattened her stylish bob.

Mary flinched. *She's attempting to purge herself of the embarrassment. And I don't blame her. How could he do this?* Slowly, so as not to startle her mother, whose motions were becoming frenzied, Mary stepped closer. "Mother?"

The bending and slinging continued, yet the robe remained tightly cinched, the bob held firmly in place by the hairnet. "Not now," she snapped.

Mary touched her sleeve. "Don't you want to wait? I'll help later, when—"

Clothes flew when Mother spun around. "How do you know what I should do?"

"I don't. I just—"

"Please leave me alone." Mother stalked into the bathroom and returned with monogrammed towels, which were promptly deposited on top of the mound of clothes.

"Did you find him?" Mary moved closer to the whirling arms and legs, a catch in her voice. "It must have been awful, Mother."

All of the motion stopped. "I said I don't want to talk about it."

Mary edged closer, all the while trying to think what Paul would do. "Mother, I need to know." She touched at a stiff curl which had strayed from her mother's hairnet, willing compassion into her voice. "About the note and—"

"Why?" Mother's hand flew to her hair as she adjusted the net. "You're just like those awful reporters."

The anger that had been mounting against her father swelled to include her mother. "Not quite." Mary didn't quell a bitter tone. "He was my father."

Mother leveled her with an unblinking gaze. "Not really."

That's right. Mary's hands trembled, but she bit back a poisonous retort. *Neither of you were ever parents. Especially you.* She marched out, then slammed the door. Her old bedroom, with its soft light, seemed to rebuke her; she burst into tears.

In an instant, strong arms were about her.

"I should have never gone in there. She won't talk to me, she can't stand me, and I can't stand her, either."

"Her husband just died." Paul tried to hold her close, but she pushed past him and threw herself on the bed.

"You mean my daddy." The pillow muffled her voice, but not the pain, inflicted not just by her father, but by her mother as well. "And she didn't love him, anyway."

"Don't say that." There was an edge to his voice. "How can you be so cruel?"

"It's true," she insisted.

"Right now, telling the truth and being cruel are the same thing." The bed sagged as Paul sat down, then gently moved her over so he could lie beside her. "Mary," he said, his face against her hair, "you can't do to her what she's doing to you."

She curled into him then, his wisdom for the time checking her bitterness. He held her until her chest quit heaving, until her mind was able to face the tasks ahead. She'd have to help Mother, the only family she had left. Except Mam. And did Mam really count? Tears fell again, and just like a tap had been turned on, bitterness flowed back into her thoughts, bitterness she directed toward God. Grandmother was gone. Daddy was gone. *And where are You in this, God? Are You gone too?*

☧ ☧ ☧

The truck loaded, Paul had gone to get gas. Mary strolled through her old neighborhood, watching boys toss a ball in the Novaks' old yard. A wave of nostalgia swept over her as she remembered the tastes and smells of the homey basement. And what was left to show that the Novaks had lived there? Only an overgrown flower bed, Mrs. Novak's beloved asters abandoned and left to die. Gone now too.

They'd helped Mother tidy up the nasty little messes Daddy's suicide caused. At Mother's insistence, Mary got rid of his things. Paul cleaned his car and sold it. Mary felt numb, as if she were watching this happen to someone else. Just hours after the mass, Mother asked them to leave. After regaining her voice, Mary invited Mother to come to the farm with her and Paul, but when Mother declined, Mary was glad.

✤ ✤ ✤

Mary pumped her arms harder, her shoes thudding onto hard ground. *Why did you do it? Did you know what you'd leave in your wake?* Brown leaves clumped about the riverbank, and a dull cast obscured the usual blue sheen. It had been a year since Daddy's death, and she still hadn't gotten over it. She wiped sweat from her brow and tried to push away old memories, but it was no use. "For once, being alive. Having something to believe in," he'd said. Tears filled her eyes. It was her fault. She hadn't seen that Daddy's smiling facade was just a cover for a desolate life. A hawk soared overhead, searching for the small and vulnerable and weak. Trembling, Mary turned her back and sprinted to the haven of Luann's porch swing.

Silver curls had been combed, and Luann's cheeks bloomed like roses, yet Mary couldn't help but remember the ashen face that last year had brought the bad news. Luann had tried to comfort her with morning coffee, afternoon tea, and it had helped. But her Daddy was still dead, and nothing in the world would change that fact.

The swing groaned as Luann set down what looked like a Bible and motioned for Mary to sit. "I don't know how you can jog like that," she said, shaking her head. "Of course, I don't know how you climb up those ladders, either."

Mary sank into the soft cushion. "It's called survival." She'd blocked out Daddy's death with a new regime of exercise, the old one of work. Every morning when Paul headed to the barn, she put on shoes and ran to the river, hoping the pounding would dull the pain caused by Daddy's decision. By mid-morning, she was wallpapering a kitchen or bath, filling as many spaces in an appointment book as she thought her back could endure.

They rocked, Luann patting Mary's hand. "If you want to meet with our pastor, he's had experience with . . . things like this, and I know he'd enjoy talking with you."

Mary went rigid like she had when Paul suggested something like this. She hadn't even told him about her dabbles with suicide, and she sure wasn't going to bring up Daddy's death with some stranger. Besides, during the day, she coped. It was when the sun went down that death crept near, its icy cold fingers gripping her and not letting go. She looked at Luann, so placidly rocking. None of them could know how she raced to stay one step ahead. Pushing, pushing—she jumped off the swing. Mother would know, would understand. She'd call right now. "Could I use the phone?"

Luann nodded. "You know you don't need to ask."

When Mother didn't answer at home, Mary called the office. "Maureen?"

"Why, hello, Mary Elizabeth."

"How's Mother?"

Maureen didn't answer for a moment. "It's been rough."

Mary relaxed her grip on the phone. She had been right, after all.

"Uh, can she call you back? Your neighbors' number, right?"

Mary drummed her fingers on the counter. When the phone rang, she grabbed it. "Hello—Tylers' residence," she said, her heart pounding.

"Yes?" The usual chill iced Mother's voice.

"Mother, it's me."

"What do you want?"

"To see how you are." Mary struggled to explain, her call suddenly seeming senseless, even inappropriate. "I . . . I just thought about how tough this is for us."

"I'm fine."

"Maureen says—"

"She's just a secretary."

"She's worked for you for years. She knew Daddy, knew about—"

"You're acting like another gossipmonger, trying to get a scoop on us."

The bedroom scene, Mother tossing about Daddy's clothes, flashed before Mary, and her own venom gathered, then shot out. "I *am* us."

"No, you're not. Not really."

When Mary slammed down the phone, the vibration knocked a book off the counter. Her mother was impossible, and nothing would ever change that. She longed to hurl the book across the room, but instead, she put it back on the counter and walked onto the porch.

The swing quit rocking. "How is she?" Luann asked.

The hope in Luann's face deserved better; Mary bent over and hugged her. "As well as can be expected." Before Luann could see her tears, she turned and ran for home.

✛ ✛ ✛

Winter struck with a vengeance and by February had set in hard. Still Mary ran and worked and cooked for the two of them. By the time they both cleaned up and sat down at their tiny kitchen table, it was pitch dark, and Paul was starving. For the past month, the sight, the smell of food had sickened Mary; she had to force herself to eat. She'd suspected, of course, but Sue, a doctor on staff at the county hospital, confirmed it. She was three months pregnant.

Paul crammed another piece of soda bread into his mouth. "This is good."

Mary smiled, thanks to the compliment and the news she couldn't wait to share. Despite nausea and an aching back, she'd bustled about the kitchen, with its pine floors, yellow walls, and lace curtains, to prepare Paul's favorite meal. From time to time, she'd peer out the window at the grove of trees Paul had called his children.

Paul, finished with his dinner, made a move to get up.

"Wait." She danced to the counter, then cut a thick wedge of pie for Paul and sat across from him. She'd held the news in all through dinner, but no more.

He looked at the pie, then Mary. "What's this about?"

She played with her fingers, suddenly shy. What if he wasn't ready? What if he—

"Come on, Mary. What's going on?"

"We're having a baby." She twirled about, her body unable to keep quiet any longer, either.

He pulled her out of the chair and whirled her about the floor.

They bumped into the stove, the refrigerator, until Mary, giggling, pushed him away. "Whoa. Careful. There's two of us here."

He put his hand on her stomach. "When?"

"Next summer."

Tears filled his eyes. "Let me see your hand. One, two, three . . ."

She looked at him curiously. "What are you doing?"

"Counting the lines. That's the number of children we'll have."

She giggled, loving everything about him. And now there'd be another one to love. Part of him and her. She grabbed him, and when she kissed his cheek, it tasted of salt and sweat. Her pulse quickened, and the two of them collapsed against the wall, near boots caked with mud and manure that she hadn't even made him set outside.

Later, after he'd checked on the livestock, he joined her in the feather bed his parents had given them as a wedding present. "What's that?" He pointed to a stack of books.

Mary showed him the titles. *Prenatal Care the Smart Way. Midwifery or Else.*

"You're getting into this, aren't you?"

She scooted away so quickly a book tumbled to the floor. Didn't he know the things that could go wrong? "I want to get this right. And I don't have a clue what I'm doing."

He pushed the rest of the books on the floor and took her in his arms. "You're a natural, Betsy." He rubbed her stomach. "We'll do it together."

The wind howled and pushed its winter warning against the home, but snuggled close to Paul, Mary felt safe. Their love would serve as the foundation for their children, and her past couldn't hurt them. For the first time since Daddy's death, Mary slept through the night, the icy blast kept at bay for the moment.

✿ ✿ ✿

Spring came early, birds chirping before dawn, the sun coaxing shoots from the ground. They usually ate dinner on the deck Paul built, even if they had to wear their coats.

"There's a nest up there." Paul pointed to one of the oaks he'd planted.

"How many babies; can you tell?" Mary squinted to see the nest that the mother had anchored between forked branches. Safe. Secure. Mary stuck out her chin, determined to be like that. *Nobody will dare hurt my child.*

"Two." Paul crept close, kneading tightness out of her neck. "Boys, of course."

Mary tossed her napkin at him, knowing it was all in jest.

When the baby kicked, Mary shuddered and then smiled. "Feel."

He put his hands on her middle, a grin spreading over his face. "It's really in there." He squeezed her until she groaned.

"Paul, I can't believe it. A few more months until I'm a mother."

"Speaking of mothers, what did your mother say?"

Mary picked up the dishes and started inside. She didn't want to get started with Paul on this topic. Not tonight.

"Mary?"

She kept her back to him. "I haven't told her. I don't want to get her involved."

"She is involved. She's your mother. You have to tell her."

"Why? She'll just ruin it for us." Mary tried to breathe deep, to keep calm as Sue had cautioned, which was nearly impossible when she thought about Mother.

"Maybe it'll help." He took the dishes from her. "Like it has you."

"How do you know?"

"Things can change."

"Not her."

Paul half-pulled, half-guided her into the family room. "Why don't we talk to Stan and Luann's pastor? Maybe even visit his church?"

"Why now? And what does that have to do with Mother?"

"Because on both counts, it's what we should do. Especially now that we're going to be parents." He pulled Mary close. "We've got to be a good example for her . . . or him."

Mary frowned. Her family had only sporadically attended mass, same as Paul's. Why should they initiate a meaningless ritual that did nothing but heap guilt on top of guilt? Once again, she tried to temper her emotions. "What good will it do?"

"Well, Stan and I've been talking, and—"

Mary bristled and stalked into the kitchen. Why would he talk to a neighbor about something so personal? And if God were so important, why hadn't she and Paul hammered the subject out before their marriage? "What all did you tell Stan?" she asked, banging dishes in the sink.

Paul shook his head. "I won't argue with you over this. Just think about it."

☩ ☩ ☩

It took Paul to penetrate the barrier Mother and Mary had erected. He called Mother and, as he later explained it, manhandled her into visiting. He'd even agreed they'd come get her when she claimed the traffic was bad for her nerves.

Before Mary could even ring the bell, Mother opened the door, her suitcase by her side. "Good heavens," she told Mary, "you're bigger than a hippo."

Mary took her mother's bag and turned for the car. Why had Paul insisted on this? She'd told him nothing would change. She gritted her teeth. "I'm carrying a large baby. And the doctor's monitoring my weight."

"That *female* doctor?"

Mary bit her lip, only Paul's squeeze of her knee keeping her quiet. For twenty-four years she'd tried. But what good was it to try to draw close to someone like Mother?

They rode in silence past acres of corn stalks dusted with snow. When they pulled into their driveway, Mother pointed at their house, a sneer on her face. "That's it?"

Mary counted to ten before answering. "It's good enough for us."

"It's just a bogsider's hut."

Her words slashed at Mary. How dare she belittle the home they'd made, a real home, not just bricks and mortar? "I am a bogsider," she stabbed back. "And so are you." Mother's pale face made Mary wish she'd employed the counting technique again.

Mother unpacked while Mary retreated to her kitchen. She chopped and minced and sliced as if creating a perfect stir-fry could get the visit off to a fresh start. While waiting for the wok to heat up, she glanced out the window at a lake so tranquil, yet so full of life. Red-winged blackbirds nibbled bright berries. Mallards swooped onto the silvery surface. Peaceful. *So different from Mother.* Mary filled the plates and set them on the table.

Mother breathed deep, then speared a forkful of peppers, carrots, and broccoli. Sighing, she sopped up soy sauce with homemade flatbread. "Delicious," she said, when she finally stopped chewing. "Where did you learn to cook like this?"

"My store, Mother. Haven't you had Chinese food before?"

Mother shook her head, too busy eating to say a word.

Mary bit her lip. The realization that Mother had never tried her cooking made Mary ache from a different hunger, one all the stir-frys in the world would not satisfy.

Paul paused from his usual shoveling and stuffing. "She's a great cook." Soon his plate was empty; to Mary's surprise, so was Mother's.

Mary made a move toward Mother's plate. "Are you done?"

"No." She motioned toward the stove. "More, please."

Mary gaped at her. Had Mother forgotten her own rules? *Don't be greedy. Only field hands need second helpings.*

Her eyes closed, Mother inhaled again, then sighed. "I like this."

"You do? Here. Have some more. After all, you're going to be a grandma." Mary refilled all of their plates, realizing she didn't have that pit-in-the-stomach feeling that she usually did when Mother was around. And she was talking, freely, without worrying what Mother might think. "Do you feel like a grandma?"

Grimacing, Mother pointed to her gray hair. "Every time I look in the mirror."

"Mother, you look great."

"Not too bad for an Anne from County Clare."

Mary's voice caught. She tended to forget Mother had stood on the very cliffs where she'd stood, had felt the same cold spray, the same harsh wind. With all her heart, she wished she understood Mother better. But what had Paul said? It's never too late? She pushed back a curl. "Did you hear the names we picked?"

"Hopefully not Anne, Mary, or Mary Anne."

"It might get confusing," Mary agreed. "How about . . . Caprice if it's a girl?"

Paul slapped the table. "In honor of my favorite Chevy."

"Of course, I always liked the name Destiny," Mary continued.

Mother rolled her eyes. "That would set her apart."

"Okay," Mary said. "Let's settle for Zanzarita." She leaned across the table and took Mother's hands, wanting the love, the joy, the fun she and Paul shared to seep into her very bones. "That'd set their teeth on edge during roll call."

Paul pounded the table. "We need some boy names. So how about Habakkuk?"

A tinkling like lambs' bells froze Mary in her seat. She stared, open-mouthed. It was the first time she'd ever heard her mother laugh. The sound set off a contagion of laughing about the table. For so long, she'd wanted to see Mother happy, for them to have a relationship. Now, both things seemed to be starting.

✟ ✟ ✟

Mary's smile turned to a frown. "What's the matter?"

"I . . . can't talk about it." Sally had done all she could to suck in the sobs, but it was no use. *Lord, help me. This isn't the place, the time. Once I open those floodgates, it'll never stop.* She wiped away tears and tried to do the same with the image of the tiny blue sock hat that her dead baby had worn. If she changed the subject, surely Mary would pick up on it. Wouldn't she? "You named her Claire, right?"

The frown had disappeared from Mary's face. "All eight pounds, five ounces. Sue delivered her right there in our feather bed." You've met Sue, haven't you?"

"Yeah. I took Ed to her clinic."

"Two weeks, and Mother and I didn't have a single argument. I thanked God for Claire's safe arrival and then stuck Him back on the shelf until I needed Him again."

"Oh, yeah? What happened next?"

Mary patted the Bible prominently displayed on Sally's table. "The inevitable."

CHAPTER 22

Jesus shed His blood for me,
died that I might live on high, lived that I might never die.
As the branch is to the vine, I am His, and He is mine.

—William McComb, "Chief of Sinners Though I Be"

It had been four months, yet Mary still thrilled to touch Claire's downy cheek. Just her daughter, her husband . . . it was all she needed. Mary swaddled Claire in a blanket, then settled into a rocking chair. The joyous sounds of carols streamed from the radio. A small lamp cast an arc of light on a crucifix that hung over the bed. Outside, snow carpeted the farm, insulating them from the outside world.

"Holy infant, so tender and mild . . ."

With the precious bundle in her arms, Mary opened her heart to the import of the Christmas carol as never before. And she was sure Claire sensed it at some level as well. *The perfect Baby who came to deliver us all. Jesus Christ, the newborn King.*

"What are my girls doing?" Paul had crept in, then knelt on the floor beside them.

Mary traced the outline of Claire's tiny ear. "Listening to carols. Both of us."

A smile played with the corners of Paul's mouth. "She's a baby."

"And maybe that's why she understands."

Paul arched his eyebrows.

With a tiny finger, Claire seemed to gesture toward the wall, the blank one except for the crucifix. The room was reduced to the sacred music. The creaking chair. And the presence of God, which Mary felt with certainty.

They embraced in a rather awkward way, Claire and Mary in the chair, Paul still kneeling on the floor, through the next song and the next. Mary thought of all her loneliness, all the times she'd wanted a family to love. She thought about the question that had hounded her for over twenty years—whether she was or wasn't Irish—and with the Spirit hovering, as it was right now, she didn't care.

✠ ✠ ✠

Mary held a screaming Claire in one arm and jostled Paul with the other. "Honey, I'm scared," she kept saying.

Paul groaned and pulled a pillow over his head. "Of what?"

"Something's wrong. She won't quit crying."

"Babies do that." His face full of sleep, he rolled toward the clock, then groaned again. "It's three in the morning."

She plopped next to him and got right in his face. "Don't you think I know that? We've been up since two. I tried to feed her, rock her—I even took her out on the deck."

For emphasis, Claire erupted in an even louder wail and waved her arms.

"Just put her down, then."

Mary glared at him. "You can't mean it. What if something's wrong?"

"Betsy, just put her down. When *you* settle down, maybe she will."

She tried not to scream at him, but how could she settle down with Claire in this state? "What's the matter with you, for heaven's sake? She's not one of your calves."

He rubbed his eyes and propped up on his elbow. "Don't overreact to this."

Mary bit her lip. She hated it when he used that know-it-all tone to tell her not to overreact. "Here she's sick, and you're just going to lie there like a bump on a log."

Paul sighed long and deep, then pulled them close. "It's all right. Babies have kept parents up for centuries, and I imagine they'll continue."

"What do you know about it?"

He flipped over, his back a wall between them. "You can't control everything." His voice came out muffled.

She stood and paced, both Claire's crying and her temper gaining momentum. "I'd settle for controlling your know-it-all attitude."

He hesitated before he answered. "I think we need to go to church."

"Why are you bringing that up in the middle of the night?" Her face got hot. "What difference will that make? And what does it have to do with anything?"

"Maybe everything."

Mary sighed. After weeks of simmering on low, religion had moved to the front burner. She'd heard about all she could stand about Stan's peace, Stan's freedom from drink and drugs. Her pacing slowed; she allowed herself a smug smile. She'd used them both and quit on her own. And she'd started to trust in God again. "Our life's pretty good right now," she finally said.

"Pretty good. But could it be better?"

Mary bit her tongue. Was he saying she wasn't a good wife and mother?

"Listen, Mary." He pointed to Claire. "See? She quit crying, and you didn't even notice." He turned to face her. "Now how about that other thing?"

"What?"

"Church. The one Stan and Luann go to. Tomorrow."

"That little one out in the country? Isn't it Baptist?"

"I don't know. I think so."

"Huh-uh. We're Catholic."

"Mary, it's an hour into town. And with Claire . . ."

"Well . . ." Mary tried to remember what she'd read, what she'd heard, about Baptists. "Aren't they against dancing and drinking and—"

Paul threw up his hands. "When's the last time you drank? Besides, it's the same Jesus, isn't it?"

Suddenly, Mary became very interested in the crucifix on the wall and didn't answer. She didn't know if it was the same Jesus or not.

✙ ✙ ✙

Mary fussed with her hair for the tenth time. It was just a tiny chapel, safe and innocent-looking in that stand of oaks. Why was she so intimidated? Besides, she was the one who insisted Stan and Luann not bring them. She picked up the infant carrier and peeked at a sleeping Claire, then followed Paul inside. As quietly as they could, they slid into aisle seats on the back pew.

Light streamed through stained-glass windows and seemed to melt away all Mary's doubts and fears.

"*What a friend we have in Jesus, all our sins and griefs to bear . . .*" He is the way, the truth, the life. He died so you could live. Accept Him as your Savior. "*At the cross, at the cross, where I first saw the light . . .*"

Mary rubbed her eyes as the preacher made closing remarks. Somehow, the service had both stretched on forever and flashed past like a meteor. Mary had heard some of it at different times and through different people, but it had never resonated within her soul like it did now. Yet questions arose. *What does it mean to accept Him as my Savior? Wasn't that handled by infant baptism? Catechism?*

After the last *Amen*, they hurried to the sanctuary door, hoping to slip out.

The minister was already there. He gripped Mary's hand and introduced himself.

Stan and Luann rushed up to say hello, as did a number of people with flushed, happy faces. Mary did her best to make small talk, yet she needed fresh air. She needed to think. She finally caught Paul's attention, and nodding and smiling, they made their way to the parking lot.

On the bumpy ride home, Paul sang; Claire slept. Mary stared out the window, questions coming at her along with the scenery. How could Jesus be the only way? What did it mean to die to your sins? She'd settle one question, but like weeds, two more would sprout up in its place.

Paul pulled into their driveway, his smiling face making it clear how he felt. "What did you think?" he asked.

"It's interesting," was all she said.

✣ ✣ ✣

Every week, they crept as quietly as they could with a baby into the back pew. One Sunday, Pastor Jordan caught up to them as they were leaving. "Could I drop by sometime, just to chat?"

It was Paul who nodded.

"Great." He smiled at Mary, then Claire. "How about tomorrow?"

Paul nodded, then looked at Mary. "Sorry. I should've checked with the boss."

"Oh, no, it's fine." She tried to ignore the gnawing in her stomach. "Around ten? I'll have coffee, something sweet."

Pastor Jordan tweaked Claire's toes and turned to the next person in line.

✣ ✣ ✣

Pastor Jordan was greeted with a comfortable chair, a roaring fire, the scent of Mrs. Appleby's cinnamon rolls wafting in from the kitchen, and a nervous Mary.

"Thanks," he said, taking in the view along with a mug of coffee and a roll. "What a beautiful place." He licked his lips and wiped his mouth. "And this is great."

Mary thought of Mrs. Appleby's rosy cheeks and smiled.

The two men chatted. Mary bounced a fussy Claire on her lap, glancing at the pastor when he wasn't looking. *He's so . . . ordinary, so casual. How can he be a minister?*

". . . the men's Bible study. We'd love to have you. You could come with Stan."

"I think I'd like that," Paul said.

"And there's a women's study, Mary."

She felt as if she was on a treadmill and someone had ramped up the speed. "Oh, I couldn't. With Claire and all." *How can I expose myself to women I've never met? They'll never accept me. Not me.*

"Just bring Claire. There are at least two grandmother types who'd fight over her."

"Thanks, but—" She stopped when the pastor's gaze caught hers.

"Do you have a Bible?" he asked, his voice low.

She nodded, her head spinning. She'd had a Bible; where was it?

"Here." He handed her a worn-looking Bible. "Read John. Romans. Matthew. The Psalms when you're at wit's end. Which is probably often, with a new baby."

Mary looked away from the fervor in his eyes. He was throwing this whole religious thing at her, and she wasn't sure she wanted any part of it. She'd been to parochial school. The nuns had taught her about Christ. What more did she need? Nodding, she took the Bible and set it down, then handed Claire to Paul. Trying to smile, she gathered up the dishes and took them into the kitchen.

Later with Paul in the barn and Claire asleep, she dusted and mopped, her eyes drawn to the book on the couch, the same book that had fascinated one of The Health Food Shoppe patrons, the fiery-eyed seminary student. What was in there that made it so important? Why did people live by it? Die for it? She sat down and rifled through thin pages. *"I am with you always."* She looked away, just for a second. *So it had been You on the cliffs, Lord. I thought it at the time— now, I know.* With urgency she flipped faster and found another underlined section. *"You must be born again."*

Several times, she read it, puzzling over each word. She agreed with Nicodemus, whoever he was. She couldn't be born again even if she wanted to be. The reactionary language, the dire warnings upset her entire way of thinking.

Mary kept flipping back and forth, reading where a word caught her eye. *"In this world you will have trouble." "You will hear of wars and rumors of wars."*

She shut the Bible. Why was it all so gruesome? Wasn't it enough just to be a good person? God and she were playing a bizarre type of tag. When she chased

Him, He dodged her. Then in an abrupt about-face, He'd come at her, and she'd be the one to turn away. The sad cycle, for decades now. She was weary of it all.

✟ ✟ ✟

The lightning bolt knocked out the power and set Claire to screaming. They got through dinner, thanks to a kerosene lantern and Sterno. It had been a long day for all of them, and Paul's wasn't over yet, not with a pregnant and very nervous heifer in Stan's barn.

Something about the eerie shadows on the wall, the creeping chill in the house made Mary clutch Paul's hand as he got up from the table. "Do you have to?" she asked.

He looked at her strangely as he pulled on rain boots and a poncho, his face further illuminated by another flash from the sky. "What's the matter, Betsy?"

Her heart still pounded from the last boom, yet she spoke with what she hoped was a carefree tone. "Nothing. I'm fine." How could she tell him about the icy chill that warned of another change? A bad one, she was sure of it.

His hand on the door, he gave her one last look. "I promised."

What if she never saw him alive again? She nodded and watched him go, the irrational thought nearly paralyzing in its intensity. Death again, dark, remorseless. "Don't wait up," he yelled as the door banged shut. "It may be a while."

The minute Paul left, Claire erupted.

Mary bounced her, gave her a bath, nursed her. All the while, sheets of rain thrummed the house and made the windows translucent, adding to the trapped-in feeling.

Claire screamed louder.

Mary forced herself to take deep breaths. What if something was really wrong?

Claire's face turned nearly purple, she screamed so loud. Her legs stiffened, and she railed at Mary with tiny doubled-up fists.

"You've got to quit this," Mary kept saying as she carried her into the kitchen, the den, finally into the bedroom, hoping the change of venue might placate her baby and quiet the storm that was rising within her.

Claire shrieked louder.

"Stop it, I said!" Mary plopped her onto the bed.

Claire's breath caught from the jolt. Then she let out a piercing wail.

With a snarl on her face, Mary picked up her daughter, shook her hard, then thrust her down onto the quilt.

Claire's eyes and lips formed perfect circles, echoes of Mary's own shock. Words tumbled through Mary, words she could not stop. *You're not good enough to be a mother.* Words getting louder, louder . . . She clamped her hands over her ears, but it didn't work. *You've never been good enough. What do you think Paul would say if he saw this?*

Mary plopped onto the bed next to Claire, who continued to scream and kick. It was as if her eight-month-old daughter was agreeing with the nasty voices.

The sky and a voice somewhere deep inside Mary thundered a response. *Stop it. It's not true. And it's not her fault. She's an infant.*

Mary stroked Claire's head, the vulnerability of her daughter as frightening as any of the rest of it. She was grateful now for the darkness, which seemed to hide the despicable truth that she'd taken out her frustrations on an innocent child. With trembling hands, she put Claire in her baby bed and raised the rail. She covered her ears, rushed to the kitchen, and tried to pour a glass of water. It spilled all over the counter. "You will not—cannot—won't," she kept telling herself, desperate to stop all the noise. "My God, help me. Please help me."

Claire continued to scream, so loud that the universe was reduced to the sheeting rain and her raging cry.

Mary flew to the bedroom door and slammed it, praying the whole time. The screams seemed to abate—of course they would with the door closed. Yet the words she had read in that tattered Bible began to come to her; jumbled, but still, they came. "Green pastures . . . he leadeth me . . . be still and wait . . . I *am with you always . . .*"

She rummaged through a kitchen drawer, found a flashlight, hurried into the den, grabbed the tattered Bible, then sank onto the couch. With a trembling finger, she found a passage she'd read earlier. "*Believe in me. I am the way, the truth, the life. No one can know the Father except through me.*" She grasped at the words like a person drowning; it was as if her hands were slippery and she could not catch hold. "Jesus? Are You there?"

"I am with you always, even unto the end of the age."

She clutched the Bible. "Help me. Help me. Help me."

"Cast it all on me. Your burdens. Your anger. Your sins. For My yoke is gentle."

Had the words actually been spoken? It didn't matter; they struck Mary with such force, she slid onto the floor. She opened the Bible, its words illuminated by the beam of a cheap flashlight. As she read, years rolled away, and she glimpsed scenes from her past. Sister Helen in her tiny room. Grandmother explaining the gorse. A dozen other images flashed through her mind as clear as if they'd happened yesterday. But the images weren't the only things clear to Mary now. Christ was her Savior. He had died for her sins. He had died so she could be free. From the past. From the present. From herself.

Mary's heart lightened. Though she felt she might float to the ceiling, she continued to lay prostrate on the floor. *Oh, Jesus. This is what they mean. My Savior.* She wept and prayed, her forehead against a braided wool rug.

"Yes, Jesus," she exclaimed. "I'm done fighting. I give it all to You." She basked in the presence of a Savior who could control it all for her. He was the Son of God, as she'd read in the Bible. As she'd heard from the priests, the nuns, Grandmother, the preacher.

For years she'd tried to do it herself, and it had never worked. She'd made her goal acceptance by others, and even though He had sent them all, their acceptance wasn't enough. Only the Son of God could make her whole.

Pieces of her life, some ugly, continued to flash by as she sprawled on the rug, but they didn't wrench her gut. They were more like reminders of why she had come to this point, this place. And she knew that He could reassemble them.

Finally she got to her feet, her fears dissolved and replaced by a calm, sure presence in spite of the rain that continued to pummel their house. A lightness so pervasive, she felt light as a—her heart leapt to her chest. *Claire? Claire!* She ran into the bedroom. Claire lay curled against a bumper pad in her crib, sound asleep.

Careful not to wake her, she kissed her baby. "Thank You, God. Thank You," she kept saying. He had saved her from harming Claire. Saved her from eternal damnation. He . . . had . . . saved . . . her. She darted another glance toward the crib. Thanks to Him, they both were safe.

✤ ✤ ✤

Mary knew she should sleep, but she kept turning those pages, the flashlight and the words illuminating so many things . . .

Paul stood in the bedroom doorway. "It's the middle of the night. What are you doing up?"

Mary smiled at his wet clothes, grimy ball cap, and filthy boots. "I'll tell you in a minute. How was it?"

"Twins." He looked at her more closely. "Now what's going on?"

"I think I get it." She pointed to the Bible in her lap. "About God. Him being Savior and all."

Paul's mouth dropped. "What are you talking about? When?"

They sat cross-legged atop a pile of quilts, Mary doing her best to explain what had happened in her heart. Then she snuggled close to him and they prayed.

By the end of the summer, Paul had accepted Christ as his Savior too. Pastor Jordan baptized them both in the pond.

☦ ☦ ☦

Barefoot, Mary pattered to the deck, a cup of herbal tea in one hand, her Bible in the other. As the sun peeked over the lake, the Bible's words leapt up to greet her, as well. She smiled. God was giving her a crash course in His Word.

"If you forgive men when they sin against you, your heavenly Father will also forgive you," she read. What Jesus said stabbed at her. Daddy had died before she'd forgiven him. Yet her mothers . . . The Bible closed with a thud. She'd better do it, and soon, while she still had time.

"Yoo-hoo." Luann, a note in her hand, peered around the side of the house. "You've had two calls already," she said, her face noncommittal.

Mary took the note and glanced at it. "Thanks. Did she say what she needed?"

"She just said to call." Luann made her way to the deck and sat where Mary had been. "I'll listen for Claire; you go on."

Mary kissed Luann, then hurried down the path worn smooth from neighborly visits. When had her and Mother's relationship deteriorated into messages on slips of paper? And not from Mother, but from her secretary? She shoved a branch away. First had been the unsigned congratulatory card, Mother's sole reaction to her first, her only grandchild. Then three years of refusals to visit their farm. In spite of her hurt feelings, Mary tried to keep in touch, but her world was so rich with Claire and Paul that she hadn't thought much about Mother.

Tripping up Luann's porch steps, Mary fought the truth: she treated Mother no differently than she ever had. Before she picked up the phone, she prayed: first, for God to forgive her, and second, to be able to start the process of forgiving Mother.

On the second ring, Maureen answered.

"Hi, Maureen. It's Mary. How are you?"

"I'm fine, Mary, but your mother's not doing so well."

"What do you mean?"

"Uh, we've had a few problems with paperwork."

"It's a mess, isn't it?" A prayer still on her lips, Mary twisted the phone cord round and round her finger. "Maybe Paul and I'll come up. He's good at—"

"Mary, I don't know how to tell you this, but your mother is . . . she's ill."

Heat rose to Mary's face. Was something really wrong, or was Mother just being difficult? They'd taken Claire up to see her—when was it, six months ago—and she'd been fine. Hadn't she? "We'll drive up tomorrow. And thanks, Maureen."

She returned the other call and sprinted home.

✛ ✛ ✛

"What's this about?" Paul, starving as usual, came up behind her as Mary put the last dish on a table groaning under the load of vegetarian lasagna, Caesar salad, and still-steaming sourdough rolls.

She smiled, glad he'd noticed the candles, the roses. "I'm hungry. Aren't you?"

He gave her a lingering kiss. "Always."

Unable to keep it in, she flung her arms around him. "So am I. Now that I'm eating for two again."

"Oh, Betsy." His love, his hunger, his joy, blossomed into an embrace which jarred the table and nearly smothered her. "When?" he managed to ask, between kisses.

"Next summer."

His eyes bright, he pulled her toward the door. "Let's tell Claire."

"Let her sleep." Despite the joy brought by the second phone call, the first one had nagged at her all day, and she was tired. She tried to smile, but it faded.

As usual, Paul noticed her conflicting emotions. He pulled out her chair, then slid into his. "What's wrong?"

"Maureen called." Mary tried to keep her voice light. "She wants me to come up there tomorrow. Something about paperwork."

Paul let out a deep breath. "The old woman's cookin' the books, huh?"

Even though Mary laughed with him, nausea engulfed her, and for some reason, she didn't think it was morning sickness.

✛ ✛ ✛

Sally shook her head. As far as she was concerned, Mary was a saint, to put up with that mother of hers. Of course, God said to honor your father and your mother, but—a question popped into her mind, and after careful thought, she decided to ask it. "After you became a Christian, did your feelings change toward your mother, or did you just do what you felt like you had to?"

"The latter, without a doubt. I was just going through the motions."

Sally nodded, not blaming her a bit.

"Christ had changed me, had shown me what was right, but I kept trying to do it under my own power," Mary said hurriedly, as if the words embarrassed her. "And that wasn't enough."

CHAPTER 23

Cast care aside;
Upon thy Guide lean, and His mercy will provide.
Lean, and the trusting soul shall prove Christ is its life and Christ its love.
—John S. B. Monsell, "Fight the Good Fight with All Thy Might"

In the rearview mirror, Mary watched the precious three-year-old in the pink parka get smaller and smaller, and the old resentments rushed in as strong as ever. *Why have You saddled me with her? She doesn't even love me, she never has, and I—*

The still small voice moved in as she drove past desolate fields. *Take captive every thought. In everything, through prayer and petition . . .* With effort, she thanked God for Claire and Paul and the little one she was carrying. The road lay before her, so flat, so familiar she let instinct take over. She passed her old school, her old church, and couldn't help but be reminded that she missed none of this.

When she pulled into the driveway next to an unfamiliar car, she didn't bother to unload but hurried up the sidewalk, a black fist gripping her heart.

The door opened. "I'm sorry, Mary Elizabeth. I didn't mean to startle you." Maureen's face was pale, her brown hair laced with gray.

Mary clutched her chest and tried to catch her breath. "It's all right." She took in the stacks of magazines about the family room, the thick layer of dust blanketing the once-gleaming entryway, and knew something was terribly wrong. "Where's Mother?"

"In bed now. We just got back from the doctor's about an hour ago."

"The doctor's?" Mary's bag slipped to the floor. Still breathing hard, she made her way down the hall. As quietly as she could, she opened the door. The drapes were drawn; the beam from the hall illuminated a huddle of quilts, nothing more. Hearing deep, regular breaths, she closed the door and, with slower steps, went into the front room, moved a stack of mail, and sat next to Maureen. "What did the doctor say?"

"A fracture." Maureen sat still, yet her lip trembled. "She's in a lot of pain."

"When did this happen? And how?"

Maureen looked at the floor, at the wall, everywhere but at Mary. "Yesterday. She didn't want you to know."

Humbled by Maureen's loyalty, Mary took her thin hand. "Thank you so much."

Maureen raised her head. "I've . . . I've known your mother a long time."

Now Mary had trouble looking at Maureen, a woman she barely knew even though she'd devoted years to her parents' business. "How long?" she asked, wanting to know Maureen better. Wanting to know Mother better.

Maureen bowed her head. "Forty years. She gave me a job when no one would." Teary eyes looked at Mary. "I had a baby but no husband." Her face crumpled. "I wish you could've known her then. Ran her businesses with an iron hand but a soft heart. Saved my life, she did." She buried her head in her hands and cried.

"Oh, Maureen, I'm sorry you're going through this." Mary drew the older woman close, yet questions about Mother burned in her. She yearned to have seen that side of Mother, to feel even a fraction of Maureen's loyalty.

"No, Mary, it's me that's sorry." Her voice, muffled by her hands, came out husky and broken. "There's something I have to tell you. I can't live with it anymore."

"Wha—what is it?"

Unable to speak, Maureen shook her head.

Mary felt her arms go rigid. Had she embezzled money? Retaliated against Mother after a severe lashing? She tried to keep her tone soft. "It's okay. What is it?"

"I've lied to you, Mary Elizabeth. She's been like this for—" She struggled to compose herself. "When I told you she couldn't come to the phone, it was true. But she wasn't in her office. She was holed up in this house."

"You mean . . ."

"She hasn't worked for months." Maureen wiped her eyes. "I tried to fool everyone. The clients. The regulators. You." She clutched Mary's arm. "I'm so sorry."

The bleakness of Maureen's countenance cautioned her against hurting this friend of Mother's—of hers, too—by a retaliatory retort. She grabbed

Maureen's hand, recalling the words she'd read just yesterday about forgiveness. "It's okay," she said, continuing to smooth Maureen's hair. "You were trying to do what she wanted."

"I kept thinking if she'd just rest, she'd get better. I hate seeing her like this."

The room closed in, and Mary, her hand clutching her throat, moved away from Maureen. *Like what?* Still, she tried to keep calm. "What do you mean?"

"You call the doctor. He'd best explain it." She collapsed into Mary's arms.

"Now, now, you've been through enough," Mary cooed as she patted the older woman. "Get some rest. I'll take care of it."

"But what'll happen to the business?" Maureen asked, clinging to Mary's sleeve.

"It'll be okay," Mary assured her, borrowing some of Paul's favorite words. The business was the least of her worries. She needed to check on Mother. Talk to the doctor.

✠ ✠ ✠

"Thank you for taking my call, Dr. Oliver."

"Not at all, not at all. Where are you, Mary?"

"Here. At Mother's. Her secretary told me what happened."

The genial tone was replaced by that of a professional rustling through a medical chart. "Hairline fracture of the left hip. Three cracked ribs. And there's the other thing."

Mary shivered and clutched at the phone. "What other thing?"

"Reduced motor coordination. Cognitive impairment." Papers rattled. "Signs of mental deterioration. We don't know the tack it'll take, but I expect it'll progress."

Mary crumbled into a chair. *He's wrong. He doesn't know Mother. Besides, we just saw her.* "We were here a few months ago," she said, repeating her earlier thoughts, "and she seemed fine. Oh, forgetful, stressed, but—"

"Your mother's a sharp woman. She's probably been covering up. Plus, the disease can progress rapidly."

"Surely there's some medicine, some therapy. Once we get her on that, it'll get better . . ."

"She'll need full-time care. Otherwise, there's not a lot we can do. Pain pills as needed for the fracture. Close monitoring of behavior. See to her needs. Keep her comfortable. If you'll hold, my nurse can recommend some caregivers."

The phone became slick with sweat. Mary knew she should be rummaging for a pen, asking questions, but all she could do was listen and try to keep from falling apart.

✠ ✠ ✠

When Mary checked on Mother the fourth time, a wizened old woman, barely visible in a sea of quilts, sat up, staring at her with beady eyes. "Who ye be?"

A soothing answer died in Mary's throat.

"Get away!" Bony arms waved and pointed. "I won't have ye here."

It was hard not to collapse on the dusty floor to see Mother, always so nicely turned out in designer suits, matching shoes, and bag, looking like this. She racked her brain to remember their last conversation. Mother had mentioned a missed appointment, had her usual litany of complaints. But certainly nothing that would hint at this. Of course, the nurse had cautioned that stress from the fall could exacerbate things.

"Who ye be?" Mother continued the screeching. "I'll call the guards."

"For heaven's sake, Mother." Mary hummed as if her purpose here was to dust off a bedside table cluttered with vials of pills, used tissues, half-filled glasses. "It's Mary."

"Mary Elizabeth?"

She nodded, warming up to her caregiver role. "Dr. Oliver told me what happened." She smoothed hair off of Mother's forehead. "What hurts?"

"Mary, ye are? Where ye been?"

"At home. I've had some nausea." She swallowed once or twice, not just from morning sickness, but from guilt. "You know, from the new baby."

"Another babbie? That's nice." The revelation seemed to transform Mother. She nestled into her covers and stared dreamily into space.

Mary's mind whirled as she tried to piece together the unreturned calls, the curt tone, the desire to be left alone. There was so much she didn't know, yet so much to do . . .

Mother's eyes grew wide. "Where's the babbie?"

"At home, Mother. With Paul. Now, I'll go to the store, get us some—"

"The store? No." She jerked up as if something had stung her. "They can't have it."

"Mother, it's all right." Mary tried to keep alarm out of her voice, tried to keep her strokes rhythmic, slow. "No one's taking anything."

She shoved Mary away and clawed at matted hair. "Don't let them have my babbie." Her eyes narrowed, her body tensed. "They took 'er, you know."

"Now, Mother, I'm your daughter, and I'm right here. Nobody took me."

She flailed her arms and kicked away the covers. "Not you. The other one."

Mary's stomach wrenched. *So the doctor's right.* She kept smoothing the sheets as if that would cover up the stark reality of Mother's condition. She'd stop it somehow, with time, medicine . . . Mother needed her, and Mary was determined to come through.

✠ ✠ ✠

Mary scrubbed the house, hired aides, had a phone installed at the farm, and, with Maureen's help, plowed through Mother's papers. She'd called Paul last night, elated to use the new phone, then got so choked up when Claire came on the line she could barely talk. Paul confirmed what her heart begged: it was time to come home.

Her bags packed, she stepped into Mother's room. "I'm going to leave now," she told her. "Claudette's here. I'll call when—"

"Who?"

"Claudette. You met her yesterday." Mary stepped to the door. "Claudette?"

"Yes?" A rich alto voice resonated down the hall. She stepped into the room.

Mother pointed a bony finger. "Who's that black devil? Get her out o' here."

Claudette seemed unperturbed, her hips swaying as she made her way to the bed. "We're goin' get on just fine." She smoothed down Mother's hair, making little clucking noises all the while. "Just get on home, Miss Mary. We'll be fine."

Her home. Paul and Claire. "I'll be back soon, Mother. I'll check—"

"Get out. I don't need ye." Her jaw set, she glared at both of them.

Somehow, Mary managed to smile and say good-bye, keeping resentment at bay until she got on the freeway. "Why, God? She's not even my real mother." She slammed her fist on the steering wheel and screamed at a trucker who swerved in front of her. *You're always cutting me off, just like that. I prayed for forgiveness; this is Your answer?* She switched on the radio, then just as quickly turned it off. In spite of her determination to forgive, she resented Mother more than ever.

✠ ✠ ✠

Leggy weeds had nearly taken over the garden, but Mary found little time to work in it with her increasingly achy back and the demands brought on by Mother's condition. But Claire loved digging in the dirt, so Mary brought her out here as often as she could.

"Look, Mommie!" Her brown eyes shining, Claire held up a dirt-encrusted potato as if it were a gold doubloon. She grabbed an old bucket, the potato seeming to provide enough incentive for her to dig on.

Mary wiped her brow. The heat, the humidity had combined to make her feel even more achy than usual. But with the new baby coming soon, these lazy days with just her Claire, nearly four now, needed to be grabbed hold of and savored.

When the bucket was full of rocks, dirt clods, and a few potatoes, Claire handed it to Mary. "Can we go to Ireland now, Mommy?" Her curls bounced, and her eyes shone.

Mary nodded.

Claire dashed toward the vine-covered shed they called Ireland, leaping over a puddle as if it really were an ocean.

Both hands protecting her balloonlike belly, Mary ducked under the low door and into a room she'd modeled after Grandmother's kitchen. Bits of lace adorned the windows. Plastic teacups and a vase of dried wildflowers adorned a vegetable crate.

Claire bustled about, gathering cups and holding them to the lips of a mangled rag doll and a china doll whose porcelain face had cracked. "You sit here," she ordered, "and don't move. We'll go to the market later."

Laughing, Mary nearly fell off the stool she'd managed to lower herself onto. For hours, they'd played like this, Claire coming alive as Mary poured tea and shared stories of Grandmother, at least the ones that didn't still tear at her. "Ye look just like her, Claire. But Grandmother would waggle her finger at you. Like—" A cramp gripped Mary's abdomen, and she leaned against the vegetable crate.

"Ye drink this, right now, ye hear?" Claire skipped from doll to doll, holding the cup close to faded lips. "You too, Mommy." She shoved a cup at Mary.

Mary gripped the crate. An oaken table, moon-shaped faces guzzling tea. Cup after cup . . . The ache in her heart grew, as did the cramps. How could it still hurt so?

"Mommy? I told you, it's—why are you crying, Mommy?" Claire stared with unblinking eyes, as did both of the dolls.

"Baby, it's okay," Mary managed, in spite of the pain, the memories roiling like a cyclone now. "M–Mommy doesn't like tea, remember?"

Claire stomped her foot and screamed.

The room whirled faster; Mary had to gasp to keep up with it. She was back in that other room, on the cliff . . . *What's to be done with the little eejit? Get 'er out!*

Claire screamed again, and it was then that Mary saw the furious swarm of hornets. Stools and dolls and the crate toppled as Mary scooped Claire off the floor. She flinched at the first stab, just at her temple, then smothered Claire in her arms. When the next insect buzzed, then struck, she flinched again but stifled a scream, not wanting to scare her baby. She willed her legs to run, but they refused, and she wobbled out of the place they called Ireland with her baby—both babies.

She passed the garden in slow motion, it seemed. A cramp—she staggered, then cried out. No wonder they'd hurt so. It was her baby, coming, coming . . . Sweat and fear poured off her. If she could make it to the barn, to Paul . . . Her world was reduced to blurs of color as she sloughed through what seemed to be a mire. *Help me, God. Just a few more steps.* She kept moving, kept praying . . . There it was, the comforting orange blur of the barn. A blur that each thud on the soft black dirt brought more into focus. A blinding pain took over, but before she fell, she managed to set Claire down and point her toward the barn. "Daddy! Get Daddy!" she yelled. Everything went black.

✠ ✠ ✠

"Are you sure about this?" Paul asked.

The pain in his voice made Mary's resentment spread until it shrouded Chloe's difficult birth, the plague of infections, the doctor's pronouncement that they have no more children. Over it all, Mother. Always Mother. "It's my turn," she managed.

Mary tried to unclench her fingers as she nestled Chloe and Claire into car seats and loaded the truck. For the past three months, Mother's care had fallen to Paul, whose major issue had been dealing with the rapid turnover in aides. Of the original hires, only Claudette had survived Mother's tongue-lashings. While Mary was on bed rest, Paul had made so many trips to Lisle that he checked traffic patterns like a commuter.

"If it weren't for the sick calf, you know I'd do it again."

"I know." In spite of doing her best to keep her voice light, she'd failed, and that knowledge made Mary even more miserable. "It has to be done."

Though his face was lined, Paul remained calm as he helped load the car. "It'll be okay, Mary. Just take it one step at a time."

Mary glared at him. "No, it isn't okay. Why has He dumped this on us?"

"We have two beautiful daughters." His voice trailed off as he glanced toward the girls. "Don't lose sight of that."

Mary crammed the last of the baby paraphernalia into the truck, for once miffed at Paul's constancy. Didn't he see that it was all Mother's fault? After the briefest of pecks on her husband's cheek, she hopped into the truck and headed to Lisle.

☦ ☦ ☦

"Mommy, it smells funny." Claire clung to Mary's legs, something that had occurred with great frequency since Chloe's birth.

"It's okay," Mary whispered. Somehow she made it to the bed without tripping. "Mother, I'm—we're here." She tried to sound cheerful.

Mother, swathed with her usual pile of quilts, folded her arms and glared.

"This is Chloe." She put Chloe in her mother's arms, praying, hoping, that the radiant little face would communicate love and hope to a personality ravaged by disease.

Mother took one look and sneered. "I've seen more meat on the neck of a scrawny old chicken than on that thing. Whatever are ye feeding her?"

Mary felt bile rising in her throat. How dare she, who'd never had a baby, pick apart her angel? Somehow she clamped in the words she longed to hurl. "Our doctor is most satisfied with her growth curve," she said as she drew Chloe close to her bosom.

"And that young'un." Mother pointed a bony finger toward Claire. "Why is she clinging to you like barnacles on rocks?"

Before Mary could respond, Claudette tiptoed into the room, no easy feat for a foot-pounding woman. "Ma'am, could I have a word with you?"

"Of course. Go ahead." It was nearly impossible for Mary to keep the smile on her face, yet she had to. For Claire's sake, if nothing else.

Claudette lowered her voice. "In private, ma'am."

Mary put Chloe in her carrier and set it next to Claire, then stepped in the hall. Leaning against the door, she gathered her resolve. Whatever Claudette needed, Mary had to provide. For without her . . . "Yes, Claudette. What's going on?"

"I don't know how much longer I can do this." Claudette kneaded her hands, then tried to smooth a black skirt over her hips. "I can't please her. That cleaning she wants hurts my back. She don't want me to bathe her like you asked. And feedin' her . . ."

"Well, Claudette, I don't think we can afford to pay you any more than—"

Claudette shook her head. "It ain't that. Y'all more than generous. All of us, we just can't take it much longer. Lord knows I've tried, but—"

Mary nodded, a desire to let out her own resentments shoving away her constraint. "I can barely deal with her on the phone. I understand, believe me."

"I hear how she talk to you. Lord, have mercy!"

"Get in here, or I'll have yer black hide."

Mary's hand flew to her throat, and she stepped back. How could Mother speak like that to a woman who changed her diapers, cleaned her sheets . . . "Is she always like this?"

Claudette rolled her eyes. "No, ma'am. Usually it's worse."

"Please," Mary begged. "I need you." She patted a meaty shoulder. "I know it's hard. I'll work something out. Please stay until I do."

After a moment, Claudette nodded. "Lord Jesus goin' help me. I give you my word, Miss Mary." She shuffled toward the kitchen.

"Who brought these filthy things in here?"

Mary flew into the room, trembling all over from the hate in Mother's words.

"How can a body rest wi' such a racket?"

"Those are your granddaughters," Mary retorted.

"Yer lyin'! Now pull the drapes, or the sun'll be the death o' me."

"Listen to me." As Mary stalked to the bed, she could feel Claire boring holes into her back, yet that knowledge didn't change what she planned to say. "Can you hear me?"

Mother just glared at her.

"Answer me. Now."

Mother continued to stare. Finally, she nodded.

"All right. I'm your daughter. I have two children and a husband who need me."

"Where have ye come from?"

Mary's breath whooshed out. "Mother, the farm. Indiana."

If Mother heard, she gave no indication. She tilted her head toward the window.

Talking in a forced tone, Mary continued. "Look at me."

When Chloe began crying, so did Claire.

Mary hurried to her daughters, scooped them up, and soothed them with kisses and whispers. When they got quiet, she lugged them to the bed and sat down near her mother. "I need to explain this to you," she said. "Please, please listen. Okay?"

Mother didn't answer, yet she seemed to settle when she saw the girls.

"You've got to make an effort to get along with Claudette. It's a three-hour drive here, and we can't come every time there's a problem." She paused, hoping to see tacit agreement in Mother's face. Instead, the eyes bulged, the lips drew back in a snarl.

"I need you to cooperate with me, Mother," Mary continued, her own face getting hot. "That is, if you want to stay here in Lisle."

As soon as Mary got the words out, Mother sat up as straight as her crumbling spine would allow and crooked her finger at all three of them. "Get out," she shouted. "And stay out. And ye won't get a dime o' my money."

Mary, her daughters in her arms, leapt up. "I wouldn't touch it." She picked up the carrier, bundled up the girls, strode past a shocked Claudette, who was stationed outside the door, loaded the girls into the truck, and stormed away.

All the way home, the girls sensed Mary's angst and tried to outdo each other with whines, which disintegrated into wails. Mary cranked up the radio and tried to let it take over the dark thoughts—all about Mother. And after a solid hour of screaming, both girls slumped forward in their car seats, succumbing to exhaustion.

When Mary pulled in the driveway, she checked on the girls, who were still sound asleep, then jumped from the car and flew to the barn.

Paul dropped the bale of hay he was carrying when he saw her. "What's wrong?" he said, wobbling a bit as if her news might be more than he could bear.

"I've had it," Mary announced, her arms across her chest. "We're done with her."

Paul's eyes narrowed. "No 'I've missed you' hug?" He strode past Mary, craning his neck toward the driveway. "And where are my girls?"

"Asleep in the car. They were exhausted from listening to Mother's tirades." Mary tossed her hair about, even though Paul wasn't looking. "And so am I."

"That's all you've got to complain about?" He strode back toward the barn.

Mary gritted her teeth. Since when couldn't he stop working long enough to talk to her? Besides, why couldn't he see that Mother was the problem here? "I'm sick of dealing with her," she shouted. "It's time to think about . . . some other arrangements."

He turned, stepped close, and put his arms around her. "We'll get through this somehow, with His help."

Mary turned, too, from him and all his hopeful talk. She stomped past neatly piled bales, spotless stalls, and the husband she'd never really had a blowup with. How dared he tell her about God? He didn't have a clue of what it was like to live in such a screwed-up family. Couldn't he see Mother was the problem here, not her?

✦ ✦ ✦

Sally found it hard to picture the meanness that oozed from Mother. She'd always sworn she'd never put Mama in a nursing home. But what if Mama acted like . . . Mother? It wouldn't be so easy, would it? Suddenly she felt even more defensive of this new friend. "You did offer to take care of her."

"I was just getting myself off the hook," Mary said, not meeting Sally's gaze. "I never intended to do it. I knew she wouldn't take me up on it. I was so hateful."

Sally could picture the cold sneer, the rigid spine. "She's a hard one to love."

"And I never could've done it, without God's help."

CHAPTER 24

Peace that flows from sin forgiven, joy that lifts the soul to heaven . . .
—William McComb, "Chief of Sinners Though I Be"

The phone rang. Mary jumped, still not used to the shrill sound, especially at six thirty in the morning. The aides called at the beginning and end of their shifts, but never this early. Unless . . . Herbal tea slopped out of her cup as she hurried to answer it.

"I give in."

At first Mary thought it was a crank call, a wrong number, the voice muffled as if someone was cupping a hand over the receiver. She stared straight ahead, the lights of their Christmas tree suddenly too bright, the tinsel too cheery.

"Come get me, Mary Elizabeth."

Mary eased herself back onto the couch. It was Mother, her voice heavy with defeat. "Mother? Mother?" Nothing but static came across the line. Mary stared out the window. Sleet glazed the hardwoods, and a chill went through Mary.

"I'll not let those strangers in, ye hear? I'm done with them." An edge had crept into Mother's voice.

"Mother, where's Claudette? Where's—"

The line went dead.

With stiff fingers, Mary dialed Mother's number over and over. Busy. Finally she hung up and hurried to the barn, where she found Paul wedged under the tractor. "There's something wrong," she said, shivering.

A wrench clattered to the ground.

"I think she's by herself. When I tried to call back, the line was busy."

Paul scrambled out from under the truck, then pulled Mary close without bothering to wipe oil off his hands.

"I've got to go to her. Now." Mary did all she could to hold back hot tears as visions of baking cookies with Claire and caroling with friends melted in the cold reality of Mother's condition. When Paul rubbed her shoulders, she could keep them in no more.

"Not this time, Betsy. We're all doing it together. We were going up Christmas Eve, anyway. It's not that big of a deal."

"But the farm, the animals . . ." Her words disappeared in a spate of tears, and she rested in Paul's support. God's support.

Too soon, Paul drew away. "Come on. I'll make some calls; you pack."

The tension that had flowed out began its creeping buildup as she packed. It wasn't just the illness that upset her, but the way Mother ruled, even from her bed. *She's ruining our Christmas. Will it not end until she ruins our lives?*

They sped north, the girls in deep slumber. As sleet changed into snow, all Mary could think of was Mother's icy stare. Snowflakes fluttered as they passed cars full of happy people, Mary imagined, zooming toward blazing fires, fragrant kitchens. The storm, and Mother, insulated them from a world eager to celebrate the Savior's birth; Mary felt distant even from Paul, who was humming a carol. She bowed her head, exhausted by it all. *God, help me*, she prayed, with an emptiness she hadn't felt since she'd accepted Christ. *I can't do this alone.* After a glance at the girls, she slumped against the window and tried to sleep.

When they reached Lisle, the snow had changed back to sleet.

"You go on in," Paul said. "I'll unload."

Pellets of ice stung Mary's cheeks as she rushed to the door and unlocked it. "Mother? Claudette? Mother?" she kept calling. The house was as cold as a meat locker, and Mary couldn't stop shivering.

A moan came from Mother's room.

The sound took hold of Mary; for an instant, she couldn't move. It was not unlike the sound of an animal so deeply wounded it could not summon the strength to move.

Mother moaned again.

"Oh, God." The sound again tore at Mary, managing to drive her into action, the blinders removed from her heart. She saw her mother as desperate for love, like she too had been, before she'd come to the Lord. "Oh, God, let it not be too late," she kept saying as she ran through the house. She rushed into the room, then slowed.

The bed reeked of human excrement and urine. Lacy curtains were pulled back just enough to illumine a figure huddled under a tangle of sheets. Mary's heart sank, not from the soiled state of the bedding, but from the thin arms curled about knobby knees, the drawn-up legs so intent on returning to the fetal position that once had granted safety and comfort.

Sobbing, Mary shoved back the soiled bedding and years of bitterness and curled in beside her mother. "I'm so sorry," she cried as she drew her mother into her own bosom, tucking the bowed head under her chin. She stroked a cheek soft as a rose petal. *So much like my baby's,* she kept thinking.

It was as if Mother understood. Gradually, she uncurled and, groaning, turned to face her daughter. Her eyes, crusted with mucus, fluttered open.

The spark that had been ignited in Mary's heart glowed brighter as she lay there on that bed, brighter, even, than the sun, which had dared to battle the storm and beam into the window. Her mother was no more miserable than she was. And if Christ had forgiven her, she had to forgive Mother. Love Mother. "You poor thing," she said as she stroked her hair. "I'm here. Lizzie is here." From time to time, she dabbed at Mother's red, encrusted eyes. How long had she waited for Mother to love her when the whole secret had been to accept Mother without stipulations? To love Mother first?

"Lizzie? Lizzie?" The eyes fluttered as Mother repeated Mary's old nickname like a child pronouncing a new word. "A nice name." She patted her daughter's head twice. Then she smiled.

Mary had held Mother close, but now they became one entity, there on that bed. Music filled Mary's heart—Mam's night music, Grandmother's folk songs, the beautiful hymns she'd learned at church—and it flowed out in a jumble of words and tears and melodies. In spite of all their failures, Jesus' sacrifice had provided the way for them to love one another. And Mary did love Mother now, with a love that transcended her human shortcomings, with a love that was heaven sent. Passionate. Forgiving.

She lost all concept of time. Paul came, then quickly left. When Mary did arise, she was no longer mired in the resentment that had weighed her down for so long. She was free, and whatever lay ahead with Mother, with Christ's help, she could handle it.

✠ ✠ ✠

Tears streamed down Sally's face.

"For two weeks, we flurried about the house like snowflakes, cleaning, packing. Maureen sold the house in three days."

Sally nodded. "So you moved her here?"

"To the farm, until it became impossible to manage. Then we moved to town."

"So she's the mother you care for now."

Mary nodded. "Day after day, I dress her and feed her and guide her into a rocking chair. She creaks away the afternoon much like Mary Ellen did. I undress her and tuck her into bed." Mary glanced at her watch. "That's my story. Why I am and am not Irish. Why I was so bitter about my first memory." She looked toward the window. "How He taught me to forgive." Her stomach tightened as she thought of the chores that awaited, the daily struggles of caring for an Alzheimer's patient. *How I still struggle with it every day and have to give it to Him.*

Sally stretched her legs and rubbed her eyes. "But why did you tell me, of all people, after all these years?"

Mary studied those steady blue eyes, still unsure of it all herself. Could she tell her it was God? She thought Sally would believe it, was almost sure of it, but something held her back. She tried to make her smile convincing. "I've always wanted to share it with someone besides Paul, and almost did one time. But something held me back."

When the sun blared its final drama into Sally's front window, Mary stood to leave. Time to fix Mother's dinner. Yet there was one more thing she wanted to say.

"I've been thinking about something," Sally said, just as Mary was about to speak. "Ah, can I write this?"

The lights in the room seemed to brighten as Mary sat back down. "What do you mean?" she asked.

"Like in a book."

Mary's spine stiffened. How could Sally think she'd want her private life exposed for all to see? Things she'd never told anyone except Paul, and a few things she'd never told him. "Absolutely not."

"Can I at least meet your mother?" Sally asked in a quiet voice.

"Of course." Mary smiled, glad to grant one of Sally's requests. "It's time you came over, anyway." She lingered a bit, right there on the lumpy couch, wondering how to broach the topic that after all these years still nagged at her.

"I can't wait to see your house. And to meet your mother. It's hard to—"

Mary's bag thudded onto the floor. "I can't get something out of my mind."

Sally moved closer until their knees nearly touched. "What, Mary? Tell me."

"Why did she do it?"

"It makes perfect sense." Sally leaned against the back of the couch. "The affairs, being the mayor's wife. And—"

"I'm not talking about Mother." Mary jumped to her feet and flew to the window, yet her mind was thousands of miles and over forty years away, back on the cliffs.

"I'm sorry," came from behind her.

Mary's shoulders drooped. Here she was, yelling at the closest friend she had. Always that temper, that resentment looming in the background, ready to pounce. "Oh, Sally, it's me that's sorry. I can't quit thinking about the other mother, the one who sent me away. Those cliffs. Why God didn't let us have a relationship."

"Did you ever write her that letter you mentioned?"

Mary turned to face her friend, yet looked past her to the magnolia still life hanging on the wall. The creamy white flowers, almost decadent in their beauty, promised vitality and life. When her voice came out, it was, in sharp contrast, devoid of emotion. "We exchanged Christmas cards. I sent pictures. She wrote about Grandmother's death, like I told you. When Claire was seven and Chloe three, I decided they were old enough to go over. I wanted them to meet. I planned to settle things." Her voice quavered, but she kept talking. "A month before our trip, Kelly sent a letter. Mam was dead. Leukemia. I didn't even know she'd been sick."

Silence enveloped the room.

Finally Sally found her voice. "I'm so sorry." She threw her arms around Mary.

Mary swallowed down the pain as best she could. She had to explain this calmly. Rationally. "My heart breaks for what never could be." For the third time, she rose from the couch. "And why would God want it that way?" She walked toward the entryway, which the setting sun had transformed from pink to scarlet. "I know the Christian line: it wasn't His will. But why? I've accepted it, but it still eats at me." She paused to wriggle into her coat. "You'd think as I got older, it would get better. But it seems like it's getting worse." She accepted a hug from Sally. "I've got to go. I'll call."

"Mare?"

"*What?*" Mary whirled about to face her friend.

"Mare, I am so sorry."

"*What* did you call me?"

Sally backed away. "Mare . . ."

Though Mary stepped forward, time turned back to the lonely girl at the statue, the girl who had prayed and prayed . . . "That's a nickname a best friend would give you," was all she managed. She kissed Sally on both cheeks and scrambled into what remained of the snowy day.

✠ ✠ ✠

"Wow." Sally took in the oversized entry, the leaded glass, arched passage-ways, a Klimt print. "I feel like I need to be wearing a bustle and carrying a parasol."

Mary giggled. "Come on back. I've made us something." She led Sally down a hall lined with portraits of Chloe and Claire and a jovial-looking man who Sally assumed was Daddy. They paused on the threshold of a room dominated by a massive bookshelf, an ornate fireplace. Mary pointed to a cluster of pictures on the mantel. "Paul's family."

It was hard not to be intimidated by the crowd of stern-looking men and women. For a bit longer, Sally studied them. "They're very . . ." She struggled to describe this somber crowd, her mind on the rollicking Flowers clan, who barely got through the annual reunion photo without cracking up.

"German," Mary finished for her.

"All those years, Mother refused to have her picture taken." Mary's voice be-came somber as she led Sally back into the hall. "And she destroyed all Daddy's pictures. Except that one." She pointed to the portrait Sally had already noticed. "As far as my Irish folk, I've got nothing. Not even a snapshot. How I wish . . ." Her voice trailed off as they walked into the kitchen.

Sally sat on a pine bench. A lone calla lily stood at attention in a crystal vase. Everything gleamed, as if a photo shoot was about to occur, yet there was a warmth in every inch of the place that expensive furnishings and no amount of cleaning could instill. Sally leaned back and inhaled the lily's fragrance, cin-namon and . . . something else. "What's that smell?"

"Nut bran muffins. Here." Mary set down a steaming basket.

Sally broke a muffin in half and popped it into her mouth. "Delicious. What's that weird taste? Kinda woodsy."

"Cardamom."

Sally downed the drink. "This is delicious too. What's in it?"

Mary lifted her eyebrows. "You don't want to know."

"Why not?"

"Okay, Sally. Wheat grass and persimmons and—"

"You're right. I don't want to know. But it's really good," she hurriedly added.

"Come on," Mary said after they chatted a while. "I want you to meet Mother."

They walked into a sunny room at the back of the house. A print by Cassatt, a blue and white and gold Impressionist wonder of a smiling mother and daughter, captured Sally, and for a moment, she lost herself amid the swirls and bursts of color. When the chair creaked, she stepped back.

There, in the rocking chair, was Anne McNamara Harris. Mother.

"Mother, this is Sally. My best friend." Mary put a hand on her mother's shoulder.

"Hi," Sally said, her voice shaking. It was easy enough to conceive of this wrinkled old lady, impeccable in a starched cotton blouse, tailored suit, nylons, and laced-up shoes, as the icy woman of Mary's story. She sat with the ramrod-straight posture of a school marm and rocked forward and back, forward and back. For the five minutes that Sally stammered through small talk, Mother never changed expression.

"Is she always like that?"

"Sometimes."

"Does she know who you are?"

Mary shook her head.

All Sally could think of was the book she wanted to write as she stared at Mother. She willed her voice to stay steady. "Did you ever learn about her past?"

"One day she was watching TV. I was cleaning upstairs. Suddenly she screamed. I flew down here. 'Don't let them take my babbie,' she kept saying, shaking like she had chills." Sally's eyes got big. "We don't know, Sally. We just don't know."

Snippets of Kathleen's story came back to Sally, prickling her arms. "Do you remember what she said about not letting them take the child? Do you think—"

Mary massaged her mother's shoulders. "Probably not. Just her illness."

✣ ✣ ✣

"Hello."

"Good morning." Mary kept her voice level even though her hands shook. For years, she'd expected it, even—God forgive her—at times wanted it. She wasn't sure why she was calling Sally. Maybe she just wanted to hear the voice of her best friend.

"Hey, don't you know it's rude to call before eight?"

Normally Mary loved Sally's giggles, but not today. She bit her tongue and tried to explain how she'd gone in like she always did; how Mother was curled into her bed like she always was; how this day, unlike many days, a peace seemed to hang in the room like a cloud of incense; how, when she touched the withered cheek, she knew, before she checked her pulse and all the other things, that Mother was gone. She tried to tell Sally all these things, but when she opened her mouth, nothing came out.

"In the South, anyway. My crazy mother'll just let it ring and ring and—"

Mary gripped the phone cord until her knuckles went white. "My mother's dead."

"Wha-what? She was fine two weeks ago!"

A wave washed over Mary, and tears flowed. Welcoming tears for His perfect will. He knew her conflicting thoughts—glad that Mother had passed, yet sad to see her eyes forever closed. And there was no condemnation from the One who knew her best. Suddenly drained, Mary dropped into a chair. "I know, Sally. But she's . . . dead." *And I pray to God she's at peace.*

"I'm coming right over."

"No, you're not. It's okay."

"Have you called the paramedics?" Sally raced on, speaking so rapidly Mary could not catch all the words.

"I don't need the paramedics, Sally," she said. "She's dead."

"I—I can't believe you're so calm."

"The police took care of it." Mary winced, the words sounding harsh. How could she explain that her body, her mind were drained of nearly everything but the realization that this was God's will? "It's been a long time coming," she finally said.

"Can I do anything? A casserole? Ham?"

Mary swallowed. "No. But thanks." She hung up the study phone, which sat on the bookshelf right below all the Freeman pictures. *It's over, all of it. Both mothers dead. No chance to ever know.* A wave of despondency swept across Mary so severe in its intensity she doubled up. She had nothing left from her side of the family. Nothing.

CHAPTER 25

And when the fields are fresh and green,
I'll take you to your home again.
—Thomas P. Westendorf, "I'll Take You Home Again, Kathleen"

The mailbox had become a symbol of connection. Would she hear from Sally, who'd moved away three years ago? Had Chloe settled into the new semester long enough to write home? She'd just heard from Claire, who was in law school, but communication with her baby, who'd struggled a bit in college, had been a different story. Terse phone messages. One-line e-mails. Worst of all, the yawning gap where there was nothing. Mary pulled out a stack of mail and rifled through it. She smiled at the yellow envelope plastered with happy face stickers and ripped it open:

> *February 15, 2001*
>
> *Mare,*
>
> *Thanks for the Cassatt print! And for calling last week.*
> *How did you know it was a perimenopause moment? Hot*
> *flashes, mood swings, and teenagers, all at once!*
>
> *Hope things are better with Chloe. Suzi and Ed are hardly*
> *ever home, and I've got lots of spare time since they've cut my*
> *teaching hours. Again.*
>
> *Since I'm twiddling my thumbs and baking brownies, I*
> *wondered if you'd reconsider letting me write your story. It needs*
> *to be told. And I want to tell it.*
>
> *Sally*

Mary headed inside, determined to read Sally's letter again later. She flipped through the other mail, hoping to see Chloe's spidery script. There was a bill. Junk mail. She pulled out one envelope, addressed to both her and Paul. The university return address reached up and grabbed her by the throat. She ripped open the envelope.

February 13, 2001

Ms. Chloe Freeman
Foster Hall, #210
Bloomington, IN 47405

Dear Ms. Freeman:

Per our Code of Student Conduct, this letter is a follow-up to our meeting on February 10 wherein you admitted to partaking of alcohol in your room and serving it to other students under the legal drinking age. Based on your taking full responsibility for your actions, we've sanctioned you to one year of residence hall probation. If at any time you violate other policies, you may be referred to the director of student judicial programs, who may sanction you further, up to expulsion.

Pursuant to our policy, your guardian of record will receive a copy of this letter.

Sincerely,
Jon Winters, Residence Hall Director

cc: Donald Moore, Director of Student Judicial Programs
Guardian of record for Chloe Freeman

✠ ✠ ✠

The phone blasted Sally out from under her down comforter. All she could think about was how, on her one day to sleep in, someone had dared to call so early. "Hello." She made sure to make her voice chirpy.

"Hi. I know it's before eight, but yes, you can."

Sally shivered at the metallic coldness in Mary's voice as she struggled to pull the covers around her. "I can what?"

"You can write it."

Write what? Sally wondered, rubbing her eyes. Then it hit her, on two levels. Mary had given her permission to pursue her dream, but the voice was so flat, so dead, Sally knew something was terribly wrong. "What's going on?" she asked.

For too long Mary remained silent. It was enough to make Sally hustle out of bed and get down on her knees. *Please, Lord, help Mary through whatever she's dealing with. And help me to know when to talk and when not to.*

"A Southerner left speechless." Mary broke the silence, her voice shrill as it always was when she used sarcasm to cover up pain. "Now, that's something to ponder. That on the heels of the shortest letter I've ever received from you."

Sally cradled the phone on her shoulder. "What's going on? What made you change your mind?"

"Let's just leave it as a yes for now and not discuss it." Mary was speaking so loudly Sally held the receiver away from her ear. Then the line went dead before Sally could ask any more questions.

Awake now, Sally went downstairs and slopped the coffee Sam had left into a mug. She set her stopwatch and worked the daily crossword with ink, like always, but a question niggled at her: What's wrong with Mary?

⊕ ⊕ ⊕

Mary punched in Chloe's number for the fourth time, then slammed her cell phone shut when the message with the bizarre music—something Chloe called ska—almost burst her eardrum. With one hand on the steering wheel and her mind on an auburn-haired freshman, she veered into the soup-kitchen parking lot. Yellowed newspapers skittered across cracked pavement, and dandelions dotted the overgrown yard. "Out of control," she whispered as she flipped open the phone. Just like Chloe.

She dialed for the fifth time, then uttered a single profanity when she got the message. This was her baby. In spite of how they'd lavished affection on her, had raised her in the faith, Chloe had descended into the pit of substance abuse, just like she had. And if Chloe kept drinking and running with the wrong crowd . . . , what if she influenced Claire, it could aggravate Paul's blood pressure, and she wasn't sleeping, and wasn't insomnia a sign of cancer, and Mam had had leukemia, and didn't that kind of thing run in the genes along with . . . She wrestled with the pit bulls of angst and anger. *Stay calm.* She dialed again, got the stupid song, vowed to leave a nice, clear message.

"Chloe, it's Mother. I, ah, got a letter, and . . . Chloe . . . Chloe . . . baby, I love you." She managed to shut the phone before great heaves convulsed her shoulders. She raked her hands through her hair. "Oh, God, please don't leave her. Don't let her do this. God."

She sat broken until she heard patrons stirring about the gate, then checked her watch. It was time to feed her people, who were hungry, lonely. People like drug addicts and the homeless and drunks. People like her Chloe.

Desperate to keep a hold on reality, she returned sunglasses to a case, hooked her keys on the purse attachment, and took measured steps toward the soup kitchen.

✚ ✚ ✚

Sally gnawed on her pencil and stared at the magnolia painting, begging it to inspire her. Nothing. With a sigh, she flipped open an outdated atlas. There. Ireland. She stared at all the pastel-shaded counties. Nothing.

For several weeks, words had flowed until she'd gotten to the part about the cliffs and what Mary had called a black sea. Then the words dried up faster than exposed bread. The only ocean Sally knew was the Gulf of Mexico, where bubbly blue waters had slipped over the feet of her precious Suzi and Ed, then kissed a benevolent sandy shore. Over and over, a blessed communion of nature and man. She tapped against her desk as if that would conjure up a word picture. And cliffs weren't that rugged, were they?

Sally picked up the phone and dialed Mary.

"Yes."

"Hi. It's Sally."

"It's hard to hide that drawl."

"And your caller ID, of course. We never have gotten that. I mean, my mother says that if someone really needs to get ahold of you—"

"Is everything okay, I mean, with the kids? We just talked yesterday for thirty minutes." Mary sounded every bit as nervous and curt as she had for the past two weeks.

Sally took a deep breath. "Everything's fine. Except I need to see these cliffs if I'm going to write about them."

"There's scads of pictures on the Internet. Go surfing."

Sally drummed the table instead of the pencil. "Will you take me there?"

"Just like that? No hour-long explanation? No travel guide description of what you need to see?"

Sally winced. *Why is she being so rude?* "I mean, I haven't talked to Sam, but if it's okay with him, will you do it?"

"There you have it. Sam. Let him take you. That's what husbands are for."

"Uh . . . I really need you to show me. Plus, I hear they drive on the wrong side of the road over there, and—"

"And why would I return to where my heart was cut out not once, but twice?"

"Hmm. Well, I hadn't thought about—"

"Get someone else."

"It really won't work unless you—"

"No. I can't do it."

"Will you at least pray about it?"

Such a long pause followed, Sally wondered if Mary was about to hang up. *I wouldn't be surprised, with her temper.* She did what was best when Mary was like this: she prayed. And waited.

"I'll think about it, Sally," Mary finally said.

When Sally hung up, her hands were sore from gripping the phone. *What if she won't go? How will I do this?* She prayed for God to take captive her anxious thoughts.

✟ ✟ ✟

Her back straight as a rail, Mary strode to the check-in desk at Sue's office. In spite of the cheerful prints, it triggered memories: lifting Mother into a wheelchair; waiting for hours; having them prod at ancient veins to find even half a vial full of blood; and of course, all the people peering around newspapers, diagnosing you with bulbous eyes. It took all her strength to keep from turning around and walking out.

A glass partition slid open. "Can I help you?" asked a smiling woman.

Mary bit back a retort. Already today she'd been rude to Sally, Paul, the clerk at the grocery store, and no telling who else. As if it were anyone's fault but her own for the mess her daughter was in. "Mary Freeman. An appointment with Sue—Dr. Lee."

The woman nodded and smiled. "It'll just be a moment." She walked to a shelf packed with manila files and found Mary's. "Has your coverage changed since your last visit?" she asked, without looking up.

Mary shook her head. Other than check-ups, they hadn't needed a doctor in years.

A nurse in casual pastel scrubs appeared. "Mary Freeman?" She ushered Mary to a weigh-in station and took her vitals, then led Mary to another room, where she could sit and wait some more. And still, nothing constructive was being done to help her baby.

The door opened. "Mary. How's Paul? The—what's going on?" Sue, her gray hair pulled into a tight ponytail, rested her hand on a counter, concern in her gray eyes.

It was hard not to break down in front of the woman who had delivered her Chloe—had delivered both girls—the one woman, besides Sally, who knew snatches of her own story. But Mary managed. "Chloe's drinking, and she won't get help." She looked hard at Sue, wondering if she dare tell the rest of it.

Sue's eyes were steady, her tanned face a greenish-beige under fluorescent light. Without taking her eyes off Mary, she slid onto an examining stool. "She's a freshman now, isn't she? What, eighteen? Nineteen?"

Mary jumped out of her chair. "I can't let her throw her life away. She might end it all. What if it affects Claire? And Paul, with the farm, he—"

Wrinkles creased Sue's brow. "Mary, sit," she ordered, pulling out a pen. With a flick of her finger, she opened a chart. "How long has your mind been racing like this?"

Mary let out a sigh so long, it had a beginning, middle, and end. In a way, she was glad Sue had noticed. But that meant it was serious, didn't it? She scrambled to decide what to tell Sue and finally gave up. "I don't know," she said. "A while."

Sue studied her, gathering evidence. "Trouble sleeping?"

Mary nodded.

"How long?"

"Oh, I don't know. Since Chloe started her shenanigans, I guess."

Sue lowered her voice. "And at other times, prior to that?"

Mary nodded.

"Lots of highs and lows?" When Mary nodded, she made some notations. "Mary, have you had any hallucinations?" Her voice was even softer now. "Visions? Delusions?"

Mary clenched her fists and stared. "What do you mean?"

"Seeing things that aren't there. Hearing voices."

"Of course not." Mary jumped up and paced the floor. Would that count the fragments causing a traffic jam in her brain? The voices? She clamped her mouth shut. She wasn't mentally ill. That was supposed to be hereditary, and her parents hadn't been—

Her heart rose to her throat. The Irish folk weren't crazy, were they? Despite an effort to stop it, Mary trembled. Perhaps they were crazy, Mam or the handsome Johnny who, according to Mam's letters, was her father. And perhaps she was too.

Sue motioned for Mary to get on the examining table. She checked Mary's eyes, ears, nose, throat, and heart, then motioned for her to sit up. "I'm referring you to a psychiatrist, Mary." Her sympathetic tone had been replaced by a brisk professional voice. "The good news? She's a Christian. The bad news? She's in Indy. An hour and a half away."

"A psychiatrist?"

Sue nodded. "I want you to have a complete evaluation."

Mary had expected Sue to suggest counseling for Chloe, perhaps both of them, but never this. "Why?" she asked.

Sue studied Mary before answering. "Depression can be hereditary, environmental, linked to substance abuse. For example, did your parents suffer from mental illness? Any suicide or—"

Mary jerked back as if she'd been slapped, then tried to act nonchalant. "Of course not," she managed to say, but her hands shook. Had Sue noticed? And had she heard about Daddy's death from some gossipmonger? But Daddy wasn't blood, so . . .

Sue questioned and probed. Mary struggled to shrug, nod, do anything but reveal the thoughts that might confirm that she wasn't normal. She longed to fly out of this sterile room, past the gaping mouths, to her truck, then home. Yet there was no peace there, either, not with thoughts hounding her even as she tried to scrub and cook and run them out of her system.

"—a correlation between heredity and certain mental illnesses."

Mary's fists became tight balls. Had Mam, or Johnny, been plagued by this . . . thing that would haunt first her, then her daughters? She interlaced her fingers, which were slick with sweat. But with Mam dead, Johnny a mystery, would she ever know? Were there records in Ireland that might reveal the truth? Witnesses? She screamed at God, silently, but with an intensity that made her body shake. *Is this what You want, for me to go back there again? For Chloe's sake? Claire's sake? Her sake?*

"—let the receptionist schedule . . . Mary? Mary?"

Mary summoned all of her resources and tried to smile. "I'm sorry, Sue. It's just a bit hard to stay focused when all I can think about is Chloe."

The look Sue gave knocked away any semblance of a smile on Mary's face. "Get the appointment scheduled before you leave here. As your health care provider, I strongly recommend it. As your friend, I insist."

She had to nod to get out of the office, so she did. But there was no way she'd expose this mess to a shrink. She'd go to Ireland before she did something stupid like that.

✟ ✟ ✟

Sally tensed every time the phone rang. Everyone she knew chose this week to call for a chat. Her old college roommate in Mississippi. Her cousin Laurie down in Dallas. Everyone except Mary. She cleaned the kitchen and plopped in front of her computer. Yet words did not come. She fiddled with the cap of her pen. Something tugged at the edge of her mind, then evaporated when the phone rang.

"If you're still game, I'm ready to go."

Sally dropped her pen, then picked it up. If she kept hanging around with Mary, she'd better get used to being speechless.

"Get a pencil. Here's the flight information."

Sally scribbled onto a tattered phone book.

"I've got to find out about them," Mary said, her intuition, at least, doing fine. "Plus Paul says he'll feel better if someone goes with me. With it being spring, he's tied up even worse than usual."

"Sure." Sally wasn't about to disagree, since her prayer had been answered, but she couldn't help wondering what Mary thought she'd find out there on those cliffs.

As Mary rattled on about the farm in a style quite out of character, Sally pushed away negative thoughts. Here Mary had invited her on a trip that just might write the ending to the best story Sally had ever heard. And if she could be there for Mary, help her get over a few rough spots, the whole thing would be a gift from God.

"You understand, don't you?" Mary asked.

"Sure, Mary." And Sally did understand, at least partially. "Of course. You want closure on this whole thing." Even though Sally wasn't exactly a tidy person, when it came to personal things, it was always better when loose ends were tied up neatly like the laces of new tennis shoes.

"Yeah. That too."

After she hung up, Sally stared at the phone. Something just didn't seem right about Mary's responses, but she really didn't have time to dwell on it now, not with Sam to convince and arrangements to be made. It was probably just menopause or nerves, or maybe a lethal combination of both.

✢ ✢ ✢

Mary arrived at Sally's on a cloudless spring day. They set out for the airport, the misty rains of Ireland about to be closer. It took both of them to heave Sally's peeling Samsonite bags into Mary's trunk. "You got dead bodies in there?" Mary asked.

"No, but just about everything else," Sally answered as she climbed into the car. "They're like sausages," she retorted. "You really don't want to know what's in them."

They bantered back and forth about their packing, almost as if afraid to broach more serious topics. Sally had packed her Bible even though it was shedding pages like last year's phone book. She'd borrowed an L.L. Bean parka that was guaranteed to keep out anything, even Irish rains, gale-force winds. Mary had enough fruit and nuts to reopen The Health Food Shoppe and had managed to fit scarves and hats and gloves and all kinds of things into two designer bags that were as thin and stylish as she was.

As they got closer to the airport, Mary's responses to Sally's questions became monosyllabic, then stopped. She tinkered with the radio until she found a news station.

Sally popped the tab on a Diet Coke, alternating slugs of caramel-colored chemicals with bites from a chewy candy bar, and tried to decide how to best ask the questions that needed to be asked. "Mare? I forgot a hat and gloves . . ."

For the first time in a while, Mary smiled. "Don't worry, I've got extra." She seemed to relax her grip on the steering wheel.

It had worked. Sally had softened her up. "Why did you decide you wanted to go back over there, look for your family?" She finished her candy, sat back, and waited.

Mary stared at the oncoming traffic. "I told you. To see if anyone can tell me about them. To see where Mam's buried. And because I think it's what God wants."

Sally started to warn against such high hopes, then remembered how God had answered her prayer about writing. He could do anything, and she wanted to be there with Mary when He did. "I feel the same way."

Her words seemed to encourage Mary. "There's something else." Her knuckles whitened as she gripped the steering wheel. "Chloe."

A convoy of trucks zipped past, shaking Mary's compact car.

Sally put her hand on Mary's arm. *So that's what has upset her.*

"She's drinking. A lot. And I ought to know, since I did the same thing." Suddenly Mary burst into activity. She set the cruise control, adjusted the seat.

"Oh, it can't be that bad," Sally said, then bit her tongue.

"But it is. It's a flashback to Marquette; this time, in living color." Mary's sigh shook her whole body. "She's been put on probation, and the way it's torn me up, I might as well be on probation too." She darted a glance at Sally. "From life. I can't stand it."

Even though Sally nodded, she couldn't help but think of her Suzi, who was breezing through her last year of high school without so much as a glitch. Guilt assailed her, and she tried to put herself in Mary's place. When she did, she wanted to punch somebody; namely, Chloe. "I don't blame you. Here she is, partying up there while y'all have—"

"No." Mary ran her hand through her hair. "Something's behind it."

"And you think Ireland will help you figure that out?"

"I don't know," Mary admitted. "But I guess we're about to find out."

✠ ✠ ✠

"Flight attendants, prepare for landing."

Sally rubbed her eyes, gradually waking after a deep sleep. From the way Mary looked, she'd barely slept at all. *God help her*, she prayed as she buckled her seatbelt.

The plane descended into massive cloud cover, congestion swirling so fast Mary got airsick. Sally patted her back, praying this wasn't an omen. Seconds later, the clouds parted to reveal a verdant checkerboard of greens and browns. As they landed, cultivated patches of farms and stretches of rolling hills came into focus.

Mary stayed huddled in her seat, her head down, her legs curled under her as if she expected a crash. Other passengers jumped into the aisles, eager to stretch their legs.

God, help her. Answer whatever she's laying at Your feet. Sally patted Mary on the arm just as the flight attendant said, "Welcome to Shannon."

CHAPTER 26

Erin, thy silent tear never shall cease.
Erin, thy languid smile ne'er shall increase.
—Thomas Moore, "Erin! The Tear and the Smile in Thine Eyes"

Things sure had changed. Banners decorated with shamrocks and leprechauns hung from bustling airport shops. Expensive designer bags, watches, and chocolates filled gorgeous window displays. Mary remembered nothing like this. Of course, it had been thirty-four years.

A young flutist, sitting cross-legged near a baggage claim area, coaxed a minor-key melody from a wooden flute and set off the old question: Is Ireland home or not? Mary tossed a few Euros into the boy's plaid wool cap and scanned the crowd for Sally. There she was, perched on a display case at the bookstore in a full-blown conversation with some man.

"This is Patrick," Sally gushed as Mary approached. "My first friend on Irish soil."

She'd crossed six time zones, traveled more than five thousand miles to help her daughter. They needed to move on. Mary forced a smile. "Let's be headin' out," she said, her hand firm on Sally's arm.

"Nice to meet you, Patrick," Sally called over her shoulder.

As they rode in the shuttle van, Sally babbled on.

Mary managed a half-smile, not blaming Sally for falling in love with the land. After all, hadn't she done the same thing on her last visit? Yet the cliffs loomed before Mary, and a chance to help Chloe. To help all of them.

Another agent, dressed in what looked like a green leisure suit, directed them to a compact car so small Mary was glad she'd packed light.

In spite of a sprinkling of rain, Sally rolled down the window and breathed deeply. "Where are we going?" she asked, her hair a tangle of colors.

"My mother's old place." *The one she sent me away from. Twice.*

"How long will it take?"

"Less than an hour." *Almost forever.*

"What are we looking for?"

"I don't know." Mary checked the map, then shifted the car, and they lurched forward, rolling up and down the hills of County Clare. Along the lanes, the gentian showed their first deep blues to the country people, hinting of a splendorous spring. Hinting of hope.

Sally bounced on the seat, oohing and aahing at every bend in the road. "It's like I'm a schoolgirl again."

"What do you mean?" Mary asked.

"All the greens in the big box of Crayolas. Mother bought me a new one every year. Just look at this. Jungle green and chartreuse and pine and cerulean." Sally rattled away. "Tornado green. Astroturf green."

Mary felt like a schoolgirl too, but in a different way. *We don't want the eejit. She's got to go.* Over and over, the voices mocked her. She turned on the windshield wipers; they mocked her too, with every swish. *She's got to go. She's got to go.*

"Look." Sally pointed out the window.

The moss-covered facade of a centuries-old castle loomed its immensity, lending a sense of the medieval to the landscape. Yet as they streaked west, piles of lumber and clusters of machinery spoke of progress, building, and expansion. Money.

"They've discovered a new shade of green over here: one that's minted." Mary pointed to a realtor's sign announcing a thatch-covered cottage as the perfect second home. "Last time I was here, it was nothing like this." She shook her head. *Can't call us filthy bogsiders anymore, can they?* She loosed her grip on the steering wheel.

"Well, now, Mary, uh, that was how long ago?"

"Over thirty years." Mary peered through whirring wipers. Vines and brambles tried to camouflage everything, but they hadn't hidden stone walls, which lined the road, then branched erratically into the fields, up the hills, and out of sight. Her pulse quickened as she squinted to see the turnoff to Glascloune. They'd tried to cover it up, but if she had her way, she was going to shove back the facade of this mystical country, expose the truth. "There!" She threw on her brakes and tapped the window. "That's it." Nailed-up boards bleached ecru from nature's sandblastings were all that remained of the old settlers' hangout, except for the Keep Out sign. Mary managed a bitter smile. They weren't keeping her out anymore, not when it involved her daughters. She shifted her focus to the road and turned north toward Mam's old house.

The color spectrum shifted from greens to grays as they neared the cliffs. They crested the hill, the fields to the west plummeting into the sea with no warning. A foreboding of a primeval encounter penetrated Mary as silvery mist mingled with smoldering soil and foaming waves. Her skin tingled as if she was not in another country, but in another geologic age, those cliffs pulling her back, back, back . . .

She glanced at Sally, who had also become more reticent. *Are we really here or am I dreaming?* As if to answer her question, rain pelted the windshield, obliterating her vision. It was rain and sky and sea and soil and memories.

Mary put the car in park and used a wadded-up sweater to wipe off the fogged windshield. She rolled down her window and tried to see past a rise in the pasture. Squinting hard, she made out a barn, a house . . . "That's it. I think."

"Your mother's?"

"I think so."

"You walked here from that store?"

Mary nodded as the mist permutated into sleet. The years rolled away like the icy droplets splattering against the car. Were days up here so gloomy Mam had turned to the bottle? Or was it etched into her DNA? *And mine and Chloe's?* She tried to refocus and yanked the gear stick into reverse. "Maybe that's not it."

Thunder boomed over the cliffs as if to argue with her, and clouds shifted across the horizon, dipping down occasionally to streak an azure sky with their dark wrath.

"This place is kinda scary."

Mary bit her lip. *You don't know the half of it.* For a moment, she was tempted to unburden herself of her load and tell Sally about the visit with Sue, but just thinking about it made her hands shake. Instead, she gripped the steering wheel, maneuvered past a gigantic pothole, and veered onto a rutted lane. She rolled down her window and craned her neck. Was it this way? That way? It was all a blur of rain and land and sky.

"Aye, are ye lost?"

Mary jumped. Sally let out a yell.

A strapping lad dressed in work clothes and carrying a coil of rope appeared from nowhere. Gray eyes peeking from beneath a wool cap, he leaned close to Sally's window.

Sally rolled down her window. "Good . . . good morning."

"And a fine mornin' to ye, ma'am. I'm Liam O'Loughlin. How can I help ye?"

Mary parked the car, jumped out, and offered her hand. Squinting, she could make out—were those the farmer's barns? "I'm Mary Elizabeth O'Brien," she managed to say, in spite of the memories trying to overcome her. "I used to live around here."

A grin brightened an already handsome face. "Jesus, Mary, and Joseph!" he exclaimed. "Kathleen's daughter?"

Mary leaned against the car. "How—how did you know?"

"I've heard talk of you since I was a wee lad."

Sally jumped out, and she and Liam chattered in spite of the chilling rain.

Mary only halfway listened. "Liam," she asked, interrupting one of Sally's yarns, "could ye tell me, where's my mother's old house?"

"Aye, the McNamaras'." He pivoted, then pointed. "'Tis that first one north."

Mary stood on her tiptoes so she could see past a hedgerow. It was the house she'd seen earlier, barely visible through the fog and the rain. "I thought that was it," she kept saying.

Liam shook his head. "Haven't heard o' the likes o' them for a spell."

Mary sighed. It was as she had feared. "Do you know where she's buried?"

"Nay, but Pap will." He pointed past a cow and calf huddled together in the middle of a verdant field. "You'll find him in there."

Mary, with Sally close behind, hurried to the barn. As they ran inside, they almost collided with a white-haired man wearing knee-high Wellingtons, a woolen jacket, cap, and knickers. He plunked down a bucket and stared at them.

Mary spoke first. "Are you Colm O'Loughlin?"

He eyed them warily. "And who's asking?" The condensation from his breath puffed into Mary's face. "If yer not the constable or the devil, I'm he."

Sally shrunk away, but Mary stood firm. She'd never forgotten the sunny farmer who'd let her rest on his knee, who'd given her a four-leaf clover. "I'm Mary Elizabeth O'Brien Harris Freeman. This is my friend Sally."

His mouth flew open. "Jesus, Mary, and Joseph. All those names for a fire-haired lass this tall"—he stretched out his hand—"when ye left these parts? I remember it well. 'Twas 1953."

Home. Mary felt her heart swell. She *had* been special to someone in this desolate land. He wasn't her blood, but still . . . She found eyes as blue as a mountain lake. "I'm so glad to see you," she cried, throwing her arms around him.

"The pleasure's mine, lass." He slapped her in the small of her back.

"Mr. O'Loughlin—"

"Nay, lass. Colm to you."

"Colm, can you tell me where my mother is buried?" Words tumbled out, and so did tears. "I want to see . . . where they laid her."

"No, lass, I'll not tell ye where she's laid to rest."

Mary stared down at muddy water. So it wasn't to be.

"Of course not. I'll take ye there. Right now." He tipped his hat to Liam, linked arms with both women, and headed back to the car. "I've never forgotten ye," he told Mary, brogue thickening his words. "Ye remember pestering me to play at cliff's edge?"

"You warned me of sea monsters." Years rolled away to a forgotten memory. The farmer had pulled off his cap and swooped it toward the rocks. Screaming, she'd leapt back, sure she'd spied a huge tail rising from the foam. As Colm recounted the adventure, the three of them hopped into the car, and Mary pulled away.

Colm rambled on about Abigail and his five children, rains and crops, and a 200-year-old house while Mary deciphered more and more of the thick brogue. She glanced over at Sally, who looked like she couldn't understand a word.

"Top o' the morning." Colm tipped his hat to a man who plodded toward them, shouldering a gigantic spade. "Aye, the gravedigger. One gent ye better be nice to, for sooner or later, he'll have his paws on ye."

Mary laughed but felt a sudden chill. Death again. Unstoppable. Always near.

"Right here, lass." After a final bump, Mary parked before a grassy knoll pinnacled above the surrounding country. A wrought-iron gate marked the boundaries of the sacred space. Ornate Celtic crosses, their intertwined circles both simple and complex, loomed like watchtowers over the graves.

Mary dug in her pocket and found gloves, which she tugged over shaking hands. Mam, dead. *And she never really knew me. Or my girls.*

When Colm yanked open the gate, it creaked in protest. He led them to an elevated plot that bore a simple cross. The granite marker read, "*Here lies Kathleen McNamara. May she rest in peace.*"

Mary stood as still as the marbled angels and granite saints that guarded dust and bones and buried memories. A cold wave pummeled her body, like those that crashed against the rocks a few thousand feet north. *Dead, and I never did make peace with her.*

Sally knelt by the grave. "It's so peaceful."

Colm nodded. "Aye, more peace than she ever had."

Mary jerked forward, her body stiffened. "What do you mean?"

Colm lowered his head, seemed about to speak, then stepped to another stone.

"Please, tell me." Words and tears spilled from Mary. "Why wasn't she at peace? And why wasn't I told? I could have helped." Her voice lost all coherence, and she cried out in concert with the seabirds that circled overhead.

Colm rushed to her side and draped his arm about her. "Aye, there's sorrows in this world. Sorrows we can't fathom." He took her elbow and led her bent form to another grave. "And here's yer stepfather and half-brother."

"My half-brother?" Mary ripped out of his hold. "Gerard's dead?"

"Nay, lass. Yer mother bore twins, didn't ye know? Gerard was a twin."

Mary clenched her fists, the words a tornado sucking one vital part from her, twisting up, and dipping in to destroy again. How many things had they kept from her, and why? A gust of wind caught the gate, and it creaked an evil response. *You weren't hers. She didn't want you like she did the others.*

"He passed at birth, he did. No will to live in this dark world."

Colm's words quieted Mary. She ran a finger over the baby's name and the dates of his birth and death, etched in the cold stone. "A twin half-brother I never knew. Another chance. Gone." Her sobs competed to drown out the sound of splattering rain.

Colm took her arm. "We best be leaving, lass."

The rain echoed his sentiments, pummeling the three, darkening the marble etchings. Sally helped Mary into the car. Colm followed and clicked the gate shut.

They'd barely gone a kilometer when Colm cracked a joke, and Mary roared in the artificial way she usually disdained. Perhaps it was better for him this way, but it wasn't better for her and her daughters. She shoved the gear stick into third. She was going to get him to talk about things that really mattered. And soon.

"Hurry me home, afore the gossips tell Missus I'm wi' two handsome Yanks."

Mary laughed again, loud and long, then cleared her throat. "Colm." Her voice caught when she saw his eyes framed in the rearview mirror, but she kept going. "I've got to talk to you. Your wife. Learn about her." *And my father.* The car fell silent, all the gaiety of the last few minutes sucked out.

Colm jumped out, his face noncommittal. "Wait. I'll see if the missus is up to it."

As soon as the door slammed, Mary's voice shattered the silence, and the whoosh of her gloved hand against the steering wheel made Sally jump. "How could they do it? Not even one word to me about a brother." She pulled her gloves off and twisted them into a knot. "Thought they owed me nothing." Her voice got louder and drowned out the rain. "I wasn't human to them." When she hit the steering wheel with bare fists, the gloves slipped to the floor. "Why? Why did it have to be like this?"

Sally, usually so cheery, so perky, leveled Mary with a gaze. "I don't know, Mary. But you may be about to find out."

CHAPTER 27

Thou hast called me thy angel in moments of bliss,
And thy Angel I'd be, 'mid the horrors of this . . .
—Thomas Moore, "Come Rest in This Bosom"

A silver-haired woman flew from the porch like a hawk. "Who do we have here?"

The anger rolled off of Mary, as did the years. Standing before her was the woman who had smelled of yeast and flour, who always had a smile . . . and a piece of bread. She stepped closer. "This is my friend Sally. I'm . . . I'm Mary Elizabeth. Kathleen's daughter."

"Of course ye are. And praise be to God for it." Abigail shooed them down a narrow hall and into a sitting room, furnished with chairs and little else. Stacks of almanacs crowded the hearth. A clock hung over the fireplace. "Over here, now." Like a mother hen, she clucked about the room, pulling chairs closer to the fire, then practically pushing Mary and Sally into them. "Would ye like coffee or tea?" she asked, straightening the stack of almanacs.

Sally leaned toward the fire, rubbing her hands together. "Either would be—"

"Neither. We just ate." The questions were choking Mary now, forcing her to abandon any pretense of social norms. She needed to know. Now.

Abigail plopped down next to Mary. "Ye got 'er cheeks and brow," she sighed, her face getting a faraway look. "I loved her. We were close, ye know."

The urge to know grabbed Mary even stronger than before. "No, I didn't know. I didn't know anything."

"She was a poor soul, I tell ye the truth."

Mary gripped the arms of the chair. "What do you mean?"

Colm, who had just come in, darted a glance at Abigail. "Wet the tea, Mum."

Abigail fluttered toward the kitchen.

"No, really, we're fine." A note of stridency entered Mary's voice.

Abigail froze, then seemed to sink back into her chair.

"All those years in America, lass," Colm began, his voice booming over the crackle and pop of the fire, "do ye think it was good that ye left?"

Mary could hold it in no more. She leapt to her feet and stalked toward the fire. "Good? To be torn from my mother at five? Good by the devil's standards."

"Did ye not go to live with Killian's sister Anne, her husband?" Abigail's brow furrowed. "Chicago, wasn't it?"

"Oh, I went there, all right." Mary paced back and forth, the room suddenly suffocating her.

"Aye, I remember Anne." Colm smiled, his voice trailing off. "Eyes gray as a Cheshire's fur, they were. A sound lass. At five, thinking and talking like an old lady."

Abigail leaned closer to Mary. "Did ye not take on there?"

Mary whirled. Was it possible that Abigail knew? Abigail understood? "No." She rushed on, desperate to get it out. "'Twas cold as the wind right out your door."

Colm folded his arms across his chest. "Ye should have stayed right here."

Now Colm became the target of Mary's stare. "Do you think I had a say in it?" Mary's words seemed to hang in the air, like smoke.

"'Twas good ye left," Abigail finally said.

Mary leaned forward. "What do you mean it was good?"

"No matter what it was in the States, lass, yer mum's house was worse."

"What do you mean worse?"

Abigail looked at Mary, then Colm. "I've got to get on with the tea." She rose from her chair.

"Tell me now," Mary insisted. "Why was it worse? Why was I bad? Why did they do it?"

When Abigail sat back down, the chair creaked. "I don't know how to tell ye," she said. She bowed her head and folded her hands in her lap.

For a moment, Mary thought she'd explode, spewing unanswered questions all over the walls. She closed her eyes, her lips moving in a silent prayer. When she finished, she reached toward Abigail, palms uplifted. "Please, Abigail. Tell me."

Again, Abigail looked at Colm, then Mary. "He beat yer Kathleen. He beat everyone." It seemed to hurt Abigail to say the words. "His own sisters, his very flesh and blood. Yer Anne too."

A spark leapt from the fire and seared Mary's white jacket, but she barely noticed.

"I've got to fetch tea," Abigail said for the third time.

Mary slammed her hand on the arm of the chair. The pure white light of truth had begun to expose decades of dirty secrets, and she refused to let anything stop it now. "Forget the tea. Just tell me about her."

Colm's laugh was nervous. "Jesus, Mary, and Joseph. You've got to have tea."

"No!" One look at Abigail, who'd slumped back into the rocker, and Mary regretted her tone. She cupped her hand over Abigail's. "I'm sorry. I've waited for so long. Can you understand what this means to me?"

When Abigail and then Colm nodded, Mary continued. "I've prayed for so many years to understand. Now God's sent me five thousand miles to talk to you. Tell me about her. Tell me about them." She squeezed Abigail's hand. "Please."

Abigail nodded. "He was a raging maniac. Full o' hate and fury. The things he did to his own sisters. And then yer mum."

Mary's stomach churned, but she kept her voice as calm as she could. "Why didn't anybody stop him?" An image of Killian's twisted smile invaded her memory, and the calm tone vanished. She seared Colm with a glare. "Why didn't *you* stop him?"

Colm bent his head to his lap; when he raised it, he looked like a haggard old man. "'Twasn't done. Ye didn't meddle in a man's business." He shook his head. "And we weren't sure. At least not for a spell."

"How did you find out *for sure?*"

Abigail broke a silence so thick it was an entity in the room. "She had bruises."

"All the time?"

Abigail nodded. "Oh, she always had excuses for 'em. She was 'polluted.' 'Thick.'"

Mary slumped forward. So it was true. And now her Chloe would have to pay the price for it. "So my mother was a drunk," she said, more to herself than the others.

As if in rebuttal, Colm waved his hands. "Of course she wasn't. Not her."

Abigail took Mary's hand. "But 'twas the very worst on that day."

"What day?" Mary's voice was a whisper.

Colm's eyes fogged. "Early on the mornin' they carried ye off, we found her on our doorstep. At first we thought she was plastered, the way her eyes were glazed."

Abigail nodded. "Covered with purple and blue, she was."

"'They've done it,' she kept whimpering, like a dog hit by a car. She begged for us to help."

Abigail shook her head. "It was too late."

Mary bowed her head, both saddened and relieved. "So she did care."

Abigail reached across the chair and tried to embrace Mary. "You were her flesh and blood. Ye think she didn't want ye?"

"I never knew. One night, I slept in her arms; the next day, I was whisked to another country, to another woman who said she was my mother. Now she's gone."

"They're all gone," Colm said. "Except Gerard. And maybe Kelly."

Mary sprang to her feet, her heart thumping. "Where are they?" She'd find them, tell them she was their sister. It wasn't ever too late, was it? In spite of the ghastly revelations, she allowed a smile to crease her face. Irish relatives. A chance for family remained.

"Kelly left years ago. Gerard's still up there."

The half-smile blossomed. So there was a chance for good to come from this.

"Aye, and rotten to the core, just like his pap."

A clod of turf burst into flames.

Mary stared at red and yellow sparks. So it was not to be. *The children will be punished for the sins of their fathers, to the third and fourth generation.* The fire seemed to paralyze her, that and the horrid truth.

"Gerard beat yer mam too."

In spite of her proximity to the fire, Mary's blood ran cold. "He beat his own mother?"

Colm doddered to the fire and stoked it. "'Twas a wretched house. I'm glad ye left."

Mary stared at Sally, who hadn't moved, and then the fire. So awful, so unbelievable. So true.

"Did ye write her?" Abigail asked.

Mary's mouth fell open. "She didn't tell you?"

Now it was Abigail's turn to shake her head.

"I thought you were her friend," Mary shot back.

Abigail shrugged yet did not meet Mary's gaze. "Aye, 'tis different out here. Some things ye don't tell."

"When I was nineteen, I lugged my suitcase down this very road." Mary's voice took on a metallic tone as if it were someone else's story she was telling.

Abigail threw out her hands. "Ye don't mean it." She and Colm eyed each other. "We'd heard gossip but didn't believe it."

The store's old settlers, without a doubt. "I trod on these very stones. I rounded the hill, and there she stood, asking who I was, not wanting me to meet the children she kept."

"Jesus, Mary, and Joseph!"

It was deathly quiet except for the mantle clock ticking, ticking, ticking.

"She was afraid, lass," Abigail finally said.

"Afraid of what?"

When they didn't answer, Mary banged her fist on the arm of the chair. "You've gone this far. Finish it."

Husband and wife eyed each other. "There were rumors."

Colm jumped to his feet. "Woman, shut yer gob. You don't know."

"What rumors?"

"Misusing all o' them. Not sparing his own sisters."

Mary flew to the window, stumbling over her chair. Incest. Satan at his best, horribly perverting God's plan. "Oh, God, no," she moaned, words pouring from her soul. "Oh, God. But thank You. To be spared from that. But my mother. Oh, God. Why?"

The only sounds in the room were the whooshing of the wind down the chimney and the ticking clock. Mary thought of the hours Mam had endured in that unspeakable place while she'd been safe in Lisle with Daddy and Mother—the curtain parted, the knowledge almost knocking her down. Mother, Killian's sister, hadn't been safe, not as a girl. Her mother, Anne; another victim of Killian's abuse.

Mary clenched her fists and moaned, losing all desire to maintain a semblance of civility, wanting to shatter the glass, to shatter how she'd viewed the woman who had adopted her. *How could I not have seen it? No wonder you were so cold, Mother.* Words and thoughts detoured onto a freeway to hell. Could Mother have even had children after what her brother had done to her? Would she have wanted to? She bit her lip and tasted blood. "God," she screamed. "Why didn't You stop it? How could You allow it all?"

A sudden gust of wind hurled its power against the walls of the old farmhouse, and the windowpanes rattled a feeble response. Spent from the shocks, Mary leaned against the glass and let its icy transparence chill her brow.

"*Who is this that darkens my counsel with words without knowledge . . . Have you seen? . . . Do you know? . . . Can you hold? . . . Do you give?*"

Mary bowed her head to the still quiet voice, turned from the window, and returned to her chair. She sat and stared and stared and sat, letting the shattered pieces of her life rearrange into a pattern formed of her latest knowledge. Years of pieces that didn't quite fit, edges that weren't shaped quite the right way falling into a mosaic glittering with memories, dark and light. She sat, and she thought, and no one else said a word.

The ticking of the clock seemed to get louder.

At least Killian wasn't blood of my blood, bone of my bone. But who was? Mary sat up straight. "Now I want to know about Johnny."

"Who?" Colm asked, but there was no surprise in his tone.

"My father."

"I don't know about that."

"I think you do," Mary said, determined to finish. She heard Sally's sharp intake of breath, yet pushed on. "You bogsiders know everything about each other."

Abigail's hands fluttered as her eyes darted about. "She has a right, Colm."

"Please." Mary spoke in a low voice, her energy almost spent. "It's the last thing I want—I need to know."

"You'll not be getting me to litter her mind with more garbage." Colm shook his head. "Things ye don't know for sure."

"I don't know what happened to him," Abigail said.

"Then what do you know?"

Abigail took a long look at Mary, then the fire. "Johnny had a sister. Last I heard, she was living in the Connemara."

"Where's that?"

"Up north. 'Tis a wild place." Quiet as a mouse, Abigail scurried out of the room, then back in. "Josephine O'Neill. Jo, we used to call her. Here." She handed Mary the address.

Colm glared at his wife, and this time, she lowered her head. Some signal acquired after decades of marital life passed between them, and whatever had compelled them to share the secrets now compelled them to silence.

The turf fire flickered and faded, thousands of years of compressed energy spent. In the same way, the tension seeped from the room.

Colm smiled, pulled his chair closer to Mary's, and patted her knees. "What about America?" he asked, returning to his original question. "Did ye make a life there?"

Mary managed a thin smile. "Yes. I have a husband, two beautiful daughters."

"End o' the story. It's good ye left." Colm once again was the robust-looking man who'd greeted Mary.

The clock ticked, ticked. Her questions answered, Mary rose to her feet.

"Speaking of leaving, we have to get on." She embraced the O'Loughlins, her sights now set on another part of Ireland. And another woman—her aunt, no less—who had another story that Mary, with all her being, determined to hear.

CHAPTER 28

Here speaks the Comforter, tenderly saying
Earth has no sorrow that Heaven cannot cure.
—Thomas Moore, "Come Ye Disconsolate"

M*am, a crust o' bread. A spot o' tea!*

Mary's hands shook so, she had trouble steering. It had been like this ever since they'd left Kilkee, where they'd stayed a few nights. She cast a glance at Sally, who was transfixed by the scenery, and wondered if Sally heard the voices too.

It was the hungry children from Potato Famine days groaning for bread. A side of Mary was sure of it; another side insisted that ghosts didn't exist. Yet Peggy, the proprietress of the Kilkee B&B, claimed she heard them on windy nights. And John, that farmer Sally had met at the pub, had shown them the lazy beds, those furrows etched into the hills . . . just like the screams were etched in her brain. Mary stared at undulating browns and shimmering greens as she drove toward the Connemara. Those poor farmers gasping, panting as they dug their trenches higher and higher on the rolling hills, trying to outclimb the black death that was rotting every last potato. She clutched at her hair. It couldn't be helped. Death was rolling, rolling in.

✝ ✝ ✝

Brakes squealed in protest to another S curve on this sinuous highway, one which Mary nearly failed to maneuver. Sally glanced sideways at her friend, whose lips were moving again. At Kilkee, she'd seemed fine as they strolled by quiet tide pools, searching for starfish among swaying kelp. And last night, when that old sod pulled his fiddle from a tattered case and coaxed out a jig, Mary actually laughed when Sally had jumped on the chair and stomped to the beat.

Sally hummed the words she could remember. "*I hope the next ones will rosin the bow. Will they resemble old—*"

Mary cleared her throat. "Sally, please. I'm trying to hear this."

Sally's heart plummeted. What was she talking about? The radio was off.

✠ ✠ ✠

The voices of the children faded as Mary drove through a land checkered with green and browns and cratered with lakes of silvery blue. Yet memories cried out to her, memories evidenced by lazy beds and stones and abandoned dwellings. What memories had this Johnny given her, things she didn't even know yet? Oh, she could guess, but what was the good in that?

She spotted the sign for Killary Fjord and turned into the parking lot. It was deserted except for one man, who stood near the shore and stared into ice blue waters. Breathtaking cliffs encircled the majestic waters and bowed out of respect to their frosty beauty. A cluster of lambs appeared to be huddling somehow in the center of the fjord.

"'Tis quite a sight, 'tisn't it?" The man sidled close to Mary, as if he wanted nothing more than to settle in for a long chat.

"What's wrong with them?" Mary asked, the lambs' bleats tearing at her heart.

The man laughed. "'Tis a tiny islet. Can't see it now, but thanks be to God, 'tis there. The silly ninnies go out at low tide, after that sea grass." He pointed toward the cluster of lambs. "When the water pours in, they're stuck. Island prisons, lass."

Mary covered her ears.

"They'll survive. 'Tis a fact the young ones have to learn. They only do it once."

Mary yearned to pull the frantic lambs to safety. That was a mother's way, and if nothing else, she was a mother. But would they learn the lesson of the fjord if someone intervened? Her mind wandered to her youngest, the one who was stumbling just like these lambs. How could she help her? What would it take? The problem seemed insurmountable, and her spirits sank.

It's all meaningless.

Mary shivered and steeled herself not to look behind her. Were the black voices disguised as dead children dogging her again? Would they engulf her, then drag her into a deep more dangerous than the waters in front of her? She stared at all the blues, representing the shallow, the deep, the known, the unknown waters, and prayed. Then she hurried back into the car, Sally right behind.

Once, Mary glanced at her friend, who'd barely spoken all day. *Sally looks as scared as I feel.* But that thought didn't soothe Mary a bit.

A few kilometers later, they pulled into a drive with a sign, Connemara B&B, Proprietors J&J Tierney, discreetly displayed near the mailbox. Hills tattooed with more lazy beds surrounded a country-style house and two barns. Dogs yipped and nipped a pack of sheep into a lush meadow. Mary couldn't help but think of a certain farm back in Indiana that looked so different from this, yet caused the same pounding in her heart. *Could this, too, be my home?* She slammed the car door and tried to do the same with the thoughts, the hopes incubating in her mind. With stiff fingers, she smoothed wrinkles from her jacket. "I'm so nervous, Sally," she said. "With Colm and Abigail, it was so sudden I had no time to think. What if she kicks us out?"

Suddenly Sally seemed like her old self. Grinning, she patted Mary on the arm. "She won't kick us out. We're paying customers."

They hurried up a stone walkway. Mary rang a bell. The door opened.

A woman towered over them, stylish in a tailored pantsuit, her silver hair cut in a chic pageboy. Her eyes sparkled as she held out her hand. "I'm Josephine. Welcome."

"Hi. I'm . . . Mary. This is Sally. We're here about the room."

"Aye." Josephine pointed up a steep staircase. "It's right up there. No heat, ladies, but the electric blankets will keep ye warm. I'll light a fire down here." She handed Mary a stack of towels. "Spread out, dears. You're the only guests."

Both women shivered as they unpacked. From time to time, Mary was drawn to the view out the dormer window, a view of hills and grass and cattle and sheep. In the same way, she felt a pull to this aunt who didn't know, couldn't know, that she too loved the farm life. In spite of the chill, she flung open the windows. The scent of Ireland, hay and grass and salt and loam and the overwhelming attar of wild roses, poured into the room.

After layering on nightgowns, sweaters, house shoes, and shawls, they descended to the sitting room. Sally sprawled on a hooked rug spread in front of the fire and wrote in her journal. Mary paced about, picking up books, studying paintings.

The parlor door opened.

"Hi, ye poor dears."

"Good evening."

"Ye might as well climb in the flames, as close as you're parked to 'em."

When Sally's chortle went on and on, Mary had to suppress a desire to scream.

Jo sat on a love seat by the fire. "Tell me, why are ye here? 'Tisn't the season."

Mary cleared her throat. Wouldn't it be better just to talk about the uncommon scenery, to smile blandly like typical American tourists? She cleared her throat again. No. She'd come this far. It was too late to turn back. "I'm Johnny's daughter. Your brother Johnny. My mother was Kathleen McNamara."

Jo jumped up, her tan paling to sickly beige. "It—it can't be."

"He knew my mother before . . . his marriage. They had . . . me."

The news seemed to have frozen Jo. "I . . . I don't know what to say," she finally managed.

Mary tried to choose her words carefully. "I know this must be difficult for you. It is for me too. I got your name from the O'Loughlins. We visited them earlier this week."

Color returned to Jo's face. "Abigail," she whispered. The room came alive as Jo, her cheeks wet with tears, stepped close, then flung her arms about Mary.

Family. Tears flowed from Mary, but not the hot bitter ones she'd experienced at Abigail's. With every soothing word, every warm caress, Jo communicated that Mary was family. Family that wanted her. Perhaps even loved her.

Later, Jo led Mary to the couch, and they huddled together. "I thought he couldn't have wee ones. 'Tis the reason for the drink,' he said." Jo's laugh was bitter and seemed to resonate from deep inside. "So many reasons he gave for the drink—to get up. To go to bed. To get a job. To forget a job. Because he lost a job."

Words poured, and Mary listened.

"A blitherin' drunk, he was."

Mary visualized that wild-haired girl at Marquette, stumbling into the dorm . . .

"He had aches no bottle could soothe."

Desperate to fill the ache in her heart . . .

"He always needed something more. Aye, there was a longing in him."

Always that need for a friend, lonely in a room thronging with people.

"It started when I was in the trundle. He'd pick me up, eyes fiery like his hair."

Mary touched her temple, a chill prickling her skin.

"Red as . . . yer own." Jo pulled Mary near, then studied her face. "Praise be to God. You've a trace o' my fine Johnny Kennedy in ye." She sighed deeply. "Oh, he was a handsome rogue. The lasses loved him, they did." She grew quiet again.

Mary slumped, her head bowed. To wonder and to have it all confirmed was some consolation for—she raked a hand through curls—such bitter truths.

"His eyes were always rovin'; except on nights o' the full moon, which he gifted to me. Handsome Johnny would scoop me out o' bed, and we'd sail to the banks o' the rushing river and sing and laugh till the moon disappeared."

Mary clung to every word as if her father were speaking from the grave.

Jo looked past Mary and out the window. "He'd pluck blooms off the wild roses and braid them into my hair." Her tears fell like rain now. "Oh, sweet, sweet Johnny. 'Twas the devil and his bottle stole ye away."

Mary nodded, sure now of the next thing. "Yer pap too."

Jo jerked back. "How did you know?"

Mary didn't say a word.

"All o' them, cursed by the drink. All o' them gone."

Mary could do nothing but stare at the fire. So she had been right. They were dead, all of them, and her Chloe was heading down the same road.

"But you're here now. My flesh-and-blood niece. That's what counts."

The two women talked as if there had been no yesterday and would be no tomorrow. Sally said good night and slipped up the stairs.

✝ ✝ ✝

Mary arose even earlier than usual, her mood in severe flux. At peace over Jo's comforting acceptance. Shaken by the truth about Johnny. She walked about the room, touching sturdy oak bed posts, an English dressing table, the chilly window ledge. She belonged here with family, just as she had belonged at Grandmother's. But would she be sent away? She threw on her robe and hurried downstairs.

Lace curtains were pulled back from a kitchen bay window to reveal the rolling green hills of the Tierney land. Clusters of sheep nibbled at waving grass, and except for a clump of gray clouds far to the west, the day promised to be tourist perfect.

Jo handed Mary a cup of tea and a plate of scones and fruit, then sat so close to her that their chairs touched. "Good morning, dear niece. Sugar and cream?"

Mary hesitated. Maybe it was time to change some old habits. Start some new ones. "Sure. Why not?" She sweetened her tea, then looked about. A sideboard groaned with English china. The walls proudly displayed pictures of Tierney children and grandchildren. "Your home's lovely, Aunt Jo."

Jo put her hand on Mary's. "It's your home now, dear. Ye won't think o' leaving until we set a return date. I can't wait to meet yer girls. Yer Paul." With a sigh, she lumbered out of the room and came back with a dog-eared picture. "Yer pa."

Her hands trembling, Mary drank in every tracing on the faded print. A tall man, perhaps twenty, held a little girl with light hair. He had a smile so wide it made Mary smile too. His eyes bore into her as if, from the grave, he wanted to know her. His lean, muscular body bespoke natural athleticism. She moved closer to Jo. "How did he die?"

Jo's eyes misted over, and she swallowed several times before she spoke. "'Twas a dreadful accident. Fell off Croagh Patrick, he did. Right near the chapel at the summit."

Mary stiffened. The urge to block out unsettling information, coupled with the need to know everything, threatened to rend her in two. A father that was not only a drunk but committed—she slumped in her seat. Was it suicide? She mustered the strength to say it. "Did he—"

"'Twas an accident. No more." Cutting off any more discussion, Jo busied herself with the dishes.

Jo's tone and demeanor destroyed Mary's appetite. She put down her fork, determined to press on with the last few questions. "Aunt Jo, did you know my mother?"

"No, dear." Aunt Jo shook her head emphatically. "'Twouldn't have been done."
"Why?"

"Certain things, ye just didn't do. He ne'er could've married her."

"I don't understand," Mary stirred her tea, working to keep the anger out of her voice.

"It just wasn't done. It wasn't proper." Jo brushed crumbs off the tablecloth as if getting rid of that topic. "Last night ye spoke of Anne. How did ye get on with her?"

Mary took a sip of water, slumping again. "Not well. Rigid as rock, she was, and I directed my anger toward her. I hated her."

Jo gestured with her hands. "Yet in a way, you were inflicted on her, do ye see? They dumped ye on her."

"What do you mean?"

"Sending a child to America was a way out. A way to get a mouth fed."

Mary's body became rigid. No wonder she'd felt like a castaway; she was. Did both her families feel that way? For a time, she'd thought she was needed to further Daddy's political career. Didn't every All-American family have a child? But Mother and Daddy were really helping a desperate relative. She thought of the beatings, the abuse. Desperate in more ways than one.

Jo melted her with deep, warm eyes. "Can ye imagine having to choose? Send 'em off or let 'em starve? Like I said last night, 'tisn't as simple as it seems." She patted Mary on the shoulder. "Did your new mother have her own children?"

Mary looked at her lap. "No. When I came, she was forty."

"Good heavens!" Jo's hands fluttered; her eyes got big. "Can ye imagine at age forty being landed with a five-year-old?"

Mary shook her head, but what she really wanted to do was weep at yet another misconception about Mother. How hard it must have been to finally tear away from the cliff's horrors, to start a new life, to find fulfillment as a businesswoman, and then to have a child thrown at her, a child who dredged up nothing but painful memories.

"What year were ye born?" Jo asked, interrupting Mary's thoughts.

"I was born in 1947."

Jo looked out the window, seemingly transfixed by a ewe nursing her lamb. "How on earth was yer mam not put in a home? 'Twas an absolute miracle she stayed free o' that."

"What do you mean?"

"Have ye not heard of the Magdalene homes?"

"What are they?"

Jo's laugh was bitter. "Workhouses, they were, for unwed mothers."

"Church homes?"

Jo nodded. "Places of refuge, they called 'em, named for our blessed Saint Mary Magdalene." She bowed her head and made the sign of the cross.

"How many were there?"

"Ten, I think."

"What about the babies?"

Tears filled Jo's eyes. "Aye, that was the worst of it. Took 'em away, they did. Ye hadn't a clue what happened to yer wee one."

The new information seemed to hover just outside of Mary's understanding. "Why?" she asked.

Jo pursed her lips. "Don't ye know? 'Twas a terrible embarrassment. They had to be hidden from proper folk."

"Why didn't people stop them?"

"Oh, it's not so clear-cut." Josephine sighed. "Who could care for the poor dears? The homes were seen as a way." She shook her head. "'Twas a desperate time."

Mary continued to struggle. "So it was a good thing?"

"God in heaven, no. They were absolute slaves there." Jo's voice gained more momentum. "Given new names. Forgotten. Locked away for one mistake." Her voice lowered to a whisper. "And some were victims of incest. Rape."

Mary's breath caught. More pain and abuse. At what point would her mind overload and quit taking this in? She closed her eyes. *Oh, God, help me. Keep me sane.*

"What I want to know is how your mother avoided this," Jo demanded.

"She ran away. To Dublin," Mary managed to say.

"She was lucky, dear."

Mary picked up her fork and toyed with a strawberry. Magdalene homes, or Killian? Perhaps Mam sounded lucky, but Mary wasn't sure.

Sally bounded into the dining room, her sunny smile brightening the pale yellow wallpaper by several shades. "Top o' the morning, ladies." She gave both women a big hug.

"Sally, I take it ye slept well."

"Oh, it was great." Hands waved, hips wiggled. "I just burrowed in that bed—it's cool how you put the blanket down first and the sheets on top. It was great, it really was, until those roosters started their little show."

They all giggled.

Jo brought Sally oatmeal, toast, and coffee, then headed for the door. "I best be goin'. Class at eight. I'll leave ye a book about the homes, Mary dear. On your dresser."

"I've heard enough." She pointed to Sally. "But she'll read anything." A chuckle contradicted the tightness in her chest. *How can I stand to read about more suffering?* She felt like a teacup overflowing with boiling water. Yet the Pourer kept adding more, more, more . . .

As if she understood, Sally touched Mary's arm. "She's wonderful."

Mary tried to block out a blackness that threatened to wash her tenuous hold on what was good, wholesome, and true. She pictured Jo, so crisply efficient, yet so warm, and smiled. The blood that coursed through Jo's veins was in hers too. "She's a teacher like you, Sally. And so is my uncle Joe."

Sally's eyebrows arched. "Uncle Joe?"

"Around midnight, Jo roused Joe out of bed." She rolled her eyes. "You should've heard the ruckus."

Tears glistened in Sally's eyes.

"They want me to bring Paul and the girls over."

"You've found them, haven't you?"

Mary felt drawn to the window, the voices near again. *You must know. You must go. Come. Come.* She pulled herself away and turned to Sally. "There's one more thing I'd like to do."

"What?"

"Hike Croagh Patrick."

"What's that?"

"The mountain St. Patrick climbed to pray and fast." She took a deep breath. She'd seen where Mam was buried. Now she'd see where Johnny had . . . died. And where her grandmother had done a penance Mary now thought she understood.

Her heart beat faster and so did the voice, imaginary drums pounding a rhythm now. *Come. Come.* She'd do it, like untold scores of Irish brethren, including the great saint who had besought blessings from God for this, her beloved land. "You might want to stay here. Work on your writing . . ." Mary eyed Sally. In a way, she wanted Sally to be there. But on the other hand, it might complicate things.

Sally shook her head so hard, everything jiggled. Even her charm bracelet jangled. "No way. I'm going."

Of course, she'd insist. Mary set her lips in a thin line. *So that's how it'll be.* She felt Sally's eyes boring into her and kept her voice light. "There's a path to the top. I just want to walk. Pray about Chloe." Her head lowered, she glanced at Sally. *I'm not going to tell her about the voices. She might try to stop me. And nothing's going to stop me now.* She closed her eyes and prayed with such intensity that she lost all awareness of time and space and didn't move until Sally nudged her toward the stairs.

CHAPTER 29

Pilgrims dwelling in the midst o' foes,
Preserve us from danger, in Thine arms repose.
—Thomas Kelly, "Through the Day Thy Love Hath Spared Us"

Sally wiggled in the seat like an excited child. "I can't believe we're climbing a mountain," she said, her eyes sparkling.

Mary tried not to stare at Sally. *I can't believe you are, either.* She focused on the scenery, willing Sally to get quiet. And Sally complied.

They streaked through County Mayo, a stunning mosaic of meandering blues, siennas, and greens. The land Mary loved, yet feared.

"You look like your father," Sally finally said.

Mary tensed. *Father.* The elation at putting a face to her father's name had quickly been replaced by the shame that he was just another Irish drunk. So why was she so torn by that faded photograph? Her fingers gripped the steering wheel. It was simple. Chloe's lips. Claire's forehead. The crimson that had found its way, to varying degrees, into all their hair.

"He was a hunk," Sally continued.

Mary nodded. She saw him as if he were sitting right beside her. A mop of red flecked with gold. A jaw too strong to call handsome. Eyes that blazed the sobering reality that for him, one drink was always too much. Almost against her wishes, she darted a glance at herself in the mirror, then forced herself to see the rest of him. A mind that raced in and out of the realm of sanity, staying put just long enough for others to think he was all right. Moods that swung from heaven's gates to hell's dungeons. The stuck record, playing the same thoughts. Restless mannerisms that others interpreted as high-strung. Arched eyebrows that questioned if the pain would ever stop. *Like you.*

She was her father's daughter, not just as concerned the drinking, but the unquiet mind as well. For a second, she closed her eyes to the worst case scenario—had she passed it to Chloe? Claire? Her precious blood, marrow, and bone? Her soul screamed out even though she clamped her mouth shut and tried to concentrate on driving. *Oh, God. Help!*

"Mary, what's wrong?"

Mary tightened her jaw and turned up the volume on the radio. "Please, Sally, just leave me alone." Sally's lip trembled, but Mary didn't care. She was too busy listening to the whispering voices. *Come to me, and you will see. Come . . .*

They pulled into a nearly empty parking lot. Clouds shifted restlessly in a gray firmament. Tiny islands sprouted out of the water like wild mushrooms. The cone-shaped peak called Croagh Patrick loomed over all, a sentinel guarding ingress from the sea. Would it protect her from the voices?

✠ ✠ ✠

Mary zipped up her parka and jumped out of the car, Sally puffing to keep up. She wasn't one to grumble, but she couldn't understand why Mary was in such a hurry.

Near the supply kiosk, Mary waited, then threw out her arms, her eyes glued on Sally's shoes. "You're going to climb a twenty-five-hundred-foot summit in those?"

Sally shrugged. "They're all I've got." She clapped Mary on the back, then waved at a passerby. "Hey, will you take our picture?" she asked, determined not to let Mary's attitude dampen her spirits.

With a nod, he snapped shots of them by a sign that warned against hiking during inclement weather. Then they started off, Mary jerking Sally away when she headed toward a restaurant right near the trailhead. Only a few stragglers, a young girl cloaked in a black trench coat and hikers equipped with walking sticks and boots, passed them. *Perhaps the smart folks are stayin' home.* Her smile a bit dimmer, Sally hurried after Mary.

The women stepped across rills snaking through silvery blue shale. Soon the incline steepened, and Sally slid several times on slippery rocks. Mary's athleticism became evident as she edged ahead, yet Sally remained calm. *Just go at your own pace, girl.* That's what Mama always said. *Take time to smell the roses.* She gazed back at Clew Bay and gasped. Dots of green in a globe of blue. Her heart soared. Now she knew how the astronauts felt seeing the earth from space. She fished in her backpack for her camera, finally found it, and shot a picture. When she shouldered her pack again, Mary was gone.

Sally's body, reacting to the desertion, exertion, and hormonal imbalances, broke out in a serious sweat. She set her backpack on a flat boulder, removed her borrowed parka, and knotted it around her waist. Before she'd taken a dozen steps, she heard a whoosh that almost knocked her off the path.

"Careful." A woman, skin so wrinkled she must've been a sun goddess fifty years ago, stepped close. She wore combat boots and a cotton dress.

"Thanks. I'm Sally from Illinois." She wiped sweat from her brow. "Actually, Texas. Louisiana—oh, well. The South. Well, now the Midwest. America."

"I'm Cliona McBride."

They shook hands and kept walking.

"And where are you from?" Sally asked.

Cliona pointed east. "Over there. I hike this every month." Next she pointed to the water. "See those islands? Three hundred sixty-five of them. One for every day of the year."

"It's beautiful. You must be so proud. Are they inhabited?"

Cliona cackled. "Just spits o' snuff."

They chatted a bit longer, then Clionia hurried off.

The warmth of a friendly Irishwoman brightened the gray sky. *Mama'd love Cliona.* God had given Sally this trip as a gift, not just to write, not just to help Mary, but to meet people. Praise Him! Then she frowned. Where was Mary? *Oh, well, just look at that view. It was so amazing what He'd done. Getting a girl from the Flowers clan over to Ireland.* She craned her neck for a better view. *That water. Blue and green melted together like a waxed-paper-and-Crayola creation.*

When Sally took a step, her foot hurt. She unzipped her shoe, dumped out pebbles, and jammed the shoe back on. A gust of wind caused her to shiver. When she felt about her waist for the parka, it was gone. *So that's what the whoosh had been.* She leaned against a column of rock, trying to push away a cold that seeped up from deep inside. She shivered again, her smile long gone.

"Where are you, Mary?" Sally shouted to the whistling winds. "I could use some help. You've brought me here; now you've up and left."

When it blew again, the wind brought a different message. *Where does my help come from? It comes from the Lord.*

Sorry for her anger, Sally stopped to pray. *Forgive me, Father, for calling on You after the fact. Get me through this. If it be Your will, help me find the jacket. In Jesus' name.* When Sally tried to pick up her bag, trembling fingers dropped it. She retrieved it, then glanced behind her. Fog had obscured the gorgeous view and managed to cloud her optimism as well. Had she made a terrible mistake?

She craned her neck and tried to see Mary, but the only thing visible was a looming, craggy peak.

✣ ✣ ✣

Faster, faster, Mary walked, almost mindless of the rocks' jabs, the steepness. Again the voices started their black cackling, their moans so hellish she'd zoomed past Sally to catch up with them. Dogging not just her, but possibly her youngest back home. She clenched her hands so tightly they went numb. "You'll not get my child," she threw back at the voices. "Even if I have to die to get rid of you." The cries crescendoed with every step, yet Mary never once glanced back. It had to be done. She had to find the source of it all, had to trod the very path her father had trod years ago if she hoped to understand the mental illness which her father might have passed to her. And which she might pass on as well.

Her jaw clamped shut, her eyes fixed in the direction of the peak, although she wasn't sure because of swirling fog. She curved about the precipitous path, ignoring skittering scree. Once she slipped and fell, scraping her hands, but she rebounded determinedly. Through the dense gray, she espied a whirl of black. With narrowed eyes, she climbed on. The voices were real, after all.

✣ ✣ ✣

"Hi, I'm Sally from Illinois. I mean, U.S. of A." Sally greeted every descending hiker with the same refrain, desperation creeping into her singsong voice. "If y'all see a coat on your way down, could you leave it at that restaurant?"

When one white-bearded gentleman offered her his windbreaker, Sally declined, but she did take a hunk of chocolate from two brothers.

"What size shoe do ye wear?" one of the brothers asked, eyeing her shoes.

"Uh, nine, I think." Sally didn't want to admit they were elevens. It was so unladylike to have such big feet.

"I'll loan ye mine."

"No way."

"Aye, lass. Some climb barefoot on Reek Sunday, so I could surely do it. Only a bit more to the bottom."

"Barefoot? On these rocks?"

"I saw a woman older than my mother ascend on her knees."

Sally gasped. "Thanks, but I'll be okay. Ah, by the way, how much farther?"

"First station's around the bend. Final ascent? Maybe twenty minutes." He eyed Sally. "Or maybe thirty. But 'tis treacherous. Take your time." The brothers shouldered their packs.

"Hey!" Sally caught one of the brothers by his arm. "Have y'all seen a red-headed woman in an orange parka?"

The brothers looked at each other before they spoke. "She's your friend?"

Sally's skin prickled, and she shivered. "Where is she?"

"Aye, she rounded the bend like a freight train."

"Talking like the devil took over her tongue."

"Ranting about blackness, children—"

The brothers rambled on about penitents they'd met on other climbs, but Sally, uncharacteristically, brushed past them. Her pulse hammered, and she plunged into action like a fireman grabbing his gear.

"Mary, no. Mary." When she tried to run, a pain shot through her side, but Sally didn't stop. "Oh, God. No. God, help me—help her." After she passed the plateau that marked the first station, Sally began the final ascent, her knees buckled, her hands clawing the rocks. Sweat poured down her face, and she gasped for breath. "Help us, Lord."

✞ ✞ ✞

Mary inched onward and upward, the fog clearing just enough to reveal the chapel at the summit that Jo had mentioned.

"Jesus, I can't live with this." This time a wail punctuated the voice.

Mary stumbled, launching crumbling shale over the edge. That voice sounded like a girl, not a demon. Calling out to . . . Jesus? Her senses grasped every sound, every glimpse which the fog allowed. Who was up there? And what did they want with her?

The wind carried a cackle along with its deathly moan, stiffening Mary's limbs. Of course. The voice was a ruse by Satan or his legions to trick her. She stumbled through a final pile of rocks, through fog so palpable she tried to wipe it out of her eyes.

"My baby. How could I have done it?" Words slipped and slid through damp air.

With clenched fists, Mary stepped forward. How dare the voice weave this web, using the children like this? She squinted, desperate to confront the visage that tormented her.

Something white flashed by in stark contrast to all the gray and gloom.

Yer not foolin' me. I'm settlin' this, for once and all. Mary's breath came in gasps; she strode forward more determined than ever. Two, three, five, ten more steps. Something solid met her. "What—"

She tripped and fell, her elbows hitting concrete. Wincing, she tried to see through the fog. It was a steeple. She had fallen on a set of stairs at the base of St. Patrick's shrine. For a moment, she rested. This was a holy place. Holy—

"My baby. It's too late. There's nothing left!" As if to ward off any hope, the voice grew louder.

Mary tensed her body as she crawled up the stairs, determined to settle things with the demon. Or demons.

A cackle sent a shiver up her spine.

"It's all meaningless," the voice said. "Nothing."

Mary ignored the pebbly concrete that tore at her palms and inched toward a wooden door. She pushed against it, but it did not budge.

Shrieks grew louder, managing to dominate the wind.

Evil, it is, wi' all the tricks of Satan. Knowledge of the enemy's potency heightened Mary's determination, and she paused to collect her thoughts on the chapel's top step. "You're not going to win," she hurled toward the voice. "He won't let you." She continued to admonish the voice as she crawled around the chapel, her back arched, her neck craned. Nothing. She peered around the corner of the building. Nothing. She moved over a low wall and proceeded toward what seemed to be the cliff edge.

The cackle got louder, fighting to dominate both Mary and the shrieking wind.

Mary convulsed in shivers and crawled closer.

"God . . . help me. 'Tis the only way out." The voice sounded empty now, hope and energy and reason blown away.

God? Mary gasped. *A demon calling on God?* Shame rained on her like brimstone. Here she was in the middle of a spiritual and a physical crisis, and she'd neglected to pray since they'd started the ascent. She knelt, once again ignoring the jabs of sharp rocks. *Oh, God, forgive me for doubting You.* Her prayers were silent, but they resounded through her with the same intensity as if she'd screamed them until she was hoarse. *I give my very life, all my questions, even my sanity to You. Use it as You would. And Lord*—sobs escaped her lips—*save my baby from this.*

Stumbling, Mary got to her feet, ordering them to move with stealth.

The mists parted, revealing a precipitous drop-off not ten yards from where Mary stood. A caped figure huddled near the edge, convulsing like an epileptic.

"Be ..." Mary gritted her teeth, words whistling out. "Be Thou my vision ... my rock ... 'Lo, though I walk through the valley ...'" She inched closer, continuing to pray silently. *Whoever—whatever you are, with Him, I will face you.*

The figure leapt into motion, but Mary was quicker. She hurled her body at the black cape and gripped, her fingers hawklike talons.

"No-o-o." The figure shoved and kicked and snarled, thrusting elbows and steel-toed boots at Mary. "Get off."

Mary wrenched back a hood. Auburn curls poured out. The girl's face was contorted, her eyes wild like an animal's caught in a steel trap. She flailed thin arms and spat at Mary. To no avail. Years of fleeing her own demons, of pushing her body into mindless, purging runs had fortified her. That and her heritage of strong-boned, strong-willed women. Mary toppled the young girl with a few desperate yanks, and they collapsed onto the surface of the ancient quartzite cone.

✠ ✠ ✠

"God, no." Scree cut Sally's hands, but she ignored the blood. "No." Mary wouldn't do it, would she? Sally wailed at her own ignorance. The signs had been there, and it wouldn't have taken a tea leaf reader to interpret them. The endless mumbles. The tossing and turning. The black stares. The voices.

Sally fell, sending piles of rock tumbling down the incline. Dust filled her eyes; tears ran down her cheeks.

"How can ye know?"

A shock electrified Sally. Now she was hearing the voices. She squinted yet saw nothing through the whirl and swirl of sky.

"I do ... Nobody can ... I know ... How? I've been there ... No."

Questions propelled Sally up the ridge and sent her stumbling toward something white. The voices grew louder, clearer, and her heart fell. *She's arguing with herself. She's gone mad.* She tried to call out, but when no sound came out, Sally trembled all over. She'd had a nightmare like this, where an evil presence engulfed her, and she'd opened her mouth to no avail.

The presence loomed nearer and nearer.

"'It's all meaningless,' it tells you. 'You're nothing.'"

Sally let out a sigh. It was Mary. And she sounded ...

Sobs drowned out most of the words, and Sally strained to hear.

"How—how did you know?"

That voice wasn't Mary's. Or was it?

"Child, I've been here. Not these cliffs, but others. And not all rock, either. Cliffs of the devil's device."

"But you don't know what I've done."

"I don't, but He does. And He can save you from anything. From everything."

"But I've—"

Sally's heart clopped painfully. What was going on? She inched toward what sounded like two voices. The wind spoke, then someone answered with a heartrending keen. Words froze in Sally's throat. *No, Mary! God, don't let me be too late.* She broke into a run and threw herself at the source of the noise, mingling with two figures and dust and an almost vaporous rain. The three lay there and sobbed and sobbed and sobbed. Then one sobbed, and two comforted, as mothers do. Patting and stroking and cooing and running soft fingers over agonized features, smoothing them until they were pretty again.

Stillness settled over the majestic Croagh Patrick, and Sally heard nothing but the pounding of her heart.

CHAPTER 30

Be Thou my vision, O Lord of my heart;
Naught be all else to me, save that Thou art.
Thou my best thought, by day or by night,
Waking or sleeping, Thy presence my light.

— "Be Thou My Vision," ancient Irish hymn

The waiter grinned at Sally. "Another coffee?"

"Sure."

After the priest and the girl's parents arrived and took the girl home, the Dublin brothers had bought coffee for Mary and Sally. Some of the color had returned to Mary's face, but her lips were still blue. Sweat trickled down Sally's back as she rubbed her swollen ankle, which the restaurant owner had taped up.

"How about you?" the waiter asked Mary.

Mary nodded. "And some of that cake too."

Coffee? Cake? "You're eating cake?" Sally asked, then giggled with Mary until they began crying again. The men laughed, shaking their heads as if to say these were certainly strange Americans. Sally's heart swelled to include her two newest friends. When she'd staggered in, they'd hailed her like she was an Olympic marathoner, waving a coat like a flag. Then Mary had limped in, practically carrying the poor girl, and the brothers had sprung into action.

One brother used his cell phone to ring for the girl's family. The other ordered coffee. They'd scrounged through their supplies for aspirin and bandages and ointment. The restaurant manager had offered to call a medic, but Mary had assured them that everything was okay.

"Aye, Sally. What wi' all the excitement, ye didn't realize what we waved at ye." One of the brothers pointed to an impressive heap of hiking gear. "Yer coat."

305

Sally jumped up, then groaned when she came down on the ankle. "Praise God." She grabbed the coat and twirled it like a lasso. "Actually, it's not mine. It's—oh, you probably don't want to hear about it."

One of the brothers scooted up his chair. "'Tis our pleasure."

"If I start talking, I may never stop."

They roared like she was the headliner at a comedy club. Encouraged, Sally told them about the borrowed coat, the time she'd tried to run a marathon, and a few other things.

When Sally paused to get her breath, she glanced at Mary, who was smiling. Though her face was pale, Mary looked peaceful, and happy, like a mother still in her hospital gown after a long delivery.

The four of them chatted. Actually, three of them chatted. Mary just kept smiling. Sally drank more coffee and polished off both her cake and Mary's half-eaten piece. Then they said good-bye to the brothers and staggered out of the restaurant like bears that had hibernated all winter and couldn't get their legs to work. Mary helped Sally into the car and tossed their things into the trunk. They did not speak for miles, and then the words poured out.

"I thought you were hearing voices."

"I was." Mary rubbed at the windshield, then flipped on the wipers.

"But it was the girl?"

"It was."

"She gave up her baby?"

"You know . . ." Mary seemed mesmerized by the patter of rain against the car. Then she found her voice. "Went to England and . . . got rid of it. An abortion."

Sally shook her head. That poor girl's suffering wasn't over. "Deirdre?"

"Deirdre McNulty, she is." Mary managed a smile. "But she's got her family, and that's a start."

Sally nodded. "Did you see how her mother hugged her?"

"Like there was no tomorrow."

"Do you think"—the rain beat harder, and Sally's voice was barely louder than a whisper—"she would've killed herself?"

"I don't know, Sally. She was overwhelmed."

"And you were too, weren't you?" Sally asked, in the same quiet voice.

Mary nodded again. "Johnny's—my father's legacy was just too much. I wondered—still do—why God allowed it."

Sally turned to face her friend. "What do you mean?"

Mary's jaw tightened. "My drinking," she finally said.

"What?"

"It was just like that."

"Like what?"

"How Josephine described my father." She took a deep breath before continuing. "Sally, it's in the genes. I know it. I can't dabble with alcohol. And Chloe . . ."

"She can't, either."

Mary nodded. "To wonder all those years and now to know. Scary and a relief."

Sally touched Mary on the shoulder, her heart twisted at the tortuous path that Mary had had to follow. She looked out the window at the sea, darkened in its mandate to mirror the black clouds. "He'll help you, Mary."

"And I'll help Chloe like I did Deirdre." She shifted about in her seat. "I'm going to tell Chloe, and Claire, everything. Bring them over here. Let them meet my Irish family." Mary's eyes got dreamy. "Paul too, of course."

Sally nodded. She couldn't have planned this better herself. Finally, Mary had some pictures for her mantel. "And you can tell others too. Like the ministry clients."

"To think of all the souls that I could've helped . . ." Rain pattered harder, threatening to drown out Mary's voice. "With just a simple word or two."

Sally patted Mary's shoulder. "But you can start now."

"But—" Mary's voice broke, and the words came out so garbled that she had to start again. "But that's not all, Sally. If only it were."

"What?"

"My father's mind. His moods. I—I have it too."

Sally didn't move, but she scrambled to choose the right words.

"I'm petrified that I'll go crazy," Mary continued. "That Chloe or Claire has inherited it—" Tears rolled down Mary's face.

It was hard to watch her friend who had borne so many griefs take on yet another. Sally thought about her aunt who suffered from depression, her uncle who was bipolar, and decided this was not the time or the place to delve into the dysfunction of her own family. Bowing her head, she did the one thing that she had learned to do when the troubles of the world overwhelmed. "Oh, God, we thank You for all that's happened in this beautiful land. You are gracious and merciful, beyond our understanding. Please help Mary with this burden. Lord, renew her mind and keep anxiety at bay. Watch over our loved ones back home, Lord. In Jesus' name."

When Sally opened her eyes, Mary was staring at her. "There's something else you don't know."

When would this stop? "What?" Sally managed to ask.

"Sue suggested—no, ordered—that I see a shrink, a psychiatrist." Mary began to drum the steering wheel. "And I refused to listen, refused to admit that it's another step I need to take."

Sally heaved a sigh that sent tufts of hair flying into her face. "That's it?"

"That's it?" Mary shrieked. "My arrogance, my pride could've destroyed us."

"No." Steel infused Sally's words. "God's in control. He'll use this for good."

"How?"

"I don't know. And neither do you. But He's already started."

"How?"

"You're sounding like a broken record, Mary." A yawn interrupted Sally's words. "You saved that girl. If you hadn't been there . . ."

"No, Sally." Mary pointed her finger at Sally. "God saved that girl."

Sally nodded. Thank God, Mary was starting to get it. Now she just needed to see that doctor. The idea seemed to make Sally's eyes heavy. So much to do. So much to think about. Mary and Deirdre and Chloe and Sam and Suzi and Ed . . .

✥ ✥ ✥

"My dear." Josephine stood at the front door and pulled Mary into the room.

Sally hugged them both. "Good night, you two. I'm going up to read." Now, she was the one who needed some time alone.

The bed was toasty, thanks to the electric blanket. Sally snuggled in, then picked up the book Jo had suggested about the Magdalene homes, her skin prickling as she read the introduction. *There it is again, that same thought about Anne.* She tried to remember when it had first occurred to her. Months—no, years ago—when Mary had told her story. She had suspected it then. And now—*No, Lord. Not another burden. I don't think she can bear it.*

Pages turned, faster, faster . . . Dungeon-like dormitories. Women scrubbing laundry by hand, the harsh soap cracking their skin. Women ironing in dank rooms, the walls slimy with fungus and rot. No contact with the outside world, not even a newspaper. Around midnight, Sally slammed the book shut, unable to read any more.

She tossed in the tiny bed, battered like a ship in a tempest at the descriptions of abuse and neglect. The church had occasionally made terrible detours from Christ's Word, she knew that. But this? Suddenly on fire, Sally wiped sweat from her arms, her brow. What was wrong with these Irish folks? Back South . . .

It came to Sally in a flash. Her own roots, buried deep in the blood-stained soil of the South. Lynching, slavery, all manner of disgrace and suffering. Not just in yesteryear. Not just in the South. Wasn't Sunday morning still America's most segregated hour? Sally felt her skin crawl. So many human failings. Then she remembered another thing. A good thing. Something from God's Word.

"And on this rock I will build my church, and the gates of Hades will not overcome it."

In spite of human history's attempt to snuff it out, hope glimmered in Sally's heart. *He'll preserve His bride. Somehow. Some way.* Comforted by God's promise, she approached that other thing she'd tucked into the smallest compartment of her brain. The thing Mary either couldn't or wouldn't see. Anne, a victim of incest. Anne, forced to give up her baby. Anne, an inmate of the Magdalene homes.

Sally shoved back the warm blanket that those Magdalene inmates never had and fell to the floor. Tears streamed down her face. *Oh, God, I don't know it, not for sure. But it's so strong, every feeling, every image. And why has it nagged at me since I've heard Mary's story?* She prayed and she wept for the stern, cold woman whom no one had ever understood. She prayed and wept and prayed some more, and when she climbed into bed, she had no answers. But she slept.

✠ ✠ ✠

A slim package sat next to Sally's bowl of porridge. She ripped it open.

A bronze coin and seed pearls were strung on a choker necklace.

Sally threw her arms around Mary. She loved jewelry, like her charm bracelet with mementos from the states her family had visited. "It's beautiful. What's the coin?"

"An Irish tuppence."

The bronzed harp etched into the quarter-sized circle jarred Sally to remember the red-haired little girl, so desperate for a best-friend locket.

Mary pulled out a necklace, which had been hidden by her sweater. "I have an identical one. Kind of like . . ." A half-smile creased Mary's lips.

"Best friends."

Mary's eyes filled with tears. "Thank you, Sally. I don't know what else to say." She reached out her arms as if to encompass the whole room. "It's been a miracle."

Sally nodded. "God allowed you to see things that many never get to know."

"He rescued me. But my mothers . . ." Mary wiped tears from her eyes.

"I don't understand it, either."

They both smiled sad, knowing smiles.

"All that abuse . . ."

Sally looked out the window at the ridge of lazy beds, willing her mouth to stay shut. She couldn't tell her, not now. Plus, she didn't know. It was only a feeling. "Some things we don't know. But this I do know," she said, eager to change the subject.

"What?"

"You can use your trials to help others. Your ministry folks."

"My daughter." Mary got to her feet. "It's time to get home. Chloe's waiting."

"Hmm."

"I can't wait to talk to her. Tell her what I've learned."

Sally smiled to see the light in Mary's eyes. "I can't wait, either. To write this."

Mary's grimace was so severe, Sally decided not to mention the book again. At least not today. But her hands shook, she so desperately wanted to start writing. She kept smiling as Mary talked, but all she heard was Mama's voice. *"One day at a time, Sally. It'll all fall into place."* Mama was right.

✠ ✠ ✠

The car had been loaded except for Sally's makeup case. The flight confirmed. Mary couldn't wait to see Paul and the girls. Yet there was one thing left to do. She prayed, then hurried downstairs to Jo's room and knocked on the door.

"Yes, dear?"

"It's Mary." She'd started to say, wanted to say, *your niece*. But fear from that last question pressed in and stopped the term of endearment.

"Come in." Jo ushered Mary to a love seat overlooking what appeared to be a full-blown English garden. Trellises and arches displayed hints of the green vines that would, with proper sunshine and rain, create a verdant wonderland.

Mary's breath caught. Could this trip be integral to a new spring in her own heart? A budding of hope after a season of cold gloom?

She met the gaze of gray eyes, which danced with life just like those eyes in the old photograph. Just like the eyes of her father.

"I . . . I wanted to ask you about him . . . one more thing, that is."

"Go on, dear." Her eyes still on her niece, Jo sat down.

"Was . . . was my father mentally ill?" Mary asked, fighting tears.

The garden seemed to capture those gray eyes, so full of wisdom. Of love. Of life. Jo's eyes were filled with life.

"Dear, they didn't call it that back then. Folk wouldn't have heard talk of those things back in our day." Tears seeped about thick lashes, yet Jo didn't blink.

"Why?" Mary cried out. "Why didn't anyone help him?"

"'Twasn't done." A warm hand covered Mary's. "Course it is now."

"What do you mean?" Mary's voice was a whisper.

"'Tis a dark land at times." Jo waved her hand as if to encompass the garden, the hills of a thousand greens, then placed it over her heart. "At times, the dark so shrouds my soul I can barely make it out of there." She pointed to the bed.

"You have it too," Mary whispered.

"Aye, along with half the land," Jo snorted. "There's more than a few of us running about who aren't the full shilling. And 'tisn't anything to be ashamed of. Not with the doctors they have. The pills they have." Her head bowed, she crossed herself. "God, give us strength."

Mary bowed her head too. She wanted to believe it. Needed to believe it. And the Spirit answered, charging the very atmosphere of the simple Irish bedroom with a power so electric, so vibrant, Mary rubbed her arms. She had to believe. Had to hope. For Chloe. For Jo. For the people at her ministry. For . . . herself. There was no other way for a believer to respond to the troubles of this world.

"Here." A sparkle returned to Jo's eyes. She pulled Mary to her feet and handed her a package wrapped in brown paper and tied with string. "Pictures of all o' us. Yer dad. Yer cousins. Everything but the pet lamb." Laughing, she pulled Mary into the warmest embrace. "Anything we can do fer ye, we'll do. Somethin' we Irish have always done."

Mary nodded. It was impossible to speak with her aunt hugging so tight, her hands full of pictures of relatives she'd only prayed about, her mind spinning with ideas of how best to share her story. So she kept quiet and let her heart talk. Her spirit talk. And from the way her aunt kept hugging, communication between the two of them had gotten off to a wonderful start.

Author's Note

Rosy hexagons bordered with violet triangles. Swirls of breathtaking color. An ever-flowing pattern of diamonds and circles and rectangles.

Your life, so like a kaleidoscope: infinite in possibilities, complex in design. But sometimes God places in your life sharp-edged fragments. Have you ever wondered why? Has it caused you to reject the One who made you?

It is my prayer that this novel, inspired by a true story, will encourage you. Mary, the protagonist in *An Irishwoman's Tale*, faced the same types of pain and rejection that you may be experiencing. When you put your trust in God, you, too, can depend on Him and His promises to carry you through the struggles. A good place to start is with the Holy Bible. The scriptural foundation for *An Irishwoman's Tale* can be found at Romans 8:28 and Matthew 6:14.

I also pray that you will seek friends who believe in the gospel message of Jesus Christ and that you are emboldened to tell them of God's patterning of your own special kaleidoscope. You have much to offer, even if dysfunction has shattered your life. *Especially* if that's the case. God bless you.

BOOK DISCUSSION GROUP QUESTIONS

1. Discuss Mary as a caretaker. What are her motives in caring for Anne? Is she handling the inherent stress of that role in a healthy way? In serving Anne, is she serving Christ?

2. The point of view shifts in chapter 3. Is your response to Kathleen sympathetic or critical? Does she make the only choices possible considering her circumstances, or does she have other options?

3. Who is to blame for young Mary's predicament, which reaches a climax in chapter 5?

4. Anne is a complex character. What are some of her positive qualities? What are some of her negative characteristics?

5. How does the setting of the book-discussion-group meeting serve as a backdrop for the rest of the story?

6. What are Sally's motives for listening to Mary's entire life story? Do you have a friend who is willing to listen to your life story without passing judgment or giving you advice? With how many people could you share your entire story?

7. Michael and Paul both provide romantic interests in the novel. Cite differences and similarities between the two men.

8. At what point in the novel do you recognize signs of Mary's illness?

9. Folk, geological, biological, and geographical elements of Mary's native Ireland are interwoven in the story. In what way do these elements have an impact on Mary's life? Have you ever both loved and hated a place?

10. How does Mary's return to Ireland serve as a quest device?

11. Does the kaleidoscope metaphor fit any aspect of your life? How has God used your brokenness to create something beautiful? How can you see a pattern developing out of seemingly unrelated events? Apply the scriptural foundation of Romans 8:28 to this text and to your own story.

12. How is *An Irishwoman's Tale* different from what you might expect of Christian fiction? In what ways is it similar to what you would expect?